Praise for

INSIDE OUT

"*Inside Out* is tender, romantic and unapologetically sexy. Lauren Dane writes with an emotional depth and authenticity that always leaves me breathless."   —Lara Adrian, *New York Times* bestselling author

"A beautiful masterpiece. Every word was a gift."

—*The Romance Reviews*

"*Inside Out* made my heart melt—it gives you this wonderful warm feeling deep inside. It's full of family and friends, love and compassion. An emotional read through and through. For me, her Brown Siblings novels are forever seated on my keeper shelf, and I know I will reread their stories again and again. A highly recommended read—I adore this book with all my heart!"   —*Book Lovers Inc.*

"Lauren Dane is the master of having the reader become emotionally invested in her characters and her stories."

—*Good Books, Good Coffee, Good Life*

LAID BARE

"It's impossible not to love this story. The sex is sizzling, the emotions are raw. Lauren Dane has done it again. *Laid Bare*, quite simply, *rocks!*"
    —Megan Hart, national bestselling author of *Precious and Fragile Things*

"I was blown away by Dane's emotionally charged, deeply erotic tale of second chances and redemption. I can't say it enough: I loved this book!"   —Sylvia Day, author of *Pride and Pleasure*

"A tender love story that wrung my heart with its sweetness. Don't miss this book."

—Ann Aguirre, national bestselling author of *Shady Lady*

continued . . .

"*Laid Bare* lives up to its title . . . Dane provides a heated yet entreating second chance at love due to the tender caring in and out of the bed of each of the prime players." —*The Best Reviews*

"In a word, this book is amazing. All three characters are magnetic and thoroughly realistic. They're expertly woven into a roller-coaster story that will have you crying one moment, aroused the next and laughing with glee at each triumphant step along the way . . . This is Dane's best story yet!" —*Romantic Times*

UNDERCOVER

"Lauren Dane deftly weaves action, intrigue and emotion with spicy, delicious eroticism . . . a toe-curling erotic romance sure to keep you reading late into the night."
—Anya Bast, *New York Times* bestselling author of *Jaded*

"Sexy, pulse-pounding adventure . . . that'll leave you weak in the knees. Dane delivers!"
—Jaci Burton, national bestselling author of *Changing the Game*

"Exciting, emotional and arousing."
—Sasha White, author of *Most Wanted*

"Fast-paced action, steamy romance." —Megan Hart

"Scintillating! . . . a roller coaster of emotion, intrigue and sensual delights . . . I was hooked from the first sentence."
—Vivi Anna, author of *The Vampire's Kiss*

"Be in line at your favorite bookstore the day it comes out. In other words, it is a Recommended Read . . . one I plan on reading over and over again." —*Joyfully Reviewed*

"A hot, sexy and action-packed piece of writing that will keep you glued to every page wondering what will happen next. A fabulous read!" —*Fresh Fiction*

"Wow! This book rocks! Lauren Dane pulls out all the stops with this soul-searing, awe-inspiring read. Definitely a must read and deserving of a special spot on the keeper shelf." —*Romance Junkies*

More praise for Lauren Dane and her novels

"Drool worthy." —*Romance Junkies*

"This story has it all! There is action, drama, interesting characters, an electrifying story line and hot, passionate sex . . . a truly beautiful and sensual story . . . a truly enchanting series!" —*Joyfully Reviewed*

"Starts out hot right out of the box, and then keeps getting hotter. Lauren Dane has a knack for making readers feel the passion and excitement of a new relationship . . . it's easy to see why Lauren Dane is such a well-loved author." —*TwoLips Reviews*

"Lauren Dane has once again created characters that you can't resist . . . the sexual chemistry sparks and sizzles." —*Sensual*

"From its completely romantic beginning to its oh-so-sensual end, I loved every word . . . Ms. Dane is definitely becoming a master of the romantic pen!" —*The Romance Studio*

"Rich and sensual . . . entirely delicious." —*Romance Divas*

"Sizzling hot and fun to read." —*The Pink Posse*

NEVER ENOUGH

LAUREN DANE

HEAT | NEW YORK

THE BERKLEY PUBLISHING GROUP
Published by the Penguin Group
Penguin Group (USA) Inc.
375 Hudson Street, New York, New York 10014, USA
Penguin Group (Canada), 90 Eglinton Avenue East, Suite 700, Toronto, Ontario M4P 2Y3, Canada
(a division of Pearson Penguin Canada Inc.)
Penguin Books Ltd., 80 Strand, London WC2R 0RL, England
Penguin Group Ireland, 25 St. Stephen's Green, Dublin 2, Ireland (a division of Penguin Books Ltd.)
Penguin Group (Australia), 250 Camberwell Road, Camberwell, Victoria 3124, Australia
(a division of Pearson Australia Group Pty. Ltd.)
Penguin Books India Pvt. Ltd., 11 Community Centre, Panchsheel Park, New Delhi—110 017, India
Penguin Group (NZ), 67 Apollo Drive, Rosedale, Auckland 0632, New Zealand
(a division of Pearson New Zealand Ltd.)
Penguin Books (South Africa) (Pty.) Ltd., 24 Sturdee Avenue, Rosebank, Johannesburg 2196, South
Africa

Penguin Books Ltd., Registered Offices: 80 Strand, London WC2R 0RL, England

This book is an original publication of The Berkley Publishing Group.

Copyright © 2011 by Lauren Dane.
Cover art by Tony Mauro.
Cover design by Rita Frangie.
Text design by Laura K. Corless.

PRINTING HISTORY
Heat trade paperback edition / September 2011

Library of Congress Cataloging-in-Publication Data

Dane, Lauren.
    Never enough / Lauren Dane. — Heat Trade paperback ed.
       p. cm.
    ISBN 978-0-425-24300-8
    1. Single women—Fiction. 2. Rock musicians—Fiction. 3. Man-woman relationships—Fiction.
I. Title.
    PS3604.A5N47 2011
    813'.6—dc22   2011004514

PRINTED IN THE UNITED STATES OF AMERICA

10 9 8 7 6 5 4 3 2 1

ACKNOWLEDGMENTS

To my usual cast of characters:

Ray, who is always my safe place.

Laura, who is my friend and a fabulous agent.

Leis Pederson—thank you for all the work you do to make my books the best they can be.

My friends, who will order me not to hit send, who whip me into shape and make my world a better place every day. I'd be in so much trouble without the ability to seek your counsel.

Fatin, who is absolutely someone I'd be lost without.

Mary, ditto.

Renee, yes, you too.

Special thanks to Ryan Bingham, who is Adrian in my head. Your music was something I listened to often when I wrote from Adrian's POV.

Thank you. All of you. This is a pretty solitary business, so it's my friends and family who keep me grounded and refuse to let me wear sweats all the time.

1

It felt so fucking good up there.

Adrian Brown leaned back, letting the music flow through him. His guitar in his hands because that was where it belonged. That essential, vibrant magic that was music rode him. The pleasure of it, the joy at creation and manipulation. The way he sounded against the drums, over and around the bass.

Music was alchemy.

Music was sex.

When it was right, when everything fit together just perfectly, it was better than any feeling he'd ever experienced.

The throb of it rested low in his gut, and when he sang, he *believed* what he said. For the first time in three years when he stood up on a stage, he felt everything he did. He feasted on every detail and it showed. Music was a banquet again and he was starving for it.

Adrian Brown was back and no one was happier to see him than he himself was.

The acoustics in the club were total shit and he made it sound

good. That utter confidence he'd started with had returned and, goddamn, he liked it.

His family was there to see it, which made it worth more. To the
right of the stage his big brother was rocking it along with his wife,
also rocking it. His sister was next to him on the small stage. Rocking
it they way they had before.

I got nothing left to give
Nothing left
Taken, taken . . .

He stepped back from the mic and let the applause come, a big
grin on his face as he looked toward his sister, who grinned and waggled her eyebrows at him.

And they dove in again, leading into a song he and Erin had just
finished a few days before.

In that moment, just as his pick was about to stroke the string, he
knew he'd done right to make himself take the time away from the
business. Because he'd needed to be lost a little while before he could
find himself again. He wasn't found totally, but he was on the way. He
had a direction, and that was most of the battle.

The scent of the orange oil she used on the kitchen table carried
through the house, back to Gillian's office. Miles had gone off to school
just ten minutes before and Gillian stood, staring blankly out over the
sweep of the front yard, the pale autumn sun warming her skin.

And it did nothing to the cold dread in her belly.

She'd been holding the secret her sister had given up right before
she'd died. Holding it tight, not wanting to think on it, knowing she
had no other choice.

A little more than thirteen years ago, Gillian had received a call in
the middle of the night that her older sister, Tina, had been in labor.
She'd rushed to the hospital—in a sadly ironic coincidence, that hospital had been the same one Tina had died in just three days before.

Gillian had come home with that baby. The one she adopted and built a life and family for and with. *Miles.*

Restless, she turned from the window and headed into the family room, to her piano.

Once her fingertips touched the wood, she calmed. As she sat, she let herself fall into that place where only the music mattered. Something simple today, uplifting.

Her fingers danced along the keys of a waltz and the knot of fear and rage began to loosen as the music flowed through her.

By the time she launched into Fantaisie-Impromptu, the line of her spine had lost its rigidity.

And that's how Jules found her.

"I told you it could wait," Gillian said, turning to find her friend standing in the doorway. "You have a business to run. You can't just blow that off."

"Whatever. You sounded like you were about to lose your shit just an hour ago. Where else would I be right now? Come on. I brought coffee and some chocolate croissant. For you, I brought ham."

Thank God for friends. Gillian followed Jules from the room and into the kitchen.

Jules hugged her tight before they settled in at the breakfast nook nestled in the sunny corner. "First things first. I'm sorry about your sister. I know you two weren't close and that she was a total cow for most of your life. But she was your sister and I know you loved her."

"Thanks. I'm okay about that part. I mean, yes, I did love her, but I've known she was on this path for a very long time. I'm surprised it took so long, to be totally honest."

She gulped the coffee and managed a few bites of the croissant, more to keep Jules from lecturing her than out of real hunger.

Jules waited, saying nothing else, knowing Gillian had to process it all and giving her that time.

"Right before she died, she told me who Miles's father was."

Jules's eyes widened at that. "Do tell. After nearly fourteen years she finally dumps it on you as she's dying. Typical."

Just because Jules was supportive of Gillian didn't mean she would hold back when it came to the subject of Tina's behavior. She was right, of course. Tina had withheld this information for her entire pregnancy and the years since Miles had been born, despite Gillian's many attempts to get her sister to tell the truth about it.

"She made me promise to find him and tell him he was Miles's dad."

Jules's sleepy blue eyes snapped wide open. "What? Get out! Well, I hope you know that's bullshit. Fuck that so-called promise to her."

Gillian sighed. "I thought it over. I've been doing nothing *but* think about it since she told me three days ago. He needs to know, Jules. Miles needs the opportunity to connect with his dad."

"Dad my ass. Where was he when Tina gave that baby to you like he was a pair of shoes? Huh? Where was he when you worked round the clock to afford the mortgage on this house? When you busted your ass to pay for braces and bicycles and summer camp? Fuck that. He's some shithead who fucked a waitress fourteen years ago—without a condom I might add—so his judgment is seriously impaired."

"He didn't know. She swore to me that she never told him. I tried to put myself in this guy's place, you know? What would my life be without Miles? What if I had a kid like him out there and didn't know it? It's not right, Jules. Not right that she never told him, and it would only be me furthering that to not tell him."

"Well, damn it, Gillian, now is not the time for morals."

Gillian laughed without humor. "Jules, they're all I've got. I'm responsible for raising that boy into a man. What lesson would I be teaching him if I didn't find his dad as I promised?"

"What if he takes Miles from you? Have you thought of that? Can you really take that risk?"

"No. I can't. I have an appointment with Cal in a few hours. Before I tell the dad, I have to know my adoption is solid."

"At least you're doing that." Jules shook her head and looked back to Gillian, reaching out and squeezing her hand. "I'm sorry. I'm sorry for being so judgy. You *are* doing the right thing, and of course this is about doing what's right for your son."

"I'm scared. It's . . . He's a rock star. A big one."

"What? Really? Why didn't she go after him for money, I wonder?"

"I don't know. She wasn't all bad, you know. She had her moments and I do believe she gave Miles up for good reasons instead of selfish ones."

"Yes, and then had nothing to do with him since."

True, and yet, in the end, it had been a good thing. "That was for the best too. Miles is my son. Mine. She knew it. Even our mother knew it. Tina loved Miles in her own way. Loved me too."

Jules sighed. "So who is it? How'd she meet him?"

"She met him when she was waitressing in some diner on Sunset Boulevard, she said. She wouldn't say much more, but that she thought he was an okay guy and that he deserved to know about his son."

Jules slammed her palm against the table with a squeal. "Adrian Brown. I knew it! It's him, isn't it?" Jules demanded as Gillian gaped at her friend.

"How did you know that? Did you know and never tell me?"

"Are you shitting me? You said rock star and immediately I thought of Miles's face. And hello, have you seen Adrian Brown?"

Jules got up and tugged Gillian over to the far wall where Miles's picture hung, and pointed. "Look at that." She pulled her phone out and then shoved it at Gillian. On the screen was Adrian Brown's website with his picture.

"Well bloody fucking hell."

Cal Whaley looked Gillian over as she sat down on the bench next to him. He handed her a coffee. "I know how you get with too much caffeine, so it's decaf."

"It's that or scotch, and it's early yet. Tell me, Cal. Am I safe? Is he safe with me?"

"Yes, baby, I told you you were. Look, you adopted him legally. You've been his mother for thirteen years. You take him to the dentist, you know what his favorite foods are. You are his mother and Adrian Brown can't change that."

"He can't take Miles from me?"

"If you were like your sister, he might be able to. But you're not. You had no way of knowing who Miles's dad was until your sister told you, and frankly, I'd be disinclined to believe her without a DNA test anyway. God knows this guy is going to want one. Even so, he could fight for visitation. You need to be prepared for that. And just because he can't tear your adoption apart doesn't mean he won't try to. If you mean to do this, you have to be prepared. Who knows, he may run the other way."

"I feel like a right selfish bitch because part of me hopes he does. I can't stand the thought of it. Of someone hurting Miles or trying to take him. I do want him to have his father in his life if the guy cares. Who am I to make the choice for either of them? At the same time, he's my boy and I will be forced to cut a bitch if he gets out of line."

"Does this mean you want to go ahead with it?"

She sighed. "I haven't told Miles yet. I don't plan to. Not until I know for sure this guy won't be a jerk. But if my legal position is safe . . . well, I made a promise and it's the right thing to do. Right?"

Cal cocked his head before leaning in to kiss her cheek. "You're a very do-the-right-thing sort of woman. Miles has learned a lot from you. You're not either one of them, you know. Not your mother and certainly not your father."

"So you say. I want Miles to have everything I didn't. A safe and loving, *stable* home. He's not had a dad, but he's had you and Jules's dad too. Do you have any idea how to find him? This rock star?"

Cal handed over a file. "You have given that to Miles. As for the rock star? We can go one of two ways. His brother owns a tattoo shop in Seattle. Adrian lives here in the Northwest and he's noted for being very close with his family. I can contact his management and then go through his attorneys. Or I can contact the brother and try to go a more informal route."

"All this time he's lived here?" She shook her head, astounded. "I'll do it myself, next week. I want to see this guy in person. Not that I'd necessarily judge anyone by a family member, god knows I'd hope people wouldn't do that to me. But if I'm going to expose my family to theirs, I want to see it myself."

"Do you want me to go with you?"

"No. But I do want you to keep on representing me in this. Just in case."

"I'm here for you. As your friend and as your attorney. Keep me apprised, all right? And don't do anything stupid."

2

Adrian pulled his SUV into Brody and Elise's driveway, grinning when he caught sight of a little girl, two white-blonde pigtails flying behind her as she ran across the yard chasing a six-foot-tall man.

Rennie's head was canted back, her mouth open on a screaming giggle of, "I got you, Dad!"

Adrian moved up the walk to where his sister-in-law swayed back and forth with a bundled-up baby in her arms.

"Hey, Elise." He kissed Elise's cheek and peeked around to see Marti's face. Her big green eyes blinked, owlish, until she recognized him and gave him a toothless grin.

"Since you're here, she won't care one bit about Momma until she gets hungry, so you may as well take her."

Laughing, Adrian took his three-month-old niece into his arms, loving the weight and warmth of her as she snuggled into his chest. "Hey, punkin. You ready for a day at the zoo? I bet your sister is."

He looked back out to where Marti's big sister got caught up into her dad's arms, laughing so hard she couldn't talk. Further proof of just how magical Adrian's brother's life was.

"You were amazing last night. Best show ever." Elise still swayed, even as Adrian held Marti, until she stopped herself with a laugh. "Sorry, I just do it so often it's hard to stop. Probably keeps us both calm." She winked.

"Thanks. It felt really good. I was glad to see you both there. I know it's hard to get the time away."

"Marti slept the entire time we were gone. She cried more when my mother left than when I did, I have no doubt. I was glad to be there to see you play."

"You ready for a date with two of my three best girls?" Brody ambled over, Rennie still in his arms like a monkey.

"I lost a tooth, Uncle Adrian. I'm totally done now. All my teeth are adults." Rennie grinned and showed him the space.

"Awesome. Was there blood?"

Elise groaned.

"Not a lot. I was wriggling it and wriggling it and then Dad just up and walked over, grabbed and pulled. Can you believe that?"

Adrian laughed and Martine, Marti for short, huffed her own laugh to mimic. "I can, baby doll. He did the exact same thing to me. I was in third grade."

"He cried. You didn't." Brody smirked as he put Rennie on her feet. "Go get your coat and hat."

Rennie tore off, Elise in her wake.

"Todd texted as he was leaving with Alexander. They should be here shortly and then we can head out." Todd was their sister Erin's husband—well, one of them—and Alexander was their son. Nearly a year old, he was walking, babbling, and generally ruling the roost.

Adrian's SUV had enough car seats for all those who needed them. He liked the ability to come over and commandeer any of his nieces or his nephew at any time. Loved taking them to the park or the zoo. Loved the normal, sweet love he got in return. Better than screaming groupies any day of the week. Even if sometimes the interior smelled like spit-up and he found Goldfish crackers in the oddest places.

"Come on in. I need to get the diaper bag and stuff. I'll use the carrier rather than deal with a stroller at the zoo."

Adrian followed his brother into the house. Once bachelor digs, it was now a family home. Rennie's art was up on the walls and on the fridge. Toys of all sorts lived in bins. Bicycles, helmets, Hula-Hoops, the house was filled with it all.

"The deal is," Elise handed Brody the diaper bag, "let me feed her now and then you'll have a bottle for the zoo too."

At the sound of her mother's voice, Marti waved her little arms and leaned toward Mom and those giant breasts. Adrian didn't blame the kid one bit.

The two settled in a quiet corner, Elise rocking and nursing as she managed to also tell Rennie the location of her hat.

Brody leaned over, kissed the top of Marti's head and then his wife's forehead. "Such a multitasker."

The noise outside drew Adrian out to greet Todd and Alexander.

"Yo! Yo!" Alexander waved at his uncle.

"Yo, kid, how's things?" Adrian picked up his nephew and got a hug in return.

They went in to grab everyone else and headed just a bit down the road to Woodland Park Zoo. Rennie had requested a trip to see the elephants and get pizza afterward at Zeeks.

As Saturdays went, Adrian thought that was as fine a day as it ever got.

Brody watched Rennie, her hand in Todd's as he stood with Alexander and looked at the penguins swimming around. "She's getting so big. She paints her toenails, Adrian. What the fuck?"

"A house full of girls." Adrian snorted. "Every man's dream."

"Damn straight." Brody looked to his oldest and waved. "Never could have imagined I'd love being woken up every few hours just to see this sweet face." He bent and kissed Marti's head. She grabbed his beard and pulled so he'd give her the theatrical *ouch* she wanted so badly. "But holy shit, it's hard. I want to do it right."

"You've done it once, no, twice before with me and Erin. We turned out pretty good. You and Elise are great with Rennie and Marti. You were meant to be a father."

Brody colored just a little bit. He kissed Marti's fingers and cleared his throat. "I want this for you too. Complete with the holy-shit-my-daughter-is-going-to-be-a-teenager-in-just-a-few-years moments."

Adrian knew it. Knew he wanted it for himself too. He wanted a wife and some kids. Wanted to come home to a house filled with noise and people waiting just for him.

Rennie returned and after a caress to Marti's foot, she put her hand in Adrian's and tugged. "My ears are cold."

Adrian adjusted her hat a little. "Is that a weak cry for pizza? You gotta step your game up. Cute you'll always have, but smart and cute? Well, you'll be unstoppable."

She nodded, face solemn. "Yeah. Maybe some hot chocolate would help too."

Alexander toddled over, holding his dad's hand. Todd swung his son up into his arms, parking him on a hip. "The boy and I throw our votes in with Rennie. I'm sure if Marti could talk, she'd agree." Todd leaned in and kissed Marti's nose and she grabbed for his hair. Smart man avoided it easily and she frowned for a moment.

"Pizza it is."

They walked over and Adrian realized how much his life had changed in the last few years. He'd made the deliberate choice to slow things down and find his joy in creating again and to be with his family as it started to grow with a whole crop of babies.

"Erin told me to tell you she really loved the stuff you sent over. Those guys are lucky to have you in their corner." Todd kept an eye on Alexander as he mawed a pizza crust. "And you lit up last night on stage. I've never heard you two so tight. I thought you were good before; now I think you're the best you've been. Erin is excited about music again."

"Man, Erin and I wouldn't have gotten many of our first, big important gigs without help from local guys who'd hit it big. Getting an opening spot on a Pearl Jam tour? Gigantic for us. It's important to help. Keeps the scene vibrant. Gives back." And truth be told, it had been more fun helping produce those few tracks for this up-and-coming band than he'd had in a while.

"Now it's time to settle down." Brody and Todd nodded, like it was so easy all Adrian had to do was snap his fingers.

"It's on the list. But it's hard to find people who are with me for me. Cope up and swiped Ella and the group doesn't have any more single women hanging around. Maybe I need to get hit by a car or something, since that's how Brody netted a woman as awesome as Elise."

Even as he spoke, he pointedly ignored the two women at a nearby table who kept looking over and whispering.

"We were rooting for Karen the baker." Todd wiped Alexander's face as he spoke of the local woman Adrian had dated for a while late the year before.

Finding the right woman wasn't as easy as he'd assumed it would be. First, he didn't have the time really, so the women he dated were temporary. It didn't really matter if they only saw each other a few times and went in other directions. But now it did. He found himself looking at an entirely different set of priorities. Partly it made him feel responsible and, shit, the rest of the time he felt like a lazy dickhead for not being able to do something as simple as find a woman who didn't care about his fame and the money he had in the bank.

"My teacher is nice. Maybe you can ask her out." Rennie helped herself to another slice of pie.

"Your teacher is in her sixties. She's a little old for Adrian. But thank you for thinking of him." Brody tried not to smile, but he lost the battle. Adrian knew the feeling.

"Appreciate it, sunshine. Good to know you've got my back." Adrian grinned at her.

"You're so pretty to look at, even Momma says so. Plus you need to start having babies or you'll be too old to run after them."

Todd snorted a laugh.

"Ever the speaker of important truths, Irene." Brody managed to say this as Marti whacked his arm, trying to get some pizza near enough to eat. "Not gonna happen, tiny bug. Your mother would kill me if I fed you pizza."

Marti's goofy smile faltered and her bottom lip trembled. Adrian would have given her pizza in Brody's place just to see the smile again. But Brody was made of sterner stuff. He brought the bottle into her sight and she narrowed her eyes at him and looked to the pizza again.

"Just like your sister, eh? Don't like to be told no."

"Who does, Uncle Brody?" Todd asked, pushing his glass of soda farther from Alexander's reach.

Rennie sang to her sister and Marti's grumpy face disappeared.

"Short attention span. Babies are awesome that way," Brody muttered. "Still, the expiration date on this little outing is getting close. Martine has Mom's milk in a bottle or from the source, and smart girl that she is, she won't want the bottle."

One of the women who'd been staring snapped a cell phone picture.

"Hey, I'd appreciate it if you deleted that," he said quietly. "I don't want pictures of children to circulate."

"Will you take a picture with me and my friend, then?"

"No pictures. People should be able to eat pizza in peace." Their server bustled back over with a box for the remaining pizza. "Sorry about that," she told Adrian.

"It's okay, comes with the territory."

"A guy should be able to eat pizza with his family, you know?"

This was why he tended to stick to his favorite, most trusted places.

Still, not wanting to be a dick, he autographed two napkins and dropped them off at the table. It seemed to satisfy them.

"Erin just texted me. She and Ben probably haven't even gotten to dessert yet and she's jonesing for Alexander." Todd laughed. "Ben's just as bad."

"Tell them to get lunch to go and come to the house for a play date." Brody packed their stuff up and Adrian grabbed the rest, including Rennie, who hadn't stopped talking for longer than a breath.

"Uncle Adrian?" She stopped him once they'd arrived back at Brody's place. He bent to look her eye to eye.

"What is it, sunshine?"

She grinned and then her smile faded into uncertainty. "Do you love Alexander and Martine more than me because I'm adopted?"

He hugged her, picking her up and moving to sit with her on the big rocker out on the porch. "Irene, my darlin', I love you because you're you. How could I love you less for that? I love Alexander and Marti for who they are. Not more, not less. You're all my nieces and nephew. And your dad is Brody, got me? Doesn't matter whose biological stuff made you into the fabulous girl you are. Being a dad is about the day-to-day stuff, not DNA. Do you love me any less than you would if I was related to you by blood?"

He ached for her just then. She always seemed so confident and easygoing, but it had to be hard for any kid to get a baby brother or sister in any circumstances.

She shook her head. " 'Course not! You play Monopoly with me and you remember my favorite stuff. I know it's dumb to be worried. But sometimes my stomach won't listen."

He hugged her tight. "It's okay, you know. To feel worried or scared. That's only natural. But I want you to know you can always talk to me. Call me if I'm not here, e-mail me, text me, whatever. I love you something fierce. As do your mom and dad and Aunt Erin and Todd and Ben, Aunt Ella and Uncle Cope too. And don't forget about Alexander. I bet Marti's first word will be *Rennie*, just like Alexander's was."

Her face brightened. "Really? I don't want to bug you or nothing."

"I know you have lots of people to talk to already, but of course. I'm your uncle, it comes with the territory. It's not bugging me at all. I like talking to you. I just wish I could help. I know it's hard right now. Is there something I can do to make this better?"

She paused, thinking, and then shook her head. "You already did."

Brody came out the front door looking for them and caught sight of the two of them there on the rocker. "Everything okay?" He reached out to touch Rennie—an automatic, sweet caress of her head. It was so clear his brother loved Irene totally. And when she leaned into Brody's hand, it was clear she loved him totally right back.

"Hey, Dad. I was just talking to Uncle Adrian about stuff." She kissed Adrian's cheek and hugged him tight. "I'm better now. I promise," she whispered.

Over the top of Rennie's head, Brody looked at Adrian, worried. Adrian gave him what he hoped was reassurance, indicating things were all right.

Turning his attention back to his niece, he gave her a look up and down. "How much practicing have you done this week?" He'd started to give her guitar lessons and like her mother, she was an easy, quick study.

She hopped up. "One hour a day, just like you said. Momma makes sure I do it. You are gonna be so impressed!"

Seeing the return of his happy, ebullient niece, Adrian felt better. "I'll be in to see what you've learned this week. If you kick it like you claim, cupcakes on me."

Her eyes widened and she hopped to it, running past them and into the house.

"What's going on?"

Being caught between Rennie's privacy and Brody's concern wasn't a fun thing. But he'd been there enough between Brody and Erin to know it was important to talk to Brody. Plus, he knew Rennie would only benefit from the extra attention and reinforcement.

"She wanted to know if I loved Alexander and Marti more than her because she's adopted." He put his hand out to stay his brother a moment. "She knows it's not true. But knowing something in your head isn't always connected to how you feel about it."

"Elise and I worry. We keep an eye out for it because of course Marti gets so much more attention than Rennie does. How can she think I don't love her just as much as I do her sister? She's my daughter. Period. Do you think I show any preference?"

Adrian might get a little jealous of just how together his older brother was and always had been, but he never ceased to respect him and his heart. When Brody Brown loved you, he loved you to the bone and that was that.

"She knows you do. She does. And she's excited and happy and full of love for you and her sister and this family. That is who Rennie is all the way to her toes. But she's ten and she's growing up and with the good has to be some being scared and a little jealousy and even a sliver of anger.

"But she knows with all her heart that you love her just the same as if she'd come to you another way. It's not the *how* she came to you, but that she did. She knows she's your daughter."

"Elise says it's a good thing she's so close to you. Mind you, I agree."

Adrian laughed. "As big a cliché as it sounds, it's really the other way around. I'm lucky to have her. I love your kid. Both of them. I love that she can come to me and trust the parts of herself she doesn't think are as pretty." He was proud of it. "I guess you raised me right."

"Enough mush. Come on inside."

3

With great care, Gillian chose her clothes for the day. Miles was at school and she was heading over to Seattle to go to Brody Brown's tattoo parlor.

She bound her hair at the nape of her neck after braiding and coiling it. Not too much makeup. Subtle colors. Messages were important and she didn't want to give an impression that she was tatty or in need of money. Or looking for any interaction but the one she detailed. Men sometimes assumed things about a woman. Though it was really stupid and their own issue, Gillian had lived with enough judgment and assumption that she was a slapper looking for a few extra quid simply because of who she was related to; she didn't care for it to happen ever again.

She hadn't always had control over most things in her life growing up, but her outward appearance was something she could control. Yes, yes, she knew it was silly, but you did what you could to get through the day without maiming anyone.

Her accent had smoothed out over the years living in America. But the flavor of England was in her forever. To her bones. She'd never lose it entirely and she figured she may as well use it to her advantage. Most often she fell to the posh one, the one her piano teacher had used back when she and her mother and sister had lived in a council flat in Newham. The Queen's English. It came in quite handy with teachers, policemen, authority figures. The other, the heavier cockney she was born with, well, that one only came out when she really got angry or frustrated, and her close friends and Miles knew to be careful when she started dropping consonants.

On the drive over, she went through her short, simple speech several times. It was best if she told Adrian face-to-face. It wasn't something she wanted lawyers and third parties to handle. This was about a real person who deserved some respect.

So she ignored the nausea and nervousness and found the place easily enough using her borrowed GPS. Her hand froze, clutching her keys in her palm so hard her knuckles were white. She made herself relax, took in the surroundings. Mixed commercial neighborhood. A café next door, a hipster hardware store a few doors down. Brody Brown's tattoo shop was called Written on the Body. Hm. Nice name. Not a cliché.

It took four tries to get out. She even restarted the car once. But in the end, she found herself walking through the front door and asking to see Brody Brown.

It wasn't that she didn't expect a very large, tattooed man—the place was positively full of them. But it was his eyes she hadn't expected. Warm, friendly. His smile was genuine and open.

Gillian found herself responding, relaxing a little.

"I'm Brody. I hear you were looking for me?"

She held a hand out, which he shook. "My name is Gillian Forrester. I know this is most unusual, but I need to get in contact with your brother."

The warmth shuttered. Not entirely, but he clearly put some distance between them.

"What's this about? He has management if you want an interview or a personal appearance."

Gillian shook her head. "No. No, it's not like that. I have some information for him. I need to tell him in person. I'm not trying to be coy, though it might appear that way, I'm sure." She put an envelope on the counter. "What I have to say, I need to say in person. My contact information is in there."

Brody looked at the envelope and then at her, long and hard. She had nothing to hide, and damned if she'd do anything but look him right back. No one would ever make her feel guilty or ashamed when she was doing the right thing.

"I'm his brother; I can pass it along. You can tell me whatever it is."

"I'm sure you're a trustworthy person. It's in the eyes, you know." She brushed down the front of her sweater, brisk now that her message had been delivered. "But it's not something he should hear from anyone but me."

She stepped back. "You don't know me from Adam. I'm sure you get people in here trying to get at your brother and I respect that you're protecting him. All I can do is repeat that I need to speak with him about something very important and that my contact information is in that envelope."

He took the envelope, sliding it into the cash register, under the cash drawer. "I can't make any promises. Your best hope is to contact his management. It's at his website."

She nodded. "Thank you."

Brody watched her go with long, precise, ground-eating strides. Which was all the more impressive given that she couldn't have topped five foot one or two. Big brown eyes that, if he wasn't mistaken, deftly sized him and the shop up enough that he'd lay odds she wasn't an easy mark.

Not the usual sort of woman in the shop trying to find Adrian. He watched her turn the corner and went back to the register where the envelope was. He took it and headed back to his office to call his brother.

Adrian picked up on the first ring. "Yo."

Brody snorted a laugh. It was such a common greeting from his brother that even Alexander had picked it up.

"I just had a visitor. A woman looking for you."

"Novel."

"Har har. No, this one was different than the usual breed of starfucker who comes sniffing around for you. Graceful. The way she moved reminds me of Elise. Though she's more . . . bold, maybe? Something. Anyway. She left an envelope here with her contact information."

"Did she say what it was about?"

"She wouldn't tell me. But she did say it was important."

"They all say that, Brody. If it's important, she'll contact Jeremy and he'll tell me." Brody heard the plunk of strings, knew his brother's focus was on the music.

Brody paused. "Adrian, I think you should call her."

"Why? Dude, she's going to want something from me. A donation for a charity, a night at a bachelor auction, whatever. I have management for this. I'm sorry they come in to bug you, man. I know it's a pain."

"It's not a pain. She's . . . well, she's different. Call her. I think you need to do it yourself."

"What does the info say?"

"I haven't opened it yet. It's to you."

Adrian barked a laugh. "Christ, dude, do you always have to be so fuckin' honorable? Open it up and tell me."

"Asshole." Brody muttered it as he opened the envelope and then scanned the sheet within. "It's a sheet of paper with her name. Gillian Forrester. Two contact numbers and an e-mail. Says she has to give you some important information and she needs to deliver it in person. Apologizes for sounding mysterious."

"Fuck this noise. I have better things to do than get hooked in to some scheme with a chick looking to get laid. Seattle's got plenty of musicians; I'm sure she can get her itch scratched elsewhere."

Brody heard the world-weariness in his brother's voice. It had alleviated some in the months since he'd been home from this last tour. He'd grown concerned over the last few years that Adrian was getting too jaded. All that industry stuff was destructive. Fake. Obsessed with things that simply didn't matter. Worse, the walls between his private life and his public one as a celebrity had begun to crumble. People camped out at Adrian's front gates on a regular basis. He'd had multiple stories fed to tabloids about his sex life, most of it totally untrue. Hell, even a paternity accusation three years prior. Brody and Erin had encouraged Adrian to take a step back and put some paid staff between him and the public and thank goodness he'd listened.

What did matter was Adrian's music. Of course Brody had been proud and wanted his brother to continue to be successful. Just not at the expense of the rest of Adrian's life.

Brody's gut was rarely wrong, and it told him his brother needed to contact this woman. "She's different. I said it and I'll say it again. Adrian, what harm can it do to call her? If she's full of shit, hang up and block her number forever."

Adrian sighed and Brody knew he was putting his guitar down, moving aside the notepad and bringing his full attention to his brother. "Fine. Fine. If she asks me for money, beer and pizza is on you next time."

Brody grinned. "I can call her for you, but she wouldn't tell me what it was about when she was here and I don't think she'd do it on the phone either."

"Give me her info. I'll let you know what she says or you'll just pester me until I tell you anyway."

"Damn straight."

She sat in her driveway for a little while, just getting herself back together now that she was home. Her hands shook until she squeezed them into fists.

She'd gone and done it. She'd opened herself up to other people who could end up wanting access to her child. She knew it had been the right thing, but it sent her pulse through the roof to imagine the sort of trouble this man could cause if he wanted to. She had to hope he wouldn't. Had to hold on to the knowledge that she was Miles's mother and no one could take that from her.

Which was good because the DNA test would obviously be a match.

She could no longer give herself the illusion of that small sliver of doubt that Adrian Brown was truly Miles's father. When Brody had smiled, her son's smile was reflected so strongly it had shaken her to the core.

She'd seen that smile every single day for the last thirteen years. Most recently that morning before he left for the school bus.

She exhaled long and hard, letting it all go. There was nothing else to be done. She wouldn't tell Miles until she knew for sure Adrian Brown was interested in moving forward.

Funny how one piece of missing information could cast a different light on *everything*.

Miles had started this little garage band with his friends at the end of the last school year. They played out there, as loud as they wanted to be, and it bothered no one. He'd stuck with it and they practiced several days a week.

Until Tina had revealed who Miles's dad was, Gillian had always assumed Miles's talent for music came from her side of the family.

He'd like that, Miles would. He'd like knowing he came from a family of artists, because other than Gillian's piano and design work, the only kind of artists in her family were grift artists.

This Adrian Brown had better love her baby with all his heart or she'd have to maim him. Unexpectedly annoyed, she stomped off to finish some work for a design client and not think about any Browns at all.

Which would have been easier had her cell phone not rang with *private caller* on the screen. She normally didn't take such calls, but she answered this time, wondering if it was him.

"Gillian Forrester," she said, and Adrian was taken aback for a moment at the sound of her accent. British. Brody hadn't mentioned that.

"Yeah. This is Adrian Brown. You came by my brother's shop earlier today looking for me. I have a management company; it's easiest to go through them. My brother isn't my business manager."

She gusted a sigh and he found himself amused for a moment.

"I need just a few minutes of your time, Mr. Brown. I have to speak with you on an urgent matter."

She was very starched and prim. "Why don't you tell me what it is and I'll judge just how urgent it is myself?"

"I cannot relay this over a phone line. I can meet you at your convenience to explain everything."

"Who are you and why should I?"

She paused and he got the feeling she was pissed. Good. He was too. He didn't have time to play around with people. He'd been down this fucking road so many times just thinking about it made him tired.

"As I said, my name is Gillian Forrester."

"Why don't we cut to the chase, sweetheart? How much are you looking for?"

"*Sweetheart?* Just who is it you think you are and who do you think I am, for goodness' sake? How much for what?"

Okay, so he did feel a little guilty for being rude. "Look, I get strangers coming around all the time looking for something from me. If you need money for your project or a school or something, I give pretty regularly. But you still have to go through my manager. I'll give you his number and tell him to expect your call."

"You ought to try using earplugs when you are onstage, Mister Brown." The accent had gone very proper now. Like the hormone-riddled fool he was, he liked it. Liked the way she drew out the word *mister*. Maybe he should investigate it a little more.

"Why is that?"

Oh dear God, did he have to do that drawl thing? Despite his manners, he was sexy and her body responded in a major way.

She stifled yet another sigh and kept her uptight British in place. "Because I think you have a hearing problem. Now, I do not want money from you for anything. As I've said, I need to speak with you on an important matter. I simply want some of your time. It will take me roughly ten minutes to lay it all out."

"I don't have a hearing problem. Though I appreciate your concern. I have a problem with people wasting my time. You've received enough of it. Please don't contact me again."

Well then, that was easy enough. "As you wish." And she hung up.

Miles came in from school. She heard his clatter and the stomp of feet that seemed to grow a size every two weeks.

He was safe with her. She'd done her best. Had tried to tell Adrian Brown about this treasure and the man had accused her of trying to extort him! The nerve.

"Mum?"

"On my way," she called out.

All the annoyance and fear melted as she caught sight of him. Of all the messy he carried along with him with ease. Backpack. Kicked-off shoes. A wash of paper and discarded clothing in his wake. "Oy, don't you dare get those trainers on my carpet. They're muddy."

"You mean my sneakers?" He grinned.

"Don't give me any cheek, mister. You know what I mean. Trainers, sneakers, the message is the same. Track mud on my carpets and I shall have you for dinner." She looked him up and down. "Maybe after you've had a snack. Go on, I got more peanut butter at the market."

She wandered with him to the kitchen, leaned against the counter while he made himself a peanut butter sandwich.

"How was school? Did you turn in your book report?"

"It was okay. Yes."

A year ago, he'd be telling her every last detail of his day. But these days, he had those little teen moments that made him less than chatty.

"Don't overwhelm me with details, boy." She moved around the kitchen, pulling things from cabinets.

"Got practice tonight." He leaned his head against her shoulder for a moment and the memories came rushing back, warming her to her toes. When he was a toddler and in the early grades, he had problems connecting with people sometimes. He didn't give a lot of hugs, but he would put his head on her shoulder, or when she asked for a kiss, he'd give her the top of his head. Over time, he'd let other people in and had gotten past it for the most part. But sometimes when he was very tired, or emotionally raw, he'd put his head on her shoulder like that and he'd instantly be four years old again.

She kissed the top of his head. "All right. I'll order you guys a pizza then. I've got two lessons anyway. Do your homework first."

"You're pretty awesome for a mum who doesn't know the difference between sneakers and trainers." He grinned.

"Talk now, monkey boy! You need those braces tightened next week; I'll have a word with your orthodontist beforehand, shall I?"

He put his hands up, which he could now that he'd shoved half his sandwich in his mouth at once. Gillian winced. "Your teeth are for chewing. Use them."

He demolished another sandwich, an orange, two glasses of milk and a handful of raisins. He ate like a machine and yet remained long and lanky. Like her own father had been. She shuddered, forcing herself to remember Brody and Adrian Brown were also tall. It was better to imagine Miles getting anything from them instead of Ronnie Pete.

He paused in the doorway after he'd grabbed his backpack. "Are you all right? You look a little pale."

She managed a genuine smile. He lifted her spirits, silly boy. She hadn't told him about Adrian and at that point, she wasn't sure she would. Maybe once he turned eighteen as Cal had suggested.

"I'm good. Just had to run around a little earlier."

And then he was gone in a clatter of noise and the kitchen was peaceful and quiet again.

She had dinner at Mary's later that night. She'd fill Jules and her friends in then. Until then, she had two piano lessons and some pizzas to order.

Brody opened his front door. "Why'd you knock? You have a key."

Adrian moved past his brother and kicked off his shoes in the hall, hanging his jacket on the way.

"It was late. I didn't want to just walk in. You and Elise could have been doing all manner of things and my fragile psyche can't handle that."

"It's seven at night. You called her, didn't you?" Brody looked him up and down and jerked his chin toward the kitchen. "Come on. There are leftovers."

"Where are your fine ladies?"

"They're out with Erin and Ella. Beer?" Brody put one in front of him before going back to the fridge.

Adrian looked around the room. Drew his knuckles over the same spot on the kitchen table so many times it was smooth there. Sometimes he'd see what his brother had and be filled with a hundred different feelings.

He had a dad growing up. Until he was eleven anyway. But that man hadn't been around nearly as much as Brody had been. Brody picked him and Erin up from school so much their teachers began to talk to him about any problems. It was Brody who checked home-work.

Brody who had bought him his first guitar as a bribe to bring his failing grades up.

Truth was, he could have let himself in, yes, he knew he could. But sometimes he liked to see his brother at the door to feel that welcome and connection he only had with a handful of people.

"So tell me." Brody made a plate and slid it to Adrian before sitting across from him.

"Not much to tell. I called. You didn't mention her accent."

Brody's left brow rose slightly. "I forgot about it until just now. Nice voice. Got all starchy when I told her to either tell me or call your manager."

Like a naughty fucking governess. Yeah, that was it. Goddamn, her voice had stirred up all kinds of shit in his gut.

"And?" Brody prompted.

"And nothing. She played coy. Wouldn't tell me what it was about. I admit it, the voice did things to me. I offered to give my people a heads-up for her call. She got pissed and we hung up."

Brody looked him over. "Okay. Cut the shit. Professionally you are at the top of your game. I've heard you play hundreds of times and you are tighter now than you've ever been. This next CD is going to be monstrous for you. But what's that mean when you only talk to the ten people in the world you trust? You need more than that. You can see it, I know you can. I see how you watch the rest of us with wives and kids and all that shit. I'm not saying this chick is a love connection or anything like that. But there's a reason you're unsettled. It could to-tally be bullshit. Chances are it is. But what about the chance that it could be something extraordinary? Huh?"

Adrian ate and considered the situation. "Chances are, she's going to want something from me, and man . . . I am just so *tired* of that."

"I get that. I don't know how you do it on a regular basis. Even

Erin loses her patience before you do. But you are crispy-fried. And it's blinding you to your gut."

He patted his stomach. "Nothing wrong with it. I can't have the same belly I had at twenty."

"I'm not playing, Adrian." Brody used the Dad voice and Adrian straightened his posture automatically, chagrined.

"Fine. You really think this woman is someone I should hear out?"

"Yes. Yes, I do. I know I'm not usually in your business this much. But all I know is that I think you need to hear her out. She said she knew I was a good man because of my eyes." Brody waved away Adrian's look. "No, not like that. She didn't say it to flirt. Anyway. Meet with her. What can it hurt? You already think people are assholes. If she is, fuck that. You're still not one. You used to be adventurous, bro. Why not now? Huh?"

Damn it. The man wasn't one to ask things from his siblings. Despite their money and their success, Brody made his own way. He and Erin had to sneak attack him with gifts.

So when he actually did ask for something, it meant a great deal.

"Fine." He picked his phone up again and dialed her number.

<hr>

"And so he called me sweetheart! Can you imagine that? The cheek of a total stranger to accuse me of trying to thieve from him? I never said any such thing."

Jules snorted. "Sounds like he's been in show business too long."

Miles was out front in Mary's large driveway, shooting hoops with Cal and Ryan, Mary's brothers.

She looked out to her son and huffed. "I almost feel sorry for him. Not Miles. Adrian Brown."

"Don't. You're offering him that boy out there and he's too conceited to even listen to you. It's his loss, but you tried." Jules shrugged.

Her phone started ringing and she looked down to see the same private number designation she'd seen before.

"Hello? This is Gillian."

Jules sent her a raised brow at her tone.

"Upon further reflection, I've decided to meet with you."

She sighed. She would have said no. Wanted to say no. But she caught sight of Miles laughing with Cal and Ryan out front. The place was filled with warmth and love. The family she'd built for herself and her son. This was for Miles, she reminded herself for the two hundredth time. For him she could do anything.

"All right. I can only meet on weekdays during the early part of the day. I need to be back home by two."

Laughter burst out from where Mary had shown up with a platter of something that smelled like heaven. Gillian smiled, thankful this call happened here, while she was surrounded by her friends.

"Tomorrow at ten. There's a café next door to my brother's tattoo shop. I'll meet you there."

"Fine." She hung up and slid her phone back into her pocket.

"Was that him?"

"Yes. Turns out he does want to meet after all. Tomorrow at ten."

Jules did that little head whip she did when she was vexed. The familiar sight eased some of her anxiety. "Do you want one of us to go with you?"

Gillian let out a breath. "No. I'm good." She called out to Mary. "Where are you guys going to be parked tomorrow?"

"Um, Phinney Ridge from eleven to two. You gonna come see us?" Mary, part owner of Luxe, a mobile gourmet food truck, walked over and popped a little bite of something redolent with roasted pepper and garlic into Gillian's mouth.

She paused to appreciate the taste. "So good. I may come by after my appointment."

"He just called right now. Has changed his mind apparently." Jules rolled her eyes.

"We can park there and kick his ass if he gives you any guff." Mary winked.

"Thanks for the backup. I think I can kick butt on my own, but I have you on speed dial if I need to."

"What'd she say?" Brody asked as Adrian put the phone on the table.

"I'm meeting her tomorrow at ten at the café. Wherever she was there was a crowd. Sounded like dinner with friends." It had sounded warm and friendly as opposed to wild. And it only made him more curious about Gillian Forrester.

He picked the phone up again and called someone else he could count on.

"Yo."

"Hey, Cope, I have a favor to ask."

4

He didn't know why he'd shown up so early. He told himself it was so he could stop in and chat with Brody. But he'd only seen his brother the night before, so it wasn't as if there was much to catch up on.

He set himself up at his favorite table. In the far corner where he could see anyone coming and going. He had a mocha and bagel, but it was nervousness that brought his knee to bounce, not caffeine.

Adrian knew it was her the moment he caught sight of the dark-haired woman making her way up the sidewalk. What a fucking walk she had. Confident and yet wary.

Her clothes were nice but not showy, he noted when she walked into the café and looked around. The only jewelry he saw were some earrings, tasteful and elegant, a watch and one ring on her right hand.

She locked gazes with him, nodded and made her way over. He may have been suspicious of her motives, but his brother hadn't raised him not to stand when greeting a woman. So he did, holding his hand out.

She took it and shook. Not overlong. Not too soft or too hard. "I take it you're Ms. Forrester?"

After a quick nod, she turned just slightly to put her sweater over the back of her chair. Enough for him to catch sight of the neat knot of hair at the back of her neck. Thick. It would have been thick, and with the mass of it he wagered it hung to her ass. He got a vivid flash of the way it would look, dark and smoky against her pale, creamy, naked skin.

"Gillian Forrester. You're Adrian Brown then?"

She said it seriously and for a moment he believed it. Believed that she really was just making sure instead of knowing it was him without a doubt because she stalked his website or whatever. But he'd been through some type of this scenario more than once, so by that point, he wasn't much up to trusting anyone but himself.

"Yes. Please, sit." He indicated the table and she sat. Her voice was perfect. Smooth. Soothing even.

"I appreciate your time, Mr. Brown. I know you're a busy man."

And suddenly none of that mattered. Because he wanted a whole heaping helping of whatever the hell it was Gillian had on under those clothes. Sure, they covered every part of her, but fabric couldn't begin to hide what had to be a hot fucking body underneath it all.

He let his breath out and leaned in closer. "I was far more annoyed five minutes ago than I am now." He smiled and she returned it, not quite willingly. For some reason that appealed to him too. If she was playing him, she was a fuckin' master, which could work too. But he preferred to think she was genuine.

The server came over. "Can I get anything for you two? A refill on that mocha, Adrian?"

He held his cup out. "Great. Thanks."

Gillian frowned slightly, her lips, lush and juicy, turning just a bit. "I've already had two coffees today. Can I get a cup of tea, please? Just something black?"

"Earl Grey all right?"

Gillian nodded before looking back at him. She hadn't expected to be charmed. The man had been such a cad on the phone, she figured he'd be snotty. Instead, he was fabulously charismatic. Charming. His

speech had a cadence to it, slow and honeyed. Not southern, but something similar. As if he liked to roll his words over his palate before he
gave them up.

And, she had to admit after sneaking a few looks at his hands and
forearms, he had lovely arms. She had a thing about a man's hands.
When a man pushed his sleeves up, she looked. And she liked what
she saw.

Sun-kissed, but not fake-tan orange, a dusting of dark hair. Firm,
muscular flesh. Big hands. He had calluses. She knew from the hand-
shake. Where he strummed his guitar she assumed. Strength but not
a showy type.

His hair was a dark chocolate tousle. Tumbled around his face and
shoulders, taunting her fingers. It would be soft and cool against her
skin. A neat beard and mustache only framed lips she had a feeling
knew their way around a kiss.

And none of this was anything she should be thinking! She should
especially stop looking at his arms. Her fingertips itched to slide along
the tattoo she could see. Musical notes. On the other arm . . . she
paused. "Woody Guthrie," she murmured, not meaning to.

His smile was surprised and pleased. "You know the quote?" He
turned his arm out so she could see it better.

"My grandmother used to listen to Woody Guthrie when I was
younger. She liked to tell this terribly lurid story about how she had a
wild and passionate affair with him back in the day." Oh and wasn't
that an appropriate story.

He laughed though, and she liked it on him so much she didn't
ruin the moment.

When her tea arrived, she put her file on the table and decided to
just say it.

"Thirteen years ago my sister gave up her newborn son for adoption. To me." She licked her lips. "I've asked her several times a year
since she got pregnant just who the father was and until several days
ago, she always refused."

The teasing warmth in his eyes was gone in a second as he physically sat back, away from her.

"No."

She sighed and tapped the folder. "Yes. My sister, Tina, died last week of congestive heart failure, and for whatever reason, she finally decided to tell me who the father was on her way out. Miles and I live on Bainbridge Island." She passed Adrian a card. "This is my attorney. I have other things here. Pic—"

Before she could finish her sentence, Adrian burst out, interrupting her. "Christ. There are easier ways to get money out of me. You've got a nice enough body, a pretty face. This is bullshit. I've heard this tune before. Didn't work for her either."

She blinked several times, her face noticeably paler than it was before.

But her back was ramrod straight as she let out a long breath. "You continue to return to this theme, no matter that I've not asked you for a single thing but your time. Miles is your son. I promised my sister to find you and now I have. Fat lot of good that's done." She had the nerve to look him up and down, finding him wanting.

He stood, the chair clattering behind him, so angry he barely registered the way she flinched before she recovered her composure. "I don't give in to blackmail. I've dealt with whores and gold diggers plenty of times. You played me wrong, baby. We could have burned things up between the sheets. I'd have tossed some money your way. A lot easier than this bullshit."

That's when she stood as well, grabbed her things, tucking the folder into her bag. Her jaw was tight, her gaze narrowed. Every movement was totally precise. Sharp. "You, my son, are a piece of work. No one calls me a whore and walks without a limp. So if you want to keep walking you'll stay behind that table. Bugger it all, you're a sullen little boy. You don't deserve Miles."

She headed out, pausing to put a few ones on the counter for the tea she'd never drink.

"You'd better go! If I see your face again or you contact any of my family, I'll have you arrested for attempted blackmail."

Gillian Forrester paused at the door and sneered. "You're a pathetic little man. Never you worry, I'm done with you and it's all your loss."

Adrian did have to admire the way she sniffed at him and flounced out.

"Shall I call the police?" the server asked.

Brody spoke from where he'd been standing at the doorway. "No. It's fine. Adrian, with me." He indicated the tattoo shop and Adrian headed after his brother, ready to punch something.

She sat in her car, her hands shaking. Impotent anger, a familiar, bitter cocktail, sliding through her system as she fought tears of frustration.

What on earth was his problem? She'd given him Miles. What gift on the entire planet could mean that much? Surely the man had stuck his dick in more than one woman over the years. And yet he had the nerve to attack her?

Humiliation burned at the back of her throat, threatening to choke her. How many times had she had to face such a thing? Public ridicule had been something she'd dealt with on a regular basis back in Newham.

He hadn't taken one second to think about what she'd told him. He didn't know her and yet he'd judged her. How dare he? Adrian Brown with his carefully constructed wardrobe of clothes that probably cost more than her couch. He found *her* wanting? Oh ho! Who the fuck was he?

He'd shown his true colors, the spoiled idiot. And now she'd kept her promise and could go on with her life. Just as she had before.

Taking a long, steadying breath, she headed toward Phinney Ridge. Mary said they'd have Cuban sandwiches today and that sounded very good.

She'd tried. She really had. But she'd done her duty and there was nothing that would make her take any more abuse because the person was too blind to see the greatest gift life ever gave you.

He was a git. A bloody idjit and to hell with him and his pretty, sexy eyes and that drawl.

"What the hell do you think you're doing?" Brody pushed him into a chair.

"Did you hear that?" Adrian surged out of the chair to pace.

"I heard her tell you you had a thirteen-year-old son. I didn't hear her ask you for money. Not once. I heard you call her a whore though. I'm sure everyone in the café did."

"What the fuck is wrong with people, Brody? Huh? What did I ever do but be nice to people and look what it gets me."

Anger burned in his belly that this woman could get under his skin so deep and then use it to hurt him with what he wanted so much.

"What if she's telling the truth? Have you thought of that for one second? My god, Adrian, are you going to try to tell me you never fucked random women you don't remember?"

"I think I'd remember if I had a kid, for fuck's sake! You remember the last one. It was a baby then. We were just lucky I was on tour in Europe for six months and couldn't have been the father. All the money I had to throw at lawyers and then the fucking label was all up in my face about publicity and media this and that to make me look nice. I was hung out to dry on all the gossip sites. People called me a deadbeat, for fuck's sake. All because some stranger needed some cash and decided to pretend some other guy's kid is mine."

Brody sighed heavily and sat on the edge of his desk. "Shut up. Just stop talking for a second and *listen*."

He did stop because he rarely heard that tone in his brother's voice. Displeasure and disappointment. In Adrian.

"You can't look at the world like this. You can't just suspect every-

one because of what some people did. I'm not saying you should automatically believe her. But you're not even paying attention to what
happened."

Adrian tapped his thumb and then his pinky to his thigh, over and
over, faster and faster.

"She came here to tell you the details and you didn't let her speak.
No, you flirted with her and all. She's lovely so I get that. But then she
tries to explain and instead of getting more detail from her you yell
insults at her in a crowded café.

"She said—and I heard because I was listening—that her sister
didn't tell her for the boy's whole life who the father was. She found
out a week ago and she came to you pretty quickly."

"How the fuck can I believe her? Huh?"

"You're a stupid asshole sometimes, Adrian. Yes, some nasty skank
tried to extort money from you with the daddy card in the past. But
the guy I know and love surely understands he can't judge all and
sundry by the acts of some dumb bitch.

"You'd just turn your back on this because why? Huh? Do you
think I'd just sit here knowing I could have a nephew out there, not
even thirty miles from here? Do you think I could turn my back on a
boy who was yours? Huh? And the real question is, can *you*?"

Chastened, Adrian sat, hard.

"If she's telling you the truth, do you realize what she just risked?
If she's telling the truth, don't you want to know? If you have a kid,
how can you not follow up? Are you saying you don't care?"

He heaved a giant sigh. "I'm afraid."

His brother just listened.

"I'm afraid to hope that it's true and then what if it isn't? Chances
are it's not. That's not how this works."

Brody's anger softened and he blew out a breath. "I get that. But
you can't ignore it. Look, she contacted you. She gave you personal
details. She gave you her attorney's card. There is no reason we can't
get an answer. The boy can get a DNA test and that's all you need. If

she's lying, we can figure out if she's trying to extort money from you, or if her sister duped her too. If our kin is out there in the world, we need to know. You're a good man, Adrian. Strong. Loving to your family and friends. I know you better than anyone in the world. I love you and I believe in you. You can be a good father too. I've seen you with my kids, with Alexander and I know this with every part of my being. You have so much love in you."

"I know! I want that so much it's not funny. I've been wondering about contacting an agency to adopt if I can't find the right woman in a few years and do it that way. I want children."

He sighed as Brody sent him that damned knowing raised brow of his.

"All right. I'll call Cope, see what he's found out and we'll get my attorneys on this. I don't have to deal with Gillian Forrester at all. Not until we know answers."

"I've got your back on this. You know that. I'm here for whatever you need." Brody clapped his shoulder.

5

Gillian waved good-bye to one of her students, watching her pull down the long driveway to the road. She had students ranging in age from six to fifty-four. Most were just learning, but a small group were exceptional. She'd been encouraging the one who'd just left to audition for a spot at Berklee.

They had an excellent program on scoring and composition and the girl had a lot of promise.

Halloween was now less than a month away. Funny how fast the fall had taken hold. Tina had been dead nearly a month and though it was sad, Gillian was grateful Miles wasn't much bothered by the death of his biological mother.

They hadn't been close. Tina had simply given Miles to her sister, signed the papers and moved on with her life. She never remembered birthdays and rarely Christmas. Never asked after Miles on the rare occasions she managed to call.

But Gillian had sent her sister pictures anyway. Sent pictures of first smiles and emerging teeth, of steps and first days of school. Had sent handbills and poorly photocopied cast lists of every musical performance and play.

Of her blood family, only Gran had ever cared about Gillian and Miles. And Miles had been inconsolable after her death. For months he'd just burst into tears or would be in a bad mood. Gillian had been similarly bereft. But keeping Miles emotionally healthy had helped her deal with her own grief.

Tina had refused to allow him into her hospital room so he'd stayed with Jules while Gillian was in Portland. No use dragging him down there only to be rejected by Tina.

Throughout his childhood she'd talked to him about Tina. She wanted to be sure Miles knew Tina in some way. But Miles was *her* son. Period. It did not matter where Miles came from, only that he'd come and that was that. She simply accepted that he needed to understand the dark sides of Tina as well or he'd be vulnerable should she ever try to manipulate Miles.

It burned in her belly even then, thinking about her sister and the way she'd simply wasted her life like she had an unlimited supply. Gillian stood there in the cold on her porch, looking out over the life she'd built for her family. She'd built it and no one would tear it apart.

So Miles had assured her that he felt bad, but almost like it had happened to a stranger. He'd been true to his word, bouncing back quickly to his normal behavior. Hanging out with his friends, going to school, passing his classes, though she had to keep on him about turning his assignments in for his humanities class. The boy had actually done the work but just hadn't bothered to turn it in. Oy! She'd been right annoyed at the little monkey over that one.

She'd taken away his computer, his phone and his television and he'd suddenly remembered how to turn his work in.

Tina was a stranger to him and the ache of that lived in Gillian's heart. That her sister had given up this incredible person and had lost out on what had kept Gillian excited to wake up each day.

She had this life. With this house and her son. The vegetable garden they'd put in three years before. The paint on the kitchen walls they'd just chosen on a whim while at the hardware store. The trees all around. This was home and she'd been blessed something fierce to have it.

She went back inside and headed to her piano, pausing to turn the music back on. Benny Goodman's "Sing, Sing, Sing" filled her house and made her smile.

She cleaned up the sheet music, tucking it away for the next lesson. That month she'd taken on two new students, which would pay for the vacation she was planning to go on with Miles to Washington, D.C., in February. They'd swing up to New York after to see one of her old school friends play the Met.

She decided to catch up on some work e-mail before Miles got home from school. Maybe they'd go get milk shakes and see Cal's game.

Instead she'd opened her door to find Cal standing there. "What? Is everything all right?" She pulled him inside. "Cal?"

"I've just had a conversation with and then paperwork verifying that Adrian Brown wants Miles to submit to a DNA test to ascertain if he is indeed the biological father."

"Fuckitall. I thought I was done with him forever."

Cal laughed then, relaxing. "I'm glad you're taking this so well. I wasn't sure how you would after the way you two parted the last time."

"Oh, I'm right murderous, don't mistake me. This is what happens when you try to do something good. But Miles will be home soon and I can't lose it. I started this stupid fucking thing, now I'm stuck."

"I'm sorry. But this way it can move forward and you don't have to deal with any abuse from him. All communication is to go through his legal team. You're not to contact him in any way."

"Whot?"

Cal flinched. "Christ, we got to the place where you lose the end of your words really fast."

"That . . ." She didn't even have words for what he was. "I gave him my information at the very beginning. Since then I have not been the one to initiate contact. Each time he's contacted me and then he's been a dick on his way out."

She began to pace. "He's accused me of all manner of crimes and falsehoods, and now through his attorneys he's coming at me with some edict that I can't contact him? When *he's* doing the contacting? Making me sound like a stalker or summat. I ought to get an order that he can't contact me at all, or my minor son. Hmpf, tell me I can't do something I never done!" She paused and then laughed. "Bet you're getting right scared I'm going to go all crazy low-class London on your ass and then you'll have to clean it up and make me all right before Miles gets home."

She sighed as he goggled at her. "Oh, I know you can't do any of that. And I know you'd let me get it all out before you started to pet me and tell me I was pretty to get me calmed down again. He's a cock, but let's do this on *my* schedule. I most certainly won't be contacting him. If he is indeed Miles's father, we can move on to the next step. I'll have to tell Miles part of the story. I can't consent to having his DNA tested without his knowledge."

"For the record, I knew you'd work your way through it. I just, well, I apologize for missing just how much he hurt you with these accusations. I'm sorry for that. I know it doesn't help to tell you this happens frequently in these sorts of cases. I know one of his attorneys, went to school together. He's a good guy. I don't think they meant it in any aggressive or disrespectful way."

She waved it away. It didn't matter. She couldn't avoid it so she may as well control it and make sure it was over as quickly and efficiently as possible.

"Fine." She paused and patted his arm. "No, I mean it. Let's just do this. I'll call the pediatrician's office now. God, is that something you just make an appointment for with your regular doctor? Can't say as I've done this before."

"They would like you to use a doctor on a pre-approved list. I've got a similar list I use too, so understand that. In fact, one of these doctors here on the list is a woman I've worked with on paternity tests before. She's professional and has a very good reputation. They've offered to pay the cost of the test."

"No. How much is a test like that?"

"It's common for the male to pay the cost of the test, Gillian. Something like this will cost about eight hundred dollars."

Well, now, that was a different story. "Ouch. Fine. Whatever. Just let's do this so we can be done."

"It's just a process. Think of it that way. The father is an affluent and therefore powerful person. His attorneys are paid well to protect him from any false claims. Step by step, we do this right so we can do what is best for Miles. I know you want that, and since this guy is being an ass, you're going to have to do the bulk of the responsible stuff here."

Someone had to be the adult, but why the hell did it always have to be her? She growled and crossed her arms over her chest. "What do we need to do then?"

Erin looked at the GPS and then at the number on the mailbox. This was it. She turned up the long drive. A craftsman-style house. Well-used basketball hoop on the garage.

Current value of this place with the sweeping view of the water with trees all around sat at a hell of a lot more than she'd paid for it originally some thirteen years before.

That's what had really convinced Erin the woman wasn't bullshitting. She didn't know if the woman had been lied to about Adrian being the dad of the kid. Whatever the case, Gillian Forrester believed what she'd said to Adrian.

Erin knew when she saw the woman had dug herself into a place and built a life. Knew a woman like this wasn't the type to be looking to con her brother into a payoff to keep her quiet. A family lived in this house and had for a long time.

There were lawyers involved now. They'd built a moat around Adrian, which Erin approved of. Her brother was a good-hearted man, and she wanted him to be protected.

At the same time, Erin felt like the process was spinning out of control, into acrimony where perhaps none was needed.

So she'd left Alexander with Ben and Todd, who had finally relented to let her go see Gillian after they'd gone over her background check once more. And she'd gotten on the ferry and set about seeing Gillian for herself.

From the other side of the door Erin heard Kings of Leon and smiled despite herself. One of Adrian's favorite bands. A sign perhaps.

Erin knocked and heard the sound of someone moving toward the front door.

And that was the first time Erin clapped eyes on Gillian Forrester.

Pretty. Dark hair. Bangs that fringed big brown eyes. Her lips drew into a bow, complete with dimple at the far corner of her mouth. Petite, she wore flats and a pair of ridiculously adorable skinny-legged pants with a lovely cream-colored sweater.

Her smile was warm for several moments. "Yes?"

"I'm Erin Brown. Adrian's sister."

The easy smile went away, replaced by a calm façade. "Why are you here? You're not supposed to contact me. Your brother made sure I knew this when he had his lawyers inform me so. In writing. Served by my attorney. It was a lovely memory."

Erin knew she deserved this anger on one level. Adrian was so nervous and thrown off balance by this he'd pulled away from everyone and had been writing music nonstop. Erin and Brody had agreed to let him until they got the answers they needed. But this woman, if she was telling the truth, had taken a huge risk and had received nothing but grief in return.

"I wanted to see you myself. Wanted to see if perhaps I couldn't smooth the way a little should the test come back positive. May I come in? He's not here, is he? I checked the middle school schedule and he's not due home until after three. That really sounds stalkery of me. I just wanted to be sure . . . well, naturally I'd love to meet him, but I wouldn't do it without arranging it with you in advance."

"He's not here, no. He has math club after school today so I have to run to pick him up later on."

Erin took a step into the house and saw them. Pictures of the boy all over the walls. It was a punch to the gut, just how much he looked like Alexander. And Adrian. A sense of longing to know him and give him the Brown love he'd been missing.

But also the realization that if Erin was in this woman's place, she'd be freaked the fuck out.

"And I can see the test will come back positive. Christ." She dug in her bag and pulled out a small photo album. "This is my son, Alexander."

Gillian leaned forward and her eyes widened a little. "He's beautiful. Is this recent?"

"This one was just two weeks ago. Miles is clearly my nephew. One only has to look at him to see it. My god. He looks so much like Brody here." She moved to one where the boy must have been eight or nine, holding a cat, grinning at the camera.

"That's Fat Lucy, she's only one of his strays. We have four cats he's picked up along the way. A turtle. We had a dog but he passed on two years ago."

In that face, Erin saw love. So much love she felt a deep affinity for the woman. This was a mother and Erin wanted her to know she wouldn't threaten that.

"He brings home stray animals?"

Gillian's smile was back. "Yeah. He's hopeless and I am weak against it. He's just got so much love to give." She focused on Erin, intent. "This is why I went to your brother. How can I keep him all to myself?"

Erin ached for her, at the same time being very grateful the woman loved that child so much she'd risk a great deal by bringing him to his father. Who then yelled in her face multiple times.

"Can I come in? Have a cup of coffee? I want to know you. I want to hear about Miles. Please."

"Come in. I'll put on a pot of tea." Gillian turned and led the way through the sunny house toward the kitchen. Erin got the chance to devour every detail of the place. Pictures on the walls. Most of mom and son, some of others Erin gathered were extended family or friends.

A grand piano dominated the family room. Music played through the in-house speaker system.

The kitchen had a large table in the nook space. "Have a seat, I'll get the kettle on." She began to bustle around. "Or I can make coffee if you like."

"Tea would be lovely, thank you."

Gillian sat across from Erin, putting a plate with assorted cookies and crackers out. "Biscuits. Erm, cookies." She laughed.

"We lived in London for two months once. Way back at the beginning. Enough for me to get a craving for real malt vinegar crisps every once in a while." Erin took a cookie but didn't eat it. "Tell me about him."

Gillian's smile was back, warm and a little shy. "Miles just turned thirteen and he's often on the tussle between acting forty and, sometimes, infuriatingly thirteen. Surly. Sullen. Snappy." Gillian rolled her eyes, amused affection on her face. "He's a great kid. Smart, though he can be lazy and I have to be on him to get his homework turned in. Musical. Which isn't a surprise really. He's rather sweet. There are three girls who call here all the time and he doesn't seem to know what to do with all the female attention."

Gillian poured out as she spoke.

"Works hard, especially on things he loves like music or animals. Rarely gives me a problem except he grows out of his shoes every few months. He started walking late. Liked to snuggle in next to me and found no reason to get up and go anywhere."

Erin sipped, liking this woman more by the moment. Charmed by the way she spoke about Miles. So totally in love with the boy.

"Gentle. Not very athletic, I'm afraid. He tried for a while and then found computers and games more to his liking. Reading. Writing stories. Music. He's in a band, you know. With his friends. They're quite earnest and sometimes they're even good."

"Yeah? We started early too. I was seventeen when we started Mud Bay. We played music together for years before that. Brody raised us, you know."

Gillian shook her head. "No, I didn't know. I'm aware Adrian believes I am some sort of petty thief out to steal from him in an elaborate game wherein I get his money without actually asking for it. But I don't know a lot about you and your family."

Erin cringed, wishing she could explain all the shit Adrian had to shovel and why it made him so suspicious of strangers. "He doesn't really think that. Brody, well, let me tell you the story and then I'll fill in the other details.

"My parents died when Brody was seventeen. He'd been pretty much raising us as it was. He's the one I have all the big childhood memories with. Anyway, our parents died when I was fourteen and Adrian was eleven. We had some distant family who'd agreed to take us. But only one each. Brody gave up his place at art school, stepped in and took over. He's my big brother, yes, but in a very real sense, he's my father. He's definitely Adrian's. They have a complicated relationship, but Brody runs a tight ship and Brody has been on your side since day one. Adrian listened to Brody and now we're here. He'll be glad he did; Brody is rarely wrong. Which'd be annoying if he wasn't such an all-around great guy."

Because he understood, perhaps, what it meant to be a parent, no matter how it came to you.

"Anyway, Adrian really doesn't believe all the stupid stuff he's said.

I think he's afraid this isn't real. Afraid to get his hopes up and then find out Miles isn't his after all. You really don't know how glad I'm going to be to tell him how utterly certain I am that is not the case. I hope you'll give us a chance, even with the rocky beginnings. I know we might look out of the ordinary, but past the funky hair and the tattoos, we're just like many other families. We love each other and we want to love Miles too."

"You have a lot of money. And a lot of power. I don't have either. I'm trying to do what's right for my child, but it scares me senseless that Adrian has the ability to tie me up in court and try to take my son."

Erin nodded. She reached out and squeezed Gillian's hand. Just a brief, reassuring touch. "I'd be freaked out too, in your place. I can't take all that fear away. I hope that'll happen once Miles and Adrian meet and you get to know us better. But we're not the bad guys. I can't say I'm thrilled about your sister not telling anyone for so long. But you can't own other people's mistakes. I've learned that one, big time."

Gillian found it easy to talk to Erin. It was, well, it was lovely that this woman wanted to know Miles. Her reassurances did indeed help too.

She began to loosen up for the first time since she'd opened the door. She talked about Miles. Told stories about his life as Erin began to unfurl her own, and through that, Adrian's too.

It was simply impossible not to like Erin Brown.

"Miles is going to like you."

Erin tucked a fire-engine-red strand of hair back behind her ear and grinned. "Yeah? I gotta say I'm very much looking forward to meeting Miles. He sounds a lot like Brody. Serious. Likes to take care of people. My brother is going to be heartbroken to know he's missed thirteen years of this child's life. Angry. Jealous. Afraid. I just . . ." Erin licked her lips. "I would just very much like you to give Adrian a break. When he finds out for sure, it's going to hit him hard. I know he's been a pain in the ass so far and that you have been beyond good to him. But I'm going to ask you to give him a little bit more leeway."

Erin shook her head, tears in her eyes. "How could she not tell you? My brother is a good man. He would have been there for Miles."

Gillian sighed. "I honestly don't know. I've asked so many times. She's always refused. I don't know why she finally revealed who Miles's dad was. She just did. And then a friend showed me Adrian's picture, you know, from his website. My friend, I'd just told her about Adrian and she showed me Adrian's picture and held it near Miles's picture. It was obvious, and then I saw your older brother, Brody, and I knew for sure. They have similar smiles, my son and Brody.

"I knew it was true then. I couldn't deny it any further. Not that your brother made it any easier. Prat."

"I'm sorry he's been such a dingus. In his defense, it's hard to be where he is. It's hard because so many people have ulterior motives. It's difficult to trust outside our group. Fame like he has changes how you see everything. He'll do right by Miles. I know it. He'll be a good father too."

"He's the best I've got, you see. Miles. He came along just when I had no idea I needed him. I had other plans, as you do when you're twenty-one. None of the items on my to-do list included two a.m. feedings or moving out here. But then he was there and the nurse handed him to me and everything else on the entire planet simply didn't matter. I will do anything to protect my son. Anything. I'm not doing this to help Adrian. I don't even like Adrian. I'm doing this because if Miles is partly yours too, he can only benefit by having more people to belong to. But if any of you hurt him, you'll never know what hit you."

"I respect that. We have lots of love in our family. Plenty for Miles."

"You can't have him. Just understand that. He's mine. I won't accept anyone who feels as if my son is a place to visit every once in a while, or a prize to be won. He deserves stability."

"I totally agree with you. I feel like I'm Adrian's ambassador." Erin laughed and then laughed some more. "You have no idea, but this is totally novel to me. It's usually Adrian who is *my* ambassador, or Brody. Adrian is the sweet one. The calm one. He doesn't say mean things and he sure as hell doesn't say them to women." She sobered. "He's torn apart. I love my brother very much. He's my best friend. I just wanted to thank you for opening your life up this way so that he can have his son."

Gillian hadn't been close with Tina. Couldn't have trusted her the way Erin so clearly did her brothers. But Erin spoke to her mother-to-mother, and that made a difference. Made some of the fear ebb enough so she could take a deep breath for the first time in a week.

Her phone rang. "Excuse me a moment, it's Miles." She answered. "I'll be leaving in about five minutes. Did you get out early?"

"Ryan's gonna give me a ride home, if that's okay? We're getting ready to leave and he saw us. He's going to drop Kaylee off first, but she's just on the way to our place."

Ryan, Mary's brother who taught at the middle school, had been part of Miles's life for as long as his sister had.

"Yes, that's okay. Hang on a moment." She looked to Erin. "Would you like to meet him? Miles? He'll be home in about ten minutes."

Erin's eyes widened and then she nodded.

"Come straight home, all right?"

She hung up.

"I . . . I really appreciate this. What do you plan to tell him? Does he know about Adrian?"

"The DNA test was yesterday so I had to sit him down and explain it all. Not the identity of his dad. I didn't want to do that until we had proof and I'd spoken with Adrian in depth about how their meeting would go. Or I suppose after Cal—that's my attorney—speaks to Adrian's attorneys. Whatever. I just don't want to upset Miles's schedule or his life. Thirteen is a hard age."

"All right. So I can be a family friend for now. Then I can be his aunt. And don't fret too much about the lawyer thing. It won't be that way forever. Adrian will come around."

They spoke for a few minutes more until Gillian heard Ryan's car out front.

Erin laughed, picking up her bag and heading out with Gillian. "I can't recall the last time I was so nervous to meet a thirteen-year-old boy. Probably not since I was thirteen."

She needn't have worried. He got out of the car at the base of the driveway and the guy pulled away with a wave.

"He hasn't noticed yet," Gillian said quietly.

Miles walked up the driveway at a pokey pace until he saw his mother and smiled. Erin warmed at the sight. Further evidence that the boy had a good life.

He sped up a bit and stopped cold when he really caught sight of Erin.

"Come on then, slowpoke. Come and meet Erin. She's on her way out just now, but I thought you might want to say hello. You know, as one bass player to another."

Oh. He was a bass player too? Erin had remembered he played in a band, but knowing the kid played bass like she did warmed her heart.

She held her hand out and he shook it nearly off her arm. "Wow. This is so awesome. I never knew Mum had famous friends I'd actually recognize. I love your music. I'm trying to learn 'Lashed' right now. Well, *we* are, my band and me. I. Whatever. Wow. Just wow."

Gillian, grinning, stepped closer to Miles and put her arm around his waist because he already towered over her. "Easy there, kid, she needs her arm to tote around her baby and her guitar too."

He laughed, letting go, and Erin so badly wanted to hug him. She settled for another smile. "I'd love to help you work it through sometime. You'll see me again, I promise."

"Go on." Gillian indicated the house with a tip of her chin. "Homework before you even touch your phone or the computer."

"Aw, Mum!"

"Listen to your mother, Miles. It was my pleasure to meet you. I need to go, anyway. My son has been spending the day with his fathers and they'll need the rest."

Miles stammered another greeting and ambled off to the house.

"He walks like Adrian does. That slow lope. Good lord." She looked back to Gillian. "He's a beautiful kid. Thank you for this. Can I call you? Perhaps spend some more time with Miles? I mean, obviously I can't speak for Adrian, but I can speak for myself and I want to know Miles *and* you too."

"Yes. They said the results would be back within two weeks, probably sooner. So once Adrian gets his answers I expect this will all begin to move. Thank you for being so understanding about why I didn't come forward sooner."

"You can't own what someone else did. We talked about this already. I learned that one myself. I'll be speaking to you soon."

She drove away and headed straight to Adrian's.

She didn't bother buzzing him at the gate. Though the siblings had decided to let Adrian lick his wounds for a few days, time was up. She keyed in the code herself and parked, smiling at the sight of one of Rennie's soccer balls near the side of the house.

She headed straight for the studio, where she found him smoking one of his forbidden French cigarettes, bare feet propped up on a table, a yellow notepad at his right hand and a guitar in his lap.

"Your son plays bass."

She came in, shoved his legs off the table and sat, tossing her bag to the side.

"What?" He sat forward. "He does what?"

"I figured there'd been enough talking through lawyers. This woman is your son's mother and she deserves respect and courtesy. Plus I wanted to take her measure myself so I went over there today."

He blinked. "You lie."

"No. I've just spent three hours with Gillian Forrester. Moreover, I met your son. He practically shook my arm off and told me he was learning the bass line from 'Lashed.'"

Adrian pushed from his chair. "You had no right to give her any more ammo against me."

Erin didn't bother with anger or even annoyance. She knew he was hurting. Still, he needed to stop wallowing. "Is that what this is to you?"

"We're not supposed to be contacting her!"

"Sit down and be quiet for a minute while I take you to school, smart-ass. I went over there ready to kick some butt if I had to. This is my family and I will protect it. But then I pulled into her driveway and saw that house and I knew then she was not out to extort or harm you. She's built a life there."

He handed her a bottle of water.

"So she opened the door I knocked on and recognized me after a moment, and though it took me a while to win past the hole you've dug with your attitude toward her, I got to know her a bit. She made me tea. She talked to me about Miles in the way only a woman totally in love with her kid can sound."

"What's she like?"

"She runs a design business. Websites, corporate logos, brochures. That sort of thing. Good work actually. I've seen some of it around town. She gives piano lessons a few days a week. They live well. Not this kind of well." She waved at the home studio Adrian had built for himself. "But the house is good. Solid. She's got a life, Adrian, and there is nothing I saw today that made me think she'd try to raise herself up by hurting anyone else."

"And the boy?"

"Say his name, Adrian. Let yourself believe this. I only met him for a few minutes. He'd just come home from school. Math club, she said. Anyway, he walks just like you do. Christ, he has Brody's smile and his way of things. There is no doubt in my mind that he is your kid. Sweet. A little shy. Super excited to meet another bass player. Ha!"

The ache he'd had in his belly since that very first meeting with her in the café dulled just a bit. A deep slice of yearning replaced it. "You really think he's mine?"

She leaned forward and took his hands in her own. "Yes. I have absolutely no doubt about that. You have a son, Adrian. Happy father's day."

It hit him then with such force he had to sit back to breathe. The reality he'd been holding at bay, telling himself it probably wasn't true, crashed back into his life.

"She took him over to get his DNA test. He knows what it's for, but she hasn't given him any details on who his father might be yet."

"I need to see it for myself. Need to see him for myself. But I don't want to upset him or his schedule."

"He's in school all day. She works from home. Chances are you could catch her there. Call and make an appointment to see her. I like her, Adrian. She loves that boy enough to risk the most important part of her life. This is all for him."

"I can't believe you went over there. Do Todd and Ben know?"

"Yes. We fought about it for a few hours, but I had to see her for myself. I needed to know if I had to cut a bitch or if I had a nephew. I'm glad to say it's the latter. I gotta get home to my boys. You want to come over for dinner? Alexander and Ben spent the afternoon with Annalee. They went to lunch and then the park. Todd said he had plans to grill tonight. You know there'll be enough for a thousand people." She stood and held her hand out.

He didn't take it, hugging her tight instead. "Thank you."

She hugged him back. "How many times have you done stuff like that for me? Huh? That's what you do for your people. You've hid out here long enough. Come back to us."

He had a son. Christ.

6

He knocked at her door three times, stepping back and working on his facial expression. Erin had lectured him on his delivery and the way he'd been with Gillian thus far. He truly didn't want to have an acrimonious relationship with this woman so he needed to try to get things back on track with her. He'd charmed plenty of women in his time—he could do this.

She opened up and her loveliness hit him square in the gut. Soft and feminine with all that hair and those big brown eyes peeking out from the fringe of French roast–toned bangs.

She smelled good too. Sweet and spicy.

He sent her a charming smile. "Hi. I—"

She slammed the door in his face before he could finish his sentence.

He stood there, struck stupid in love with Gillian Forrester. Though he wouldn't know it for a while yet.

Before he could knock again, she yanked the door open, those gorgeous sexy eyes of hers honed in his direction with an angry violence. "You! How dare you come to my doorstep knocking after you sicced your lawyers on me forbidding me from any contact?"

Fascinated by her, by the way her accent had sharpened from that smooth flow to sharp-tongued barbs, he stood, struck mute. Goddamn, he wanted to take a bite.

But not until they got past this thing between them.

"I want to add that I never contacted you after I gave my information to your brother. It was always *you*, you contacting and then you send me a letter telling me I can't do something I never done! You are an arse. A big-headed, too-good-looking-for-his-own-good dickhead."

Well now. This hot governess of a woman was all kinds of dirty underneath. She just threw the gloves off and sent a shiver through him. He took a step closer and found himself half inside her house. Murphy Oil Soap? He breathed in deep.

He let her go on as he tried not to have a fantasy about her polishing the table in nothing but an apron and some heels. Clearly he had some fetish about cleaning and housework. This needed investigating.

"Are you even listening to me?"

"I had to protect myself. Okay? I'm sorry. It was shitty and I was a . . . What did you call me? A good-looking asshole?" She was like one of those little dogs just then, the energy in her radiated outward. She would jump on his back and scratch his eyes out to protect her son. His son.

That mama-bear, elegant-and-modest-on-the-outside, hot-as-all-fuck-on-the-inside thing was ringing his doorbell. And God help him, he knew it was beyond inappropriate to be making up fuck fantasies about this woman right then, but he couldn't help it.

"Leave it to you to choose to interpret what I said that way. The ego on you! Astounding is what—"

And his mouth was on hers, and her words morphed into a groan so sexually tortured his entire body got hard.

Her back hit the wall and she practically climbed up his body to keep the kiss. Her fingers tangled in his hair as his taste first hit her.

She gasped it in, coffee and an Altoid. Stupid to get wet over it, but

Forrester women never had very smart pussies, and that's what was doing the thinking just then.

His tongue slid into her mouth like it was made to be there. Not a single bit of hesitation in him. Adrian Brown owned this kiss and that only made her madder for him.

The sexual tension that'd been stewing, deepening, thickening between them burst over her skin, into her system, taking hold like a frenzy. He was warm against her front. One of his hands cradled her ass where she rested against his thigh.

Dragging her nails over his chest and then down his belly, she shivered and swallowed his tortured moan. The way he had her propped and balanced between the wall and his body brought her thigh against his cock.

One of his hands had been at her waist but he'd slid it up to cup her breast. She arched with a groan and the door slammed closed, bringing a surprised start from them both.

Adrian looked back to her, leaning closer to get back to the kiss, and then he froze.

She managed to extricate herself to turn and look at the picture she knew he'd just seen. Miles on the first day of kindergarten. He'd lost one of his front teeth, on the top, and he cheesed it up, making sure the grin was extra wide.

"Shit."

She saw it on his face. The wonder. The joy and then the sadness that he'd come to it so late. It was at that moment she let go of her anger at him and let herself sympathize.

"That's Miles on his first day of kindergarten. Right out front, as a matter of fact. Would you like to come in and sit down? I can make tea. I've got something stronger if you've a need."

She walked ahead of him, into her house, and let that get her balance back. The kiss, the way she'd totally come undone the moment he'd touched her, had sent her reeling. Gillian was not a kiss-a-total-stranger type of woman. It was the opposite usually. It took her a long time to trust someone enough to get sexual in any way. But when his hands were on her, his mouth, she lost all her rules and fell into their insane chemistry. This bore a great deal of thinking and care. Too bad her hormones were far more interested in jumping on him than thinking.

He'd be reeling too, she knew, for entirely different reasons.

She put a kettle on and moved to the bookcases at the other end of the room. Selecting some photo albums, she brought them back to him. "Would you like to see some pictures? I'm not saying you have to meet him before the test comes back. But I thought . . ." She shrugged, feeling suddenly self-conscious.

"I'd love that. Thank you." He patted the couch next to where he sat. "Please, I'll need you to narrate."

She sat, trying to keep her thigh from touching his.

"I *would* like to meet him as soon as possible. I understand this might be a surprise for him and I want to do this right. But I want to start getting to know him. Being his dad. At this point, the test seems, well, a foregone conclusion."

Fear nibbled at her insides as she held on to the knowledge that she had control here. She was Miles's mom and nothing was going to change that.

It still scared her. The thought of losing him, even if it wouldn't happen in reality, made her sort of woozy.

"All right."

"I appreciate this. The way, well, you brought him to me and you didn't have to. And then I treated you badly. You invited me into your home today. I'm grateful." His lips curved upward just slightly and she repressed a shiver. Oh yes, they had high-octane sexual heat. Which was stupid because this thing between them was foolhardy. He would need to focus on Miles and she'd help him because it was the thing to do. And it would make Miles happy.

"These are organized by year. Yes, I know it's sort of obsessive of me, but for a time when Miles was an infant I made scrapbooks for people to pay my bills." She tried to sound nonchalant, but the truth was, she was proud of those scrapbooks. Had spent a great deal of time and creative energy on them. But suddenly it seemed intimate to share that. So she didn't.

"These are amazing. I can't believe anyone could make something so beautiful. All this detail. He'll have this forever."

She ducked her head a moment. "Thank you. Obviously this is his first year." She touched the first picture of him. A blurry shot she'd taken in the hospital. The card had read, "Baby Boy Forrester," and she had it there, tucked into the page, along with his identification bracelet.

"He was little."

Gillian laughed. "He was premature. But you know he was only in the hospital for a few extra days. We were lucky." Lucky he hadn't had to go through drug withdrawal or suffered any long-term effects from the life Tina had led while pregnant.

Adrian turned the page, amazed at the scrapbook he held. Amazed by her generosity in sharing it with him.

She moved quickly to get the tea and bring it back. She smiled, tapping her finger on a picture of a baby about Marti's age sitting on an elderly woman's lap.

"That's my gran. She lived here with us for a few years until Miles got a little older and I had a steady income. They were inseparable. I don't know what I would have done without her. Especially at the beginning."

On it went, she showed him picture after picture in the first several albums. It was surreal, watching his son grow and change. Knowing other people got to watch him—love him—and all the while Adrian was less than thirty miles away.

"Miles is going to be home in about two hours. Would you like to have some lunch and perhaps talk about how we'll move this forward?"

His stomach growled. "I haven't had much of an appetite, but apparently that's back now. I'd like that. I'm a pretty good helper."

She looked him up and down and seemed to doubt that, but he left it alone. She'd just opened herself up to him and he appreciated it more than he could say.

"You're in luck. My friend runs a food truck and she took pity on me and Miles and brought by a huge amount of food last night." She put several containers out on the counter. "Plates are just behind you, in the cabinet."

He got them out and moved to the island where she poked open containers and hummed her delight.

"Lucky you to have such friends."

She shrugged. "I'm very lucky indeed. Miles too."

He bit into a piece of spanakopita. "Damn, this is good." He sighed. "Why didn't she tell you, Gillian?" He hadn't meant to sound angry, but there it was anyway.

"I don't know. Tina was impulsive, flighty and pretty self-centered most of the time. But I do believe she didn't say anything out of some sort of misplaced duty to Miles."

"How could she look at him and think it was all right for that boy to grow up without a father? That wasn't her choice to make."

"She didn't look at him. She never held him, not a single time. She signed him over to me immediately and then the adoption went forward very quickly. She never named the father on the birth certificate, and to be totally honest with you, I figured she just didn't know. She was a girl who loved a good time with a lot of people. She was reckless and thoughtless a lot of her life, but I never knew her to be malicious."

She poured them some juice and returned to the island. "And no, it wasn't her choice to make and I'm sorry she robbed you of your son and Miles of his dad. All I can do is try to make it right from now on."

His anger ebbed a little. "Thank you. I can't understand it, why she'd have the baby and then give him up without even contacting me."

She looked him dead on. "My sister is dead. Her reasons were her own. She never shared them with me, though I did ask. She liked . . . attention. Whatever those reasons were, there is nothing to be gained in your going over it again and again. I'm not trying to rob you of your anger; you have every right to be mad. Talk to a professional if you need to, and heaven knows you might. But she's not here. Miles is."

"Last night my sister told me bitterness was useless in this situation."

Gillian shrugged. "You said you wanted to move quickly and start being a dad. Would you like to come for dinner tomorrow night? It'll give me a chance to talk to Miles first. Prepare him. I need to be there for this first meeting and it should be small and on familiar turf."

"Did *you* talk to someone about this?" His emotions ran riot, but he continued to be impressed with how she put Miles first over and over.

"I did, yes. Cal, that's my attorney"—she paused to send him a look—"he hooked me up with a counselor he's worked with before. She gave me some handouts." She left the room and came back shortly. "Here. This is what she gave me. It might help." She thrust an envelope into his grateful hands.

"I'd love to come to dinner. I appreciate how supportive of all this you're being. I don't know what I'd do in your place."

"Parenting is hard work. The hardest job I've ever had. What else can I be? Even if you don't like me, I'm Miles's mum and I hope we can work through this mess if for no other reason than to make things better for him."

"I'm surrounded by parents and I guess I assumed it would just come naturally."

She laughed and his desire roared back to life. They'd both played it cool since the kiss, but neither of them had forgotten it. She'd looked at his mouth enough that he was sure of that fact.

"Miles is a good kid, but he'd try a saint sometimes. Naturally? I don't know about that. Maybe it's just me, but I wouldn't say it was natural as much as trying, but alleviated by the fact that you love this person so much you'll endure attitude and having to harp on silly stuff to train them to be good adults. Though I'm not really surrounded by parents. Miles has a lot of aunts and uncles, but I'm the only one in the group who has kids. I could be mucking it all up but not know it."

He doubted it. She seemed eminently capable.

"Anyway. Why don't you show up around six? Would you like to help make pizza? The papers said that an activity might be good, to keep the nervousness at bay but also start building a relationship."

"Hell, I'm the one who's nervous," he mumbled, not used to the feeling at all.

"Come tomorrow night. I'm biased, but Miles is a fabulous person. He's smart and fun and he's going to love you. He nearly passed out after meeting Erin yesterday."

As it was designed to, it made him feel better. "I'll be here at six."

"It's a Friday night so you might have plans, but if you don't, and if you wanted to . . . we have a guest room and you're welcome to it. The ferry is great and there's always the bridge and driving around, but when it's late, it's late." She shrugged and he caught her blush.

"I'll see you tomorrow with my pajamas packed. We'll play it by ear, as they say. But I'm . . . well, I'm grateful to you for sticking this out even when I was a total dick."

"Try not to be one tomorrow and I might forgive you."

He didn't wipe that stupid grin off his face for hours.

Gillian looked at her son across the table. "So, I need to talk to you about something important."

He paused momentarily in between giant shoveling bites to give her his attention.

She hoped she managed to do this with a minimum of scarring.

"I turned in all my homework, I swear. I did get a C minus on my math test."

She made a mental note to scare him into confessing things more often. "No, not that. Though I'm glad to hear about the homework, not so much about the math test." She took a deep breath and forged ahead. "You remember the test you had to take? The DNA test?"

He put his fork down and wiped his mouth, all his attention on her.

"We found your father, Miles. I've met him and he'd like to meet you. Would you like that?"

The line between his eyes deepened as he thought. "Well . . . what do you think? What's he like? Will I have to go live with him?"

She got up and moved to sit next to him, hugging him tight. "Miles, I am your mother. Period. You live here with me. This is our house. I never would have sought him out if I wasn't totally sure my rights as your mum were protected."

He swallowed hard and nodded, brightening enough to shove half a dinner roll into his face. " 'Kay then. So what's he like?"

"He's a musician." She snorted a laugh.

"Oh my . . . *dude*! It's Adrian Brown. That's why Erin was here." He jumped up. "Are you kidding me? *Mum!*"

She laughed and took his hand. "How'd you know?"

"Isabel, you remember her? She said I looked like him and then all the other girls, they said it too."

A year ago, he'd have said it with mild disinterest. Now, well, now he thought it was pretty cool, she could tell.

"It's not every day awesome rock-star bass players just come over for tea and biscuits. I can put it together. Anyway, why'd he bail for so long?"

"He didn't know. I told you, Tina only finally admitted who the dad was in the hospital. I had to track him down. I don't know him that well, but I do know he's really excited about you."

"Yeah? I guess that'd be all right. Here, right? With you around?"

He looked very young just then, vulnerable, and she vowed that should Adrian Brown ever harm her baby, she would cut his bollocks off with a rusty fork.

"I thought it would be fun, and sort of you know, low key, if we made pizza. He could come over and make them with us. Would that work for you? I'll be here the whole time," she added at his questioning look.

Admittedly, she felt a little better. She didn't know what she thought. That'd he'd see the shiny daddy who is a rich rock star and perhaps forget about her? Petty and silly, but it had been a worry, albeit a very small one.

"You'll stay? For the whole time?"

"Of course. Look, if you don't feel ready, that's okay too. We can start out with a phone call or two, or even some letters and e-mails. You don't have to do anything you don't want to."

"I think pizza could be all right. As long as you're here."

"Definitely."

7

Adrian juggled the photo album, a bottle of wine and the box of cup-cakes to raise his hand enough to ring the bell. A bicycle was parked against the side of the house.

His son's bicycle.

Before he could have a panic attack over it, Gillian opened the door and took his breath away. Her hair was in a high ponytail. She wore an argyle sweater of all things, but holy shit she filled it out. Couldn't see any skin other than at her wrists and yet she looked ridiculously sexy anyway. Black pants hugged her legs and led to bare feet with deep red toenails.

She wore glasses and absolutely no makeup. And she was hotter than the sun.

"Hi, Adrian. Come in. We're in the kitchen." She took the bakery box and he followed her through the house and found himself in the kitchen, face-to-face with his son.

"Adrian, this is Miles. Miles, this is Adrian Brown."

Miles looked as nervous as Adrian felt. He'd asked Brody's opinion as to whether he should hug the boy. Elise had urged him to just let

Miles lead. To be open and affectionate, but to respect the boy's space and also his nervousness.

"Hey." Miles tipped his chin and Adrian tipped his back, only with a grin. One the boy mimicked and sent a shock of recognition through him.

"Hey yourself. Big week, huh?"

Gillian laughed, taking the wine and the photo album, making sure he saw where she'd placed it on a nearby table.

"Okay, Adrian, we're rolling out dough and cutting up toppings. Do you have a preference?" The take-charge way Gillian spoke seemed to calm Miles down as it did Adrian.

"I'll wash up." He pushed the sleeves of his shirt up and caught Gillian looking. She blushed and turned her attention back to the island where Miles was shredding cheese.

Well now.

Forearms? Guitar playing had given him decent ones, he supposed, looking at them as he scrubbed his hands.

He turned and took the towel she held out.

"I'm a good hand with dough rolling. I worked at an Italian restaurant for two years back in the day."

"Nice!" She pointed at the balls of dough covered with a cloth. "There they are. Pans are oiled and there's a dusting of cornmeal on them."

He began to work, letting the simplicity of the moment and what they were doing roll over him. "So, Miles, I just wanted to tell you how proud I am to be your father. I apologize for not being in your life before this. But I hope you'll let me make it up to you."

Miles looked up from the cheese and then over to his mother before nodding. "Okay."

"What's your favorite subject in school?" He had to get to know his kid sometime; it seemed good to start with the easy stuff.

"Science."

Gillian moved around with quiet efficiency, slicing onions and mushrooms. She poured a glass of juice and put it at Miles's side. Miles leaned his head over toward her, touching her just briefly. She smiled, closing her eyes for a moment and while that easy intimacy reminded him of how he had lost out on thirteen years of Miles's life, he also found himself comforted by it.

"Adrian, would you like juice? Water? Beer? Wine?"

He paused, not knowing. He'd brought wine, but he didn't want his son to think he was some drunken rock star.

"Why don't you start with some juice and we can have wine with dinner? Does that work?" She poured herself a glass and he nodded, grateful.

"Thanks."

"What was *your* favorite subject in school?" Miles surprised him by asking.

"History. I still love it."

"What period?"

"All of it really, but I have a soft spot for American history. Especially 'round the end of the nineteenth, beginning of the twentieth century."

"Industrial revolution."

Adrian let his breath out and grinned. "Yeah. What about you? You like history?"

Their conversation wasn't deeply emotional. It was, well, rather like the conversations he had with Rennie, only thirteen-year-old boys were definitely not as chatty as a ten-year-old girl.

They ate pizza and salad and devoured a few cupcakes.

"I just remembered I need to call a client to check on something. I'll be right back. Adrian, that photo album you brought is on the table there."

She ducked from the room and Miles eyed him warily.

"I thought you'd maybe like to see your family. The other side of it, I mean. Your aunts and uncles and cousins. They're all very excited to meet you." Adrian opened the first page to pictures of the Brown kids and smiled.

"Is that you?" Miles scooted closer to peer at the page.

"Yeah. Me, my sister Erin and our older brother Brody." Adrian brushed a fingertip over the three of them, frozen forever, mid-cheese for the camera. Erin had a big smile, her mouth full of perfect teeth. Adrian's grin had plenty of missing teeth, though. "It was a summer trip to . . . your grandpa's hometown. Cleveland, Ohio."

Miles raised one brow. "I went to Cleveland two years ago. Youth jazz band competition. It was all right. Hot though."

"Jazz band, huh?" Adrian turned the page. "Me too." He pointed at a picture of him in black slacks with a white dress shirt. Hair too long. Holding the guitar Brody had bribed him with. "Never went out of state though. I hear from your aunt that you play bass. Sheesh, boy, she's already insufferable about her bass thing. You couldn't play guitar instead?"

Miles's laugh felt like victory to Adrian.

They continued to go through the book, page by page, as Adrian filled in a rough sketch of his life. Miles asked more questions as the time went by.

And that's how Gillian found them when she returned nearly an hour later. Oh, she'd stood at her office door and peeked at them, had watched to be sure Miles was all right. And he was. He'd warmed up considerably to Adrian and that was a big relief.

It made her warm to see them, to see this man love her son, *their* son, in his own easy way. Miles had plenty of men in his life with Ryan and Cal, but this was different.

Miles licked his lips a few times, the way he did with her when he wanted to ask a question he wasn't sure of the answer to. She sat across from them, waiting for him to speak.

"So, um, you wanna see my room? My bass?"

Adrian's gaze cut to hers and it was so surprised and touched, she couldn't help but smile at him.

"Yeah, I'd love that."

Miles grinned and hopped up and they left the room, Miles chattering as he landed on a topic he loved so much.

She sat back and let out a long breath. She'd always had a vision of how her family would be. Always wanted normalcy and stability. And she'd ended up a single, unmarried mother. At first glance it looked like what her own mother had been, and that had left her shaken. But once she'd dug down a few layers, she realized there were far more differences than similarities.

She pushed from the couch and headed into the kitchen. Above her, she heard the tromping of both males and then shortly thereafter, the thud of the bass being played.

The kitchen was a mess, so it gave her something to do while Miles and Adrian were upstairs, wanting them to mix and mingle, happy they seemed to be making a success of it.

Adrian Brown was nothing like she'd imagined.

He was without a doubt the most compelling man she'd ever met. He exuded charisma without trying. His allure was that he was a refreshingly complicated man. He looked like the star he was. She sighed, thinking about his voice. Every sentence had its own sort of flow. It was, she thought with an amused and slightly horrified snort, like being hypnotized.

He could walk into any room and instantly grab everyone's attention. His hair, so sexy and tousled. Browns with the occasional auburn hue, it hung to his shoulders, framing a face that had featured itself in no less than three masturbation sessions since that kiss in her hallway.

It had been delicious between her fingers as he'd kissed her. She imagined what it would feel like trailing over her breasts as he made his way to her pussy. She squeezed her thighs together just to ease the ache.

He was long and substantial. A high, tight ass that she really wanted to take a bite of. Wanted to feel that ass against her calves as he fucked her and she wrapped around him.

If he fucked like he kissed, she'd have a very good time. They'd be hot, sweat slicked as they slid, skin to skin. She got a pretty good feel of what he was packing when she'd been against her hallway wall, his body pressing against hers with just the right amount of pressure.

She shivered. A dominant kiss from a laid-back man. An image of him fucking her from behind, her hair wrapped around his fist, sent a flash of desire through her so hot she found herself sweating.

Whew. She had to pause and fan her face with a towel. So totally inappropriate! Yup, she was going to have a date with her showerhead five minutes after he left.

"So, how do you feel about getting to know each other?" Adrian really liked his kid.

"How do you mean? Like tonight? Or like hanging out regular and stuff?"

"Both. I'd like us to hang out. I'd like to become part of your life and I want you to be part of mine. I want you to meet your aunts and uncles and cousins. I want to be your dad."

"Okay, that would be cool, I guess." There was a *but* at the end of that sentence. Adrian could see it.

"Miles, I want to do this right, but I've only been a dad like two days and I have to apologize in advance for all the messing up I'm going to do. But I'm going to try really hard and I can do a better job if you talk to me so we can figure this out together. I know you don't know me well, but you can trust me with what's bothering you."

"I like it here. I like my school and my friends and I love my animals. And I love Mum. I don't want to leave her, or make her sad by ignoring her. I know Tina never told you and that sucks. Don't tell Mum I said that one." He grinned, sheepish, and Adrian let some of the tension go even as the resentment about Miles's birth mother stoked. The woman wouldn't let Adrian have his son but didn't keep him herself either. She robbed them both.

But it wasn't Gillian's fault. While there was no doubt in Adrian's mind that Gillian would move mountains for their son, there was also no doubt that she hadn't known and had mothered his son. Their son.

"I know it's not your mom's fault. And I would never make you be anywhere you didn't want to. I'd like you to spend time at my house. I've got several rooms for you to make your own. I even have a home studio if you want to jam. I want you to feel at home there too." He leaned against the doorjamb, trying to remain relaxed and feeling all out of his element.

"Cool. Mum got me a cell phone for my birthday. I'm only supposed to have it on after school, but I could give you that number and maybe get yours." Miles tipped his chin casually.

This would be all right. He took the phone and put his number in, letting Miles do the same.

"Dude! You have Willie Nelson's phone number? That's awesome."

Adrian grinned, nodding. "It is awesome. He's a very cool guy and I was lucky enough to do some work in the studio with him two years ago."

"It's pretty sweet that you know people like Erin and Willie Nelson. Did Mum tell you she named me after Miles Davis?"

"Mum?" Miles clambered downstairs and across the house to her. He was so happy it brought a prick of tears to her eyes.

"That's me."

"Two things. One, I invited Adrian to spend the night and he said you already had so he's staying over and will you make French toast tomorrow? And, tell Adrian the name story."

Adrian looked just as happy as Miles did. "Miles told me he was named after Miles Davis. And then he said you tell the story best. Lay it on me."

"All right. On one condition: it is eleven and you need to head to bed after the story. Also, that was three things. Yes, I'll make French toast tomorrow." She kissed Miles's forehead and he agreed.

She looked back to Adrian, pleased that Miles had put his arm around her waist and his head on her shoulder.

"The day I brought him home from the hospital, he didn't have a name yet. But he was sweet and snuggly and we hung out as I tried to figure out what to do with a baby because I didn't have the slightest idea." She laughed at the memory.

"I kept looking into his face saying different names. He'd screw his mouth up or look sour, sometimes he looked bored or angry. He got fussy and we danced around the hotel room, me calling him Albert and William and Levi. But none fit.

"And Miles Davis came on the television. *The Cool Jazz Sound.* This documentary about him." She met Adrian's gaze and realized he knew what she meant. "I said, *Lookie here, Baby Boy Forrester, it's Miles Davis.*"

Miles snuggled into her side and she snorted a laugh. "He stopped fussing immediately. He looked up at me with those big green eyes and blinked. That was that. I could have checked to see if he liked John since Coltrane was on the telly too. But I said, *Oh, and there you are, Miles. Big name for a wee boy.*" She said it in the same tone she always told it in, putting extra English into it, and Adrian laughed.

"And so I became Miles Blue Forrester." That Miles always said it so proudly made her deeply happy.

"Erin will love this story," Adrian assured her.

"We had a deal. To bed with you. I'll see you in the morning."

He let her hug him a little extra, and clung a little longer than normal. "I love you. I'll be up in a few minutes, all right?"

He blushed. "Mum!"

"No shame in liking to have your mom tuck you in. I'll see you in the morning." Adrian and Miles clasped palms, each of them not quite knowing what to do yet. Gillian found the awkwardness of it sweet.

"Why don't you go get your stuff?" She turned to Adrian once Miles had left. "When I come back downstairs I'll show you where the guest room is and, if you like, we can have a fire on the back deck and share a bottle of wine if you're not too tired."

"That would be most welcome." He moved to go and stopped just at her front door. "And thank you. For him. For this."

Smiling, she went up to her son.

He'd managed to change into pajamas and get his face washed.

She sat on his bed. "I love you." She kissed his forehead. "Big day for you. You okay? Want to talk?"

"He's all right. He has Willie Nelson's phone number. How awesome is that?"

"Pretty impressive."

"He's a big star. It's weird. He doesn't act like one, but he is."

She knew what the boy meant.

The wonder wisped away, replaced by fear. "Do you think he's disappointed that I don't play sports and have a million girlfriends and stuff?"

"No. I don't. Not one bit. I know I'm your mum and all, but he sees what I do: a fabulous, smart, talented kid. You're musical, just like he is."

"Like you are, too. I got it from you first."

Oh, he was determined to make her cry. She shook her head and kissed his forehead again. "You got it from both of us, I'd wager. Anyway, I get the feeling he likes you for you, not for your potential RBI. He's a decent man, from what I can tell. He's your dad, he's going to love you for you."

"Are you sad? That you have to share me? 'Cause, Mum, I still love you best."

She laughed, squeezing his hand. "Right back at you. And mother-love doesn't work that way. I love you because you're my son. He loves you for that reason too. It's hard to open our lives up to a stranger. I worried, I'll admit that. As long as he respects our life and works with me like he should, like I should with him, things will be fine. This isn't about me anyway, it's about you. I never like sharing! You know how I am about my crisps, and you're far more important to me than that."

He snuggled down in his blankets, a smile on his face that made her feel a lot better.

"Sweet dreams. I'll see you in the morning." She stood.

"Love you," she called as she trailed down the hall and toward the stairs.

"You too, Mum."

8

Adrian stood at his car for long moments once he'd gotten outside before he finally gave in and called Erin. It was late. She was a mom, but he knew she'd be waiting for an update.

"God, it's about time," she said as she answered. "So. Tell me."

"It's really, really good. He's an amazing kid. Sweet. Heart-on-his-sleeve kind of sweet. He's got all these strays." He laughed. "Four cats. Christ. Gillian seems to just roll with it. I'm going to stay over here and have French toast in the morning."

"I'm so happy for you. I really can't wait to get to know him. Invite him and Gillian too, for dinner next weekend. He'll feel better if she's with him the first time, and I think it's wise to include her. I like her."

He did too. A whole hell of a lot.

"I do too. I'll ask them both. Plan something at my place, invite the immediate family."

"Do it here so Todd can grill. You know how he loves that damned thing. Anyway, yes, it'll be a birthday party."

Adrian had to clear his throat to get past the emotion from that statement. "Yeah. Exactly. Thanks. I'm going to go. I just ducked out to get my bag. I'll call Brody right now so he won't worry."

"Good. He called once to ask if I'd heard from you yet. I love you. Come over when you get back so you can tell me all about it, okay?"

"I will. Love you too."

He hung up and called his brother, giving Brody the same info and promising to get together when he got back home.

Standing there in her yard on her big lawn with its beautiful view of the water in the distance, he could see the stars so bright above. His breath misted around his face as he turned to go back inside.

He liked her house. It had an easy feel to it. She had a few really great antique pieces. A sideboard served as an informal divider between the dining room and the kitchen while still leaving it open. The chest serving as her coffee table probably sat in someone's attic for a good thirty or forty years until it got put out at a garage sale.

There was a lot of color on the walls. A deep but bright yellow in the kitchen. The bathroom he'd used was blue. Miles's bedroom had a ceiling painted blue. He liked that about her.

The space they lived in was eclectic and vibrant, just like, he was beginning to discover, Gillian was.

"Clearly you've got a green thumb," he said, pleased to find her coming into the room. Plants hung and perched, they popped up on windowsills, on tables and shelves. Everywhere.

"Well, it's been a trial sometimes. Miles and his cats." She rolled her eyes, but the affection was written all over her. "Lord above. One of them, Fat Lucy, well, she's a plant eater so I had to be sure all the plants I have in the main areas and on the patio are nontoxic. Lucky for her, Jones protects her and swats at her big dumb head when she gets near something she's not supposed to be near." She grabbed the bottle of wine and two glasses. "Still up for a fire outside? You don't have to. You must be tired and maybe just a little shell-shocked by all this."

"I'd like that, though it's really cold out there."

"Grab that blanket right there." She indicated the blanket with the tip of her chin.

He followed her out the back and across a deck. "This is great."

"Thanks. This place was rickety when we first bought it. Over the years we've added things. Painted. Replaced windows. All that stuff. We have friends over a lot so it's nice to have a good outdoor space."

She drew him down the steps and toward a paved, circular fire pit surrounded by chairs and benches. One flick of the switch and a fire sprouted merrily. She smiled and sat on a small bench, putting the wine and glasses down. A black cat streaked through the yard, rubbing across her legs on the way.

He leaned back, happy to sit in the quiet and sip a glass of wine. She wasn't always trying to make noise for the sake of it. He liked that about her.

"My place has this sort of quiet, but even so, it's in the city. This is real dark out here."

"Makes the stars very easy to see."

He paused, tucking the blanket around her and then himself. "*Thank you* seems a pale tribute for what you've given me." He snorted and then breathed deep. Someone somewhere had a wood fire burning.

"I think Miles had a great time. He was positively giddy about you having Willie Nelson's phone number." She laughed and he wanted more.

This place, this moment, it was beautiful and relaxed. He felt safe and comfortable and able to be who he was without having to be on guard.

"At least he's got good taste in music, even if he plays bass. Erin's never going to let me hear the end of that. She likes you." He licked his lips and her eyes moved to his mouth. The echo of that appraisal shot straight to his cock.

"I found your sister impossible not to like back. She's straightforward and protective of her family. She took a risk in coming here."

"She's a force of nature."

"A good way to describe her. And how are you, Adrian? A lot has happened to you over the last month or so."

"Birds flying high, you know how I feel. Sun in the sky, you know how I feel. Breeze drifting on by, you know how I feel. It's a new dawn, it's a new day, it's a new life for me," he sang softly.

"Fish in the sea, you know how I feel. River running free, you know how I feel," she completed. "I must tell you I feel much better about you that you'd quote Nina Simone to me."

He burst out laughing. "I was just thinking the same thing. Relieved you didn't think it came from a commercial." He reached out to squeeze her hand and the moment shifted back to what they'd had in her front hallway only the day before.

The tail of her hair was so close. He gave in to his desire to touch. And the soft, cool strands against his wrist sent a hum of pleasure through him. In the moonlight and the glow of the flames, her skin looked even better.

Her pupils nearly swallowed the iris of each eye. Her lips parted and he heard her gulp. Part of him registered relief that she was as off balance and drawn to him as he was her.

"My brain wonders why I'm out here with you, when it would be far safer inside, in the light, in the open." She made no effort to move.

"I've had similar arguments and have decided to just accept two things I find utterly true. First, that Miles is my son and I plan to be part of his life." He paused, making sure she got that that was his top priority. "You've been good to me in making that happen and I hope I can continue to count on your help. Because Miles is my family and that means you are too. That's just how it works with us Browns. *That* is separate from *this* other thing I also know as true."

"Yes? And what's that then?"

"We have something." He twirled her hair around his finger, fascinated by the way her lips canted up just a whisper.

"Do we now." It wasn't a question at all. It was a tease and he liked it.

"Oh yes. Yes, we do."

"What do you plan to do about it?" One perfectly shaped brow rose.

"I don't know. This is . . . has the potential for trouble. I want to do this right."

She nodded, humming when he drew the pad of his thumb over the hollow just below her ear. "You're not helping me be clearheaded, Mister Brown."

"Just being here with you has made me totally fuzzy headed." And hard everywhere else. "And"—he set his glass down before scooting closer—"perhaps I prefer you less than clearheaded. Because . . ." He hesitated, his lips so very close to hers. "I think I'd love it if we could take this inside and I could divest you of your clothing and perhaps set out to make you unravel a few times."

"Is that so? That's a bold statement."

"It is." He nodded before leaning in to run his mouth along her jawline. "You should let me prove it, to protect my honor and reputation."

"I—I . . ." She groaned. "Can't have your reputation impugned. It's just I'm quite demanding when it comes to sex. I'll put you through your paces. Won't let you slack."

He smiled against her flesh, loving the frantic beat of her pulse against his mouth.

"Will you grade me? Because"—he burrowed a hand under the blanket and slid it up her belly to her breast—"I have to tell you how much that appeals to me." Made him feel like a naughty schoolboy in all the best ways.

"It's like that, is it?" Her fingers dug into his shirt and the muscles of his shoulder.

"It is."

She pushed back a little, sitting next to him. "I am not prone to this sort of rash behavior. I'm certainly not prone to anything that could harm Miles, and this could. I think we should talk first. Set some ground rules." She licked her lips and he forgot what she'd said for a moment or two.

Finally, he found his words again. "Yes, yes, okay."

"We have to keep this"—she waved her hand back and forth between them—"separate from your and my relationship with Miles. I'm not looking for forever, but I'd like to remain low-key, especially in front of him. He's a smart, very observant kid. He's going to notice at some point if we do this more than once."

"We will definitely do this more than once."

She made a cute, sort of frustrated sound. "He's going to figure it out eventually."

"I agree we need to be careful, especially around Miles. I'm not going to jump on you in front of him."

She licked her lips again.

He groaned. "You gotta stop that. I can't think when you do that."

She smiled. "This may be crass, but I'd just like to establish up front that should this end. When. If. Whatever, let's keep that private and never let it touch Miles."

"Not crass at all. Responsible. You're his mother and you put him first, and yes, of course, I agree that should things end that we never let it affect Miles. I'm asking you to let me co-parent our son. I expect us both to put him first." Not that he had any plans at all to stop getting all up in Gillian Forrester's panties any time soon. Still, he appreciated the reminder and, he supposed, the parenting lesson.

"I'm a very private person. My sexuality, what I do and what I like, none of it is for public consumption. I like a space between who I am behind closed doors and who I am out there." She indicated the rest of the house.

He nodded. *Um, yes, please.* If he could have extra helpings of that he'd take it with gravy. The whole thing got him hard and hot. So cool and unruffled and then, something altogether sultry once the shades went down.

"I look forward to learning a few things about what you do and what you like. And I have zero problems with privacy. I take it every moment I can get it. I like to keep my private life off the radar. I want to keep all this private. The out there and the in here both."

Her smile brightened for a moment and he knew she was pleased. "All right then. I'm down with whatever you can cook up."

At that a full flush moved through him from head to toe.

And just like that, she stood. "All right then. Clock's ticking, Adrian Brown. Dazzle me and I might just give you an A."

He grabbed the blanket while she took care of shutting the fire down and bringing the wine and her glass inside.

She flipped lights off, locked doors and led him down a hall to the north of the kitchen where he grabbed his bag.

He paused at her doorway, surprised.

Red.

"I've got to say, I've imagined your bedroom many times since yesterday alone, and this never entered my mind."

"Is that so? And why is that?" She moved around him to close and lock the door.

He turned to catch sight of her pulling her hair loose and the cascade of it around her shoulders and back.

"I expected to find roses and cream. Not shiny red walls and bamboo hardwoods. It's unexpected. Sexy." He backed her up to the door, caging her with his body.

Gillian laughed, albeit a little nervously. First that he'd expect roses and cream, ha! And most important, the way he'd hemmed her in, his body just barely touching hers, features intent, sent her pulse racing.

Sex was complicated business.

Which didn't stop her from having it, of course, because she loved it. She'd given in and accepted that one's baser urges weren't all bad and liking sex didn't make her her mother or her sister.

But this. This thing with Adrian Brown was foolhardy. Yet she knew she wasn't going to stop it. Their little talk had assuaged some of her fears, but it was as if she was totally intoxicated and under the influence of Adrian Brown.

He set her on fire and the burning was the best part.

"I like red," she managed to stutter out as he leaned into her, pressing his open mouth against her throat, where it met her ear.

And then he breathed her in, his face in her hair, and paused as if he savored her. It made her weak in the knees.

Made her want more.

As if the world had slowed down, he drew her against his body, arm banded around her waist.

And he swayed to the music she'd turned on when they'd entered the room.

Just a slow, full-body touch. She pressed her face into his chest, eyes closed, and leapt into whatever this experience would bring her.

As if he'd sensed this certainty in her, that mouth of his smiled. "There you are." His words were drawled, like he did sometimes. When he did it, the sound of them would stroke her senses.

The shuffle must have been on, because it went from Kings of Leon to the Stones. Which also seemed to work because suddenly her sweater was up and over her head.

"Well now, look at you, Mister Brown."

"Goddamn, I love it when your accent does that." He drew his hands up her sides, skin to skin, as he stared at her breasts. Thank the fates she'd worn the hot bra instead of one of her plain ugly comfortable ones.

"I can't believe what you've got goin' on here, Gillian. You are fucking spectacular under those clothes you hide yourself with. And damn it, the Rolling Stones." He paused a moment to listen to "Soul Survivor." "Hot. You have awesome taste in music."

"Just another one of my fabulous personality traits." She returned the favor, removing his shirt and taking him in.

"That's what I'm afraid of," he murmured, popping the catch on her bra to reveal her breasts.

She slid her palm up his chest, pausing at the nipple ring. If she was spectacular, then he was a universe more. He was all rock-and-roll bad boy once the shirt was off.

"Wait." She pushed back from him to look better.

If she'd expected him to be shy, she'd have been wrong. He let her look her fill, that sexy smile of his planted on his mouth.

She shivered, thinking about his mouth a moment as the music shifted to Vivaldi.

He stood there in her bedroom, hair tousled, sexy-mouthed rock star. Complete with three gold hoops in one ear and a bar running through his right nipple.

Broad shoulders led over a tightly muscled chest down to a narrower waist. On his belly lived an intricate Celtic tattoo. "Is that a serpent?"

He made a sound, sort of a growl, as she traced over it. Warm, hard skin pebbled under her touch. She wanted to purr at the power of that moment.

"Yes. I've got another you might want to see."

She laughed, charmed.

"Another tattoo? Or another serpent? Never mind, I'll see both."

"If you don't kill me first."

"Now why would I do that? Today, anyway. Perhaps you'd have received a completely different answer to that question a week ago."

"Seems my luck is looking up. Your tits are the most incredible things I've ever seen. Just so you know and all. I'm going to be spending a great deal of time getting acquainted with them." He caught his bottom lip between his teeth and worked it.

"Cheek." She shook her head, trying to be stern and failing.

He held his hands out as if to surrender, and her attention was again snagged on his body. On those hot and sexy forearms she'd seen a glimpse of earlier. All covered in water and then later flour from punching and rolling out the dough.

Now she got the whole package. "I must admit to you that there's just so much to look at I feel a little faint."

"Take your time." He slid his hand up his belly, flicking his nipple ring. "Because I will be getting all up in you when you're finished."

Whoo. Boy.

"You're very good at the foreplay. Whatever will you be like when you're buried in me to your balls?"

His smile changed, just a little bit. This one drew her in closer as she ran her palms over powerful hands and wrists, sliding her fingertips over knuckles and the sensitive wristbones on her way to the tattoos.

"You're a dirty girl."

She looked up, holding his gaze. "I know what I like."

He leaned down and took her mouth. Hot as a fever, need crawled through her belly. A delicious, nearly painful pleasure twisting through her.

This kiss was slow and deep. His tongue tasted, teased, danced along hers. His taste dizzied her, sent signals to every part of her body. Her cunt, already slick for hours, was so sensitive and ready that every time she moved, just that small bit of pressure sent little shocks of pleasure skittering through her.

Her nipples slid across his chest, making it worse. Well, no, *better.*

When he broke the kiss, it left her a little off-kilter for a moment as she gripped his arms, looking into his face. She licked her lips, wanting more of his taste, and he groaned.

"You have no shirt on. This is very distracting."

"I can say the exact same thing." She stepped back and indicated him with a tip of her chin. "Look at you! Those jeans fitting you just right so that now all I really want to know is if you've got yourself a pair of the other kind. The ones that are threadbare on the back pocket where a wallet was carried." She reached out and drew her nails up the front of his jeans, over the zipper and his very hard cock. "And here on the front. The kind with a hole in the thigh, frayed at the hem."

"Now I know what I'll wear the next time I see you."

She'd look at him some more *after* they both came. She made herself that promise. But for the moment, she had to get him in her, on her, against her.

"You should take those off."

"Oh, are we at that portion of this evening's events?" He said this as he unbuttoned and unzipped his jeans and slid them slowly over his hips and to the ground, stepping out of them, his underwear and socks too.

"I'd just sort of made a deal with myself to look my fill at you after we both came, but then you go and show me all of you."

Sun-kissed, just like the rest of him. A dusting of dark hair covered long, muscular legs. Tight calves, powerful thighs. A cock so hard it tapped his belly.

"And here I thought I'd have to use my showerhead after you left tonight. This is much better," she murmured, staring at him like the visual buffet table he was.

"Never use a showerhead instead of me. Unless I'm there to watch." He sighed, happily eating her up with his gaze. "We'll need to get back to that later. Now, I took off my pants, English. I have to propose you do the same. It's only fair."

Aware he watched her every move, she slowly drew the long zipper at the back of her pants down before stepping out of them. She left the panties on. Because, well, duh.

"Wow. That's. Whew. Gillian, each layer you peel back is more amazing than the last. And while"—he circled, looking her over—"these panties are hotter than the sun, I want to see all of you."

He kissed her shoulder, tripping his fingers down the line of her spine.

When she'd kicked her panties to the side, he gulped and shook his head.

"Curves that lure a man to explore in every way possible. I want to eat you all up."

As if she'd complain?

He fell to his knees, brushing his lips over her belly.

"I can smell how much you want me."

That hit her right in the gut, wrenching a small groan from her lips.

"Now I think I need to taste how much you want me."

He surged to his feet and flopped himself on her bed. She scrambled on, straddling him as she crawled up his body. He put his arms above his head, distracting her with his bulgy pecs and the tats.

"I sure like the look of you. Perched up there, your pussy sliding along my cock like that. Nipples so dark and hard it makes my mouth water."

"These?" She cupped her breasts, testing their weight, all the while loving the way he stuttered out a breath.

"I'm really going to be getting even with this." He said it as he began to do it, using a long strand of her hair to play over her nipples.

"Dazzle me, rock star."

His sleepy green eyes went half lidded, his touch slow and sensual as he replaced the teasing touch of her hair with the roll, tug, pinch of her nipples.

She arched to get closer and he hissed. "You're so fucking hot and wet. Now I'm the one who doesn't know where to start."

She leaned across him and fished around in a vase on a nearby table, pulling out a condom. "This is step one."

He laughed. "Not yet. On my face. I want to taste you."

He was so delightfully filthy she wanted to throw her head back and laugh with the joy of it.

"Hands on your headboard. Don't let go until you come. And remember . . . be quiet. We don't want anyone to hear me licking your pussy until you want to fly apart."

She closed her eyes and let it all go, shoved everything but this man in her bed far, far away.

He urged her upward with his hands, wide, strong, callused hands.

She positioned herself over his mouth and barely had enough time to grab her headboard before he brought her to his lips, kissing her cunt like it was a lover.

As her fingers gripped the wood of her headboard so tight she wondered if she was hearing it groan against the pressure, Adrian's fingers dug into the muscles of her ass and thighs, holding her in place.

Right how he wanted.

He held her tight to his mouth, using lips and tongue and even the gentle slide of the edge of his teeth. He licked at her like he couldn't get enough.

Struggling to keep quiet, she bit her lip so hard she was sure she'd taste blood. Knowing she couldn't scream out or even groan very loudly only made everything hotter.

Her thigh muscles trembled as he suckled her clit, tickling the sensitive underside with the tip of his tongue. His pace was relentless, his touch just perfect, riding that line between too gentle and too much.

And when she came, she had to turn her head, pressing her mouth into her arm to muffle the cry.

9

It wasn't until he'd laid her back on the bed and she looked up at him, eyes glossy, hair a wild dark river around her body, that he realized one taste of this woman would not be enough.

He licked his lips and she shivered. "You taste so good."

"I wonder if I'm fattening."

Surprised by her dry humor, he laughed, but it died as she reached out to grab his cock and squeezed it just right.

He watched, unable not to, as she slid her thumb over the head and brought it to her mouth, sucking it inside.

"Whoa."

"You don't taste too very bad yourself."

She got to her knees and he resolved to get her that way as much as he could, she looked so fucking delicious.

She moved down the bed, running hands over his skin, adding the scrape of short, neat nails when she got to his thighs.

So bold, she held him at the root, angling his cock and sucking him into her mouth slowly and deliberately.

Hot and wet, she took him deep, swirling her tongue around his cock, giving extra attention to the space just under the head. He groaned, giving in and sliding his hands into the shadowy mass of her hair, cool and so very soft.

Settled on her knees between his thighs, she locked her gaze with his as she sucked his cock and he was entirely sure he'd never seen anything so very hot.

And then she changed her angle, taking him as far back as she could and her hair swept forward, only giving him the briefest of glimpses of her face and mouth.

Sweat beaded at his temples as he was hypnotized by the rounded sway of her ass. Her fucking curves . . . his fingers itched to touch. To dig his fingers in and clutch as he fucked into her body. That lush, beautiful body.

"Wait." He managed to get his tongue unstuck from the roof of his mouth. "I want to be in you."

She pulled up and off his cock slowly, with one last swirling lick of her tongue. She sat back, on her knees, smug smile on lips swollen from his cock.

"Tell me something good, Adrian Brown."

Whew, he had *not* expected this . . . this hotness just under the surface.

"I might be able to do that if you had condoms."

Then she crawled past him on her bed, that round ass swaying past as she fished around to retrieve the condom she'd brought out earlier.

It was only with the greatest of concentration that he was able to get the condom on. "I want you from behind."

She got up from where she'd relaxed after tossing him the rubber. And then she turned around and he nearly lost his mind at the sight of the bounty before him.

Not wasting another moment, he moved to her, licking up the line of her spine, delighted by the way she moaned and arched into him. Lining up, he nudged her open, shocked at how hot and wet she was as she enveloped him, bit by bit, as he sank into her cunt.

He exhaled long and hard, concentrating to keep from coming. She felt so fucking good. Then she pushed back, taking him those last few inches and they both gasped and sighed.

"Yeah, right there." He ran hands over the curves of each side, over the flesh of that magnificent ass.

Every inch of his skin was hypersensitive as he dragged himself nearly all the way out of that heated inferno and then pushed back in.

Her hands fisted in the blanket and the strangled little sounds she made, especially that she was trying to keep them quiet, only made him hotter.

She clutched with her inner muscles as he gave in and grabbed those hips, sinking his fingers into her flesh and holding on as he began to fuck her hard and deep.

He was already close. His emotions raw, his feelings so very near the surface. Having been teased by her scent and her manner all evening long, and driven nearly senseless by her mouth on his cock, her taste on his mouth, he was holding on by his metaphorical fingertips.

And that was before she began to thrust back at him, swiveling.

He snarled and she laughed.

It was that laugh he found so ridiculously hot. The way she *knew* she was tormenting him and loving it.

"I'll get even for that one," he muttered as he increased his pace, the pleasure rushing through him so hard and fast it nearly hurt.

"Promise?"

That was it, that last little push and he fell hard into climax. He came so hard he saw stars and his thigh muscles jumped as he nearly yelled out at how good he felt.

"Christ," he hissed as he pulled out, after he'd gotten his breath back, bereft at the loss of that snug heat. Managing to lever off the bed, he stumbled into the bathroom to get rid of the condom, pausing in the doorway to watch her on her bed on his way back.

He liked Gillian. A lot.

He really liked the way you dug down a bit and found a whole other side, a filthy-talking woman who loved sex.

"I'm pretty sure my teeth are numb."

She laughed, sitting up to take a sip of her wine.

"Don't get too comfortable, we have hours until Miles wakes up, right? Lots of time for us to get a few more rounds in." He waggled his brows.

"Miles used to be up before the sun."

He settled in beside her, sated for the moment, but hungry for details of his son.

"Tell me about him."

"He'd get up at five and build giant Lego cities that would span several rooms. He made machines with moving parts, houses, businesses, fortresses. He'd have these intricate stories about each place and each thing, each person who owned or used it.

"When I'd give lessons, he'd sit just outside the room and color for the entire time I was working. And then when my student had left, we'd have a snack I let him help me make."

"Is he a good cook?"

She laughed. "Not at all. But we still try." When she smiled, a dimple hollowed and called to his mouth. He leaned in and kissed it.

He swallowed her soft sigh, liking the way she felt against his body, loving her taste.

The kiss was lazy and soft. The kiss of two people who knew there'd be more later so it could afford to meander and play. He broke away, unable not to smile at her.

"Tell me more."

"We found the bass guitar at a garage sale. He had some money saved up from birthdays and chores. A friend of ours knew enough to teach Miles some basic chords. I traded piano lessons for guitar lessons and after several months he didn't need them anymore. He'd watch a music video and have the song down."

"I was like that." Pride warmed his belly.

"I'm not surprised." She smiled and he picked up a long strand of her hair, playing as she spoke. "Of course he got older and he stopped waking up so early. I remember falling into bed at night and praying he'd just give me until six thirty. Now I have to turn on his light, put the music very loud and yank the blankets off to get him up for school."

"He's shy."

She nodded. "He's Miles. He's different and that's hard. It's hard to be different and to wear your heart on your sleeve when other boys aren't that way. He's not sporty. He's not popular. He's a sweet boy most people like because how can you not? He's generous and compassionate, gracious, silly, old-fashioned in many ways."

She saw him so clearly, and that went straight to his heart. "He's lucky to have a mom like you. Some parents would try to shove him into a role to make things easier."

"You can't make yourself be anything but who you are. He's got friends. He has his band. He's got music and now there are a few girls sniffing around at school events. I'm not entirely sure he notices really."

"He will soon enough. After they start getting boobs."

She turned to face him. "Ah is that when you noticed them? When they got boobs?"

"Boobs are one of God's finest creations, Gillian. Don't mock. Yours are spectacular and singular specimens, by the way."

"Whatever. They're lovely and all. Who doesn't like to see a nice pair of tits?" Gillian groaned. "I can't believe how fast this is all happening. He was just taking his first steps and now he's going to be looking at boobs. I feel totally unprepared for that stuff."

"I'm sorry I wasn't around before." The bitterness of it still burned in his gut. The years of Miles's life Adrian totally lost.

"It wasn't your choice. Anyway, I figure you can get some basic training in and then I'm going to turn over the sex talks from now on. I have no penis, as you may have noticed, so the recent discussions were harder. Since you have one, you're more qualified."

What a completely odd conversation to be having after a scorching-hot sex session. And yet, it felt—for want of a better word—normal. Natural.

"He doesn't have any men in his life?" On one hand, he wanted her to say no. Didn't want to have to come out from the shadow of anyone else. But on the other, he hoped Miles had had male role models because it would be better for him.

"Cal and Ryan have been in his life since he was about six months old, actually. They live up the road a ways. Or they did. But I see them both all the time and Ryan teaches at the middle school. Cal's my attorney."

Something less than pleasant slid through his gut. "What about dating?"

One of her brows rose imperiously. "I don't think Miles should date until he's fifteen and then in groups."

Blasted woman was going to make him say it?

"Ha-ha. I mean you. Do you date around? Anything serious?"

"I date from time to time. The man has to be very special for a number of reasons."

And she left it at that, which made him crazy. But he'd find out those reasons soon enough. For the time being, she was his and that's all that mattered.

And in a lot of ways, this sort of quiet thing they were building here was like a sweet secret. He liked that.

He took the wineglass from her fingers and put it down. "We've got two more condoms. I think we should use all our resources."

He rolled on top of her and her legs wrapped around him, bringing him right up against her cunt.

"I hope you don't need a lot of sleep to get through your day."

10

"Can you show me one more time?"

Gillian nodded as she scooted over on the bench to play. "Rach-maninoff comes from here." She placed a palm over her belly. "It might be different for you. But if you want to play him, you have to find a way to translate all that power. You can hit all the correct keys in the correct order and still, if you don't feel it, it's going to sound cold and perfunctory."

"Do you think I should play a different piece for the audition?" Shannon, one of her advanced students asked, clearly nervous.

"I think you have all the talent you need to play this piece. It's not as technically difficult as some other pieces you could use. But the key is your spin, your interpretation, and that means you have to *feel* it."

"If you say so. You make it look easy."

Gillian laughed. "I have been playing piano longer than you've been alive. At Juilliard I played this piece for hours every single day. I'd better make it look easy."

Shannon moved off the bench. "I'll watch from here."

Smiling, Gillian centered herself, slid her fingertips over the keys and found that place inside, opening herself up to it. And began to play.

The start—slow to draw the notes, to paint with the sound. As she played and changed her pace, faster and faster, the music had consumed her. The piece ebbed and flowed, boiled over and wisped away like smoke. She let it lead her, ceased thinking and gave the music free rein.

When she'd finished, she opened her eyes to Shannon's wild applause.

"I don't know if I can ever play it like you."

"Play it like you; that'll be better."

After the lesson ended, she put on Florence + the Machine, smiling as she headed into her room to change for a client meeting she needed to be at in less than an hour.

Hopping to it as she hummed to "Dog Days Are Over," she found the skirt she'd been looking for and paired it with a twinset in pale lavender. Cashmere.

She didn't have a lot of clothes. Always when she was confronted with something for herself it was hard to make that choice instead of something for the house or for Miles. So she had a few very nice pieces she found on sale racks and thrift store shelves and filled in with other, less expensive items.

She'd clawed her way to where she was now and had no plan to ever go back to a place in her life where she was grateful for scraps and wore shite and pretended it was queen's robes.

No one would think her naff or poor to look at her now. No one would wonder how quickly they could get her on her back. She was not in *anyone's* shadow, not judged against them because she'd made herself into something more than she'd been as a kid in England.

Brushing her fingertips over the sweater, she carefully pulled it from the hanger and put it on her bed as she moved through the room.

She looked at herself in the mirror as she secured her hair. Then her gaze was drawn to the marks on her hips, a slice of which she saw above the top of her knickers. Pale bruises where Adrian's fingers had dug in while they fucked.

A delightful shiver surfaced as she slid the skirt up and zipped it. The man had sex like he meant it. He didn't handle her like she was fragile. He was base and dirty and she was right chuffed to have had him in her bed.

She'd been more forward than she'd ever been the first time she had sex with someone. One of the reasons she never had casual sex with anyone was that she wanted to trust her partner enough to let the carnal side of herself show.

She wasn't Tina, or their mother, but she liked sex. She liked it hard and rough and with a side of dirty talk. There were myriad things she'd apologize for in her life, but liking sex wasn't one of them. It was part of who she was, and as long as she kept it where it was meant to be, her *private* business, she had nothing to be ashamed of.

Still, a flush warmed her neck and chest at the memories of the things she'd said and done, at the things *he'd* said and done to her. She couldn't regret it. Sex with Adrian Brown had been everything she thought it might be. Three times over. He did have a lot of stamina, a very fine quality when coupled with a sensual imagination, tireless and never-ending.

She'd enjoyed herself very much. Enough to not be embarrassed at her own rawness. Enough to hope it might happen again, though she steeled herself to accept it probably wouldn't. Things were complicated, she knew. Hell, she felt it all too.

Things had shifted in the week since he'd first come to dinner. He called every day to talk to Miles. Adrian had to make a quick midweek trip to Los Angeles, and when he was in California, he and Miles managed to do face time via their phones.

Miles seemed more confident, even if in need of a little more reassurance and love from Mum to let him know that though things had changed, some things never would. His mum would always love him. Nothing would ever change that.

Even if Adrian Brown hadn't totally turned their lives upside down with his presence. Easy. Laid back. Sexy. He had a quiet confidence about him, a sort of unruffled and unmistakable air that he knew what he was about and if it needed handling, it would be handled.

And he appeared to be smack-dab in love with Miles, which only made him about eighty billion times more attractive to her.

She slid her shoes on, smoothed her sweater, adjusted her glasses and blotted her lipstick, and upon consideration in her mirror, approved mightily. This new client was a sizable one. If she landed the job, it would mean she could get the car fixed without having to tap into her savings and even be able to tip quite a bit into Miles's college plan as well.

Portfolio in hand, she headed out the door and toward Tart, where her informal coffee meeting was to take place.

Jules looked up and grinned when Gillian came in. "Hey, you. All ready for the meeting? I've got you a table over in the corner. Away from traffic so you won't be bothered. Plus the light there is marvelous. You'll look even better, if that's actually possible."

Gillian had walked around with a perpetual blush at Jules's manner when they'd first become friends. By that point, she knew Jules didn't make compliments lightly and if she said it, it was true.

"Always watching out for my best interests. I'm a little early."

"No shit. My darling woman, you are beyond punctual. If you were ever late, I'd worry. Go sit. I've got a pot of Earl Grey steeping. I'll bring it and we can chat a while before he arrives." Jules waved her away, rolling her eyes and Gillian headed to the table her friend had indicated.

Tart had belonged to Jules's parents. They'd run it as a small café for several decades. Until Jules's father came home one day and announced to them all at a family birthday dinner that he was leaving Suzy for the just barely adult girl who'd lived a few doors down.

Suzy had made him sign over the café and then had given it to Jules and left for a yearlong trip around the world with friends.

And Jules had made the café into Tart. Sensual. Beautiful tarts, pastry and pie. Tart was one of Gillian's home places. A sanctuary from all the bad things outside. Being situated where it was also made the location convenient for business meetings.

Jules was, as Cal Whaley said, a long, tall drink of water. Bright and lightning quick, her pale hair and brilliant blue eyes were a contrast with Gillian's darker looks. But the two shared a friendship deeper than anything she'd had with anyone other than Miles and her gran.

"Here." Jules put down a pot of tea and two mugs. She returned shortly with a cup of coffee for herself and shoved a slice of persimmon tart Gillian's way. "Eat it. I know you probably haven't eaten all day. Don't want to bottom out on energy during this meeting."

They chatted idly until her client-to-be showed up, and when she left an hour later, she headed straight to the bank and then dropped her car off at the shop, and even got a ride home from the mechanic whose son she gave piano lessons to twice a week.

She hoped his gratitude at how far his son had come in the last six months would merit her a discount, but took the ride thankful either way.

And who should be on her doorstep but Adrian Brown, looking every bit like a sexy-tousled rock star even when he wasn't wearing anything more posh than jeans and a fisherman's sweater.

"I suppose you'll need a key," she called out as she headed up the walk, pleased to see him. "Miles will be thrilled you're here. You'll be staying for dinner?"

He took her portfolio when he met her at the bottom of the steps and surprised her with a kiss. Nothing salacious, but it was more than a friendly peck.

"Hey. Where's your car?" He looked around.

"At the shop." She unlocked the door and went inside, heading straight to the heat to turn it on. "What brings you here today?"

"I wanted to see Miles and you said I should feel welcome to come by."

She handed him a key on a small fob bearing a plastic image of a vintage woman holding a cup of coffee and a slice of tart. When Jules had first opened her doors, all her friends got together and presented them to her as promotional items for the shop.

"Here. This way you won't have to wait in the cold if I'm out. Would you like some tea?" She began to move around, turning on the stove to heat the water, grabbing the teapot and mugs, measuring out tea. "Miles won't be out of school for a few hours."

"I know. I mean, I know Miles won't be back until two forty-five. He told me." Adrian's smile was sweetly charmed; it stripped her reserve away. He held the key up. "Thank you. I appreciate the gesture. Knowing I could come here today and see him, knowing you'd welcome me . . ." He paused, watching the way she put out placemats and then the cups and tea.

"Sit. Of course you're welcome. This is your son's house and so that means the door is open to you." She poured out, enjoying the smoky sweet scent of the tea. "It's jasmine green tea. Low on the caffeine. Miles was over the moon every time you called. I wanted to be sure I told you because of course he's not a very chatty phone person and I didn't want you to think he wasn't pleased."

"Thank you for that. For being our mediator of sorts as he and I try to figure out our relationship. It's a big help for both of us."

He ducked his head again and she was, again, charmed.

"I wanted to see you too. I've thought about you all week."

She looked to him over the rim of her mug. This was stupid really. She knew what his life must be like; she'd seen a small slice of it, and that was just the classical music world. His universe was . . . well, certainly filled with experiences and people far outside her life here on the island.

She wanted him anyway. The time she had when it was just Gillian and Adrian was something she enjoyed greatly. She *liked* Adrian Brown in a way she hadn't liked a man in a very long time.

"Say something."

"It occurs to me, Mister Brown, that you're entirely unused to being befuddled, thwarted or told no."

"It only makes my cock harder when you get very prim and British. Almost as much as it undoes me when you lose that uptight and you start dropping consonants and get filthy and sort of bitchy." He winked and sat back, sipping his tea. "This is nice. I love the scent."

It wouldn't do to encourage him, but she couldn't help but smile at his comments as she squeezed her thighs together under the table to quell the ache he'd brought. "I thought about you this week too."

"You did?"

"Yes. Don't pretend you're surprised. Are you fishing for compliments?"

"If I was, would you give me one?"

She sniffed, extra prim just for him. "You eat pussy like a gold medalist."

He put his mug down and threw so much smolder her way she nearly gasped.

"As compliments go, that's a winner. I thought about that all week too. The way you tasted as you sat above me, your cunt, hot and slick, against my lips. Do you know how many times I fucked my fist, imagining it was you I was inside?"

Things fluttered in her belly. A novel sensation. She wasn't usually prone to that sort of breathless reaction to a man. This one though, broke through all her rules and regulations.

He fussed up her ordered world with gleeful abandon. And for some reason she couldn't quite explain to herself, she couldn't find the energy or the will to fight it.

"How many times, Adrian?" she asked, feeling so free with him to unleash that part of herself. It was just the two of them there.

His gaze went hooded. He moved his chair back, away from the table. His long legs stretched out. She watched, ensorcelled by the way he ran his palms down his thighs. "Twice a day. You make me feel like a sixteen-year-old boy, Gillian. And even that wasn't enough."

"Show me."

If she'd been expecting him to get shy now, she had another thing coming. Her breath caught as he reached upward, unbuckling his belt. Her muscles jumped slightly at the metallic sound as he moved it aside, opening it before moving to his buttons.

Pop.

Pop.

Pop.

Pop.

Pop.

Some American things were simply undoubtedly better. Button-down jeans were one of those things. A zipper was sexy enough, yes, but that sound as the metal button cleared the denim seemed to mainline straight to her clit.

The room heated up as he opened the vee of the denim wider, shoved his shorts aside and pulled out his cock.

She may have let a small sound of longing slip out. One of his brows rose and his smile hitched up a notch.

"You sound hungry, English." His voice changed at the very end, when his thumb slid through the bead of pre-come on the head of his cock, smearing it.

She crossed her legs, lazily kicking one foot and wishing the friction was enough to help get her off.

"And what if I was?"

"You keep teasing me like that and you'll get your answer." He said this as he began to slowly thrust his cock through his fist.

"After you've finished, you can give it to me."

She meant to joke, but it wasn't. He didn't take it that way either, only locking his gaze on her though she couldn't look away from the way he handled himself.

Sure. Aggressively masculine. Rougher than she would have. She licked her lips and made him groan. That only made her ache more.

"Still not as good as what it feels like in your mouth. Or your pussy."

She stood and walked toward him. He continued that thrust, thrust, thrust as she approached, though his mouth quirked up at the corner. Behind him, she leaned over, her breasts to his back, mouth at his ear, gaze back on his cock, slick, hard and dark as he drew closer to climax.

"Watching you jack yourself like this makes me wet," she whispered.

He strangled out a curse, sped his pace.

"When I make myself come I'm going to think about this moment. When my fingers slide between my legs, into my panties, I'm going to play with my clit and think about the way your cock looks in your hand."

He groaned, tipping his head and turning it, meeting her mouth in a desperate kiss. She stretched, her fingertips brushing against his hand as he came, the warmth of it a brand against her skin.

Adrian tasted her mouth, groaning as he came, groaning again as she broke the kiss and circled him, licking her fingers covered with his seed.

She had no real idea what she did to him, he could tell. Didn't matter really. He'd have her, and by the time she realized it, he'd be dug in deep. Like a tick.

He grabbed some paper towels and she helped get him cleaned up, even gently tucking his cock back into his shorts.

"Now, I believe you had an answer to give me?" She had this way of smiling at him. He watched her enough, well, a lot, to know she didn't use that smile with anyone else. Teasing. Sexy.

That smile made him sort of dizzy.

He bent his knees and caught her with his shoulder, hefting her up and toting her down the hall to her bedroom.

He tossed her on the bed and she laughed. "You've hauled me around like a sack of goods!"

Her laughter died when he got to his knees and took the hem of her skirt and inched it up, dropping kisses against her hose.

Stockings actually. Her skin was warm just where the edge of the material met her thighs.

He began to yank and she sat up with a squeak.

"Oy! That's my skirt, you're going to rip it."

That was unexpected. He hit a nerve there.

He held his hands up in surrender. "I'm sorry, darlin'. The stockings were a surprise. Got me all hot and bothered."

She got up and carefully stepped from the skirt, hanging it in her closet and then doing the same with her sweater and little shirt thing she had on.

And then he forgot what he'd been worried about because she was standing there in thigh-high stockings, sheer panties and a gorgeous pale blue bra, her tits mounded at the top edge like something he had to have a taste of.

"Now, where was I?" He crawled across the floor to her, slowly moving up her legs to place an openmouthed kiss at the back of her thigh, right against the top of the stocking.

"That's a very nice place to pick up." The burr in her voice had smoothed again and he relaxed, pausing to squeeze her ass, kiss each cheek where it met her thigh.

He kissed his way up her side, over the delicious curve of her.

"Your body is off the chain," he murmured, mouth against the swell of her belly, enjoying the way she clutched at his shoulders to stay standing when he dipped his tongue into her belly button.

"That's a good thing?"

He'd reduced her to breathless. Good. He didn't want to be alone.

He popped the back hooks on her bra and within a breath her breasts were in his hands, nipples burning into his palms. Grabbing the material of her panties with his teeth, he pulled them down and she stepped from them. This left her in nothing more than those stockings of hers, her hair still bound at the back of her neck.

"It's a very good thing." He surged to his feet, embracing her, pulling her in close.

Petite and nearly naked, she should have felt fragile against him. But she didn't.

"I've been dreaming about licking you until you made that quiet little sound. But now no one is here and we don't have to be quiet." He drew her back to the bed and she came with him, pulling her hair loose as they went.

They landed on her bed, side by side and he went back for a kiss. Soft at first, teasing her sweet lips open, making way for his tongue.

He wanted to lose himself in her, just lay with her here for hours, kissing and touching.

But now they didn't have time for that so he'd take what he could get, what she gave him so willingly.

He moved away, reluctantly, from her mouth and over her closed eyes, across her cheeks and against her temple. Her mouth curved up as he paid homage to her jaw and down her neck.

The phone in his back pocket sounded and with a groan he sat up to turn it off.

She watched him with a shiver of delight. There was something about being totally naked against him while he was fully clothed that really pushed her buttons. He was tousled, flushed from arousal; his eyes held a gleam that told her he had wicked intentions.

"Today is a very good day."

He tossed the phone on her dressing table and moved back into place. "Is it now?" He licked over one nipple and then the other, scraping his teeth across it until she arched.

"Yes!"

He continued the erotic assault on her nipples and tiptoed down her belly with one hand, carefully spreading her labia and exposing her clit to the air, tickling it just a little with his fingertip until a ragged moan made its way up from her gut.

"These tits drive me crazy."

He flattered and it wasn't empty. The awe was there in his voice, in the way he touched her body and definitely in the way he looked at her.

Then she couldn't decide if she was upset that he moved away from her nipples and promptly forgot about that as he kissed and licked his way down her belly.

And she lost all coherent thought when he spread her wider and took a long lick with a little swirling flourish against her clit.

Giving in, she let herself touch him, let herself slide fingers through his hair. Let herself tug him upward as she rolled her hips to get more.

He groaned, the vibration sounding through her, setting her senses aflame. She did wince a little when his fingers dug into her hips again and he paused to see what was wrong.

"Bruise from last week. Don't stop now! It's fine." She tugged and tugged until he gave his own ouch. He moved up to kiss the fading bruises.

"I'm sorry."

"Don't be. I like them. And I really liked where you were there, you know, your face in my pussy? Can we get back to that, please?"

"I like it when you get all panicky about your orgasms." But he did get back to work quickly and she sighed happily when he found that rhythm again with the licks and swirls.

She wouldn't last long; she knew this about herself. It was very easy for her to get off, and having a man who so obviously loved oral sex with his mouth on her, his tongue whispering sweet nothings to her clit, was already getting her 90 percent of the way.

So she held on, and gave in to the heaviness of her eyelids, letting them close with the image of that dark chocolate hair bent over her.

And then she was coming, hard and fast, as pleasure filled up and up and then up even more until she nearly shouted.

When she finally opened her eyes on a satisfied breath, he was there, looking at her. "You're a noisy little thing when there's no one else here."

She sniffed. "Well, only when I come that hard. So I suppose you've taught me my lesson. Which is that you give great head."

He kissed her, tasting of her and himself beneath that. She liked it. Thought the combination was quite lovely.

"Who knew you'd wear thigh-high stockings under those school-teacher clothes? I like it."

"It's cold, in case you hadn't noticed. I had to go out and meet with a client and I wanted to stay warm. Are you going to stay over?" She'd asked it naturally but then felt uncomfortable, like she'd gone too far. This could be a drawback of the whole fucking-your-son's-father thing. Was she his lover, or Miles's mother, or what? Sure, they'd had a discussion about it, before the first time they'd slept together, but this would all take a lot of careful thought.

"I'd like to, yes, if that's all right with you."

"Of course it is. We're having grilled cheese and tomato soup."

"What?"

"Grilled cheese sandwiches? You know the ones you fry up and melt? Have you never had a grilled cheese before?"

"Oh yes, loads of times. It was one of the things Brody could cook. No, the other thing."

"Tomato soup?"

He grinned and she realized he'd been having a laugh.

"I love the way you say tomato."

"Ha, bloody ha."

Grinning, he gave her a quick kiss to smooth her agitation, which wasn't really agitation, but she had no plans to discourage kisses, for goodness' sake.

"How long will your car be in the shop? Why don't you and Miles ride with me tomorrow and I'll bring you both back Sunday afternoon?"

She hadn't forgotten about the dinner his sister and brother were having. Miles was in turns thrilled and excited and scared to death. No more than she. She didn't even belong there!

Not that she'd leave Miles to face the occasion on his own, of course. He'd made it very clear he wanted her there, and in his own way, she supposed, Adrian had as well. So she was in it and that was that.

"All right, thank you. They had to order a new part so it won't be done until Tuesday they said."

"I have an extra car if you'd like to borrow it for a few days. Just until the repairs are done."

Of course he did. "No." She paused when she realized how vehemently she'd said it. "Thank you, but we're fine. Miles takes the bus to school, we've got groceries and if I am in a bind there are many people I can call to give me a lift. Really. I appreciate the offer though."

He looked her over carefully so she jiggled just a little, snagging his attention and moving away from the topic.

"How long until Miles gets back?" He'd gotten that look again, and she rubbed herself against him with a happy groan.

"We've got about an hour."

He sat quickly, pulled his sweater off, shimmied from his jeans and underwear and rolled onto his back.

"Then let's use it wisely, shall we?" He held up a condom.

She grabbed it, ripped it open, donned his cock and scrambled atop him. "It's better to look at you from up here."

"If you're expecting any—*fuck, that'll do it, Christ you're tight*."

It pleased her to get him all befuddled and speechless.

She sank down on him, letting her body adjust, taking the time to look at his body. "I love that tattoo on your belly."

"To finish my first thought—I have zero argument with you riding my cock. This way I can look up at you and you have to do most of the work as well. It's a win-win situation for me."

She rose and fell, sighing as she rolled her head on her shoulders, stretching and relaxing. He felt thick inside her. Big and thick and very, very pleasing. "I must tell you, your cock pleases me."

He laughed briefly, before she started to move again.

She liked fucking him this way. Liked the way he looked all spread out below her, looking debauched. Liked the way he continued to touch and caress, as if he couldn't *not* touch her.

Big, sure hands ran all over her torso, returning time and again to her breasts, where he rolled and tugged her nipples until the tension inside her nearly vibrated. She'd thought herself sated after that last orgasm, but now a new one built.

Dragging her nails up his sides, she leaned down and licked over his nipple, tugging on the ring. She'd never been with anyone with all this ink and a piercing. It was not an overrated experience.

His breath caught when she flicked her tongue over the bar quickly. Her angle had changed, leaving them belly to belly as she pushed back against him.

"Yeah, that's the way. Fuck yourself onto me, English."

He turned her to goo when he used that rough and dirty voice.

Even more when he banded an arm around her waist and began to lever himself up into her, holding her in place and fucking her hard and deep.

The length of his cock stroked over her clit with each thrust, sending a full body shiver through her each time he did it. Drawing her inexorably closer to climax.

His chest, tight against hers, slid across her nipples, including his nipple ring. A sound, low and needy, came from her mouth like a stranger had put it there.

"Tell me," he murmured. "What do you need?"

His words played through her senses, honeyed, seductive.

"Fuck me. I want you to come. I want to come. I just . . . want."

He snarled, just a little, enough to excite her senses even more, and before she knew it, climax rolled through her, stealing her breath, leaving her with no other choice but to writhe helplessly as pleasure ravaged her.

He pressed in deep and groaned so hard she felt the vibration through his belly into her body.

He'd watched her as she worked in her office. They'd lazed around for a while after that spectacular welcome-home sex and then she told him she needed to get caught up, especially if they were going to be gone the entire next day.

So she'd been on the phone and her computer, had moved around the room pulling things from shelves and drawers.

He'd seen some of her work, though she didn't know it. In the packet of background information Cope had given him there'd been credit reports; she had a small savings and lived within her means, which were solidly middle class. Even had a college fund started for Miles. Something he intended to do himself as well. And there'd been a menu she'd created, graphics for a friend's pastry shop that he frankly thought brilliant. Retro woman holding a slice of pie, a cup of coffee and a smile on shiny red lips. There'd been mailings and some other stuff of the sort. Enough for him to be impressed with her eye and her talent.

And to have realized it was never about money for her. Not ever. That shamed him. He'd compared her to the series of nasty people who'd tried to shake him down for one reason or another. Brody had been right. He hadn't been fair to her. It seemed absurd that he'd ever suspected anything like that from her when she was, well, Gillian, amazing mother, beautiful, sexy woman, creative and successful business woman and his . . . well, whatever they had.

Miles came in, a shy smile on his face, and Adrian's heart lifted again. "Yo, kid."

"Yo, um, so what am I supposed to call you anyway?" Miles looked at Adrian's shoulder.

Brody had told him to just go with what he felt. To be natural with

Miles and Miles would feel it. In truth he was scared as hell to fail this amazing kid, but he'd do his damnedest not to.

He reached out, taking Miles's shoulder gently to get his attention. "You're my son, Miles. I know we didn't know each other last month, but I love you. And we'll keep getting to know each other and hopefully one day it'll be as easy between you and me as it is between you and your mom. Call me what feels best to you. Adrian. Dad. Whatever."

Miles blushed and kicked the toe of his sneaker against the floor. "Okay. That sounds okay."

"You wanna jam?" Adrian asked. "My guitar is in the guest room."

Miles's eyes widened and he gifted Adrian with one of his rare, open grins. Shy was Miles. He must have gotten that from Gillian's side of the family because no Browns were shy. But Adrian liked it on his son.

"That would be monumental. Mum!" he called, surprising Adrian. She poked her head from her office door. "You bellowed?"

"Me and Dad are going to jam. You should too."

Dad. Wow. Adrian was so caught up in that moment that he nearly missed the fact that Miles had asked her to jam with them. He hadn't heard her play piano yet, and that seemed ridiculous. Especially as he'd seen her pussy up close and personal more than once.

"I've got to finish this. You two go on and I'll get dinner started when I finish. I'm keeping the door open so I can hear you though." She smiled at Adrian before going back into her office, making him wonder if she really did have more work or if she was giving him time with Miles.

"We're working on 'Creep' right now." Miles followed him to the guest room so Adrian could grab his guitar.

Miles stuttered to a halt, eyes wide as saucers, wonder stamped all over his features. He reached out, only to snatch his hand back. "Wow, that's your guitar? Wow. Wow."

Adrian wasn't a stranger to people admiring his music or his guitar or whatever. But this was different. Made him feel proud in a way he'd never experienced outside his immediate circle. And this was even better than hearing Brody tell him something was good.

He looked down at the guitar and saw it through Miles's eyes. "Yeah. I've had this guitar just a little longer than you've been alive. It's still my favorite."

He turned to see Miles's eyes wide as he looked at the guitar. He held it out. "Wanna try it?"

Miles backed up a step, his hands up. "Oh, I don't know. Wow. That's like. Like a 1959 Sunburst?" He dragged his gaze from the guitar back up to Adrian's face. "I looked it up. You know when you first came around I looked you up on the Internet. Is that weird?"

Adrian couldn't help his laugh. "Nah, dude, this whole situation has been wild. I'm glad you looked me up on the Internet, but also, if you want to know about it, ask me. I know we've got a lot of stuff to learn about each other."

Miles nodded, ducking his head in a way Adrian recognized in both Brown brothers. He tipped his chin to indicate the guitar. "I don't think I've seen one for real. Just, you know, on the Internet. This is a special thing. You know, the few of your things that's so special you're allowed to be a bit greedy over."

Adrian liked Gillian even more right then.

"Yes, this guitar is totally my special thing. But I get to be greedy with her all the time. I've used this guitar on every single CD I've made but the first one." He ran his fingertips along the little modifications he'd made over time. Hardware swaps and additions.

This guitar, until Miles had come along, had been his most precious thing. And his son got that. Christ, he was a lucky man.

He held the guitar out toward Miles. "I can share my special thing with my son. That's the sort of thing dads are supposed to do, right?"

Miles couldn't hold the edges of his excited smile back as he stared at the guitar. "Dude, take it. You're not going to break it. You know how to hold an instrument. I'm not worried." He handed the guitar over and moved past Miles out toward the stairs, wanting to show just how unconcerned he was that Miles would be anything but careful.

It made Adrian ridiculously happy to share it with Miles, with someone who understood the beauty of your own guitar. With his son. Damn.

They set up in the garage, where Miles's band had the practice space.

"Mum jams with me in the house, but when we practice, she comes out here." Miles pointed to the stand-up piano in the corner.

"Is she good then?"

Miles plugged his bass in and then returned to Adrian's guitar, sliding his fingers along the smooth-worn spot just below the strings, the spot he'd wear on his own guitar someday.

"Yeah, she's mag. I never heard anyone play like her, even her friends she takes us to see when they come to town."

He had a piano in his studio; he'd have to see if he could lure her into playing something for him. And maybe the story about why she didn't pursue it professionally other than as a piano teacher.

Miles handed him the guitar.

Adrian grinned, plugged in and gave the strings a brush, eliciting a Brody-like grin in return.

For the next hour they went over the chords for "Creep," a simple enough bass line for Miles to learn. Also a great bass line to show just how integral a bass player was to a band. And then they noodled around with other stuff, just playing and riffing off one another.

"Tomorrow," Adrian said as they put things away and headed back to the house, "we should get your aunt to get in on this. She's been pestering me to play with us." He laughed, because it had been true.

"Yeah? But you guys are like, wow, well, rock stars and stuff. I'm just a kid."

He turned, clasping his son's shoulder. "You're my son. You're her nephew. We started at your age. Music runs in the family, it's what we like to do, you know, like the family business and all. It's fun, isn't it?"

Miles's features lit up, excited again. "Yeah. I'd play all the time if Mum didn't make me go to school and take out the trash and stuff." He paused. "Not that I'm complaining. She's a great mom. She wants me to get an education and be responsible."

"It's okay, I know. She is a good mom. I like that you call her Mum." They climbed up the deck and went through the house just as Gillian wandered past, laughing at something a man he'd never seen was saying.

"Cal!" Miles moved to bump fists with the other man, who looked at Adrian's son with affection clear on his features.

"Good to see you, my man. Your mom tells me you were out jamming with your dad. How'd it go?"

Adrian relaxed slightly.

"Awesome. He taught me some new stuff. You staying for dinner?"

"Well, I . . ." He turned to Adrian, clearly taking his measure. "I'm Cal Whaley. Gillian's attorney and a friend too."

"He's pretty much a member of our family. Miles, take your things to your room please." Gillian moved past them into the kitchen. "Cal, you know you're welcome, though it's grilled cheese and tomato soup night so you'd probably get better if you showed up at Mary's looking hungry."

Adrian shook the man's hand. "Adrian Brown, nice to meet you."

"Mary told me I was on my own. You know how she can be some Fridays." Cal sent a look to Gillian, who laughed.

"Mary is my friend, she runs one of those mobile food trucks, called Luxe. She's a master cook. Never made a thing I haven't adored with all my taste buds. But sometimes on Friday nights she calls in pizza, hunkers down and does not answer her phone. Cal's her brother."

"Yeah, well, six days a week she's always happy to have me at her table and if I'd begged or sucked my gut in, she would have found something for me in her fridge. She likes to take care of people. I figure every once in a while I can leave her alone to have a Friday night to herself. So if you don't mind, Adrian, I'd like to stay for dinner, get to know you a bit. Gillian and Miles are part of our family, you see. I've been charged to get the inside dirt, as Gillian has forbidden Jules to come over."

"That's a bloody lie, Calvin Whaley!" Gillian called out from where she'd just turned the soup on. She was easy around Cal. Relaxed and affectionate. Adrian tried not to be grumpy as he watched Cal coax the ginormous Fat Lucy into his arms where the furry traitor purred and enjoyed being scratched behind her ears. Slutty cat.

"Whatever the truth, I'm in. I'd like to get to know the people in Miles's life better." Adrian sent the man a charming enough smile, but also he hoped enough seriousness that he saw Adrian would be also checking them out.

"Well, good then. Want a beer?" After depositing the cat on her perch, Cal moved past Adrian into the kitchen as Miles came back downstairs.

The man sure was at home in Gillian's house. Hm. He seemed to also have great affection for both mother and son. Adrian wondered how much he had for the mother.

"Yeah, thanks."

Cal popped the top on a bottle, poured it into a glass and put it at Gillian's elbow as she sliced cheese for the sandwiches.

"Thank you, darlin'." Which sounded more like *daw-lin* in her accent. Hot.

To Adrian, he handed a bottle, as he had himself. "She's got that thing about glasses." Cal laughed, assuming Adrian knew the story he of course did not.

"Nothing wrong with liking to drink from a glass. I'm at home. Dishes are clean. Why not drink from that instead of the bottle? Set the table, Miles. Cal's going to stay."

"Awesome." Miles moved to the cabinets and began to gather plates and soup bowls.

"I've got ham, tomato, pickles and mushrooms to go on the sandwiches if anyone wants."

Adrian moved to her, wanting to be near. "Here, let me help."

The smile she gave him was plenty reward. "All right. How about you assemble and I'll get them started?"

"Tell me about yourself, Cal."

It was Gillian who spoke though. "Miles likes ham and pickles on his sandwich. With mustard."

"Like a Cuban sandwich of sorts."

"Yes, exactly. I blame Mary for that too. I'd never had such a marvel until I met her. Now Miles and I are addicted. Not enough to make them pressed the way she does, though."

By the time the sandwiches were ready and they'd all sat at the table, Adrian knew Cal Whaley was an attorney, the one his attorneys had been dealing with. He needed to talk with the man one on one, alone, about that stuff later.

"Do you have a wife or a girlfriend or anything like that?"

Gillian laughed in her delightful way and then chided Miles to not eat an entire sandwich in one bite.

"I'm afraid he gets that from me." Adrian shrugged, looking guiltily down at his own plate.

"Figures." But she wasn't angry. In fact her smile pleased him. It held intimacy and affection. He didn't feel as suspicious of Cal just at that moment when she looked at him and he knew all her secrets.

"And yet, so many boys his age don't know the Heimlich and I worry he'll choke on half a bag of Cheetos because of it. There's no food shortage, boy, slow it down."

They hung out for a while and after dinner, Miles and Adrian cleaned up while Cal and Gillian moved into the living room.

"So does Cal have anyone? He didn't answer my question." Adrian kept his voice down, nonchalant, as he and Miles loaded the dishwasher. An ancient model that had clearly seen better days.

"There was Angel; he and Cal lived together for three years. I was bummed when they broke up. I was only seven though. He was a cool guy. Then for a few years there was Callie. She was hot. But they broke up last year. I know he dates. He says he doesn't want to bring anyone fleeting into my life. They all want to protect me, Mum says."

Gay, okay he could deal with that. It meant, well, it didn't mean shit. Ben, his sister's other husband, liked men too, and he managed to have both. But hearing the man was careful about who he brought into Miles's life was a good thing. Almost as good as the way Miles had seemed to make clear Cal and Gillian had nothing romantic going on.

Not that he should care, but of course he did and he was too damned old to pretend otherwise. He wanted Gillian. And he wanted to slowly work into a situation where they could be openly affectionate in front of Miles. But the two of them wanted to be slow and careful about it. Which wasn't such a reassuring thing when other people saw Gillian for the wonder she was.

"Thanks. I just . . . you know want to be sure people around you and your mom are good to you."

Miles grinned.

When they came out, Gillian and Cal were near the front door. "Just in time! Cal's got to run now."

Cal hugged Gillian before kissing her cheek and whispering something into her ear that made her roll her eyes and shake her head.

"Good night, Calvin." She said it primly, and it got to Adrian the way it always did.

Miles hugged Cal, who then ruffled the boy's hair. "Two weeks until cards and junk food."

"Yeah. I'm on it. See you later, Cal."

"I forgot something in my car. I'll be right back. I'll walk out with you, Cal." Adrian grabbed his keys and slid into his shoes.

"I imagine you wanted to talk to me alone." Cal paused near his car door.

"Nice car. I nearly bought this model." Brody joked that one of these days Adrian would have to move to a house on some land so he could have all the cars he really wanted. Looking at the sleek BMW just then, he wondered what land went for on Bainbridge.

Cal nodded his thanks, waiting for Adrian to speak.

"You must think I'm a dick."

Cal shrugged. "Are you?"

"Sometimes. My lawyers are when they need to be."

"Look, I get it, okay? I know the whole thing about DNA and all that wasn't personal. But it *was* to her. She's special to me. Miles is special to me. You hurt her and she never showed any of it to Miles. You need to understand what you've got in *both* of them. I see how you look at her. She's not a passing phase. That's not the world Gillian inhabits."

"I know it upset her and I've apologized directly. I'm sure she shared that."

"You don't know Gillian at all if you think that. Gillian doesn't share that sort of detail. If she felt it was personal, she'd keep it to herself. Jules probably knows. They're tight that way. And of all the group, she's the one to worry about because she loves Gillian and Miles fiercely."

Adrian didn't really know her. Which he supposed was part of his problem. "You're right. I assumed she'd share, but upon reflection, that's not really how she is. It's just, you're clearly important to her and to my son and I want to clear the air. Things started off badly. I reacted strongly based on other things having nothing to do with this and ended up causing some hurt."

"I imagine being Adrian Brown, international superstar and business mogul, comes with a hell of a lot of people who are after things from you. I'm sure Gillian wasn't the first woman to claim a child had resulted from some indiscriminant one-night stand."

"No." He shrugged. "Success comes with downsides too. Three years ago a woman came forward with a baby. Said it was mine. Wanted money, of course. But I'd been in Europe on tour for six months and she'd been here in the States. It turned out fine, but I don't like being shaken down. But it'd be stupid to complain about all that when I have platinum records on the wall of my home studio and a hundred-and-eighty-degree of view of Puget Sound. I know I started out on the wrong foot with them, but I aim to make it right."

"I'm going to give you a tip; Gillian is not Tina. Never in a million years would she be."

"You're going to think I'm a dick again, but I don't even remember her."

"Tina was a broken, fucked-up woman who failed to understand the difference between offering herself up to anyone who'd take her and affection or love." Cal paused. "Anyway, Gillian won't say it but I will—her sister was a manipulative whore and Miles is far better off that she never sought to use him the way she could have. Gillian loved her sister and her fucked-up mother more than they deserved.

"Tina Forrester was a calculating bitch. She died young because she led exactly the kind of life that ends up with you dead at forty. So be glad you don't remember her." Cal took a deep breath. "I've said more than I should. Gillian is a very private woman. You don't remember Tina, sure, but Gillian is the kind of woman you'll never forget."

That was the understatement of a lifetime.

"I appreciate you telling me all this. I love my kid. I don't know him as well as you do, but I will be a good father."

Cal laughed. "Gillian wouldn't let you anywhere near Miles if you weren't worthy. He's crazy about you."

11

Gillian got up early, tiptoeing past the guest room where Adrian had shifted only a few hours before after passing a considerable amount of energetic time in her bed. Her exhaustion reminded her of those first six months with Miles.

This was a satisfied sort of tired. Adrian had brought a whole new kind of muscle ache into her life. She smiled to herself as she set up at the piano. She had a lesson to give in an hour, so this would be her own time.

She'd warned Adrian about it, putting earplugs on his bedside table. Miles wouldn't stir, being the layabout he was. But he was used to the noise.

Bach today, she decided. She hadn't played Bach in a while. She decided this as she opened the front drapes and the sun tumbled in.

Her piano. The sight of it brought a sort of tenderness. The wood was smooth and firm beneath her fingertips as she slid them over the curves she loved so much.

Her very finest physical possession. Gran had given it to her when she'd moved into the house.

She'd thought her days playing on a grand piano like this one were over when she settled in with Miles here. And Gran had shown up with a moving truck one day and the piano delivered the next.

Gillian sat and fell into the ritual of it. Of the weight and sway to discover the keys and feel that upswell of love and connection.

An extravagance her grandmother couldn't afford, and yet she'd sold her home and all the land it was on. She left San Francisco and had shown up with a house she'd bought for them to live in.

Gran settled into the house and one day Gillian came home to see the piano dominating the space. A Steinway grand piano. A thing so stunningly beautiful she'd nearly wept at the sight of.

She and Gran had argued about it. Gillian had insisted her grand-mother return it. It was an extravagance. It had hurt to say it out loud when she wanted to reach out and touch it so badly. But no one else in her life had ever loved her like Gran had and there was no way she could have accepted such a gift.

Gran had told her she'd been saving to buy Gillian a proper piano since she'd first heard Gillian play.

Bach it had been that day.

Gillian breathed in and out and then touched the keys and lost herself in Bach.

As she had those years before when Gillian's mother had come home to their shitty little council flat and announced their dad was in the nick for killing some teenaged girl he'd been banging.

They'd packed a few bags, not having much more than that any-way, and had ended up living with Gillian's father's mother. Gran, who had cut off contact with her son, but who had been trying to keep a relationship with her grandchildren.

Gran, who took them in, and it was then, in those first months she'd been in America, that she began to breathe deeply.

In her grandmother's grand front room of her ranch-style house an hour or so outside San Francisco, she'd coveted the piano until her gran had asked her if she wanted to play it.

Her mother had smiled proudly. A small bit of affection from a woman who'd at best been a distracted adult who lived with them rather than a mother.

Candace Forrester had possessed many flaws, but she hadn't been all bad. She'd scrimped and saved so that each daughter could take a lesson of some sort. Tina had received dance and voice lessons. Her sister's voice had been beautiful. Their mother had decided piano lessons would be best for young Gillian. Pretty girls got tap and singing and Gillian would be good at something you didn't need looks for.

"You gotta work what you got, Jilly," her mother used to say. "Show some cleavage. You got yerself a nice pair of titties, girl. Use 'em."

Tina and their mother had cast off their past and jumped into being American. Her mother wanted to be called Candy now and Tina, just barely eighteen and in possession of a fake ID, had already taken to bar hopping with their mother.

Gillian wasn't a Jilly. But she was free of the knowing glances and suspicious stares when they entered a store. Free of having to see her father's name in the papers.

For Gillian, America had been a new start too, but instead of going the way her mother and sister had, which in a sad parody was pretty much what they had back in England, Gillian had decided to make the most of this clean slate.

"G'wan, Jilly, play the piano for your granny."

"What would you like to hear?" Gillian had asked, expecting to hear Beethoven or maybe Mozart.

"I should like to hear you play Bach."

And she had.

Now as she played through her Gran's favorite parts of the *Goldberg Variations*, she did it on a piano her grandmother had found at an estate sale. She did it on this piano because her gran had sold the one that had sat in her own parlor for thirty-five years to pay for Gillian's tuition at Juilliard.

Even though Gran had passed several years ago, it felt to Gillian that they were together every time she touched a keyboard.

The doorbell sounded and she started. An hour and a half had passed and she hadn't realized it. Lesson time.

Adrian couldn't help but feel nervous as he made the last turn down his street. He wanted Miles to like the house. To like what was his too. Wanted Gillian to like it.

Gillian had tried to sit in the backseat, but he'd said no. Kids didn't sit in the front, moms sat in the front. They'd taken a little bit of a public step that morning when he'd held her hand, just for a few moments, as they'd been loading into the car. It had felt right, to touch her and guide her, carrying her overnight bag.

Miles hadn't cared either way where he sat. He'd been talking about manga and anime nonstop as Gillian smiled faintly, looking out the window at the passing scenery. Every once in a while she'd ask a follow-up question or help with a detail or two. He appreciated how much subtle help she sent his way. Knowing her, it was subconscious on her part, wanting to take care of Miles and Adrian both. It felt good to be taken care of that way.

His gate slid open and he wondered what all this looked like through their eyes. The cops had come by earlier to roust the three young women who'd been camping at the bottom of the drive. He knew this because Cope had made sure of it and texted him about it. The last thing he wanted was to freak his kid out, for god's sake.

Despite the end-of-the-drive issues he constantly had, he did love the house. And he couldn't deny he wanted them to love it too. Her house was so warm and open, he had to admit he was a little envious and wanted that here for them as well.

"Let's get your bags in your rooms and get you settled that way." Nervousness jumped inside him, skittering through his muscles.

Miles unfolded himself from the car and looked around, wide-eyed. "This place is awesome."

Well, okay, that made him feel better.

He took Gillian's hand without thinking and she stumbled a bit, but adjusted, keeping her hand in his.

"Glad you approve. Come on in." He grinned at Miles, who didn't see it because he was too busy gaping when Adrian pushed the front door open.

"This is beautiful," Gillian murmured.

He squeezed her hand. "Bedrooms are this way." He led them up a floor and went to Miles's room first.

"Holy cow." Miles paused at the door, dropping his bag at his feet.

"Do you like it? It's the biggest room here other than mine and I wanted you to have the space. There are other rooms if you prefer."

Gillian put two fingers over his lips. "It's a great room. You did a good job." He took her hand then and kissed it without thinking. Just totally pleased. She looked to Miles and then smiled back at Adrian. He supposed they were "out" about this little romance between them with that kiss. She didn't seem nervous or upset about it, which did relax him a little.

Miles went into the room, tentative at first, just looking and not touching. Gillian stayed him when he began to speak.

And so he'd watched Miles learn the space in his own precise way. Sometimes so much like an engineer. He examined things and then he looked at them again and began to touch.

When he did finally speak, Adrian was glad he'd waited. The look on his son's face would last him through a thousand shitty days. "This is awesome. Mum, do you see this room?"

"I did, it's marvelous, isn't it? What a lovely view."

The room had a view of the water and a deck. Adrian had put in a big bed and had built-in shelving and drawers installed. A big-screen television was set up in the far end of the room with several gaming systems. A computer and printer as well.

Erin had supervised it all over the last week when Adrian had to go back to Los Angeles to deal with a number of business meetings with management and label people, accountants and lawyers. He'd told her what he wanted for the room and she and Brody had made it all happen.

Miles threw himself on the bed and laughed. It felt so good, that perfect moment. Adrian looked back at Gillian, liking how it felt to have them both in his house.

"Come on then." Miles jumped up. "Let's see your room, Mum."

"You're downstairs." Adrian pointed to the hall on the other side of the second floor, an atrium-type ceiling soaring in an open space sitting between. "I'm over there."

He led them down and around the corner to the guest room that Ella had volunteered to deal with. At first Adrian wanted to create a lush, sensual room for her with deep, rich colors. But then Ella, wonderful, sweet and insightful Ella, had suggested Gillian might feel uncomfortable with a room like that in someone else's home until she knew them better.

She'd been totally right. He knew that for sure as Gillian stepped into the room and began to look around. She kept her hands clasped as she moved, but her gaze ate the place up.

Gillian hadn't known what to expect when he'd brought her into the room. What she got was a delight. Pale blue walls with chocolate brown accents and the very occasional splash of green.

"Do you like it? I'll take credit for it if you do. But if you don't, I'll tell you my friend Ella took care of putting this room together this week when I had to be out of town."

His quirked-up grin was of the sideways persuasion that always made her weak in the knees. Like hands and forearms, of which his were all manly and tattooed and muscled and it drove her crazy to look at them.

She turned before she went any further than that.

Inappropriate! She shook herself and gave herself a mental slap. She met his eyes in the mirror above the dresser. The bed reflected in between them and she swallowed hard at the look on his face. And then the moment was gone with the next breath and she looked away.

And still, something had shifted between them. Subtle, which is why she wasn't having a stern conversation with him. The hand-holding and then the affectionate kiss to her fingertips had happened in front of Miles.

She knew it would come, unless they hid their relationship totally, which wasn't to her liking either. This would be about managing expectations so Miles wouldn't be thinking something unrealistic like his parents would get married in a week or what have you.

Adrian was respectful to her. Touched her with gentleness and a sort of Old-World chivalrous air. She liked it.

She turned back to Adrian and Miles with a smile. "This is beautiful. Really. You and your friend Ella did a great job." She wondered who these people were going to be when she met them in a few hours. Wondered if they'd like her or if they too believed as Adrian once had that she was out to get something from him.

"Oh good." His face lost some of its hesitancy. "Through those doors is a patio. You can follow it down toward the water, or you can head left and get to the backyard. The bathroom is through there, as is the closet."

She wandered back, through the huge bathroom and into the closet. Drawers, shoe racks, pegs for hats and bags.

"Erin is in charge of all the soap and other foofy gear in the house. It's just that I'm hopeless and she gets some insane charge out of making me try all this stuff she stumbles across. She used to dress the dog up too. She's bossy like that. Anyway, there's all sorts of bath and body goop in the linen closet over there. I have no doubt she and Ella tucked all sorts of female regalia all over the place for you to use while you're here. If you need anything, please let me know. I want you to be comfortable."

And there was the charming again. He made her swoon with some of things he said and did.

"Thank you. It's lovely."

He shrugged, casting for unconcerned, but she saw the slight blush at his neck. Which she'd been looking at and then wishing she could lick it.

Going straight to hell for this.

They'd gotten settled in and Adrian had given them the tour of the backyard and side gardens. It had pleased Gillian to see the pink bicycle with the fringed handlebars. Balls of all sizes sat in a box on the deck near the back glass doors.

"Rennie, my niece, she likes to head to the park nearby and ride her bike. Miles, that's yours over there." Adrian pointed to a brand-new mountain bike. "Of course I got him a helmet and that stuff to go with it. I got you a bike too. You know, so we can all go riding to-gether when you're here."

She appreciated his generosity but the level of extravagance made her nervous. For Miles it was more that she didn't want to suddenly thrust wealth into his life, especially not without consulting her first to work on how to handle it.

Gillian had watched her mother and sister selling themselves short by hitching their lives to men. She made her own way.

A woman who made her own way didn't owe anyone anything. She didn't have to turn a blind eye to philandering or a heavy hand with the drink or fist. A woman who made her own way had choices.

"I appreciate that, Adrian." She paused. "Miles, can you go and change your shirt and wash up? We should be leaving soon for dinner."

Miles looked at Adrian, sympathy on his face. "Good luck, mate."

She shushed him and shooed him with her hands. "Get on with it, boy."

He obeyed quickly.

"Did I make you unhappy with something?"

Of course he looked all innocent-like and she immediately felt guilty for being annoyed. "It's just that all this is a lot. Do you under-stand?" She softened her original tirade. "You can't just spend all this money on him. Or on me."

"I'm sure I owe you a few child-support checks. I want to give him things, Gillian. I wasn't there for a long time. I—I want to do for him, take care of him."

And she got that. She did, and it tempered her frustration and even the fear. "I understand that. And I appreciate it. He does too. But he's a middle-class kid. He's got a middle-class life. You can't— I'm asking you to please take that into account when you buy things for him."

"You got to give him presents for thirteen years, Gillian." Adrian began to pace. "All that time I could have been with him at birthdays and Christmas and I wasn't. I think it's pretty fucked to expect me to not want to give him the benefit of my wealth. He's not a middle-class kid anymore. He's the son of a millionaire. And it's a fucking bike."

Having a man, even one who looked and acted like Adrian, use that kind of language when they were angry around her really pushed buttons. "Look, you." She planted a hand on her hip and pointed an accusing finger at him with the other. "You'll speak to me with some respect. You don't use those words when you speak to me. I don't give a toss about who you are at home or how much you've got in the bank. That is my son and I've done a very good job at teaching him to value what he's got and to work for what he wants."

Adrian lost his anger and stared at her. If Miles hadn't been around, Adrian would be on her right then. Damn, she was fierce and pissed off and protective of their son.

"Don't you get that look either."

He took a step closer. "I apologize. But whatever do you mean? What look is that? Hm?" He nuzzled her neck and she sighed softly, the rigidity of her spine loosening.

"You know the look I'm talking about. Sex won't get you out of this." She pinched his side but there was no real effort in it. He jumped back anyway, needing the space to lose the hard-on he could pound iron with.

"I can't apologize for getting him a bicycle. Or you one. I bought a bicycle for Rennie. And a tricycle for Alexander. Marti has a wagon.

I wanted us all to be able to go on rides. And he needed a room here. I want him to spend time with me. I want him to be at home. And you too."

"Adrian . . ."

He wasn't having it. "No. Look, you and I have something. Something I'd like to follow up on."

"You don't even know me. You're going through a lot right now. You'll get more accustomed to being a dad and you won't need me around. It's going to happen."

He backed her against a nearby post. "Is that what you think? All this energy between us is just me nervous to be a dad?"

And when her eyes widened and she licked her lips he tasted victory. She could claim otherwise all she wanted. But she wanted him as much as he wanted her.

"I—I don't expect anything from you."

He took a deep breath. "I know you don't. But I expect something from you."

"Wh-what?" She sucked in a breath when he nipped her bottom lip.

"Do you know what? Finding Miles has taught me to be open to all kinds of great things I never expected. You're one of those things. I want you, Gillian. And I know you want me too."

"Miles is—"

"He's in the other room. Also he's old enough to know his parents date. And why not date each other? Novel, huh?"

"Let's take this slow." She looked him over, suspicion clear on her face. "And you'll speak with me and at the very least inform me when you plan to make some large purchase on his behalf. Please. I know you want to do things for him. And it *is* unfair that you missed so much time. At the same time, I think it's really important he retains gratitude and having to work for what he gets."

It actually was a reasonable request. "All right. I want to go skiing at Whistler in a few weeks. I have a house up there. Will you both come?"

Before they could speak any more, Adrian heard Miles's footfalls and eased himself away from Gillian.

"We'll talk later. Let's get going to Erin's."

He let it go but knew he'd be back to it.

Are you sure we shouldn't have brought anything?" she asked him, unsuccessfully hiding her nervousness as they approached Erin's door.

"You already made me stop and pick up dessert at your friend's shop on the way over. I love that logo. Clever, retro. Sexy."

She blushed and it shot straight to his belly. "Who doesn't like pie and tarts with coffee? And thank you. I assume you know I designed it."

Before he was able to knock, the door whipped open and it was Rennie who stood there, a huge grin on her face. "Uncle Adrian!" She threw herself at him as he knelt toward her, hugging him tight.

"Yo, Rennie. I missed you, sunshine."

After he delivered a few kisses, he put Rennie down and straightened before stepping into Erin's place.

Rennie, being Rennie, didn't waste any time. She planted herself in Miles's path and stuck out her hand. "You must be Miles. I'm your cousin, Irene. But everyone mostly calls me Rennie. Did you know they have four gaming consoles here? It's awesome. You have pretty hair. Most boys like your age have dirty hair. Yours is nice."

Miles seemed caught off guard and charmed by Rennie, as everyone else always was upon meeting her. He nodded respectfully as he allowed her to pump his arm up and down several vigorous times as she shook his hand.

Brody came into the room, toting Marti, who laughed and reached out when she caught sight of Adrian.

"Come in, please." Ben stepped forward, extending a hand toward Gillian. "I'm Ben Copeland. I'm one of Adrian's brothers-in-law. Jeez, Adrian, where are your manners? Invite them in and let's get their coats."

Gillian shook his hand, looking as if she dealt with this sort of thing every day. Adrian had to admit to himself how impressed he was, especially as she looked even smaller compared to Ben's bulk. Miles looked him up and down, a little awed.

Adrian took coats and her bag. He handed the bakery boxes to Elise, who took them with a sweet smile of reassurance.

"Gillian Forrester. Thank you for having us today."

"We're glad to do it." Ben smiled and turned to Miles. "I've been waiting to meet you. Welcome to the family, kiddo."

Miles nodded and stammered his way through a thank-you. Adrian noted the way Gillian would touch him every once in a while, just to give him a little reassurance.

Erin pushed her way through the group, who'd been creeping closer but hadn't quite broken through their manners to be their normal, nosy selves and push into Gillian and Miles's personal space.

"Hey there, Miles." She hugged him, and he seemed a little stunned but then went with it.

"Hey."

"Gillian, it's good to see you. I hope you two are hungry. Todd's out on the terrace grilling up a storm."

"Let's get the introductions out of the way." Adrian put an arm around Miles's shoulders and a restraining hand on Gillian's arm to keep her from sidling away. "Everyone, this is Miles and Gillian. We don't expect you to remember names; there's a lot of us. But here goes."

He pointed Miles toward Brody. "This is Brody. He's my older brother and your uncle. The baby is Martine and we call her Marti. That pretty blonde there is your aunt Elise. She's Brody's wife and Marti and Rennie's mom."

Gillian gasped, surprising Adrian. "Oh my goodness. Elise Sorenson! I've seen you dance many times. I'm a huge fan." Gillian blushed nearly as deeply red as Elise did.

"Really?"

"I saw you dance *Coppelia* four times. And *Giselle*. Oh, and the *Sleeping Beauty*. Brilliant. You're amazingly gifted."

"You did? Where?" Adrian and Miles stood back and watched the two.

"The Met most of the time, and then Lincoln Center. I lived in New York for several years."

"I'm very flattered. Thank you. Those are some of my favorite roles. You've made my entire week." Elise smiled at Gillian. The two women did have that sort of elegant, graceful manner. Brody had been right about that. Funny how he and his brother seemed to have similar tastes.

"Irene, wait until Miles has met everyone before you go dragging him off somewhere." Brody looked toward his daughter and she sighed heavily.

"Fine. I just was gonna show him the *Mario Kart* game."

Miles appeared shell-shocked and Gillian subtly moved a little closer, sliding a hand up and down his back.

"Okay, everyone, let's stop crowding. Why don't you two sit down." Adrian ushered them into the living room and sat with them. "So you met your uncle and aunt and two of your cousins. And you met Ben." He'd discussed the situation with Gillian and they'd both been up front with Miles about it. Miles didn't seem to care one way or the other, so they left it at that. Gillian told him Miles would come to her if he was having any problems.

"You met Erin. That's Todd, Erin's other husband, and Alexander, their son."

"Yo! Yo!" Alexander waved, pushing from his dad's grip and heading to Adrian, who scooped him up, settling the boy on his lap.

"Hello, young man." Gillian took Alexander's hand and shook it as he tried to gnaw on her. "Oh my, someone is teething. Vexing, that." She smiled at Alexander, who stopped his pursuit of her knuckle to gaze at her adoringly.

Todd waved at them.

"Last but not ever least are Andrew and Ella Copeland. Andy is Ben's brother and his lovely wife, Ella, is an old family friend."

"It's very nice to meet you." Gillian nudged Miles, who parroted her words.

"All right then. Miles, would you like to play a few video games or go out on the terrace and check the view?" Elise asked.

Erin took Miles's hand. "None of the above. I'm going to show Miles my bass collection."

"Hey!" Adrian got up to follow them, the siblings joking and bickering as they went. He was still holding Alexander, who patted his chest over and over as they disappeared around the corner.

Gillian grinned as she watched her son trail down the hall, listening to every word Erin said as if it were gospel.

"She's so excited. Probably almost as much as Adrian." Brody spoke in an undertone as he settled in across from Gillian.

"I suspect it's the bass-guitar thing." This would be good for her son, and that made her very happy. But this day had been illuminating for a whole new set of reasons. It had obviously occurred to her that there were differences between Adrian's life and her own. She accepted there was no real competing with a dad who could drop the kind of money he had without thinking on high-end bicycles, electronics and remodels for his house. It continued here in this giant, open apartment that dominated an entire half of a floor of a building.

Money and power were adversaries she could not defeat. This had been with her since finding out who Miles's dad was. But being confronted with it like this set her on her heels a little.

Some small part of her worried Miles would forget about their simpler life and crave this. Who wouldn't? Would she lose him, then, to something she couldn't begin to imitate?

Or would he be swallowed up by these people with their big, charismatic personalities? Would he lose himself in the midst of it? Feel bad? Her mother heart worried for him and that heart he wore on his sleeve, even as it loved him fiercely for exactly that and expected that everyone else should too.

It made her want to clutch Miles against her and rush away. Instead, she swallowed it back. She simply had to trust in what she'd built. Anything else wouldn't allow her to do it at all.

So she'd do it and make the very best of this new direction her life had been thrust into and get over the fear with time.

Brody Brown was far more than an older brother. She saw it in the way he interacted with Erin and Adrian. And with the others in this tight-knit group. He was the one they all seemed to look to, the father figure for the whole crew. He watched her with eyes that held kindness and no small amount of respect. "I wanted to thank you for sticking with this. Even when it got unpleasant. You gave my brother something more important than anything else he'll ever have or want."

One thing this man was, was down to earth. She liked that about him. It countered the fear about this life going to Miles's head. The Browns seemed to be grounded, humble people.

"Thank you. Adrian tells me you got in his face a few times to urge him forward." She'd liked how Adrian was when he spoke of his family. At times he could be vary wary, but when it was about them, he was open and warm.

And she liked that Brody Brown had been on her side since the very start. She'd never mention that she knew to him. It would only make him uncomfortable. But she knew it just the same.

Elise came over and sat next to Brody, smiling at Gillian. The baby she held had Brody's serious eyes, and that pale as sunshine hair her mother had.

"I hope we haven't totally overwhelmed you."

They were, she saw quite clearly, a team. A unit. Brody and Elise were so in tune and in love with each other and this life, Gillian could do nothing but smile at them.

Gillian looked around the room at the people gathered there. "This is good for Miles. That's what's important. Eventually he'll be part of you all and he won't need me to be around."

Elise gave Brody a look and he snorted a laugh.

Elise explained. "I should tell you the Browns, Copelands and Keenans happen to hold family as very important. Miles is Adrian's son. You're Miles's mother. You'll always be part of this if for no other reason. That's who they all are."

It barbed into her belly for a brief twinge, realizing she'd begun to wonder if the thing developing between her and Adrian was something more than fleeting. Fear that it was for her and not for him. Excitement at that new-relationship feeling. Exhilarating and nauseating all at once.

"Would you like a drink?" the pretty redhead, Ella, asked from her place across the room. "We've got juice and water, soda, beer, wine, margaritas in the blender too. Not only is Andrew pretty to look at, he makes a mean margarita." Her husband, the ridiculously gorgeous aforementioned Andrew, grinned her way.

Gillian looked back toward the hallway, trying not to worry about Miles. That's when Brody took her hands in his, leaning forward.

"Miles will always be safe with us. I know the tattoos and piercings can be a little off-putting at first."

Gillian couldn't help it, she laughed. "Honestly, that is just not on my list of concerns. Not at all. I'm not bothered by the ink. I think it's beautiful, actually." She shook her head, hard.

"That's my baby in there. I'm his mum. It's my job to worry about him. It's not about what you look like. He's . . . shy and quiet and"— she paused to glance around the room—"that's a little rare around here. I know he's thirteen and I know Adrian loves him and I know you're all good people."

Mortified, she batted back tears.

Elise helped her up. "Ella, how about one of those mango things you make, without the tequila for now."

Ella smiled reassuringly and handed over a pretty glass.

"Thank you." Gillian might be on the verge of losing her shit, but she still remembered her manners.

"Why don't we take a walk? The terrace is gorgeous. Marti loves it out here, even when it's cold like today."

It was cold, especially at the elevation they were at, but Elise hadn't lied about how pretty it was out there. At least the cold would give her something else to think about aside from her worries for Miles and yet more evidence of the difference between her life and this . . . this abundance.

"I can't imagine what you must be feeling," Elise said as they took a stroll along the terrace. The baby was snuggled against her mother in a carrier, a jaunty little cap on as she strained to see all she could from the confines of her bundle. People were everywhere, but everyone seemed to fit together so well. A lot like her own group of friends. That did comfort her in a sense, but at the same time, this wasn't about her. She felt out of place because of that even as it comforted her that Miles would have this tight-knit community to be part of as well as the one he already belonged to.

"For years I lived in fear that my ex-in-laws would take Rennie. They tried several times. It was hard to get past that terror of losing her. Even when I knew in my head that they couldn't take her, that she was mine and I was a good mother. And then I met Brody and everything changed." She laughed.

"I see the way you are with your son and it makes me like you. Mothering is a hard job, thankless, exhausting. You did it on your own for a long time and now you have to share your beautiful son with others. That's the hard thing. Am I right?"

"Partially." She paused, watching Marti, missing the weight of a baby in her arms.

"You don't know me very well, but I'm a pretty good listener and nothing you say to me is going to be repeated. I hope you can trust me enough to talk to me, but if you don't, that's all right too."

Gillian paused, trying to find the right words. "I knew I'd have to share Miles when I started this process. Just as I knew it was the only thing I could do because it was the best thing for him. But the reality of it is beyond what I had imagined. It's hard not to let fear and distrust color everything." She waved a hand, indicating the view. "I can't compete with this. I can't compete with a man who can drop the kind of money Adrian can on things it takes me years to save for. I worry how this will affect Miles. I worry about what it will be like for my middle-class son, who brings home strays and uses his allowance to buy feed for the birds and the squirrels instead of video games. I worry he'll feel out of place in the midst of a family full of rock stars and ballerinas."

She looked over the city. "I apologize. That was rude of me."

Elise waved the apology away. "Of *course* you'd worry about that. All I can tell you is that we're good people and we love each other. Adrian Brown is one of the most humble people I've ever known. Sensitive. Kind and loving. My kids adore him. He's an amazing uncle and I know he's going to be an amazing dad."

Elise laughed softly.

"So, when Marti was about a month old, Erin and Ella convinced me to come to get a facial and a manicure. The shop is about two miles from our house. Now, I'd left Rennie with Brody many times. He's a great father. But Martine was just a month old. Would he remember how to get the breast milk out of the freezer? What if she got upset and wouldn't stop crying? She'd had a fussy few days.

"But they argued and wheedled, as did Brody, who gave me that sort of stern puppy-dog face and said it sounded like I didn't trust him to take care of our daughter for less than two hours."

Gillian laughed.

"I needed that hour and fifteen minutes. And when I got home, the place was a big mess, but Brody and Rennie had managed to do just fine with Marti. Of course he put the wrong size diaper on her and her clothes were too big because he'd put on the ones I'd put aside for her next growth spurt. But they were all fine and I'd done something good for myself, and for Brody too. And also, it's good for a kid to have Dad be in charge sometimes. They can be washed off. It won't kill 'em to have Popsicles for breakfast sometimes. And if things get too bad, there are no less than seven other people within a fifteen-minute radius who are available to help."

"Are you promising not to break my son?"

Elise grinned at her, laughing. "Yes, exactly that. And this group of people here? If anyone knows how to love and respect that people are different and to celebrate that—it's them.

"And because of the fame Adrian has, their lifestyle is very protective of that. They're not lavish people, though they are generous. Especially Adrian. I—well, can I be perfectly honest with you?"

Gillian nodded.

"He's going to try to do for you and Miles, and I take it from some of your earlier comments that perhaps he already has and you're feeling a bit uncomfortable about it. He has the means. More than enough means. And he's made it a sort of personal journey this year to spend more time at home with his family, doing what's important and taking time off from the road for a while. He gives because he can and because he loves his family. It's not meant to make you feel bad."

"It's just I've spent Miles's entire life trying to teach him about saving for things and waiting to have things you really want, and in just one week of being Adrian's son, he's got a brand-new room that could be an electronics showroom, and a swank new bike I'd never be able to afford in a million years. I feel petty and selfish and maybe even a little jealous that I can't do the same for him."

"This is going to be fine, you know." Elise put an arm through one of Gillian's and they began to walk again. "There'll be bumps along the way. As such things go. You're a strong person to have done what you have in bringing that boy and his dad together. We'll work this all out because that's what family does. Over time you'll get used to all the interruptions when you're out and about. Though"—she paused to look around—"perhaps you can draw him out of this self-imposed shell he's retreated to."

"How so?"

Elise readjusted Marti's hat before she spoke again, clearly weighing her words. "I want to tell you because I think it's good to understand him. I see how he looks at you and it's not just as the woman who's been mothering his kid. He's had a few conversations with Brody about you, but they both pretend like I don't see what's totally obvious." She snorted a laugh, still managing to sound elegant when she did it.

"But he's a man, therefore he won't say anything to protect you or something equally silly. It's got to be hard, you know? Being recognized all the time. And while he loves his fans, it's hard on him to feel like he's on display every time he leaves the house. So he sticks to safe places. Our house, here, the café, the tavern and a few places we all eat as a group. I like it that he goes to Bainbridge to see you. I like that he's pushing past his comfort zone to be part of Miles's life. I think it's good for him to realize there's more than ten people and eight places he can be safe with."

Gillian hadn't known the extent of it, though his distrust of the unfamiliar was fairly obvious. Gillian knew what it felt like to not have enough safe places in your life. Knew the helplessness of it. It made her want to find Adrian and hug him.

"Thank you for saying that. It helps. As for how he looks at me . . ." Her words died as she looked toward downtown. "Well, we're . . . I'm not used to this sort of sharing, but I'm trying to learn too." She blushed and Elise squeezed her hand.

"You don't have to say anything. I get it. More than you can know."

"There you are!" Adrian came out onto the terrace with Miles at his side. "Your son and my sister just trash-talked me. Can you imagine? Where's the gratitude, Miles?"

Miles, laughing, poked Adrian in the ribs with his elbow, playfully.

Gillian couldn't help but smile at them both, playing together the way they did. Adrian encouraged Miles's roughhousing side.

"Like puppies, the both of you."

Adrian looked up with a grin and then over to Todd. "He eats like one too. Christ, Todd, you should see how much this boy can put away. He'll fit in here just fine."

At dinner, sitting at a table in a dining room that ran the length of the windows south of the kitchen, Erin maneuvered herself next to Gillian. "How's it going? This has to be a bit much."

"Funny how a glass of wine can take the edge off."

Erin laughed and Alexander looked up from where he sat with Adrian. "Mah!" He hopped down and toddled around, holding on here and there, taking whatever helping hand a nearby adult gave until he reached not Erin, but Gillian.

"Up." He added something that sounded rather like please and automatically, Gillian picked him up, plopping him into her lap, careful not to let him too near cutlery or anyone's drink.

"He loves the ladies, does our Alexander." Erin cocked her head at her son, who blew her a kiss. "I'm afraid he's just as terminally charming as the rest of the men in this family. Luckily, we're a hearty bunch of womenfolk and can whip them into shape."

She paused to look at her son with affection. And then back to Gillian. "I want you to like us. I can't pretend I don't. I'm weird that way, I guess, but when I meet people I enjoy I get excited. I promise I won't call you at two in the morning to make you tell me I'm pretty though. I have Ben and Todd for that." She laughed, Alexander mimicking her.

"I was telling your brother how impossible it was not to like you. You're rather irresistible. It runs in your family. Charm." Gillian looked to Adrian and Miles, heads bent close, up to some sort of mischief. "Adorable, the whole lot of you."

Erin barked out a laugh, though no one seemed to notice over their own laughter and talk.

"As compliments go, that's up there near the top. Thank you. I know we're sort of like the Borg, sweeping in and taking over with our bright colors and loud voices."

Gillian really did like Erin.

"Oh, you're not as bad as that. You all certainly make Miles happy. Counts for a lot with me."

Alexander leaned his head back into Gillian's chest to look up at her. "You're just as bad as the rest." She dropped a kiss to his forehead and he grinned.

"He's worse. He's a hybrid. With all these bossy men around, he's just as bad as they are. Rennie and I have decided that having you in the family makes it way better for us odds-wise. You see, we drown in all these big old alpha males around here. It's all we can do to hold our own. You even the odds, though you do bring another boy to the table."

"I like Rennie too."

The little girl had set her sights on protecting and guiding Miles through the day. Miles was being sweet with her, as Gillian had no doubt he would be. But he was extra courtly with his manners and right as she watched, she saw so much of his father and uncle in him it made her stop and stare.

"I know. It's insane. Never met his dad until a week ago and look how much alike those Brown boys are. So much Brody in him. Serious. He's protective of you, which is very sweet."

"I'm lucky to have a kid like him."

Adrian looked up at her and sent all her hormones into action.

Erin looked between them, a mysterious smile on her face.

***

She'd been standing next to the doors looking out over the view when Adrian came to the door and tapped lightly.

She'd known he would come, and yet her heart skipped a beat as she headed to let him in.

"Hey. Can I come in?"

"Of course." She stood aside and he came through the door, shutting it behind himself.

It had taken an extra two hours for Miles to finally drop off to sleep. He'd been so wound up and excited, and after they'd returned from Erin's they'd hung out in Adrian's studio, playing for several more hours.

A big day for her boy, and she was overjoyed for him. They welcomed him with open arms and open hearts. It warmed her to her toes to see these people so eager to love her son.

"You settled in all right?" He moved to stand next to her, both of them taking in the view.

"It's a lovely room. Thank you. Your home is beautiful."

He faced her and she wasn't ready just yet, so she continued to watch moonlight dance on the water.

"I need you, Gillian."

His words came in the dark, filled with emotions she didn't know what to make of. She drowned in her own, unsure, off balance. Her reality was ill fitting, like a suit from the charity shops, and it sent her reeling.

She liked it when things made sense. Liked knowing exactly where she stood and what would happen next. She was not a woman who thrived on mystery or drama.

But that's where she found herself. On uncertain ground with a man she wanted so much sometimes everything inside her ached. On uncertain ground about her future, her son's future. It was good. Mostly. But not enough to push her to want to expose all the emotion in his simple statement.

She turned to him, letting her robe fall away.

His lips met hers with a brief gnash of teeth and tongue as they left words behind.

Silently, he eased her back to the bed, opening her pajama shirt with nimble fingers, sliding it off. The cool air bit against her bare skin, her nipples tightening, readying for that first brush of his thumbs.

She pulled his T-shirt off, sliding herself against him, skin to skin, bright lights against her closed eyes at the pleasure and warmth of contact.

She landed on her back and he made quick work of her pants and his own, and when he joined her, he was as naked as she, holding her for several long moments as tenderness scratched the back of her throat with the swell of emotion.

Not slow and finessed. That's not what she needed. Not what she could bear just then.

"Hard and fast," she murmured into his ear.

The muscles on his back tensed and bunched under her hands. He moved away just a moment and returned, ready.

She was wet, open to him as he guided the head of his cock to her gate and pressed in. She swiveled her hips, rolling them to get him inside all the way.

Now.

Now.

Now.

Her skin was on fire, sliding against his, sweat-slicked. The friction brought her system to near overload with so much sensation.

She bit his shoulder to keep the words where they belonged. Her nails dug in where she held on as he fucked into her pussy hard and fast. No sound but gasping for breath and the slick slide of cock in cunt.

The silence just made it more intense. All the tension of the unsaid swirled around them both as the frenzy of desire spiced it. She nearly drowned in how much she needed him just then. How intensely he made her feel, how much more she wanted.

He gave as good as he got. Not satisfied with her teeth in his shoulder, he wanted her mouth. So he took it. Possessing it with his own, his tongue barging in, assured and bold as you please. His taste incited her, his groan when she sucked his tongue lightly shot straight to her nipples and then her clit.

He was so sure then, aggressive there in the dark. Not just guiding, but taking, pushing, driving and grabbing just exactly what he wanted, how he wanted it. It was so breathtakingly alpha and in charge she was glad not to be standing on legs he regularly turned to jelly.

She arched and he flipped, rolling to put her on top. She tucked her feet beneath his thighs and braced her hands just behind her ass as she rose and fell on his cock.

This way her cunt was exposed to him. Open as he slid a fingertip over her clit as she swallowed back a groan of pleasure.

He touched her just right. Keeping her on the edge of climax as he filled her over and over.

And when it broke, it hit her hard, shattering all around her, pulling at her composure, threatening to unravel her.

So she threw herself into it. Into that very moment as desire ran wild through her veins as orgasm turned her inside out. He continued to thrust, his muscles tight as she knew he barreled toward his own climax.

Moonlight splayed over them, just enough for her to see the drive in his features. The relentless pursuit of pleasure as he flexed and filled her completely before retreating.

Just watching him then had wedged open doors she wanted to keep shut. But there was no way she could avert her gaze. He was beautiful there, sexy and earthy. Masculine and strong.

When he came, his fingers tangled with hers, his gaze locked on her face. His kiss then was slow and tender as he came back to bed, sliding in next to her body, moving to her mouth like it was all he'd been thinking of. And she wanted that to be true more than she really wanted to admit.

He stayed next to her in the bed until the sun began to creep over the horizon.

12

"I'm having sex with Adrian."

She blurted it out, having to say it out loud and knowing Jules wouldn't judge her.

"I knew it." Jules shrugged. "Can't imagine why you waited so long to tell me. I'd say, given the way he looked at you when you were here a few weeks ago, that you two have been fucking like minks since—" Jules's eyes lit up and Gillian just waited for it.

"You have been doing naughty naked things with Adrian Brown since pretty much day one?" Jules tsked. "Wow, my estimation of you has risen even more."

Gillian sat on a barstool at Tart, drinking coffee and eating something that would go straight to her bum and she did not care one bit.

"Yes. He's just . . . I'm just . . . well, I don't know what it is but we have something really intense. Still, how can you be so casual about it? He's Miles's dad! He's wholly unsuitable for me for reasons you very well know. Talk me out of it."

Jules only rolled her eyes. "It seems to me there are two issues here. First, the Miles thing. What does he think? Does he know?"

"We've been careful to keep it slow and subtle in front of him. We talked about it the first time, well, you know. Anyway, neither of us is seeing anyone else. It's been a few weeks so the most Miles is going to see is a hand hold here and there, a quick kiss on the mouth, no tongues or anything. It's clear he knows something is happening. We're not keeping it a secret or anything."

"Miles would tell you if he was bothered. Or worried. He talks to you. I bet Miles can see you're happy and he obviously likes his dad, so why not? I just have total confidence that you handle it right."

"I'm glad you do. Me? Not so sure."

"Gillian, you are many things, and one of those things is an awesome mother. Just be happy. Miles wants that."

"What if it goes wrong?" She twisted her fingers.

"You've broken up with people before and he hasn't gone off the rails. I mean it would suck for you on a few levels, but people do it all the time. They have perfectly cordial relationships with their ex for the sake of the kids. And both of you love Miles. So part one, check. Miles is just fine. And now that we've cleared that up it's on to part two."

Gillian held a hand up. "I need a bracing sip of tea for this, I'm sure."

Jules smiled, looking sort of predatory. "Pfft. Does he get you off? Is it hot sex? 'Cause I gotta tell you, he looks like he knows what he's about when it comes to fucking."

She should have known this is how Jules would respond. Hell, maybe that's why she'd told her to start with.

"Yes. He's—astoundingly creative."

Jules's face brightened and she laughed in her quicksilver way.

"Yeah? Like how?"

Gillian had long since given up trying keep her reserve around Jules. It simply wasn't possible. "Well, to start with, he's tireless. When he stays over we're on each other every time we're alone. He's very"— she shivered, thinking about just how to put it—"intense. Dominant. Rough, but in the right way, if you know what I mean. Also"—she

took a quick look to each side before leaning in closer to her friend—
"he's a dirty talker."

Jules fanned her face. "Girl. You don't say? 'Cause, whew."

"I know." Blushing wildly, Gillian looked back to her plate for a
moment.

"So clearly you and he are a fit, and we both know how hard it is
for a woman to find a man who can deliver what she likes in the sack
when your likes might be a little unusual."

"It's not inappropriate? He's my son's father. I'm a mum! Shouldn't
I be, you know, chaste and such?" There was no need to comment on
the unusual reference in what Jules had just said. Gillian had told her
what she liked a long time ago.

"How is that inappropriate? You do know how babies get made,
right? Although, okay, perhaps that may not be a road you want to go
down."

Gillian laughed, finding levity in her friend's horror.

"He can't remember her. I don't know why it doesn't bother me,
but it doesn't. Most of the time Tina didn't even really seem like she
existed outside my childhood memories. I can't be jealous of a ghost.
Especially when she is just nowhere in my life to get in the way. I loved
her, despite her flaws. But I don't worry he'll compare me to her."

Jules nodded, thoughtful. "This makes sense. Not that he'd have
much to compare even if he did remember her. You're all curvy and
sexy. You mother like a fucking warrior. You're recommended by four
outta five."

Gillian snorted. "Well, that one doesn't count. He was a mercy
fuck. God, see how I am?"

"And how is that? Funny? Self-deprecating? Of course he wants
you. You're beautiful and talented and you smell all pretty like a
lady should, and even rock stars like that. How do *you* feel about all
this?"

She talked about it for a while, about Adrian's life and his family.
The close-knit nature that made her glad for her son and the double

edge of that. The fear they'd take him somehow, or that Miles would find her wanting in the face of all that.

Jules just listened, refilling her tea and occasionally moving to deal with a new customer.

"If he tries anything, you'll win. You're the primary parent. You've done well by Miles. That boy adores you. No amount of mansions with home studios are going to change that. You have to trust the job you've done with him. None of us would allow them to hurt you or Miles. You have to know that. Mary would drive her truck right into that pretty face of his if he even tried. You know how we had to hold her back when you came home from that meeting."

"I must be remembering it wrong then. I was under the impression it was *you* we had to hold back."

"Tomato, tomahto." Jules winked. "Anyhoo, I think you underestimate how much that boy adores his mom." She shrugged. "However, I'm so glad you're telling me all this." Jules moved to slide onto the stool next to Gillian. She put her head on Gillian's shoulder.

It had been hard, especially at first, to share her doubts. Her flaws and all the small, not-so-nice stuff in the corners of Gillian's mind. She'd lived with a mask on so long it was hard to let to go long enough to be vulnerable with someone.

But Jules wouldn't allow it. In her own way, of course. She pushed and poked and was just there until Gillian took a risk and shared. Just a little those first few years. But she'd never judged.

In the years since, Gillian had come to trust Jules Lamprey more than anyone else on the planet.

"I know you. You're trying to think about this in the way that makes you look the worst. Stop it. Let yourself enjoy this thing with him. Of course he wants you. Good gracious, he'd be an idiot or gay to not. You said he's a star in bed. Is he nice to you when he's not putting his penis in your hoo-hoo?"

Gillian laughed until tears ran from her eyes. "My what?"

"Your fertile fields. Your pink garden of delight. Your po-po.

Cooter. Cootchie. To get British—your fanny. Your cunt, pussy. Dare I say, your vagina. Do I need to have the talk with you? Last I remember, you had a few things to teach *me*, so stop pretending you don't know what I mean."

"I knew what you meant, you git. Though you know how much I love the term *cooter*. So very romantic, you Americans."

"That's us. Candlelight and soft music. All the best love words ever. Also you're an American too."

"Half, anyway." She laughed. "Yes. Yes, he's nice to me when we are not engaged in carnal relations. He's fascinating. Creative. Magnetic. He excites me sometimes with how he sees the world. I love to hear him talk about his music. I like him. A lot. And I don't know if it's that he's got this thing about him, this whatever it is that makes someone a celebrity or star. You want to look at him when he comes into a room. He has this voice, well, you heard it. That drawl thing and he sounds like sex on legs. Did you notice? Wait, no, don't tell me that. I don't want to know."

Jules took her hand and squeezed it before she hopped off the stool and wandered off. "I've never seen you so nervous and fluttery. You totally go gooey for this guy. I like that."

"I suppose I am. Which makes me distrust it. I'm not one for fluttery and gooey. I like being in charge of all my parts. He sort of takes several of them over."

Gillian ducked her head, blushing as Jules hooted laughter. "That is awesome! You deserve this, Gillian. Don't second-guess it. Let yourself be happy. Let yourself fall a little crazy in love with someone. Go a little wild."

"I'm someone's mother! I can't go wild."

Jules only rolled her eyes. "Oh, for poodle's sake, of course you can. For you wild is how other people stay sane. Eh? I mean Gillian wild, not Daisy wild." Daisy was another friend, a total wild-child artist. Gillian absolutely adored her, but they were very different.

"Well. Maybe. He"—she licked her lips, trying to find a way to say it—"I feel like I can let go with him."

Jules moved closer, though the place was nearly empty at the moment. "Then do it. Baby, how often do you let go? Really? If he rings your bell and he's doing it in a way that is not hurting you or Miles, ring it like it's dinnertime."

"I've got to go before you talk me into those strip-aerobics classes or something. I have a lesson in an hour and a thousand e-mails to deal with. I shall be taking this pear tart with me." She grabbed the pink box on the counter. "And give you proper credit with Miles, though he'll know everything baked and sweet comes from you, as I am such a disaster with a baking sheet."

"I'll see you both Thursday, if not before. And Friday night is club night. I know Mary told you to bring Adrian, so be sure you invite him or I will pester you until you do anyway."

Gillian tossed some money on the counter just as she turned to go and headed to the door, not stopping when she heard Jules exclaim when she saw the money.

"Bye, Juliet Lamprey, goddess of pastry. I will see you anon."

Miles had gone to bed, and as had been their little ritual, Gillian and Adrian headed outside. Her back deck had become one of his favorite places, he had to admit. Even as winter approached, it was still lush and the fire pit kept them both comfortably warm, but they still used a blanket as an excuse to sit close.

She'd taken the time to let him know Miles's jazz band was having a performance and he'd rushed back from a quick trip to San Francisco so he wouldn't miss it.

"Our kid is a damned good musician."

Gillian nodded and sipped her tea. "He is. I used to always think he got it from me, but apparently not so much."

"Why not from both of us? You're an incredibly talented piano player. You have a design business, which is also very creative. The boy gets all sorts of artsy stuff from each of us."

He liked when she revealed these small bits about herself. She was so reserved and guarded about her past that it was often a trial to get her to share things about her past.

"Tell me something about yourself. Something I don't know."

"Like what?"

The firelight on her skin only made her more beautiful as she turned to smile up at him.

"Anything."

"Miles didn't walk until he was fifteen months old and I was so freaked out that I'd messed up and he was delayed that my gran and Miles's doctor both had to shake some sense into me and tell me he was just fine. About three weeks later, he took his first step and was pretty much climbing, running and giving me a heart attack with all the new danger he could get into."

He laughed, imagining this buttoned-up woman in a panic about something like that.

"When did you walk? I mean, were you an early or a late walker? Apparently I was super early. Brody says it was to keep up with Erin, which is probably the truth."

"I believe it. You and your sister are partners in crime. I can only imagine what you two were like as children. I like that you're all three northwesterners, born and bred. This is my favorite part of the country out here with the trees and the water."

"I lived in L.A. for a decade. I'm there enough still, to deal with business stuff. I love the beach and the sun, but Seattle always calls me back. I can be quiet here, you know?"

She nodded. "I do. This is the place I decided to raise my baby. On purpose. I've just always felt at home here."

"Do you miss England?"

She shrugged. "There are things I do miss, yes. But this has been my home for longer than England was. I'm British at heart in many ways, but Miles is so much more American than I am."

"You never thought of going back?"

She blew out a long breath and he knew they were reaching that place where she got more and more stingy with her past.

"For the first little while I used to imagine going back when I was an adult. But really? Everyone I care about is here. My child. At the time my grandmother, and then school. I haven't been back since we left."

"We should take Miles. He should see that part of his roots."

"That has nothing to do with him. His roots are here. With me and with you." Her voice had tautened, gotten clipped, and he knew she'd be less and less willing to share after this point.

"You can trust me, you know. I understand enough that you didn't always have the best childhood. But how can I know you if you don't let me in?"

"None of that has anything to do with Miles. Or with you and me. It has nothing to do with trust and everything to do with me not wanting to talk about or give it any more time and emotion. I'm done with that part of my life."

And how could he argue with that, really? She'd told him about Miles, some about herself, and in doing that, she'd exposed herself to him, made herself vulnerable.

"Fair enough." He put an arm around her, pulling her closer. "Just, you know, don't stop sharing. I like getting to know you. I'm not going to judge you. You're safe telling me things."

13

Several days later, Adrian sat in his car on the ferry. He'd seen them only a few days before, but he wanted to see them today too. Wanted to see how Miles's day had gone at school. Wanted to know how his math test went.

Craved the sight of Gillian, the smooth tones of her words and then the sharp burr when she got agitated or pissed off.

And she most likely would be when he told her what he'd done. But it was his right as a father, for fuck's sake! He wanted to do for his son. Wanted to do for Gillian too, damn it.

Maybe he'd call first. Yeah. That would be better. Butter her up.

He called her cell and she answered right away.

"Hey there, English. Busy?"

"Hello there, yourself. Yes, as a matter of fact, I am. I have to call you back, I'm in the middle of something just now."

He heard people talking in the background about a carburetor.

"Can I help? I'm actually calling you from the ferry." He'd wait to tell her in person; she sounded agitated and he wanted to fix it.

"No. No. I'll meet you at the house. You have a key."

"Gillian, are you having car trouble again?"

"I'll see you shortly." And then she hung up!

He considered calling her back, but thought better of it. He already pushed the lines as it was. However, if her car was broken down, he'd be damned if she thought she would walk home or get a ride from some stranger when he was already on his way.

Though, he realized as he drove off the ferry and headed toward town, he didn't know where the mechanic was. It was only ten in the morning, so he drove toward Tart.

Jules Lamprey was a nice woman. He liked her and he really liked how protective she was of Miles and Gillian. He'd met her a few times, including a rather amazing dinner the Friday before hosted by another one of Gillian's friends.

She looked surprised when he came in, and then wary.

"You looking for Gillian?" Jules wrapped up something pretty delicious-looking and handed the bag to a customer, who thanked her and turned to leave. Halting dead in her tracks when she recognized him.

"Oh my god. You're Adrian Brown. Wow. Just wow! Can I get a picture with you?"

Jules looked to him and then back to the woman. "No. Sorry. No pictures with the customers. Let's respect his privacy."

Adrian sent her a look of thanks and then smiled back to the customer. "I'm happy to sign something, if you'd like."

Then she pulled her shirt back, exposing her breasts. Like she whipped them out in public on a regular basis. Chances were she didn't, but people did crazy shit around him all the time.

"Do you have a pen? I have a few at my place." She fluttered her lashes, making it clear just what she was inviting him for.

Jules came from around the counter so fast Adrian had to jump from the way. "Get out. This is a family place. My god, girl, put your boobs away."

The woman looked back to Adrian. "You sure? I'm just—" But

whatever she'd planned to say he missed as Jules literally shoved her out the door and onto the sidewalk.

"You're banned."

Adrian sighed as the other customers finally turned back to their coffee and pastry.

Jules washed her hands quickly and turned back to him. "I'm so sorry about that. I'm so embarrassed."

He shrugged. "Happens all the time. Thanks for getting my back."

"This is my place. I won't have any of that crap in here. Dumb hooker." She shook her head and he tried not to laugh. "Anyway, Gillian would have my head if I let some skeezeball shove her knockers at you like that."

He did smile then. "Yeah?"

"Stop fishing."

"She says that too. Speaking of Gillian, do you know where her mechanic is? I was on the phone with her and I know she's there. Or she was about half an hour ago."

Jules sent him a raised brow. "Normally, I'd let you suffer through her wrath for doing something you and I both know she told you not to. But she's not having a good week. Back off."

"What's going on? Why doesn't she tell me this stuff herself?"

"You're really quite pretty, but Miles clearly got his smarts from his mother. I'm not telling you where the mechanic's shop is. But I will tell you that Gillian has boundaries for a reason and if you don't respect them, this thing between you two will be over before you can really get started. She likes to take care of things herself, in her own way."

"It would help if she told me why she says and does the things she does." Frustrated, he sighed and sought patience.

"Oh, aren't you special. Have you shared all your history with Gillian then? All your bad moments and the things that fill you with shame even though it's not your responsibility?"

See, the thing about falling for a woman for the first time ever was

all this stuff was new to him. He wasn't used to uncertainty in his
personal life.

"You can tell me and I'll understand."

Jules sent him a raised brow, crossing her arms over her chest. "Oh,
you will? What about Gillian? Does she matter at all? Are you unfamiliar with how getting to know someone works? This isn't her sister."
Jules leaned in and lowered her voice. "Gillian is a very private person.
I wouldn't betray her confidences to anyone. I love her and she trusts
me and I'd never do anything to mess that up. Also, do your own work.
She cares a lot about you, Adrian. Don't be a dick and fuck it all up."

He exhaled hard, mainly because she was right.

"Fine. If you see her, tell her I was looking for her." He headed to
the door.

"She's worth it, you know."

He did.

Turns out he didn't have to look too far because he caught sight of her
walking, phone to her ear, not very far from Tart.

He pulled alongside and she ignored him until he rolled the window down and called her name. Startled, she turned and nearly fell,
dropping her phone with a snarled curse.

He pulled over and got out. "I'm sorry. I didn't mean to spook you."

She picked her phone up. "Still there?"

She paused a moment.

"Yes. Yes. I understand. I'm heading home now and I'll e-mail it to
you for approval." She hung up and looked to him.

"Are you all right?" He took a long look at her. Rosy cheeks from
the walk only made her prettier.

"I told you I'd meet you at the house."

"And you mistakenly hung up before I could tell you I'd come get
you. But none of that matters because here I am and here's my car,
which is warm inside unlike out there."

She did that thing that made him crazy about her. One brow slid up as if it could not believe his audacity. Which only made him more audacious just to poke at her and bring out her English.

"You know how hot that makes me," he said, moving close and catching her face in his hands to hold her still enough for a kiss.

"Everything makes you hot, Adrian. You're a menace with a penis." She tried not to smile. He saw her struggle against it and then give in.

"Not everything. I just got accosted with breasts at Tart. Don't worry, Jules threw said possessor of breasts right out."

"A random woman showed you her breasts in Tart? What for, and why were you in Tart?"

"Get in the car and I'll tell you."

She groaned and allowed him to help her in.

"Are these seats heated? Also, is this a new car?" She looked around at the interior.

"Yes, heated seats. I know it's ridiculous and yet, I love them anyway. Not a new car. I bought it a few years ago. But I drive the SUV more often when I'm in town to tote kids around."

He headed toward her house. "Why were you walking just now?"

"Why were you in Tart just now?"

"You're a difficult woman."

"You're a spoiled man."

He shot her a grin and liked how it made her blush. "I am spoiled and I like it that way. I was in Tart asking Jules where your mechanic was located so I could go pick you up. She wouldn't tell me so don't get that face."

"I told you I'd meet you at the house."

"Why? Why won't you let me help you?"

"Because I don't need help! I can get home from the auto repair shop. I had to stop by a client's on the way back anyway. Which I did. Believe it or not, I am capable of managing my life."

"I don't know why you're always so eager to refuse my help." He pulled up her drive and she bounced from the car before he got the keys from the ignition.

"You're right. You don't know me."

"Because you won't share!"

"Share what?" She opened her front door and went through; he closed and locked it after himself.

"Anything! I hear you had a hard week. And not because you told me, no, that would be too easy. But you didn't tell me. I want to help you, make your life better!"

She spun, hanging her bag and coat up. "You have some cheek, you know that?"

"Is that a bad thing?"

She heaved a sigh. "I run a business. A successful one. I had a client to see and I don't think having you wait for me in the car would have screamed *able professional*, do you?"

"All you had to do was tell me that. We could have met after and I'd have given you a ride. Or, even better, if you'd let me know your car was still having trouble I could have loaned you mine. Which I'll be doing anyway. You can give me a ride home tomorrow or whenever."

"No, Adrian, I didn't have to tell you that. You don't tell me what you do all day long. I trust that you handle your career in a way that works best for you and that if you need my help you'll ask. It infantilizes me that you'd assume I need to fill you in when I was just managing my damned job."

"That's not the same!"

She blinked at him and he was so annoyed he decided to just forge ahead with the rest. "And in the interest of full disclosure, I came over today not only to see Miles but to let you know a few things. It gave me an excuse to see you."

"You don't need an excuse to see your son. You know that."

"I'm talking about *you*. Anyway, I set up a college fund for Miles. And I paid off his orthodontist."

Her brows flew up even higher and she made a noise that would not bode well for him. Though he had to curse his cock because it knew they'd be burning up the sheets after they worked things through.

"I have a right to pay for his education. In fact, he can go to private school now if he likes. A friend of mine went to the Northwest School in Seattle. It's an excellent school. I spoke with their admissions people and if Miles wanted to apply, we could put him there in the fall."

"Oh, we could, could we? And how much would this little program cost?"

"I'll pay for it. Look, Gillian, I know you're doing a great job with him, but your resources are limited. Why do you have such a problem with my helping him? I shouldn't have to ask permission to do things for my son."

"You *promised* me we'd talk about this stuff first. That's how important this is to you? You'd just go do all this without even talking to me, and then you try to make it my fault. I'm not going to play this game with you. I have too much to do."

"And I won't let you make me feel guilty for having money."

"Wha' are you on about?"

Uh-oh, dangerous ground when she started losing the end of certain words.

"You act like it's poison when I offer to help. Like my money is dirty. I earned it, Gillian. I can provide for the people I love. And now you don't have to pay the orthodontist. It's nothing to me and a lot to you so why fight me?"

"It's not about that and you know it. For the record, I appreciate the help and I'm glad you set up a college account for him. I think that's marvelous." She shot him a look that dared him to try interrupting so he didn't. "When you do these things you promised to discuss with me first, you're not respecting me as his mother."

"Then you respect me!"

"I risked *everything* to bring him to you, so don't belittle it."

He heard the tears then and stepped back, looking at the situation more carefully. She was not the kind of woman who'd manipulate with tears. If she was this close to losing it, she must be really stressed out. And damn it, he wanted to fix it for her.

"I'm sorry. I just want to help. And I live over the water and I go to sleep every night without him. I wake up every day wondering how he's doing. I miss him. Let me help, Gillian. Damn it."

"How did you find who the orthodontist was?"

Oh. That.

He thought about telling her the truth. Knew he should. But she'd be mad and it sounded worse than it was anyway.

"You had my financials checked, didn't you?" She sat down heavily.

"Yes. Okay? Yes. I had to be sure you were on the up-and-up. I had to know. And then I put it all away when I met Miles. I had the envelope in my desk and the DNA test came back and I tucked it away and saw the orthodontist and your payments. It was a lot for you to handle each month. I took care of it. I want to help you and Miles." He looked at his hands, wishing he could put into words how he felt so she could understand and not look at him with all that hurt in her eyes.

"I feel"—he licked his lips—"helpless sometimes. I hate that. I'm alone and you're both here and I just want to be of some use."

For a long time she simply looked at him, clearly having some sort of internal argument with herself.

"Please tell me you understand."

"I do. More than you can possibly know."

"So you're not mad anymore?" He waggled his brows and she scowled, for real.

"Thank you for the help."

"And you still sound very disappointed with me."

"You broke a promise to me."

"I was meeting with my financial guy and he mentioned college funds and I realized I hadn't done one for Miles for school so I did. I'll get copies of the paperwork to you so you can see."

"How am I to know you won't do it again? You talk about how it makes you feel when I want you to talk to me about spending money. How do you think it makes me feel that you just ignore the things I think are important?"

Her voice hitched and she turned away. Alarmed and torn up inside, he moved to her.

"Baby, please. God, please don't do this. Don't cry. Don't shut me out. I'm sorry I didn't talk to you first. I knew you'd be mad, but not how mad, and I've hurt you completely unintentionally but it's still there." He hugged her from behind.

Gillian didn't want to be so affected by him but she was. She leaned back into the solid, warm wall of his chest and breathed him in. He kissed the top of her head, murmuring things she shouldn't want to believe but did anyway.

"Please let me be part of what you and Miles have built. Let me be your family. Be mine."

And what woman could resist this? Could resist him and what he offered? In that moment she opened herself to the parts they shared. That loneliness and helplessness she'd felt met his, and the wave of longing rolled through her.

Adrian Brown was no mere lover. Not just a boyfriend. There was something deep and strong between them. It made her attraction to him more intense than she'd ever experienced with a man.

She wanted it so much she was afraid to let herself get lost in it.

Tenderly, he slid his hands through her hair, cradling her skull as he bent to kiss her.

She kissed him back, turning in his arms as she fell into him. She'd missed him so much and it had only been four days since she'd seen him last. He and Miles had video chatted every night, even if it had only been for Adrian to ask Miles how his day went.

But they hadn't been able to talk much, and in just a short time she'd really come to like being with Adrian Brown. To being used to having him around enough that she felt it acutely when he wasn't.

Needing someone else was a risky thing but she did anyway. It didn't matter that she hadn't planned on it, or planned for a man like him ever.

But that didn't keep her from falling back onto the couch with him as the tenderness began to edge into something else.

He pulled her into his lap and she turned, straddling him. His fingers in her hair tugged the last pin free and it fell around their faces.

He plunged his hands into it, wrapping it around his fingers and forearms and using it to move her how he wanted.

"I missed your taste," he said into her mouth. Little nips and licks, sweet, quick kisses and slow, dragging kisses until she was lightheaded with it.

And then he pulled her hair, arching her neck to his mouth, and proceeded to devastate her that way.

Need clawed at him. He couldn't seem to get enough of her. Wondered if there'd ever be enough for him and knew there wouldn't be.

That she stumbled with him in this new life as a family made her vulnerable. Vulnerable like he felt, and that filled him with a tenderness he wasn't sure he was capable of before he met Gillian Forrester.

She was so real in his lap—the warm, beautiful weight of her, the heat of her cunt through the pants she wore, her breasts pressed to his chest.

His fingers curled with the need to rip the sweet pearly buttons down the front of her shirt. He wanted to strip her bare and possess every part of her he could see. Every part of her he could touch and taste.

"Off, off, off," he muttered, pulling at her buttons.

She moved his hands aside, quickly unbuttoning her blouse. He took over then, pulling the shirt open and exposing her to his gaze.

He paused to look his fill. No one else saw her like this. This Gillian—tousled acres of dark hair around her face, her spectacular tits usually hidden by her clothing, exposed in a pretty bra, mounds of creamy, sweet flesh at the top—this Gillian was all his.

He ran covetous hands all over her upper body as she arched into him. So sensual. More than sensual, she was dirty and hot and sexy and pretty much on his mind all the time.

"You're so fucking beautiful." He pressed a kiss on her chest, between her breasts, pausing to take a deep breath. "And you smell good enough to eat. At least twice."

She made a ragged sound, laced with need and something else that brought so much emotion he had to swallow it back.

She didn't reply, only looking into his eyes for a while and then kissing his forehead before taking his shirt off.

Then she started.

Kissing down his neck, nibbling on his earlobes one at a time until he was a shivering mess of a man who needed to come more than he'd ever thought possible.

"Tell me about these," she said, pausing to press a line of kisses up each forearm.

He leaned back, rolling his hips to grind his cock into her pussy, enjoying the way her breath stuttered.

Straightening his arms, he rested one in her hands, exposing the musical notes and a date. "Our first top-ten single was called 'Reflected.' This is my favorite part of the song."

Bent over him, she massaged fingers up his forearm, kneading and stroking. She had a thing for his hands and his forearms, which he found ridiculously sexy.

"I like it."

"Me too. It helps having an in with a great tattoo artist." He grinned at the thought of Brody. He switched arms. *You got to change with it* scrolled upward. "You've seen this one. One of my favorite Woody Guthrie quotes."

She dipped down to kiss the hollow of his elbow and he had to close his eyes a moment at how unexpectedly good it felt. "Your arms are so strong." She kissed up his biceps. "Why do you have Themis on your back?"

"I'm impressed you knew her name. Most people just say justice."

"I like goddesses. And I really like Themis." She said these things as she kissed her way across his chest, pausing to flick her tongue over his nipple until he arched with a hiss.

"You can tell me after I've sucked your cock," she said, sliding down his body to settle on her knees at his feet.

He nearly choked on his tongue but then she was back, undoing his pants as she licked over his belly.

She pulled his jeans down enough to get at his cock, licking over it as she kept a tight grip at the base. So fucking good it made his balls draw close to his body.

"If I can remember how to talk when you're done," he choked out.

All he could do was watch as his cock, shiny, hard and dark with arousal, disappeared between her lips over and over. Her eyes were closed, the dark lashes fanned against pale skin.

He looked on as she sucked him hard and deep and then shallow and wet. She licked up the line of his cock, just how he liked it, and then added sweet digs of her tongue in the sensitive spot at the head.

She sucked his cock like it was the only thing she wanted or needed. It wasn't that he was a stranger to a blow job, but with Gillian it was different. As everything else about her had been, he supposed.

Each suck and draw, each time she pulled back and fisted him a few times and then dived back in, taking him as far back as she could drove him toward the edge.

She hummed for one long moment, as if totally pleased, and he couldn't help but smile.

Her eyes opened slowly as the fingertip pressing just behind his balls slid back just a bit more, tickling over his asshole. All while he watched.

She pulled her mouth off, waiting for a sign, and he arched toward her. She smiled as she sucked him back in and pressed that questing finger in just a little, stroking and warming.

Goddamn, that felt fucking amazing. He slid closer to the edge of the couch and she got a better angle.

She let go of the root of his cock and reached down, sliding her zipper open, and he knew exactly what she was doing.

"Are you touching your pussy?" He managed to say all the words, which surprised him because his tongue felt as if it weighed a thousand pounds.

"Mmm."

But he'd been wrong because she wasn't fingering herself, she was bringing her sweet, slick honey up to where her other finger was, spreading it to make him wet. In more, a slight burn, but more pleasure than pain. Waves of that sensation spread through him, echoing straight to his cock, which grew harder with every bit of progress she made with mouth and fingers in concert.

His legs were hobbled by his jeans but he wanted to move so badly. Wanted . . . something. God, something more.

And she gave it to him when she slid her fingertips over his prostate. He didn't recognize the snarl of pleasure he made, didn't remember making it, didn't recall sending messages to his muscles to begin to thrust into her mouth, fucking it as she stroked that exquisitely sweet spot inside him.

He was in a place beyond forming words—unable to tear his eyes from this woman on her knees, her hair wild and loose around her naked torso, her mouth on his cock, two fingers inside him.

And when he came, arched, hips thrust, groaning, it was her name he spoke.

For long moments afterward, she rested her head on his thigh and he simply stroked a hand over her hair. After a while she sighed happily and stood, sweetly placing a throw over his lap. Then she left the room for a moment as he worked to catch his breath and get his bearings again.

"I put the kettle on for tea," she said, returning to him, still naked from the waist up.

"If the gas guy is in the yard checking your meter, he just got an early Christmas present."

She laughed with a blush. "I looked to see if anyone was out there first. I'm not prone to streaking past the windows."

Reaching toward her, he caught her around the waist and brought her to him, settling her in his lap.

"You're a goddess. That was, well, that was a forty-five on a one-to-ten scale." He thumbed one of her nipples, which stood up immediately. "I like you right here like this. Spread out on my lap like a buffet."

Without speaking, she took his hand and guided it down her belly. His cock, which Adrian had figured would be out for a while after that orgasm, twitched as it reawakened at her boldness.

"You don't know what it does to me when you're this way," he said, unzipping her pants again, sending his hand down into her panties to discover a slick, swollen cunt.

He sucked in a breath when his fingers toured each and every fold, rimming her gate before heading back to her clit.

A simple stroke of his middle finger at first as he played with a nipple with his free hand. She made little sounds in the back of her throat, her eyes closed, face turned, beautiful pale pink flush on her skin.

"I seem to remember you like this." Ever so gently, he squeezed her clit between thumb and forefinger around the hood, letting the slide of skin against skin give her the friction she needed.

Her breath hitched and she arched up, rocking her hips, riding his hand and taking her pleasure.

She undid him.

Even as she spiraled apart and began to come in a hot rush against his hand, it was he who was reeling.

After a long, sensual stretch, she opened her eyes and looked up at him. His sleepy green eyes were obscured by his hair, just a little. Just enough to make him look sort of mysterious. He'd let his beard go a little scruffy. He looked disreputable and utterly delicious, small gold hoops in each ear.

When he smiled, he teased a little, catching his lip between this teeth.

"You're a rogue. A cad and a bounder, a dog and a cheat."

He burst out laughing. "You're a The Bird and the Bee fan?"

"I love them."

She watched as he pulled his hand from her pants and traced across her nipple with his fingers still wet from her. Time pulled taut as he bent to lick across it and then drop a kiss on her lips.

"Every new thing I find out about you only makes you more irresistible," he said right before licking across her bottom lip.

"Oh yes, you seemed right pleased with me earlier."

He looked a little sad, but she still had her own emotions about it so he'd just have to work it out.

The kettle whistled and she bustled in to take care of the tea. She took a tray into the living room and settled back on the couch, intending to keep some space between them but he pulled her close.

"You asked earlier? About Themis on my back?"

She nodded, leaning her head back on his shoulder.

"I spoke to you about Erin's daughter, Adele? I got Themis when she was killed. Going through the arrest and sanity hearings and then the trial and sentencing stuff was a nightmare. It really shook my belief in the good in people."

"I can see that." She thought of her father and wondered how to tell Adrian. How did one tell their lover that one's father went down for killing his teenage girlfriend?

"Anyway, it was Brody who suggested it. To do Themis and make her sword bigger. Because justice isn't always bloodless, you know?"

She entwined her fingers with his.

"I don't know, it just—it helped me to get it all straight. I don't believe, not anymore, that justice always happens. But I still believe in people and I still believe in doing the right thing. And doing the right thing is protecting the people I love."

He turned his head and focused his gaze—which had been focused on something long ago—on her. She felt the echo of the connection down to her toes.

"I just wanted to feel like justice was real."

She kissed him because if she didn't she'd have ended up crying, or worse, blurting out the story about her father and this wasn't the time.

"I don't know how you do it, but you make everything better, Gillian. You and Miles are the best things to ever happen to me."

She wanted, desperately to believe it so she let herself, just a little.

Struggling with her words, she poured him a cuppa and handed it his way before settling in with her own cup.

"So yes, I was mad earlier. No, not mad really, just frustrated that you didn't share with me and let me help. But that doesn't erode the way you make me feel, the way I feel about you. I don't want to make you cry."

She laughed then. "I am working on sharing myself with you. But my financial issues and the way I do my job isn't up for debate. I don't need to clear seeing a client with you any more than you need to clear meeting with your agent or your manager or what have you. Lastly." She brushed a fingertip over his brows. "If you can't make someone cry, they don't care much about you."

"Is that your way of telling me you care about me?"

She sighed. "Is there any doubt? Really?" She licked her lips, which still tasted of him. "I don't do this, you know."

"Do what? Have tea with bare breasts? I vote you do it far more often, but only with me." He took her fingers to his mouth, kissed them.

"It's only you, Adrian."

"Oh, English, how you undo me." He leaned back, keeping an arm around her waist to hold her close. "Tell me something about yourself. Why is it just me? And yes, I'm fishing."

Incorrigible.

"I don't go out on a lot of dates. I don't have a lot of love affairs and I don't fuck people on my couch in the middle of the day." She closed her eyes. He'd given her insight into his heart, into his head and she owed him that sort of intimacy in return. "It's a very personal thing, what I like. What makes me hot and melty." She smiled as he made a humming sound deep in his gut. "I like sex. I like it—raw, hot, hard, dirty. It's not easy to trust someone else enough to let go and be that."

Needing a little time, she leaned forward to grab her mug. It was cold in the house so she reached for her blouse and instead, he handed her his T-shirt.

When she smiled her thanks, she caught his gaze. He watched her, she saw, understanding what she'd just said.

"So when I say it's just you, I mean that. I can be who I am with you. That's—well, it's hard to put into words what it means."

"You don't have to because I get it. Every single day when I leave my house, or leave the places I feel safe in, I have to deal with people thinking they know me and they don't.

"There are very few people I can truly be who I am with. You and Miles are two of them." He blushed, adding quickly, "For different reasons obviously."

She laughed. "I figured that."

"I'd like to talk with you about Miles staying with me on some weekends here and there. Obviously you too. As the holidays approach there'll be a lot of family events and we want him to take part."

She knew to expect this, but it was still hard to let go. "As long as his schedule is accommodating, I'm fine if he is. I don't know if he's ready for solo time yet. He might be. I can talk with him about it."

"I want you to be there too." He put his tea down and faced her fully, which only distracted her because his upper body was still naked and he looked yummy. "I like being with you. You're Miles's mom and my . . . god . . . my girlfriend. Adult words for this stuff are weird."

She was? Stunned and wildly flattered, she sought words. "Just give me the dates and we can work it out."

"And I want to give him some money."

He put his hands up defensively when she glared at him.

"Like an allowance. Or a bank account. I'd—I'd like to set up a bank account for him so he has walking-around money. He needs new strings, for instance."

"I bought him new strings yesterday."

"You have no idea what it feels like to grow up with nothing."

"Okay, first of all, are you insinuating that Miles has *nothing*? And that I have no idea? Fuck off!" She pushed from the couch, pissed off all over again. "Can you possibly imagine I don't know what it means to be poor?"

"No. Damn it, Gillian, stop trying to pick a fight. The words came out wrong. Okay? Obviously you've provided him with a great life. But if a guy can't get new strings, what possible harm can it do to be able to go to the ATM and grab some cash? Or if he wants to order something online? And as far as what I imagine, that's pretty much what I have to do since today is the first time you've really told me anything about yourself that had nothing to do with Miles."

Even in his T-shirt, she looked murderous as she glared his way.

He exhaled hard, not meaning to have said things that way. "I appreciate that you shared with me. It means something to me that you did. I'm altogether new at this relationship thing. I don't do them, really. But this isn't just a romantic relationship. We're parents too, and I'm new at that and you're not, and I just want to do something and you keep stopping me. I missed thirteen years of his life."

"I am not angry at you for doing for Miles." She paused a moment, thinking better of it. "All right, so I was angry about the bike for a little while. Silly and petty, I know. I'd been saving to give him a bike myself. But I don't think you did it deliberately to mess with my Christmas plans. It's a nicer bike than he'd have gotten from me anyway. You wanted to make him feel at home in your house. To have the things his cousins have. I appreciate that."

"I always get all prepared to be mad and stay on my high horse and then you go and disarm me with your honesty. We can do this, you know."

"Adrian, you and I are going to fight. You know that, right? Oh, I made a rhyme." She snorted and he couldn't help but laugh. "I'm not staff. I'm not a fan. I'm a real person in your life because of the man, not because of the star."

Nothing else she could have said would have disarmed him the same way. "C'mere."

She eyed him warily. "Why?"

"I want to grope you and it's much easier to do here on the couch than with you across the room scowling at me."

She sighed theatrically and moved back to him, allowing him to pull her into his lap.

"That's better."

"You can set up an account for him. I give him twenty dollars a week for his chores and keeping his grades up. I'd ask you not to go wild. I use that to be sure he doesn't muck about and gets his work turned in."

He nuzzled her neck, where he liked it best, and by the way she hummed softly, she liked it too.

"You're pretty fierce when you're protecting our son. That makes me hot."

"Everything makes you hot."

He laughed, nipping her shoulder. "When it comes to you. How about I add thirty dollars a week to your twenty?"

"You want to give a thirteen-year-old boy fifty dollars a week?"

Christ, she was not going to give him an inch.

"He wants a new bass. Now, I could give him one. God knows I have plenty of connections to give him something really amazing. Or, he could save for it with that extra thirty bucks and buy one himself."

"And Erin will give him one for Christmas anyway."

He sighed. "Well, probably. They share that. It makes her happy. Anyway, a kid his age has expenses. Dances, school trips, guitar strings, pizza for his friends."

"Adrian, precious, I want you to think back to the beginning of this discussion about the strings. Now, he makes eighty dollars a month already for his allowance. Does this not indicate to you the boy has some instant-gratification issues rather than a lack of money to spend?"

He was quiet because she brought up a good point.

"I think it's lovely that you want to believe Miles is so perfect." She laughed and then stopped herself. "I do. And he's a good kid, no doubt about that. He does spend his allowance on things like feed for the birds, the big softie he is. But he also fritters his money away on crap and wonders where it's all gone. Making him wait for new strings because he'd burned through all twenty dollars in less than a day and a half is supposed to teach him a lesson. Don't know if it will, but it makes me feel better."

"How about I match you? Forty dollars a week."

She tsked and then sighed. He was as hard to say no to as their son was, damn it.

"You have to give him chores for it. He has to do chores here, give him some at your house."

"Oh." He nodded. "That would be awesome. So you think it'd be all right?"

"At some point, you're going to have to be upset with him, you know. You'll have to hold him to a standard and he won't make it either from sheer laziness or he'll have a reason you'll find flimsy. If you give him an allowance, you have to make him earn it and you're going to have to steel yourself to be the bad guy sometimes."

He frowned and he looked so adorable she kissed the furrow between his brows. "It comes with the territory. But for now, you know, have him take the garbage out. Let him do laundry. Make him learn something for it. It'll create a new bond between you both."

"You're a lot of help, you know. Just being able to pick up the phone and ask you a question or get your advice is so big."

"Hm."

He grinned. "All right, I'll come up with chores. Which means he, and *you* too, need to be at my house more often. Like this coming weekend? We do a Halloween party at Brody's place for the kids. Miles should be there."

"He's got a party on Friday night. But after that he's free."

Adrian nodded. "All right. And for Thanksgiving, will you and Miles be with me? And my family of course. This year it's at my house because we're such a big group now. It's also Alexander's first birthday so there'll be cake. We moved the annual grudge match football game from October to Thanksgiving Day this year. Maybe Miles would like to play."

She got up to make some tea and he followed her into the kitchen.

"Normally we do Thanksgiving with Mary at her house."

"Holidays are going to be tough sometimes, I suppose."

"I want him to build traditions with your family but not at the expense of what he has now." Though the last bit about Alexander had been a very powerful lure. That little boy was very dear to her and he followed Miles around calling him Boo, for Blue, which Erin had started much to Miles's shy delight.

At the same time, structure had been what kept both she and Miles on track. He was the kind of kid who needed it and she was the kind of parent who gave it.

This storm between them began to build again. Their energy changing, intensifying. It dizzied her, tempted her to let herself fall into that supercharged thing between them.

His gaze roved over her features with such longing, such aching need, that she felt it to her core. To be looked at that way by a man like Adrian Brown had been a far-off fantasy only a short time before, and now her reality had turned inside out and he'd filled everything she didn't know needed filling until he was there.

"Look, I know it's hard to allow me in. I know you had a life before I came along. I upset the order of things and you love order so fucking much you're torn between me and it."

"Is that what you think?" She turned to look at him, trying not to allow that gorgeous face to steal her wits. She was weak, damn it all. Weak for him.

"How can I know what to think, Gillian? You keep your past locked up in a vault so all I can do is guess. Tell me something. Let me in. I won't judge you. I just want to know you."

Wretched, sweet man.

"You're an amazing mother. I mean that. I watch you with Miles and I know that despite the fact that I wasn't around for his early years, he had you and that helps. A lot."

She exhaled, charmed no matter how hard she tried not to be.

"What was your mother like? Was she a good example?"

Well now, he just went from zero to fifty in a second, didn't he? But he was right, she did need to share more, even if little by little.

"My mother was beautiful when she was a young woman. Talented. She wanted to be a dancer but she just didn't have the training." And she'd let that limit her until she died.

Adrian watched her, not speaking, but listening.

"So when my sister and I were growing up she always found a few quid extra here and there to pay for lessons for us. Tina had dance and singing lessons. She had a right lovely voice, she did." But no real discipline.

"And you? Piano?"

Gillian nodded. "Yes." She smiled. Those hours had been the best of her week, every week. Once her fingers brushed the keys it hadn't mattered where she lived or what idiot her mother had gotten mixed up with this time.

"Was she a good mom then?"

Startled out of her memories, Gillian opted for honesty. "No. No, she wasn't. She never should have had children."

He paled a little. "I'm sorry."

She shrugged. "It happened a long time ago."

"And your dad? Was he around?"

"No. And that was a good thing. My mother was a drunk." Gillian's laugh was without humor. "She also loved pills, and when we moved here, found crack cocaine to her liking as well. She also loved men who were easy to anger, hard to rouse when it came to work or any positive activity like cleaning up."

"Christ. Did they hurt you too?"

"Here and there. I got good at staying out as much as I could. Got quick and nimble." One of them had tried to break her fingers for fun. Because he'd known she loved the piano and he wanted to steal it from her.

Candace had hit him over the head with a bottle and they'd shoved him out the door. Mother-daughter bonding in Candace's book.

"There's not much worse in the world than a man who brutalizes women and children."

"True. But to my mother, those were the best kinds of men. I used to think she wanted to fix them. But I don't know if that's the case anymore. I think perhaps it just got her off. The danger. The drama. Candace loved drama and with the men she chose, she got plenty."

"Your sister . . ." He shook his head, she knew, probably uncomfortable.

"It's all right. To be curious about her." Gillian shrugged.

"It's just . . . I feel like an asshole for not remembering her, even after you showed me pictures. And then I feel like an asshole for feeling like an asshole because I'd never in a million years forget you. Your voice, the way your skin feels, the way your hair smells. You're indelible."

She swallowed back a knot of emotion at his words. At the way he gave her compliments that seemed to burrow deep and barb in her heart.

"You befuddle me."

His grin was sideways. A little crooked. A lot sexy.

"I do? How so?" He underlined this with a little head toss, artfully tousling his hair around his face, totally aware of his effect.

"Stop it." She blushed, shaking her head. "You're incorrigible, you know that?"

"I do. Erin told me once it was one of my best qualities. Take a compliment, Gillian. God knows you need a few, and I certainly don't have to lie because you're one of the most amazing people I've ever known."

"Thank you. I feel very much the same way about you."

The cockeyed grin changed a little. For a moment he looked like a sweet little boy.

"I like to hear that. A lot."

"My sister was a lot like my mother. They wanted to be loved so much they forgot themselves. The same love of addictions and shitty men. Present company excluded."

"Why do you think she never told me or tried to get money from me? I mean, you say she was like your mom. And how come you didn't call her Mum?"

"I did when I was little. She wanted me to call her Candace. And then when we moved here she wanted to be Mommy or Candy." She withheld her shudder. "My gran was a mum. I'm a mum. Once I was ten or so, I knew she wasn't a mum. She sure as hell wasn't a mommy, though Tina called her Mommy. They were close. Ran together."

"Was that hard for you?"

"You're going to think me a monster, but I was just glad not to be part of it. I always hoped they'd find in each other what neither found from anyone else." She shrugged. "I wasn't what my mother wanted or expected. I'd say something like how she did all she could with what she had, but that's a lie. She was lazy and self-centered and she had a great, gaping hole inside that she never filled. It made being around her painful. I preferred my books and my music and later, once we moved to the States, my gran."

Gillian looked to where her hand lay in Adrian's. He'd filled something inside her. His gaze met hers and she was glad she'd shared. Felt better for it. He made her want to let him in. Which scared her even as it thrilled her.

"As for why she never used Miles to blackmail you? I don't know for sure. Using him to manipulate you would have not been out of her behavioral patterns. She was manipulative, and when you were with her she still had her looks and she wasn't afraid to use them to get what she wanted. But she never did that where he was concerned. I like to think that she loved Miles in her own way. And that he was the one thing she felt like she'd done right. She signed the papers and left me alone to raise him. I'd have given her money, she knew that. I'd have done anything for him. But instead of using it, she respected it."

He couldn't know what that meant.

"The way we grew up . . . skint, we call it. You grow up with nothing like we did and it shapes you. For good or for ill, it frames everything in some way or other. My sister was a mess. I can't deny it. But she wasn't all bad. How we came up sent me one way and her another. Miles is my anchor in a way my piano never could have been. I weathered a storm and survived it. She just sort of got battered over and over until she couldn't anymore. She never stopped being a victim.

"Our mother didn't have those scruples. I paid her many times to keep away from Miles and out of our lives. I'd do it again." Hated tears fell and she brushed her hands over her face.

Most men would have changed the subject or made quick assurances to a woman as she sort of fell apart. Instead, he did exactly what she needed. He listened to her, his gaze on her steady and filled with more emotion than she could process just then.

He let her get herself together and then continued to listen as she spoke again.

"So, I choose to believe that my sister did not use Miles because she loved him and it was what she could give him. And for that, I'll love her until the day I die."

Adrian got her then. Understood the steadfast determination of hers to be independent and make her own way. Each word had come from her because she'd chosen to share herself with him. And what she'd revealed only dragged him under deeper.

Gillian Forrester was the perfect woman. So much control and discipline. She'd risen above a shitty childhood and built something not only for herself but their son too.

She understood family in the same way he did. When she said family was important, it was through the way she mothered, the way she'd stayed close with her grandmother, even the way she'd described her sister.

He'd liked a lot of women. Maybe even could have loved a few. And none of them had been what this one was.

He leaned closer, brushing his lips over hers with aching tenderness. The soft sigh she gave him in response undid him to his foundations.

"You're a mum, all right. Thank you for loving our son so much."

"Stop it now!" Flustered but affectionate, she glared his way. "As for loving him, well, of course. How could you do anything but?"

Easy, he leaned in and kissed each corner of her mouth before sitting back. "Yes. And thank you for that too."

"What about your parents?"

He drew in a deep breath, as if measuring his words. "It wasn't anything like your situation. They just weren't around much. My mother loved my father powerfully. So much that she sort of forgot anyone else existed. He liked that. Being the center of her world.

"We weren't abused or anything. It was just that they had not much left for us. He was busy. On the road a lot for his job. I've told you how much more Brody was a father to me than the one I had. I worry that I'll be a shitty father. I travel a lot too. Less now than I did even a year ago. But I don't want to be an absentee dad any more than I was already."

"Oh no." She shook her head. "Don't. Please. You're brilliant with Miles. You listen to him. You care about him. You want to ensure his well-being. You see him as much as you can. The best thing is that he knows it. Brody was your example and he's an amazing father. As for your travel, Miles is getting older; perhaps you can take him with you when you go from time to time. He'd love that."

"I want to take you both. I want to show you the world. I want to give it to you because I can and because you deserve it. Don't you see? It means something that you're here for Adrian. The guy who is trying to be a good dad. The guy who is head-over-heels gone for you. I can be that guy with so few people."

She exhaled and he caught the battle on her features. He knew most likely torn between knowing he was telling the truth and feeling like she was using him.

He laughed. "Oh, English, remind me to play cards with you some day. Strip poker would be quite fun."

"Am I that obvious?"

He took her hand, the one she'd squeezed his with, entangling his fingers with hers and kissing it. "You wear everything you feel on your face. That wasn't always true, so I feel as if we're moving forward."

14

Adrian sailed past his lunkhead of a brother and toward the end zone. He still had to avoid Todd, who lurked just ahead, wearing a smirk.

Ben then approached from Todd's left and tackled him.

Rennie cheered him on from the sidelines, Erin calling out jeers for Ben and laughing at Todd.

Gillian and Miles were there too. That part was the best of all.

Gillian had shown up on his doorstep with Miles, as she'd promised, just a few hours before. Had given up her Thanksgiving plans with her friends to be with him and his family, and to give that to Miles too.

And in doing so, she'd only made him want her more.

She sat at a nearby table looking feminine and beautiful in a knit cap and gloves, her coat buttoned up smartly.

Elise sat on one side and Ella to the other. Both women—well, hell, all of them—had gone out of their way to befriend Gillian. Erin was relentless anyway; Gillian couldn't resist any more than the rest of them could.

Miles had declined to take part in the game. Adrian had tried to convince him how much fun it would be and his son had raised one brow, indicated the size of the men playing, and had reiterated his no-thank-you.

Given that the game had broken out into two outrageously vicious fouls between Adrian and Brody once and Ben and Cope another time along with the tackle that had Todd limping, Miles did appear to have a point.

Though Adrian had noticed the more-than-friendly lingering pat on the ass Ben had given Todd when he helped him up.

'Course, he noticed this from the end zone. Ha!

"Are they like this every year?" Gillian asked, sipping some hot apple cider. This game of theirs was something Adrian had described as a *fun* thing he and his friends did every year. Fun. Hm. "Adrian assured Miles that it was just about pulling the flag things off the belt. This looks a lot more like full contact to me."

"I believe that there is called showing off." Ella sighed, but the affection was clear in her voice. "You're here and Adrian wants to look tough."

"And Brody wants to school him for being a show-off and in doing so, is also showing off," Elise added.

"Oh, those two have that relationship anyway." Erin moved back to the table to sit.

Which Gillian had noticed.

Alexander sat in Ella's lap, clapping in between shoving handfuls of Goldfish crackers into his mouth. Erin grinned at her son across the table.

"Yo!" he called out gaily, handing out a cracker to his mother.

She took the cracker. "Thanks, monkey. How's your birthday so far?"

He nodded. "Yes." He grinned before snuggling back into Ella, who kissed the top of his head.

"Yes? I'm not sure it answers the question," Erin teased.

"Yes! Yes!"

"At least your favorites don't include *no* all the time. I'll take the grin and fistful of crackers as you perch on Auntie Ella's lap to be a thumbs up."

"Yes." He had her devilish grin and it made Gillian laugh.

"Frankly, Blue," Erin called out to Miles, "you're the smart one for resisting. Certainly the only one not walking with a limp later." She winked and Miles blushed.

Miles was, as everyone else seemed to be, totally caught by Erin Brown's personal magic. The woman barreled into Gillian and Miles's life like she'd always been there. She loved Miles in her fierce, beautiful way and Miles loved her right back.

They all had gone out of their way to open their world to Miles and Gillian both. Browns and Copelands, all their noise and color, all their affection and the downright protective way they were with each other had taken up space in her life, and she was richer for it without a doubt.

"I was thinking next year we should do track racing or something everyone can do." Erin watched them all. "This was fun for the first twenty years."

Everyone laughed.

"I'm not complaining. I mean, look at them." Gillian tipped her chin toward a field full of fine-looking American stock. Big and braw. Masculine. Sweat and muscles, hair all over the place. "Still, they'd be far less use if they got too banged up."

Erin nodded. "Yeah, that's a very good point."

"I think we need to eat now. It's time for birthday cake, turkey and pie!" Elise called out from her place on the sidelines. She looked back toward Gillian and winked. "You can't let them go much longer or everyone will be limping later. Dumbasses."

"Hey!" Adrian jogged over, pausing to reach out and tousle Miles's hair. "No one even needed an ice pack this year. I think that's a record."

Of course that was the moment Brody took to barrel into Adrian, sending Adrian into the grass, which he'd probably have to pick from his teeth. If Brody broke Adrian, he couldn't continue to provide those excellent sexual services of his. Plus, well, she hated to see him get hurt.

"Oy!" Gillian stomped over, yanked Brody up by his collar. "That's enough of that, you two. Someone is going to really get hurt."

"Damn, you're very stern." Adrian blinked up at Gillian, smiling and totally unrepentant as his brother jabbed him one last time in the ribs before getting up.

"Yes. Well. It seems to me, Mister Brown, that you need some stern talking-to from time to time to keep you from trouble."

He sprang up and hugged her, swooping down to kiss her firmly on the mouth. Not so long that she'd have been embarrassed. Oh no, the man was fiendish in the way he simply knew exactly how far to push. Miles knew they were dating and *stuff*, as he'd put it a few days prior when she'd asked him what he thought of it. He'd grinned in that Brown way, as she'd come to think of it, and had said he liked it and that was that.

"You'd be my keeper then?" He grinned.

She cleared her throat. "Rogue."

They caught up with Miles and all headed over to Adrian's house where the turkeys had been roasting all day.

"I like how she looks in your kitchen." Cope looked over to where Gillian chopped vegetables at his sink, laughing with Erin.

"Yeah."

"Figured as much. Ella and I were talking about you two yesterday. Ella says you look at Gillian like you want to eat her up with a spoon. She's right."

Adrian snorted.

"Last year you and I had a conversation. I was falling in big love with Ella. Shit was blowing up with my father and brother. Erin's pregnancy was difficult and you didn't want to go on tour at all."

Adrian nodded, remembering the day his friend had come to the house with the security details for Adrian's upcoming tour.

"You were trying not to drown in it. The business, fame, all that shit," Cope clarified. "Anyway, you were like, I am so over this bullshit and I want to be around for my family, et cetera, blah blah blah."

"Clearly what I said touched you deeply." He rolled his eyes at his friend.

"It did, because I was blooming into something else. Into a man in love with a woman who changed *everything*. And right now, you have Miles and that's fucking awesome. You're coming into your own as a dad, trying to figure stuff out and not fuck him up so much Gillian notices and gives you a frown. Though, I must tell you, I did notice a distinct *zing* when she gets all prim and proper and your eyes glaze over."

"Am I that obvious? She'd hate that if she knew. She's very private, you know? She'd be embarrassed. Please don't mention it."

"Of course not. What do you think I am?" Cope socked his arm extra hard for emphasis. "What I do want to mention though, is how you have not only a son who has rocked your world but this woman who has set you on your ass. Gillian is your other half. Your key. You two have energy. Chemistry like whoa, and wow, can you two snarl at each other. It's that fire-and-ice thing. It's what Erin has with Todd."

He clinked his beer against Adrian's. "And yet you take care of her. I notice how you always stick with her at family stuff. Checking in frequently. Bringing her food and drinks. You make sure she's comfortable."

"I'm wooing her. She's prickly. Defensive. Christ, her childhood has left her less than trusting of most people so we clash that way."

"Because your snout is up in her business. And also, because you have your own baggage when it comes to trusting people."

"Yes. Yes, that's true. And so fucking what?"

"So fucking nothing. Stop being so defensive. It just means you're having to work for it. Welcome to the real world where the rest of us have to rely on our wits instead of our guitars to get women."

"You're an asshole."

Cope laughed. "I am, totally. But I'm married to the most beautiful woman in the world. The woman who makes every single moment of my life better. You're letting her in. I'm happy to see that too. You can't just live your life in the same four places with the same eight people. She's making your world bigger."

"She gets to me. Everything she does gets to me. I'm helpless against it."

"Yeah, they do that." Cope's attention snagged on his redheaded wife, who sat across the room with Elise, their heads bent together, both laughing.

"So this doesn't go away?"

Cope snorted. "Hell no. But they're worth it anyway."

"She likes horror movies." He laughed a moment, remembering the moment he'd discovered this fact about the prim and proper Ms. Forrester. He'd been looking through her music and DVD collection and had been rocked back on his heels by how many horror movies she owned.

"Yeah? That's sort of awesome. I'd never have suspected."

Brody ambled over and tossed himself on the couch next to Adrian. "Talking about the lady folk bustling around in the kitchen looking all fine and shit? Even hotter when they decorate for a birthday party. Don't know why, but I don't question these things."

"I was telling Cope about Gillian's secret addiction. Horror movies. I'm using it to woo her."

"Ah, the woo. Nice. What's the plan?"

"I have a giant screen in my media room and I'm not afraid to use it. I've got a double feature planned for later. *Rosemary's Baby* and *The Wicker Man*. Popcorn, root beer floats, some awesome scary movies. I'm going to lure her into my parlor with my projection screen."

Brody laughed, slapping his shoulder. "I knew you were a smart man. Elise loves them too. We should do a group viewing. Not tonight, so get that look off your face."

"With this group, you never know." Adrian searched the room until he found Miles playing a board game with Rennie. Alexander stood at Rennie's knee, patting it.

"He's a great kid." Brody smiled. "Probably because he's so much like me, eh?"

"I worry about your low self-esteem."

"Yeah, it's a cross I have to bear. Anyway, it's impossible to have low self-esteem when you're married to the most scorching-hot ballerina on the planet." Brody waggled his brows.

"Andy here was just making a similar assertion. Women seem to be at the root of all this stuff."

"Of course they are. You don't really get it until you find that one. There are plenty before, but once *she* shows up in your life, none of the rest matter. She matters in a way you couldn't have imagined before. And then you're stuck because you're addicted."

Cope nodded his head, each of them watching that woman. "Best kind of addiction there is."

Gillian's gaze moved to Miles, a smile on her lips as she reassured herself he was all right. Then it moved to Adrian and she started a bit to see he was staring right back.

She stood in his kitchen, the sun slanting over the floors at her feet. Bare. The woman seemed to hate shoes. Not that he had any complaints about it. Her feet were sexy, like the rest of her. It was probably the way she so rarely displayed a lot of skin, but the sight of her bare feet always got him hot.

"She doesn't seem to let go all the way with us, though. She holds back just a little." That bugged him, he had to admit. In bed it was raw and honest, but here, sure, she laughed and had a lovely time, but she deliberately hung back a step.

"This is about Miles." Brody, as usual, seemed to understand Gillian better than Adrian did. Most of him appreciated this, but a small part was a little jealous she clicked so well with his brother when he wanted her to tell *him* everything.

"I don't know if I should be offended that you get her better than I do."

"It's easy to from where I'm sitting. I'm not in love with her. This is big family stuff. It takes time and she's already a reserved person."

Then again, Brody got *him* best too, so it was really just about the way his brother saw right into the heart of the people he loved. "I didn't say I was in love with her."

"You didn't have to. It's written all over you. Please, Adrian, give me some credit. When have you brought a woman to any of our holiday stuff?"

"Well, she's Miles's mom and all. I can't very well not invite her. I mean, of course I have feelings for her that are way more than just being Miles's mom. But she's different from those other women on every level."

"Exactly. Also, you say you don't know why she holds back and then you say you invite her here because she's Miles's mom. Now, you and I both know you'd invite her regardless, but how can she know for sure until she knows you better?"

"Fine. Yeah, yeah, you're right."

Brody grinned. "Yeah, boy, I am."

The men had washed up after the meal while Gillian headed out onto the large patio with a glass of wine to join Erin and the others. This was a very good deal, she thought, given how much cake and frosting Alexander had smeared all over himself and his high chair.

Todd had disappeared to clean the boy up. Gillian really liked

Erin's husbands. Both men clearly adored their child as much as they adored Erin. Both were active, involved fathers, and Alexander thrived because of it.

"Have we talked you to death?" Erin asked, somewhat teasingly.

"How can we not?" Ella smiled reassuringly in Gillian's direction.

"My friends are a lot like you all, actually. I was thinking of having a winter mixer at the house to introduce them to you."

Erin's smile turned up a thousand watts and she leaned in, taking Gillian's hands. "That would be awesome. From what Adrian's told us about your friends, I'm excited to meet them."

"They're all quite curious about you all since I'm spending more time here. They love Miles and he talks about you nonstop."

"You too, Adrian says. Anyway, I'm sure in their place I'd be just as curious. Though you're a woman with her head and her priorities straight. I'd wager they trust that too." Elise was always so reassuring.

"Oh, Raven's here." Erin waved at a lush, ridiculously beautiful woman making her way to the patio.

Adrian had mentioned this woman in cautious terms as a close friend of Erin's who had a no-nonsense personality that rubbed some people the wrong way. As she studied those lazy cat eyes of hers and the swell of her mouth, Gillian noted the closed expression that had bloomed at the sight of Erin.

For some reason that appealed to her. Maybe it was that this woman who swept outside and into a hug with Erin wasn't entirely snug up in the family either. Maybe it was the hesitation Gillian saw on Raven's face, but there was an affinity.

Raven turned and looked Gillian up and down. Her gaze was appraising, eyes narrowed. She was being judged. Which irritated her to no end until she finally spoke.

"Can I help you with something?" She kept her accent smoothed, haughty.

Raven startled, her smile brightening. "Awesome. You're a bitch under the surface. Nicely done." And she held her hand out. "I'm Raven and you're Miles's mom. I'm glad to know you."

She smiled, taking Raven's hand for a moment. It was an odd way to say it, but Gillian was sure she'd meant to say exactly what she had said. Gillian had apparently been under some sort of test and had passed by not taking any shit.

She could deal with that sort of blunt.

"I'm Gillian, the aforementioned mother of Miles and admitted bitch under the surface."

"We should move to sit down and speak with the others or they'll continue to hold their breaths that we'll get along. You've probably heard that I've got a little bit of a reputation." Raven linked her arm with Gillian and pulled her to the nearby swing to sit.

"Now then." She handed Gillian the glass of wine she'd set down when Raven had first entered. "Hey, Ella. Elise." She smiled over at Erin. "Loving that shade of purple."

Erin grinned back. "It's so totally grape soda."

"Where's the young master? I come bearing presents."

Before anyone could say anything else, Rennie crept out onto the patio, a giant grin on her face.

"Irene Brown, how have you been, girlfriend?" Raven waved her over.

"Did you go snorkeling in Mexico? You said you might. Did you? Did you see dolphins? Did you know the salmon is my favorite animal? They smell the dirt, you know, from where they were born? That's how they get back home at the end. Isn't that cool? Imagine that. Did you see sea turtles like the last time?"

"I can see I should have a slice of pie or perhaps even cake, before I enter into the telling of my tale. But I want to find out more about Gillian. Can we work something out?"

All this said with Gillian right there.

"Are you trying to con me into getting you a slice of pie?"

Raven sent a raised brow toward Elise, who sighed, though with some amusement. Adrian had told her some about Raven and Brody's long-past romance and the trouble she'd given Elise when they'd first gotten together.

But Elise's body language wasn't tight. Her smile toward Raven just a few minutes before had been genuine, so some sort of accord must have been made.

"It's not a con if I'm being blatantly obvious. It's called being resourceful."

"Mm-hm," Rennie said in a perfect imitation of Brody.

"Is there cherry?" Raven asked Erin, who nodded. "I want a slice of cherry, and if you add some ice cream, I will totally share with you. I will also show you the pictures from my trip."

"Deal!" Rennie tore off toward the house.

"I dig that kid. Keeps me on my toes and helps her mom forgive me for being a bitch when she first came around."

Elise snorted. "You're still a bitch, but you're better behaved."

Raven looked back to Gillian. "We didn't throw down or anything. But queen serene over there would have totally cut a bitch if she had to. So what's your story?"

"You have absolutely no filters at all."

Raven pondered that for a moment and then laughed. "Erin says I'm sort of feral."

Todd strolled out with a grumpy toddler in his arms. "Alexander is freshly cleaned up from cakegasm. He's having none of us menfolk. I tried to coax him into a nap and he actually snorted at me. It's clear he takes after his mother."

"Mah! Yo!" And then Alexander saw Raven and laughed. "Ray!"

"I love that he expresses himself pretty much solely with exclamations." Raven blew Alexander a kiss and he tipped his head back, grinning.

Elise stood. "No doubt Martine has sensed her partner in crime is ready for another round and she'll be up soon too." She paused to kiss the top of Alexander's head before moving inside where Martine had been napping.

"You even changed him." Erin grinned up at Todd as he deposited Alexander into her lap. He kissed her soundly and stood back.

" 'Course I did. I can't make milk like you do, but I can change a diaper. I had to bathe him anyway; he had cake in the little folds on his arms. Plus he stunk so bad I couldn't pass him off and pretend I hadn't noticed."

The energy between the two of them sparked and Gillian's gaze scanned the room for Adrian, who was sitting near the fireplace, a guitar on his lap, Miles at one side, both singing.

She was standing before she knew it. "I need to go see this," she said faintly as she wandered in.

She perched on a nearby couch arm and simply listened as her two favorite males made music. Her fingers itched to join.

Miles's head swung up and he smiled at her. "Mum!"

"Hello, darling." She waved him back to work but he stopped, putting a hand on Adrian's knee.

"Dad, you have a piano downstairs right? Mum can jam with us now. You haven't heard her play yet."

"You haven't?" Brody shook his head. "Neither have I, come to think of it." He turned toward the open doors to the patio. "Erin, you wanna jam with Gillian, Miles and Adrian?"

She knew her blush was apparent to everyone in the room. "Oh no, that's all right. Really."

"Oh, but I have heard her play. Bach, Beethoven and Mozart." Adrian spoke with eyes just for Gillian.

He'd come to her after that morning when she'd played Bach. Had told her he lay in his bed, wondering at how much talent she had. He wanted more, she knew. Wanted to know why she was a piano teacher instead of working in the industry. He didn't understand, of course, coming up the way he had, making it at the level he'd achieved would color his perception.

One day she'd tell him.

"She's wicked talented. Come on, English." Adrian stood and held a hand out to her. "Show us what you've got."

She attempted to send him a look but he ignored it, leading them all down to his studio.

She'd looked at the piano before of course. Hello, she wasn't made of stone. But now she sat ran her fingers over the keys. Tuned perfectly. A man who kept his instruments in good shape, was Adrian Brown. A good quality.

"Play something, Mum."

"We'll jam, silly. We'll *all* play."

Elise came in holding Marti, Rennie pulling Raven in behind them.

"Will you play for us? I miss hearing piano live."

Because it was Elise and yes, maybe because she wanted to show some of what she had, she assented.

"All right. Do you have any preferences?"

"Beethoven? Sonata number Eight?"

She smiled and nodded her head. Simple, beautiful, a piece she hadn't played other than to teach for a long time.

Adrian watched her as she played. She felt his attention and in her own way, felt better for it.

When she finished Marti clapped and Rennie, who'd been dancing around, stopped and bowed toward Gillian. That little girl made Gillian wonder if she'd ever have a daughter some day. And in truth, the Browns and their crazy menagerie of colorful, loving people who've made themselves a family in their own way gave her hope.

They'd built something important and unique and very, very powerful, and it was impossible not to admire it. If her son and the odd relationship she and Adrian had could fit in anywhere it was with them and with her friends at home.

"Mum went to Juilliard." Miles said it offhandedly as he plugged his bass in.

Elise's smile brightened. "Really? How did I not know this until today?"

"Because Gillian hides her light under a bushel." Adrian winked at her.

They jammed and she had a lovely time. Playing music with all these people she liked so much was a joy. Playing it with Adrian and Miles though, that part was extra special and it was a memory she knew she'd recall with pleasure for the rest of her days.

15

"Over the first week of the winter break, would you and Miles come to Miami with me?"

She looked up from where she'd been working on her computer just a few feet away. He'd set up a mini workstation at her house and she'd begun to get used to him there.

"I have some meetings to attend. There's a producer I really want to work with for my new CD and he's going to be in the U.S. for a short period of time. I have to go for a few days and I thought it might be a fun family trip to take. And, well, I'd like to introduce Miles to my team."

At his excited nervous tone, she turned in her chair to face him fully.

It would come. She knew this. Knew that their blissful time of anonymity would end at some point and it would become widely known that Adrian had a son. His people knew already, and they weren't the only ones.

This alarmed her most. The way that something Miles had come to take for granted like his relationship with his dad could put him at risk and threaten his privacy. Already some in the press knew, like the prat who showed up on her doorstep the day before.

"I want him kept out of the media as much as is possible."

Adrian's gaze raked over her in that way he had. "Is there something you'd like to tell me, Gillian?"

Oh so much.

"A reporter came to the door yesterday. He stopped in town and spoke with Cal and Jules threw him out of Tart."

Adrian's gaze shuttered. It rarely had with her since the truth about Miles had come out. But it hurt to see just then. Hated to see that distrust aimed at her.

"What did you tell him?"

"I described that birthmark you have on the back of your thigh. You know the one, right below your arse cheek. Was I not supposed to?"

"Gillian, be serious."

"Yes, since I so rarely am. Not that you knew just how much I crave being interrogated as if I had given a total stranger the code to your front gates. I told him nothing. You might recall just how infrequently I share my personal business with total and utter strangers out to manipulate me to exploit my child and my boyfriend." She rolled her eyes. "I told him to get off my porch or I'd call the police. But I did call the school and tell them to be extra wary about visitors on campus."

He blushed. "I'm not trying to do that. It's just . . . hard to get used to the constant level of attention by total strangers. It's hard not to get taken in by it all at first."

"I get that. I do. But you have to deal with the fact that the people in your life care about you and aren't out to collaborate with the media to expose your love of root beer and jelly beans."

He grinned and the tension eased a little. "Good idea with the school. What did your friends say?"

"Cal's not a moron, you know. And I just told you Jules threw him out of the shop."

"Sometimes they get their hooks into you and you don't even know it until the story shows up. I still think you should let me see about putting Miles into private school."

"He loves his school. He loves his friends. He's built something here and I think he's had enough change for the next little while. If he wants it when it comes time for high school, fine. But for now, I don't want to upset his schedule or his life any more than it has been already."

"Stalkers are out there. I know this from experience."

She hated that his niece was murdered. Hated that such violence had touched their lives. It made her even more hesitant to tell him about her father.

At the same time, she didn't want to give in to fear and send Miles's life into further upheaval when there was no reason to go there yet. She knew he worried a lot. Knew he had reason to. But this situation was not the same. A single reporter sniffing around was not what happened to Erin and her baby.

"I know you had a horrible experience, Adrian. But this is Miles's home. Some of the kids at school know since you came to the jazz band performance and they've seen you around with him. But so far there's not been an issue. I don't want to move him unless it's absolutely necessary. Rennie goes to public school, for goodness' sake. Children of celebrities do go to public school. Not everywhere, but I don't see any reason to move to private at this point."

There was something so wrong with her, but every time they started to spar like this, the energy between them sharpened and made her all deliciously woozy. For him too. She saw the spark in his eyes, even as he set his mouth in a hard line.

"Rennie isn't my child."

"A fact that I appreciate. And still I don't see the point in moving Miles when he's happy and there is no problem. His life is far from normal. I accept that. But he should have the normal parts when he can get them."

"Are you saying I'm not normal?"

She cocked her head at him, eyes narrowed. "Are you picking a fight for some reason?"

"You're the one who said you wanted him kept safe. I offered you a way to make that happen and you rejected it."

"Oh no, you don't. I brought up safety concerns as it related to these trips and bringing Miles out into the open as your son. I didn't say I found his school or home life unsafe. I said, in point of fact, that those *were* safe. I said I didn't want to take him from school to put him in another unless it was necessary and I even gave you reasons."

"You had a reporter at your door, Gillian!" He burst from his chair. "And you didn't even tell me until today."

"I did. I threw him off my land and that was that. And if you re-call, you showed up, took Miles and his buddies to pizza and brought him back too late to finish his homework so he had to get up early to do it. And then you leapt on me and kept me awake until nearly two. Not that I'm complaining, mind you. That part is always enjoyable. When is it you needed to know and how do you propose I should have told you? Are there rules you have? If so, perhaps you should share them with me."

He got that look and she knew there would be bite marks and scratches when they finished with each other.

"When anyone in the media approaches you, I want to know im-mediately. I prefer you don't speak with them, but if you do, I'd like a heads-up on what you said."

"Fine. Fair enough. I told him to get his nosy arse off my porch or I'd call the police. Then I menaced him, which wasn't effective, as he was quite big. Then I used the broom and he got moving. If I speak to them, I'll be sure to let them know you're a generous lover and a good father. Is that to your liking?"

"You're bitchy today."

"Hm."

"I like it."

"Hm." This time he got a raised brow, but the glimmer of a smile to go with it. "If there are safety concerns, I'll move him. I'll put a bodyguard on him or whatever it takes. Otherwise, I want him to keep having a normal life."

"Can we talk to him about private school? You know, after this school year is over?"

"See? That wasn't hard at all. And yes, we can. In June. And yes, you may take your son to Miami. He's only been on an airplane once before. He'll be thrilled."

"Both of you. I know you heard that part. He's my son, but you're mine too. Anyway, it'll be a good trip. A friend of mine has a house right on the water. A dock. A pool too. The weather should be nice. I figured we might be able to, you know, do something silly and touristy, maybe even head up to Orlando and do theme parks. And we'll be traveling with a bodyguard, just so you know in advance."

She was his? Oh. Well, that made her all tingly.

"English, say yes. Let me show you and Miles a great time. Let me spoil you both. Our first family trip." He looked so sweet she couldn't have refused, even if she'd wanted to.

"I'll have to get someone in to deal with all the animals. A day here and there while we're at your place is one thing. But several days with all Miles's cats and the turtle will take coordination."

"We can board them."

She laughed. "Board a turtle? Between Mary, Cal, Jules and Miles's friends we can get people over here to feed, water and give love to everyone just fine. You have no idea what it's like to get Claypool into a cat carrier." She shuddered. "Getting that big blob of fur to do anything but eat and sleep is hard enough. If he thinks shots or anything of the like is involved, his claws come out. Thirty pounds of fat, pissed-off cat is no fun."

Adrian lost his annoyance and barked a laugh. "Erin thinks naming a cat after a bass player is pretty hilarious. And in case you haven't noticed, Fat Lucy is also gigantic. Not sure about the orange one since I see him so rarely."

"That's Pikachu. Miles brought him home when he was still obsessed with Pokémon. He's not fat, just crazy. He lives under the back porch and he likes it that way. Jones—that's the Siamese—is all about stealth and he's sleek and manly. I have to tell him this over and over so he won't get a complex about it. He's also Fat Lucy's guardian. He has a crush on her."

"Just when I think you're one thing, you prove me wrong. I do like that whimsical streak you've got." Before she could get embarrassed he continued on. "So okay, we'll get the pet-sitting in place and you'll come." His smile was so pleased she couldn't remain cross.

"I'd better. Heaven knows we don't need *that* to get to the press."

"The longer I know you, the more devious I find you. Sexy."

"Back off there, Mister Hands. I have to finish this project. Give me half an hour and then I will be available for ravishment."

He pouted, which only made him more handsome. "Fine, fine. I'll get the plane reservations made."

He pretended to work for half an hour. Put a call in to get the plane tickets taken care of. They'd arrange to pick Adrian up at the airport. Gavin, his bodyguard, would meet them in Miami.

When she turned back to him, she caught him watching. "You're a terribly impatient man, Mister Brown."

"When sex with you is what I'm supposed to be waiting for? Yes, yes, I am." He stood. "I think we need to break in that hot tub."

She blushed. "Adrian! It's broad daylight!" But he heard the way her voice changed. Knew she was intrigued.

"You have a gazebo around it and it's surrounded by big bushes and plants. You can't see it from the yard unless you're standing a foot away. Who's going to see? Hm? If you like, we can put sheets out to protect you from view even better."

Which is how she ended up naked in her backyard in the middle of the day when it was about forty degrees and misting.

"Come here," he murmured, pushing her up against the side of the hot tub. He did like to hem her in, against doors and walls, the kitchen counter, a car. It didn't matter, he liked it and heaven knew she did too.

The kiss wasn't soft and finessed at all. It came through quite clearly just how much he'd needed her in the slightly less-than-graceful way he took her mouth. She sighed into him, running her hands all over wherever she could reach.

"I need you." He broke the kiss and looked her up and down. "Five seconds after I've come and I need you again. I think about you arched and moaning, bent over my cock as you suck me off. I think about how tight your cunt is when I push into you. You make me feel like the luckiest man on earth."

She didn't blush for once because the water was so warm, but she would have at such beautiful praise from him.

"Take what you need then. I'm all yours, whenever you need me."

"I know. It makes my hands shake sometimes, not only just how much I need you but how instantly you give yourself over."

She found his cock, fisting it as he kissed his way down her neck.

"On your knees on this bench here. Face the outside."

Gillian moved to obey, shivering not at the cold but at his tone of command. She was sure she held the rim of the hot tub so hard it would break something. But that didn't matter. All that mattered was him inside her. Her pleasing him.

He moved behind her and wrapped her ponytail around his fist. She stuttered a breath at the way he used it to angle her just right, even as she arched her back to get her ass closer, to push back against him.

"I love it when you do that. When you can't wait for me to fuck you and your reserve falls away with all your impatience."

He pressed in. One stroke, hard and deep, bringing a grunt from her lips. Her ass and cunt were out of the water, which was good. Fucking underwater was not fun. But he'd moved her near one of the jets. The foam and enough of the bubbles brushed against her clit as he began to move.

"Your pussy is on fire. Hot and tight. I love being in you this deep. I love fucking you this way, the sound of the pine trees hushing over those little desperate sounds you make. I know the jet is near your clit. Mmmm, is it making you hot?" He licked over her shoulder and then bit her. Not too hard, but enough to make her give him another one of those sounds he was just praising.

That he knew without a doubt he was not only ringing her bell, but that she'd never done anything like this before, only made him hotter for her.

"Yes," she managed to gasp out.

"Good. Don't come yet. I want your cunt grabbing my cock, squeezing until I can't hold off any longer. And I want to fuck you for a while longer before I blow. And I will."

She writhed, pushing back to meet his thrust.

Her breasts called to him so he slid his hands up her sides and around to tease her nipples. Rolling and tugging, just this side of rough. Her nipples were very sensitive and he knew just how to touch her. Another thing he loved about her—the way she responded to him.

The only one. She was the only one for him. The only one who'd ever make him feel this way and he knew that to his toes.

"Do you have any idea how you look from my perspective? Your back is curved, your skin beaded with water, flushed with sex and the heat of the water. I could write a dozen fuck songs every time I think of you. Your hair wrapped around my fist as I hold you exactly how I want and you not only give in to it, your pussy gets juicier and even hotter. Your nipples, oh, English, so hard in my fingers. The only drawback of taking you from behind is that I can't lick them and suck on them until you start to pant."

Her needy sounds began to gain urgency and he knew exactly how she was feeling.

"And then you let that first *please* go. *Please, Adrian, make me come. Please put your cock in me.* You're so pretty when you beg and use your manners all at once. Though sometimes"—he paused to grab at control, which seemed very insubstantial just then—"sometimes you go another route and you boss me in that haughty way you have and I like that just fine too."

"If you don't let me come, I'm going to die. Please, Adrian. *Please.*"

"Not ready to leave your pussy just yet."

That's when she squeezed her inner muscles and added a tiny swish from side to side when she slid back against him.

He snarled a curse. "Not fair!"

"Hm." And she did it again. He knew she was close. Her cunt spasmed around him a few times, the way it did right before she came.

He'd gone through his schedule for the next week, had mentally counted all the picks he'd collected and tried to remember the book he'd heard about that morning on NPR, but it didn't work. That little swivel was more than enough to send him over the edge.

"Siren," he murmured into her ear. "Go on then, let go and come."

She gulped in a deep breath of air and used her grip on the side of the hot tub to push back harder, her movements getting less and less coordinated as her little pants began to have a soft moan at the end.

And then she was pulling against the hand restraining her hair, needing more. He braced his other hand, the one that had been on her nipple, next to hers on the tub's wall and gave it to her. Fucking her hard, sending waves of water all over the place, and she broke on a gasped whisper of his name and shoved him right over in her wake.

He came and came and came some more until it nearly began to hurt. He wanted to crawl into her body at these moments, wanted to be closer, wanted to wallow in that heat.

No porn, no show, nothing he'd ever done with any other woman had affected him on such an elemental sexual level. Or at all. Nothing and no one could have compared to what he shared with her.

Adrian stretched and stood. He'd been in his studio writing for the last six hours and his back was killing him.

Being a father had reawakened something inside him he'd forgotten about. That innocent sense of wonder about everything. He had a life full of exceptional people and experiences, and seeing it through Miles's eyes had brought him new appreciation for it.

And a creative rebirth of sorts. Since October he'd written fourteen new songs. A personal record and, if he did say so himself, they were all the best stuff he'd done.

Not all those songs were about Miles. Some were about Gillian. Goddamn, the woman had turned him upside down. Being in love was as novel as being a father. And also as exhilarating and scary.

"Jesus, Adrian. I've been calling you all day." Erin sailed into the room and tossed herself into the chair across from where he stood.

"I've been working. Anyway, not like it stops you when you decide you have something to tell me."

She laughed. "I've been playing trucks all morning, and we made cookies too. Handed a grubby boy off to a daddy and headed over here. Playing trucks is better than any therapy I've ever had."

"Miles had band practice last night. Kid's got chops." He grinned. "I was itching to join in, I gotta say. Gillian says she feels it too when they're out there. You should see them, Erin. Reminds me so much of us it makes me a little nauseated. Drummer needs more practice though."

"Did you mention that to Miles?" Erin had picked up his notepad and flipped through it, pausing here and there.

Anyone on the planet other than Erin and he'd have snatched it back, horrified to have his emotions and inner world so exposed. But she was his best friend. They'd been making music for so long she knew all his worst thoughts, all his lows and highs. It seemed only natural to have her read through them all.

"Aid, this is . . . Wow." She didn't look up from the pages as she spoke, instead picking up a nearby pen and scribbling her own notes here and there.

"Yeah? You like?"

"You know I do, stop fishing. You've got enough for a double album here. And why not? You're at a good place in your career and you've got this amazing experience to draw on."

"All the women I know love to tell me to stop fishing."

Erin laughed. "That's because you have good taste in women."

"I'm going to meet Reg Thorne in two weeks." He said it fast. He'd made light of it when he'd discussed the trip to Miami with Gillian the week before, but this producer was the kind of man who Adrian felt could put the songs together in an entirely new way. It was exciting and slightly nauseating all at the same time.

She looked up, surprise on her face. "Oh, that would be awesome."

"I can't believe I'm actually nervous about it. Christ, I've had more than enough critical and commercial success, and this guy would obviously know that. But damn, I want him to like this stuff. I think he could push me into something extraordinary."

Erin held up the pad. "These songs *are* extraordinary. You've been hiding them from me." She frowned a moment.

"Not hiding. I . . . I just had to process it all. So much has happened since September. I just—"

"Weren't ready to share. Which I get. By the way, I do hope I'm in on this one."

"He likes to work in New York, Miami and Portland. You'd be away from home for a while." Truth was, Adrian wanted her to not only be on the CD but to do tour dates as well. She'd done two surprise shows with him at the end of the summer, which had only made him more sure that it would only work if she was with him up there onstage.

"It would be doable. One of the guys would always be with me for bodyguard work. That was my deal with them. And then the other could be there with the wee man."

"Yeah? So maybe there's a chance you'd consider a tour too? A short one, of course."

She snorted. "Duh. Do you think I would let some other bass player get in on this? This record could make history, Adrian."

"Dunno about history, but it feels good."

"You're so fucking in love with Gillian." She looked through one of the songs he'd finished earlier that morning.

The song was called "Spitfire."

Erin picked up a nearby guitar and noodled a little, setting a slower pace than he'd first imagined, but it worked.

Buttoned up
Buttoned up, lashed down
Closed up tight till the lights go out
My spitfire comes
Yeah, she comes and comes again

"Yeah, that's the stuff." Erin grinned. "You're going harder here. I think it works on you. I've been meaning to go and have lunch with her, your spitfire. We've talked about it a few times but she's always so busy."

"Between her design business and her piano lessons she's busy, and then of course there's Miles and now me." He grinned.

"She does seem to take care of you like you're hers. She's good for you. That kid of yours is astoundingly awesome. You have good things in your life. And I'm glad."

"Things are good."

"I've never seen you annoyed by a woman the way you get with her." Erin continued to noodle on the guitar as he made notes and adjusted the lyrics to the tune she wrote.

"She drives me crazy. She's so thorny sometimes."

"You've never given a fuck about what any of them thought before now. Not in more than a gentlemanly fashion. This is different. You need to be challenged because your fallback is pretty boy with too-amiable arm candy. She doesn't let you get away with anything. She's a fierce bitch."

He grinned. "She's hot. God, she makes me cranky and pissed off and two minutes later, in the middle of some argument, suddenly all I want is to jump on her. I've never ever had this insatiable need for a woman the way I do her. It's like I can never get enough of her."

Erin snorted. "Listen, having insane chemistry is a wonderful thing. It's what keeps you going when times get hard. You respect each other, which is obvious, although you have a learning curve with the parenting thing. She seems like such a perfect parent, I really should get tips from her."

"The thing is, she gives me great advice when I ask for it and sometimes when I don't." He sighed. "She is good at it and they have such a beautiful relationship. I felt threatened by that for a while, but shit, now I just look at them and know they're mine. So we can argue but it's over stuff we're actually not disagreeing on, it's the manner in which things happen that we get hung up on."

"How does Blue react when you two bicker? He seems sort of amused by it."

"He is. Kid gives me advice on how to deal with his mum. Which sort of brings us closer too. It's all scary. I worry I will fuck him up. I mean, what are the odds this thing between Gillian and I will work out in the long term?"

"Are you shitting me, Adrian? Puhleeze. You two are stamped all over each other. Neither of you is the type to make allegiances easily. You're already together and neither of you makes idle promises.

"I'm probably the last person to take love advice from, but I can tell you that just because it's not mainstream or the way others do it doesn't mean it isn't real or it can't be done. It can. You two are like Brody and

Elise, different as hell on the outside, but I honestly can't think of a woman who'd be better for you. She's musical like you. She raises your son like she'd kill anyone who tried to harm him. She loves you, Adrian, without falling prey to the bullshit you have to live with to make your music. You have something extraordinary with her and Miles. Chances like this one are rare and in my totally not humble opinion, you're a fucking dipshit if you don't take it."

"Sheesh, I was beginning to wonder if you were a figment of my imagination." Mary smiled up at Gillian as she came through Mary's front door. It had been at least two months since she'd come to dinner there, and though they'd seen each other several times, it wasn't the same as sitting down and having dinner with them.

"I'm sorry. I know I've been scarce. Would it help if I told you I've missed you?"

Mary hugged her. "Yes, it would, because I've missed you like crazy. Come on through, everyone's here. Where's the young lad?"

"He's spending the night at his dad's house. Alone for the first time." She took a breath. It would be fine. Adrian was a good man and a good father. Miles would be fine. It wasn't like he hadn't spent the night at friends' houses before, and this was his father, for goodness' sake.

"I can see that argument you're having right on your face, baby. Come through and Cal will fix you up with a cocktail." Mary linked her arm with Gillian's and drew her into the house.

"Look what the cat dragged in!" Jules came over and hugged Gillian.

She smiled, looking at the gathering of the people she thought of as family. Cal waved from his place at the bar. Ryan sat at the gigantic farmhouse table that dominated Mary's dining room, already playing cards with Daisy.

Gillian dropped a kiss on Ryan's cheek and squeezed Daisy's hand on her way to Cal, who already held out a lovely, pale green drink in a champagne glass.

"Death in the Afternoon. Absinthe and champagne," Cal explained of the drink. She sipped. Lovely and sure to make her tipsy. A good combination.

"Oh, nicely done, Calvin."

Cal kissed her cheek. "He's going to be fine. Adrian is a decent guy."

She laughed. "I know I'm transparent. They wanted me to go too but I think they need some time alone and I suppose I could use some as well." She shook her head, turning back to Mary, who bustled about her kitchen, totally in her element. "What's on the menu tonight?"

"Tandoori chicken, scallion pancakes, veggie pakoras, rice of course, curried, roasted cauliflower. Jules brought some new chocolate thingy that looks ridiculously awesome."

"Sit down. Tell us about your life of late." Daisy patted a place on the long bench next to where she sat.

"Here." Mary put a platter down on the table heaping with pakoras. "Munch and chat. I'm going to see how these work out for the New Year's Eve dinner that I will tell you right now if you do not attend I will be super pissy about." She sent Gillian a look.

"I promise. I've spoken with Adrian about it already so he's in as well. Speaking of that, we're still on for Sunday right?" Sunday was the day they'd chosen to do a gathering of all the friends and family. Mary had insisted on hosting it and making a huge feast.

"Yep. I think it should be fun. I'm looking forward to meeting Erin. Miles loves his aunt. Maybe as much as me. A girl's gotta keep an eye on the competition."

Gillian barked a laugh. "The two of them are very close. They clicked right away, and as you'll see on Sunday, it's rather impossible not to like her anyway. Still, never fear, Miles's affections are not fickle. He still loves you to pieces." Gillian took a bite of the pakora and sighed happily. "This is so good."

"I bet Erin Brown can't make pakoras." Mary sniffed and then grinned. "Try them with the hari chutney. It's a new recipe and I don't know which I prefer."

"She thinks we'd hesitate in this. I find that hilarious." Cal shook his head and reached past Jules to dip the pakora in the vibrant green chutney.

Gillian didn't miss the way Jules leaned into him, just a brief touch. They had something and Gillian hoped it didn't take them forever to figure it out.

"I'm going to Miami with Adrian and Miles week after next."

"You need some clothes shopping for that trip." Jules's grin was infectious.

"I'm fine."

"Where are you staying?"

Food began to appear on the table. Mary didn't like anyone other than her designated assistant to be in her workspace, so Gillian sat and ate more pakoras than was proper but was helpless to stop.

"He's got a friend who's in Europe on tour, apparently. I didn't ask for names but it's probably someone Miles would get all stuttery over. Anyway, the guy has a house on the water, complete with boat dock and swimming pool. Adrian wants to head up to Orlando to do theme parks the last three days. We'll be back by Christmas, which he's asked quite nicely if we'd spend with his family in Whistler at his house. Of course he has a house in a ski town."

"Honey, you don't have the clothes for it. I promise to take you to some great places. We'll find good deals. Let part of it be my holiday present to you." Jules dished some chicken onto her plate and hummed before passing it to Daisy.

"I have perfectly good clothes, thank you very much."

"You need several bathing suits if you're going to be staying in a place with a pool. I know you don't have one and you'll need three."

"Three? Why would I need three?"

Jules and Mary exchanged a look and Daisy just laughed. "Y'all lighten up on our Gillian. She'll come shopping with us tomorrow before Miles comes back home. Won't you? I promise we know all the best places for bargains."

"It's ridiculous to spend all that money on new clothes."

"I bet you already set about buying Miles new things." Mary said this knowing the truth of it.

"Well, the boy outgrows his clothing at an alarming rate. He's going to be meeting with Adrian's professional team. He needs to look nice. And he needs a real winter coat if we're to be in the snow."

"And so do you. You do for him easily; do for yourself every one in a while too. Come on. Let's go shopping. You need to look nice too."

It was useless to resist them. When any of the three ganged up on the fourth it was a lost cause.

"All right. But I don't need three bathing suits."

Daisy grinned. "I know of some great secondhand places. I think you need some pretty dresses and some of those après-ski things."

As her friends took over the planning, she set about eating again, happy to be there with her lovely drink and the fabulous food as her friends spoke all around her.

Her phone rang, the silly ringtone Adrian had somehow put on his number sang out. Worried, she excused herself and picked up.

"Is everything all right?"

Adrian's laugh assured her it was. "Of course it is, English. I was just calling to discuss a little something with you."

"Mm-hmm. And what would that be?"

"I'd like to buy Miles some clothes. We're out with Brody and Rennie right now and it occurs to me he'll need clothes for the upcoming trip. So in the spirit of not making you mad and living up to my promise, can I, please, huh?"

Incorrigible. But he was right. And, she was making an effort to let him do for Miles. It made Adrian feel better and it didn't hurt the boy to have new clothes either.

"I was just discussing this with friends. Yes, yes. Go on. Thank you, and do not let yourself get gulled. It's okay to tell him no some-times."

"I already told him no when he wanted to buy a shirt with a naked woman on it. Great shirt, but you'd kick my ass. I know how to pro-tect myself."

She smiled. Thank heavens he couldn't see her or the way he turned her to mush.

"I planned to get him a parka, you know, for Whistler. And . . . a snowboard."

She must have made a disapproving sound because he interrupted the denial she planned to make.

"Look, we've all got them up there. He won't. I go up there several times every winter. He needs one and it's stupid to rent one at the slopes or a ski shop."

Jules had really worked hard on Gillian and the issue of money between her and Adrian. Her friend had made very good, albeit totally blunt points, and Gillian was trying very hard.

He was *asking* her, which he'd also been working on. And he had the money and it was for something useful.

"All right. Have fun then. Give my boy a kiss for me."

She heard the grin in his voice. "You got it. And one for me too?"

"Cheeky."

"That's me. All cheek."

"This is more true than you know, Mister Brown."

He lowered his voice. "You know what that does to me. Now who's the rogue?"

She laughed, delighted by him and this playful thing they had.

"I'll see you tomorrow afternoon. By the way, I picked up *Psycho* and *A Nightmare on Elm Street* for our viewing pleasure."

She blushed that he knew her so well. "The original, right?"

"Of course! Miles and I are doing a *Resident Evil* marathon tonight. We'll miss you."

"That was offsides!" She loved zombie movies with an insane level of glee.

"I know. But how else can I lure you over to my house tonight? You have a key and the gate code. Come to me, English. I miss you in my bed."

"It's been two days."

"And then you go being prim and you know my perspective on that. Two days ago I fucked you from behind. Remember that. Your hair wrapped around my fist."

The words were quiet. Meant for her only, and they filled her with that slow punch of longing only he ever seemed to create. And fill.

"Have a lovely dinner with your friends. And then come to me. I'll be up late. Tell me you'll come."

"I don't know. Will I?"

He laughed. "Oh yes. As many times as I can manage."

"I might be by later. I want to be here for a while yet. I've not seen my friends a lot lately and Mary's made an Indian food menu to die for. Also I've promised an excursion tomorrow before I was to meet you and Miles."

"I'll take you however I can get you. Be with your friends. I'll be here either way."

Yes, she was getting the feeling that was a very true statement indeed.

"That must have been some conversation," Jules murmured when she came back to the table.

"Stop that, you."

"Thought so."

"He's out and wanted to kit Miles up for the trips. He asked first."

"Our boy is learning after all. And you said?"

"I agreed. He did ask and Miles does need it and he is Miles's dad."

"Good girl."

Adrian knew she'd come to him. Heard the assent in her voice when he spoke with her earlier that evening. And still when he saw the panel light up indicating someone was entering the front gate, relief flooded through him.

When she came to him like this it did something to him.

He and Miles were watching the second *Resident Evil* movie still, so she'd be able to catch *Extinction* with them.

"Your mum is here," he murmured to Miles, who turned with a smile.

"Cool! She can catch the next movie from the start. Though we've seen it a few dozen times."

"I'm going to see if she needs help with her bag."

Miles rolled his eyes. "I know you two are together. You want to kiss her. It's all right with me."

"Is it?"

"Yeah. Why not? She thinks I don't know how much she does for me because I'm only thirteen, but I see it. I want her to be happy and find someone she loves. And it's good that it's you. She and I already had a talk about you. You know she worries more than she needs to."

"Loves? Do you think?"

Miles laughed. "Dude, I thought you were all cool-hand rock star and stuff."

"Your mother makes me nervous. In a good way," he amended quickly.

"She doesn't bring men around. She doesn't date much. She lets you get away with stuff she'd shoot someone else in the face over."

"Christ, she's going to kill me when she hears you say that. Stop with the shooting-in-the-face references."

Miles laughed and Adrian realized he'd been playing with his dad the way Brody had with him and hell, the way he had with

Brody. "I got it from one of the *Mummy* movies. So you know it's her fault anyway."

Adrian choked back a laugh. "Fine. I'm going to get your mum alone so I can kiss her and be mushy. I'll be back in a few. Don't start without us."

"Done."

He headed up the stairs and heard her key in the front door. She came in looking perfectly cool and elegant with her hair tied back, wearing a bright red sweater and gray pants. Her scent hit him when he got close. Just a small hint of flowers and spice.

"You made it." He swooped in and kissed her soundly.

She licked her lips, enjoying one last bit of him and undoing him in the process. "I did. I even brought you and Miles some leftovers." She held up a bag that he took from her hands.

"Your son told me he knew we were together and he was fine with it."

She blinked up at him. "He told me the same thing. That boy of ours is a smart one."

"Come on. You're just in time for *Extinction*. Let's bring back some food and drinks for Miles. Will you sleep in my room tonight?" He surprised himself by asking, and then realized how much he wanted it.

"Your bed is a lot bigger than the one in the guest room. Though I should warn you I do have to meet my friends at ten for shopping. They believe I need three swimsuits for our trip." She rolled her eyes and followed him into the kitchen were she began to make plates for both him and Miles.

"I should have mentioned this on Thanksgiving, but I really do love seeing you in my house. In my kitchen." Something about her presence there, the way she made the room the heart of the house when they were staying over, always pleased him.

She blushed as she worked on the plates and he put away the excess as she was done.

"I like being in your house." She turned after putting the plate down, sliding her arms around his waist and getting close. "I like being with you."

"You do something to me. More than one thing. A whole lot of them. Be here with me all the time." He kissed her and she kissed him back, rising up on her toes to reach him.

"I hate being away from you both. You two could live here, you know. We can convert your room to a home office."

She breathed deep. "I hate being away from you too. As does Miles. But you see us several times a week, including every weekend. Moving isn't an easy thing. My friends live on Bainbridge. I've built a life there. Miles has room to play and run and practice with his friends in the garage. If we moved here, he'd lose that."

"He could start a new band. You can take the ferry to see your friends and you have friends here too now. Erin and everyone already like you. I could wake up every day with my two favorite people with me under one roof."

"That last line saved you, son." Her eyes narrowed and he took a step back because she was *pissed off.* "Who do you fink you are?"

"Fink? Is that a Britishism?"

Her narrowed gaze went wide and he realized, too late, that she had said *think* and her accent had thickened.

"I didn't mean to offend you with that."

"Do you *think* you can just plug me and Miles into your life and all will be well?"

While she'd said *think* extra clearly, the rest slid back into her *Newham* as Miles had called it after the area she'd grown up in back in England.

Miles skidded into the kitchen and looked from his mother to his father and chuckled. "You're in big trouble, mate. When she starts sounding like an episode of *EastEnders* I usually just run for it. Protect your junk." And with that, he turned and bolted from the room.

"I don't think that at all. Come on, you know I'm just saying that you have a life here too if you want it." Jesus, he wanted her to move in to his house and she was mad at him for how he phrased something?

"Let me ask you a question, Mister Brown. In my place, if I said please come live with me and Miles and don't worry about missing Erin and the bunch, you can take the ferry to visit your old life. Don't worry about your friends, you already have a friendship with Cal and Ryan—you tell me how you'd feel."

"That's not what I meant, or even what I said."

"When I lost my gran I was a mess." She stepped back and leaned against the center island. "She was everything to me. The only real mother I'd ever had. She'd been such a huge part of my life, of Miles's life, that when she died the only thing I could manage to do was cry."

He wanted to touch her, but knew if he moved, he'd break the spell, so he remained, just listening to her.

"I never heard a thing from my mother or sister. So I made the arrangements. Or I should say I put it all into motion because my gran was a very organized woman and she had everything she wanted outlined and even paid for. And on the day of the memorial service Jules showed up in my gran's car to get me and Miles. She knew I needed it. Cal had taken it to the shop and gotten it detailed. It was Jules's plum thumbprint cookies we had to eat with our coffee and tea. They were Gran's favorite." She looked up and met Adrian's gaze.

"That's just one example, but these people are as important to me as your sister and brother are to you. I'm flattered and touched and very tempted by your invitation to live under the same roof. But I have a life already and I've never seen being with a man as a way to simply stop what I was before he came along. I want to live with you, not through you."

He took a deep breath. He got it. Understood how she could see what he said the way she did, and perhaps she wasn't entirely wrong that he'd sort of expected her to blend in with everyone as closely as Elise had, or Ella.

"I just hate that you hold back."

"How do I do that?"

"I want us to hang out with my family more. Don't you want to go out with my sister?"

"I've arranged a lunch on Sunday to have your family and friends meet mine, if you recall. I don't think it's a crime for me to like my friends. I love your sister, she's a lovely woman and I enjoy time with her, as I do Elise and Ella and everyone else."

"I just . . . it feels to me that you like them better."

"Well, of course I do!" She began to pace, muttering. Her reserve had melted away entirely. "I never lose my temper with other people this often," she tossed back over her shoulder as she continued to pace. "I like the people in your circle. But I have friends too and it's absolutely ridiculous for you to expect me to like people I've known for four months more than I do people I've known for twelve and thirteen years."

He wasn't used to fighting with women this way. With the people he'd been with before, if he discovered something that would have made him mad enough to argue over, he just would have moved on.

But as they stood there in his kitchen arguing, he realized he only bickered and fought like this with people he knew and trusted most. With Erin and Brody. With Cope. He wasn't worried this would be the end between the two of them. His assumption was that they'd fight and work it out.

Huh.

"I just realized something. Would you like to hear it?"

She turned and made an on-with-it movement with her finger and he made the herculean effort not to snort.

"I fight with you."

"Because you're a particularly vexing man who is very attached to getting his way."

He smiled despite his annoyance.

"Yes, I admit that. I only fight like this with people I love. What does that say that we've been like this since the first time we met?"

"Are you trying to defuse a fight with this romantic stuff?"

"It just occurred to me. Answer the question." He'd just told her he loved her, damn it. He wanted her to face that.

"I think it's probably true that I love you too. And quite honestly you're too vexing for any other woman with a weak constitution to handle, so I must take this on myself. You know, for the good of the world and all."

He swooped down and kissed her again, this time backing her against his fridge.

"Miles will be waiting. There's food and he left it in here," she whispered into his mouth as he slid a hand down the back of her pants to cup her ass.

He groaned.

"Welcome to parenthood."

After the last movie they'd both tucked Miles in and headed to his room. She was nervous, which was new for her when it came to Adrian.

She did love him. More than was wise, and not without a hard fight against it. God, how many times had she watched her mother lose herself in yet another man? The way Adrian made her feel had been the first time in her life that she'd understood her mother.

And it stood to reason that since her mother was a featherheaded slapper and each man she'd fallen for was as big a loser as she was, what Gillian felt for Adrian was far deeper.

Because Adrian's greatest allure was that he was a man who believed in fidelity and commitment. Which seemed funny, given that he was a rock star and all, but he was. A good, strong man who was more than worthy of her love and the return of that fidelity.

He saw through her. Which was exciting. Flattering that he hadn't run screaming. She wanted to believe everything he said and made her feel.

In the dark, the pale light of the moon outside giving enough light not to trip, his hands found her first, pulling at her clothes, getting her naked. She writhed against him as his mouth was everywhere his hands weren't.

He brought her to the rug, kissing down the line of her spine. The rustling at her back alerted her that he'd been undressing too, but even so, when he stretched against her, skin to skin, the feel of it made her suck in her breath.

She kept her eyes closed as he laid hot, openmouthed kisses across her shoulders.

"Head down, ass up," he growled into her ear as he pulled her up the way he wanted. "I'm going to fuck you right here." His fingertips wet from her pussy trailed over her asshole.

She shivered at the darkly sensual promise.

She waited for him as he briefly left her and then returned.

"We good?"

Her answer may have been different before the warm flow of lube over her hole and then the slick fingertip on her clit.

"Mmmmph," she managed to say in assent as he worked her clit with one hand and stretched her out with the other.

"I want every part of you," he said, voice taut as he stroked the head of his cock against her, the cool of the condom against the slippery warmth of her body.

She wanted him to have it just then, even as the burn of entrance rode that line between pleasure and pain.

Being fucked this way stole her wits. In that act, in the time he began to fuck her and keep her pleasured and open with his fingers on her clit and the occasional slide back to her cunt to fuck her there as he fucked her ass—in that he dominated her fully. In body, in heart and in mind.

She was utterly his, which is why it worked for her when the only other time she'd done this, it had been uncomfortable and not very exciting. Like something you agreed to because it was a birthday or an anniversary.

Each time he dragged nearly all the way out of her ass, a guttural sound came from her lips as her fingers sought purchase in the carpet. Each time he slid back inside, firing nerve endings she'd not known she had, he won his way deeper past her defenses.

She felt the throb of his cock, the frantic beat of his pulse.

His fingers on her clit got a little clumsy but kept their rhythm. Relentless until she exploded, the inner muscles of her cunt grasping at nothing, body writhing around each invasion he made with the thrust of his cock.

His groan as she came echoed through her body, and it wasn't a breath more until he pressed in deep one last time and she felt the jerk of his cock, knowing he came.

It wasn't until he'd picked her up and carried her into his bathroom that she began to rouse from the sexual stupor she'd been in.

It was as he ran the bath, hot with soaking salts included, that she fell totally in love with him. Past the point of no return.

And all she could do was smile lazily at him as he picked her up again and took them both into the bath with a sigh.

"You all right?" he murmured against her hair.

"Yes." She curved into him, letting him hold her tight against his chest.

"English?"

"Hm?" She hoped he wasn't ready to get out yet because she might just want to sleep in this bath for a while.

"Your car, the one with all the problems you keep having to fix? Was that your gran's car?"

"Yes."

"That's why you keep replacing carburetors and brakes and steering columns and other things."

Moved beyond words, she nodded and hoped he didn't ask for more because she didn't trust herself to speak.

Adrian Brown laid waste to her reserve. Barging in and taking up residence inside her. In her heart and head and damn it, it felt good. And right. He understood her, darkness and all.

She knew she should tell him about her father. Right then would have been a good time. Sort of. But it was ugly and it had been years since she'd seen him. Her mother had never taken his name anyway. Tina and Gillian had Candace's last name—Forrester—instead of their father's.

He kissed the top of her head and murmured to her that he loved her, and that closed her throat with unshed tears.

So she burrowed in tighter. He held her tighter and she let him love her.

16

"You're eating all my food, Miles!" Mary called out. Her grin was so wide it filled Gillian with joy at the sight of it.

"These are brilliant." He held up a Thai chicken slider.

"You like? I think they could be a tad bit hotter. Wanna be my test subject?" She held out another slider.

"Yeah!" He grabbed the plate as Mary sat next to him, ready to get his opinion.

The day had turned out utterly gorgeous. Clear and cold, but the sun was out and Mary's backyard was perfect for year-round entertaining with many seating areas, shade and direct sun. Tables were scattered across the pretty brick patio.

Browns, Keenans, Copelands, Whaleys and Forresters filled the space, spiced by Jules and Daisy. It had been a little careful at first, but once Mary brought out the first platter of food, everyone had relaxed.

"Your people are nice." Raven stepped up next to Gillian. "I wondered, of course. You know, if they would be cool or if they'd be stuffy. Most people are just utter fuckwads."

Gillian linked her arm with Raven's, sensing the surprise and then pleasure in her movements.

"I'm pleased you like my friends and have judged them not to be fuckwads."

"You're a trip."

"I am? I thought I was uptight and stuffy."

Raven laughed, shaking her head. "Oh no, not you." Raven studied her face intently. "You're so much more than what you give out at first glance. You have layers. One of the reasons Adrian pulls that stick out of his butt and loves you as much as he does."

Gillian couldn't swallow back her horrified laugh. "He does not! He's one of the most relaxed, adaptable people I've ever met. He does get passionate about things. He can be obstinate and fiercely stubborn. All in all, you must admit, it's compelling."

"Maybe if he and I saw each other through you it would work. He doesn't trust me and I have accepted that we can tolerate each other at events because we both love Erin and Brody."

Gillian tugged Raven toward the drink table. She wanted Adrian and Raven to get along better. She really enjoyed Raven. There was no mistaking that Raven was one of those sort of crazy women men seemed to go for in droves. Gillian didn't hold any fantasies that Raven was well adjusted, or even partially so. She tended to be abrasive. And yet, for Gillian, it was refreshing to just hear what someone else thought without any varnish.

There could only really be one Raven in your life, Gillian knew this. And yet Raven called out to the outsider who also lived in Gillian. She recognized some of the same behaviors in Raven, and wondered if she'd grown up with a similar sort of misery as Gillian's.

Whatever it was, Gillian got the feeling Raven had the same sort of reaction to her. Adrian hadn't gotten angry about the seeds of their friendship, but he did say he felt Raven wasn't trustworthy.

There was something there people deliberately talked around, and though she wanted to know what it was, she didn't want to hear it by her own request.

"Do you know the story?" Raven sipped some tropical juice thing Mary had made. "No, you don't, I can see. Well, of course you should know this is my perspective and in that, it's going to be biased, so I don't claim to be totally honest or fair."

Only Raven would talk that way.

"You do know that once upon a time Brody and I had a thing. He's a great guy and I think I wanted it to work at first. I don't know. Anyway, I was up-front with him that I wasn't always going to come home to his bed."

Gillian wondered at that. How on earth could Raven be happy with that sort of life?

"So I travel around. Don't like to stay in one place very long. I was in L.A.; I have a place down there and I work winters in a friend's tattoo shop. Of all the people in the world to be in Los Angeles, it was Adrian who saw me at a nightclub with another person I was obviously pretty fond of. He flipped out and went to Brody. I hurt Brody and that sucks because it's totally my fault and I was selfish. But I never lied to him about what I was like. I never promised him monogamy."

But if Adrian had caught her with that person he'd never trust her again. The kind of man he was, Gillian knew, would always be offended that she'd chosen anyone over his brother and that she'd betrayed Brody that way.

She understood it a lot better and didn't blame Adrian at all. Brody had told her part of the story some months back. But he said they'd come a long way and she was part of his family so clearly he'd forgiven her.

Something was broken inside Raven and it enabled Gillian to see past the devil-may-care abrasiveness and into her heart.

"Do you hate me now?"

"Of course not. Raven—is that your real name?"

Raven grinned. "And they say I'm blunt. My full name is Beautiful

Raven Haired Baby Girl. So, you can see that I had to make a choice. My mother was apparently quite the hippie with delusions of New Age–ism."

"Wow." Gillian didn't fail to notice the reference to Raven's mum was past tense. "Okay then, as I was saying, I can see why Adrian feels the way he does. Brody is his brother. He's nothing if not loyal. And I imagine you feel like a right prat for letting a man like Brody slip through your fingers."

"That sucked, yes. Especially when Elise showed up and I realized Brody never, ever looked at me like that. But I do love him, and over time I've come to really like Elise. Rennie is a force of nature like Erin. I dig that kid."

Adrian looked across the lawn to where Gillian stood, her skirt swirling around her ankles and the boots he'd given her the week before. He knew she needed them. Miles had pointed them out as ones like his mum had been drooling over. As if he could resist giving her something to keep her feet warm.

She'd hesitated when she'd unwrapped the box but had relented and he'd felt like a king for being able to do for her. She had no idea, but when she allowed him to spoil her even in small ways, it made him happier than if she'd given him something instead.

She spoke with Raven, who towered over her by at least six inches. They couldn't have been more different. Raven was in-your-face pretty. Snug clothes to show off her body, makeup always applied. No doubt she was a looker.

But Gillian, well, she stood there looking like something that belonged on a shelf for precious things. Feminine. Beautiful with very little makeup.

His beautiful woman.

"I like how you look at her." Jules approached him. "She takes care of everyone else. It's her nature. But you, you want to do for her. Protect her. She needs that." She started to speak again but closed her lips.

"No, please, go on."

"I don't want to divulge any confidences. She trusts me and I'd never hurt her that way. But she fights you on the money stuff because she grew up with a woman who routinely let loser after loser into their lives. They'd be flush every once in a while but mainly broke cause guys like that don't work and her mother couldn't be bothered. I know she told you about Candace and that's why I feel okay in sharing this part."

He was relieved this woman had been part of Gillian's life for so long.

"Thank you for that. I just want to provide for her. I have it and she doesn't. She makes it difficult, though she is getting better."

"Bet you never met a woman who balked when you tried to buy her stuff."

Adrian snorted. "Yes. Well. Gillian's not most women."

"Glad you understand that. I want you to also understand that we're her family too. We'll share her and Miles with you, but we're not going anywhere."

His back got up until he realized that comment was not a result of Gillian telling any stories to Jules about moving and their fight. She just wasn't like that, even with her best friend.

Which meant he was being obvious about it and mucking that up.

"I can't apologize for wanting to be with her and my son more often. But I get your meaning. Miles has a family in you all, so does Gillian. I'd never stand in the way of that. She tells me herself, so trust me, I hear you and I respect your relationship with them."

And the truth was, every time he saw her with her friends, he saw the softer side of Gillian. She laughed more and seemed more relaxed than she was with him and his family.

"It took Gillian three years to tell me about her sister. I know you're looking at her now and thinking about how it seems like she's closer with us and you wonder why she isn't as open with your family. I like your family, by the way. I think in thirteen more years, she'll have the same openness with you all. But Gillian doesn't throw around her affections or her trust idly. Give her time and realize it's not personal."

"You know her pretty well."

"I've had some dark times in my life, and for thirteen years it's been Gillian who has always been there for me. She is the sister of my heart and I'd do anything for her. I'm pleased to see her falling in love, and you certainly seem worthy. But she's not easy. She won't suddenly be tomorrow either."

"I can think of lots of words to describe Gillian with; easy wouldn't come up." He grinned as Gillian looked up and met his gaze. He waved and she blushed, waving back. "I've had enough of easy. She's worth it."

Jules grinned. "She totally is. Don't fuck up or I'll kick you in the junk."

"You're all a vicious cabal of junk kickers over here, I've noticed. It must by why my sister likes Gillian so much."

He watched Gillian with her friends and gained new appreciation for this woman he'd come to love in such a short time. It seemed impossible to remember a time when he couldn't pick up his phone and hear her voice, or a day when he couldn't get on the ferry to see her and touch her.

And that was only a part of it. Miles had ties to these people. Adrian considered them his in-laws, because they were all clearly family. He'd ceased to be jealous of Miles's closeness with Ryan and Cal Whaley and had let himself get to know both men enough to understand why his son liked them so much.

They'd stepped back, allowing him to be with Miles, but didn't stop being part of his life. Which was important. It showed Adrian they loved his son as much as he loved them.

If he had to miss the first thirteen years of Miles's life, at least he had the knowledge that he'd had family who loved him.

She couldn't deny how totally impressed she was by all she'd seen that day alone. First-class plane tickets. A limo that also contained their bodyguard picking them up at the airport. That had been odd, but she'd understood why he had one. Especially when they'd been approached several times by fans and autograph seekers since they'd left his house earlier that morning.

But this house . . . dizzied her. It hugged an emerald-green patch of front gardens and back lawn with a dock and a huge boat. The pool had been inside, which had surprised her until he'd explained how often paparazzi would fly over to get pictures of his friend and his boyfriend as they used the pool.

Adrian read a note the guy had left. Brandon, his name was. The lead guitarist in a very large alternative rock band.

"He says he's made sure the pantry is fully stocked and offers his cook should we want her services." Adrian took her hand and Miles trailed behind them, gawking as surely as Gillian was. "You're in here, Miles." He opened a door down a wide and bright hallway, revealing a huge bedroom. "Says it has a balcony you should feel free to use. Extra blankets in the chest at the foot."

"This is off the chain," Miles breathed out. "Brandon Federson's house."

Adrian grinned and walked across the hall. "And this is our room, English."

The room had a full view of the water, glistening in the sun, dotted with boats and other watercraft. "This is a guest room so he says we should feel free to get wild and not worry about it."

She blushed.

"He's just kidding. He's a good guy. We'll get the bags in, and then would you like to go out on the boat?"

Which is how she found herself sunning on the deck of what Adrian had laughingly referred to as a boat. The thing was massive. She barely felt the water as they sliced through it.

She'd allowed herself two bathing suits. The one she had on was a teal blue, a color Jules had assured her made her look fab. It was flattering and fit her perfectly, keeping her bits covered. Most of the suits she'd tried on were either far too revealing or those swim dresses some women wore. But she was determined to find that middle place between showing her areola and wearing a long-sleeved dress with pants to her calves beneath.

"I should tell you that suit is gorgeous. I don't know that I've ever seen this much of your legs exposed out in public." Adrian was above her, navigating expertly. Of course he could also captain a boat. There hadn't been much she'd seen him not be excellent at right away.

"That's because she doesn't," Miles called out. "Mum doesn't flash her knickers in public. This boat stuff is awesome."

"I've been considering buying a boat. Want to come with and help me pick one out?" Adrian asked Miles, a smile on his face. Gillian wanted to sigh but couldn't bear to be bristly over it.

"Where would you keep it? You can't off your house."

"There are several marinas near enough. Or I can buy a house with a dock. What do you think, Miles?"

"I think you should buy a house on Bainbridge. Have a big studio built. You could have a boat dock right there."

Adrian cocked his head and took Miles in carefully. Gillian held her breath because she'd been thinking the exact same thing but hadn't wanted to bring it up in the wake of their stalled conversation about living together.

"Would you like that? For us to live in the same place?"

"Duh!"

"Miles, what did we say about *duh*?" Gillian let the heat soak into her bones as she cracked an eye open to take in her boy.

"Aunt Erin says it."

"Your aunt is an adult and your mother just told you not to do something. That's enough, Miles."

Well.

Miles was just as surprised at Adrian's fatherly interruption as Gillian had been. But probably didn't react the same way she did. It made her all flustered and flattered that he'd parent with her that way. And it made her proud that he'd reinforced one of her rules.

"Sorry, Mum." He ducked his head a moment in a perfect Brown mimicry.

Adrian clapped his son on the shoulder. "Mistakes happen. Now you were going to tell me how you felt about us living in the same house."

Nicely done, Dad.

"I like seeing you all the time. But when I'm at your house on the weekends I miss practice with the band and miss my friends. It'd be cool if you lived nearer."

Gillian sat up straighter, but didn't interfere.

"Yeah, that's a good point. But the good part is, we can agree on the living together thing?"

"I'd like that a lot." Miles looked up to the man he resembled so strongly. His grin was huge, reminding her that he had an ortho appointment before they were to go to Whistler.

"Your mum seems to like the idea too."

She liked that Adrian used the word *mum* when he referred to her. It was a silly little thing she knew, but it still meant something. Made it feel like a family.

"I do."

Miles turned his smile to her. "Yeah?"

"Yeah."

"Seems like we need to start working on a solution then." Adrian smiled while he spoke, eyes on the horizon.

"So, tell me about this producer you're meeting tomorrow?" she asked as they sat on the back lawn some hours later.

"He's Reg Thorne."

"Ah. Yes, I know of him. He's done a great many records that are on my favorites list. Are you looking to make a change in sound?"

"Why didn't you pursue a career in music? I mean"—he turned to her—"you went to this big-time school and that means you're damned good. I've heard you play, I know you're good. So why are you doing marketing and piano lessons instead of being on a stage?"

"That's a program change, isn't it?"

"I figure we can share on this one. I'm nervous. I admit it. Humor me."

"Nervous why? My goodness, Adrian, you're not only gifted, you're very successful."

"Answer my questions."

She sighed. "Because not everyone gets a blue ribbon. You should know that more than most. Yes, I'm good. I'm very talented, as a matter of fact. Of the people playing piano, I'm up there, of course. Just not quite enough. If I'd started earlier or had more lessons. If, if, if. Anyway, I did some studio work for a while in my last years at school. I wanted to be a concert pianist and that just didn't work out. I'm good. Just not *that* good. And then Miles came along and what was I to do? I'd been living in a grotty little apartment in Hell's Kitchen, which is one thing for a young adult, another entirely for a newborn. And how would I pay for rent if I stayed home? How would I take care of a baby if I was at auditions and taking all the extra classes and jobs I could, which were often in the evenings. I made a choice and I've never regretted it. I have my music still. In fact, Elise asked if I'd be willing to do *Carmina Burana* for her school."

"She did?" Adrian grinned, kissing her knuckles. "Neither of you told me!"

"She only asked me via text earlier today. They're doing a joint performance with a choral group. There's a version of it for two pianos instead of a full orchestra. It's a challenging but really wonderful piece. I told her I would. It's in March."

"Congratulations. I can't wait to hear it. As for the rest, well, you chose Miles. Every time you choose our son." He kissed her softly. "That makes me love you even more. You gave it up for him."

"I gave it up because chances were that even though I could have made some money and gotten gigs, it wouldn't have worked with me as the single mother to a young child. Life is all a benefit/cost analysis, Adrian. You make choices much the same every day. You could be on tour right now making even more money but you chose to take time with your family. And you're making this choice to try something new because it feeds you artistically. That's important. Making good choices is important."

"I want to try something darker and harder. I've been writing a lot lately. Since I found out about Miles. I have some songs I think are pretty amazing, Erin agrees. And if Reg agrees to take me on, it could be a big bust or a career change. Either way, I can afford something that doesn't quite make as much money and I feel like I have this small period of time to take some chances."

"I'm excited for you. I can't wait to hear the songs and I have zero doubt you'll be hugely successful. How can Thorne not like you?"

"He's mercurial. He only takes projects that appeal to him on a personal level and he only works a few times a year."

"All right then, how do we make him choose you?"

He laughed. "Ah man, that's better. You make things better. Thank you. I'm going to play a few songs for him tomorrow. Just me and my guitar, he says. I told Miles he could come watch, but he has to stay in the booth. Do you think he can do it? Would you go with him?"

"Yes, he can handle it and there's nowhere else I'd rather be than listening to you."

"It won't be the whole time. There's a private, one-on-one meeting first and then if he likes my pitch, he'll ask to hear the material. Jeremy will come to breakfast tomorrow. He's on a red-eye tonight from Los Angeles. He's got a pitch worked up for me. Thank God for him, that's all I can say. We'll all go over together."

He tipped his head back and looked up at the sky. "You know, all I could think of when I was away from you both was how I was looking up at stars you couldn't see and how much I hated it. I've never been much convinced a man could have a good balance between career and personal life, but you and Miles give me hope. I feel like when I talk about music you understand. That he understands too."

"We both do. I love to hear you talk about music. It's like you open up a super secret place inside and let me in."

"You and Miles are there now too. My most special things."

She blinked away tears. "He told you about that?"

"He did. I like the most special thing idea. I like being able to talk to you and have you know what I mean."

"Well, I don't know much about how the music industry works at your level. I just know it's hard to expose what you bring out from inside to the public. And it's harder for you than it ever was for me. People fill arenas to see you. That's some serious exposure there."

He stood up and pulled her close. There, under the stars, across the country from home, she swayed with him to a song only he knew but she felt like she'd heard before. Wanted to hear it again.

"Adrian! Hey, is that you? Do you want to introduce your lady to the viewers at home?"

That this was bellowed through a bullhorn from a tiny boat some hundred yards away did not mitigate Gillian's distress. Adrian put her behind him and backed into the house where Gavin was.

"Gavin, we've got company. Paps know we're here."

"On it. I just checked on Miles, he's sound asleep, but I'm setting the alarm when I go out. You two stay in here. I'll handle the authorities."

Gavin swung his bulk from the seat he'd been occupying. Within hearing, but giving Adrian and Gillian privacy.

"Damn it. I didn't even get twenty-four hours. One of the neighbors might have tipped them off for a couple of bucks. Or they followed us from the airport earlier. Who knows. We need to move."

"Neighbors call the media? Really? You think they'd hate having the press here with all the noise and nosiness."

"People do it all the time. Once it amazed me. Now I suppose I've just gotten used to it."

"That's ridiculous! Why should you get used to people selling your privacy for money? These people live in huge waterfront mansions. Unless they need to pay for a liver transplant, selling out other humans to the media is unacceptable!"

"God help me, I adore you, English." He kissed the tip of her nose.

"Do we really need to move? This house seems very self-contained. I'm fine with whatever you decide, but I don't necessarily think we have to move right away. Will they swarm up onto the lawn?"

"No. That's private property. They'll camp on the street out front and then on the canal outside, all waiting with cameras to get a glimpse. I'm not as exciting as some others, or hell, as exciting as Brandon is, so there'll be five instead of fifteen. But that's five people with cameras trying to get a picture of my son. I'm not down with that."

She took his cheeks in her hands and tipped his head so she could reach up to kiss him. "I love when you protect him."

"Of course I do. He's my son. You're my woman. You don't need to have pictures of every trip to get gas or coffee run on gossip sites. I have to deal with it, but you two don't. I won't have it."

Gavin came in some minutes later. "There's another who just showed up. Cops arrived, chased them off but they know just how far to stay offshore. Stick to the roof or the indoor pool and you'll be all right. Cope wants me to ask you about adding another person to security while you're here, and also if you'd like to move to a place in a high-rise? He's got several contacts through the record company. Pap-free building, though you'd be losing the pool." He shrugged.

"What's your perspective on it?" Adrian asked, patting his pants pocket. Looking for cigarettes he'd ceased smoking some years before, she knew. Old habits die hard, as she knew very well.

"This house has great security. Anyone comes onto the dock and lights and sirens come on. Anyone tries to enter the house and same. I do think two of us running interference would be good, especially as you'll be heading into town tomorrow and then up to Orlando. If you do the parks, it'll be nice to have us around just to give you some space in case you're recognized."

Which of course he would be.

This made her appreciate Seattle even more. Most of the time he was left alone and she knew he liked it that way.

"I'll talk to Cope myself. But let's get the extra guard here. I want him on Miles and I want someone with weapons knowledge."

"Weapons knowledge?" she asked weakly.

"I told you it could get hairy out there sometimes. Chances are we won't need it. But should anyone even try to throw down, you'd be amazed at what a former Navy SEAL or an ex–special forces Marine like Gavin here can do to defuse it."

"I'm going to go check on Miles."

She knew he was all right. Knew it in her heart and also trusted Gavin on his word, specifically because Adrian did. But she had to see him herself.

"Go on up, English. I've got calls to make. There are movies in our room you might want to check out. *Audition* is one of them."

She shivered. "That one is so creepy. I won't start without you, I promise."

After standing over Miles where he'd sprawled on the big bed, she also checked the door to the balcony, making sure it was bolted, which it was. She left his door open, knowing she'd feel better if she could hear him if he woke up.

She liked this house. It was palatial, yes, but someone lived here too. It was nicer than a hotel room would be, though she'd go along with whatever Adrian and his team decided.

"Andy, tell me the news," he said when Cope answered.

"First things first, everyone all right?"

"Yeah. Pap just yelled from his boat asking if I wanted to introduce Gillian to the readers at home. Fuck. Um, no, I don't! I don't want my kid in the rags and risk him seeing twenty-five-year-old losers living at home ripping his appearance to shreds. Or saying Gillian isn't pretty enough or that she should wear makeup to Tart or whatever. I sure as hell don't like it when they do it to me. I'm not going to tolerate my family being pulled into it."

"I know, man. I've got several alternatives if you'd like to stay elsewhere. A penthouse or two. All with great views. A few more houses. Hotels. What do you want? Merrill is on his way. He was in Maryland so he's already en route." Merrill was one of the guards Adrian had used on the last tour.

"Good. She doesn't want to move unless we have to. Gavin says this place is secure. I don't want to scare her or Miles."

"The area you're in is pretty good. We can have a bodyguard on routine front-gate duty to chase off squatters. Jeremy also told me to tell you the label would send a helicopter tomorrow to get you to Reg's place. You're pretty big news, I guess." Cope's snort made Adrian laugh and relax a bit. "Gavin says you've got a secure situation and plenty of room. Miles is with you, as is Gillian. You can't just move around like you normally do. Why don't you give it another day to see? If you wake up to a street full of dipshits with cameras tomorrow, fuck it. Get out and we'll handle it all. I'll come out myself, if need be."

Adrian hung up and spoke with Gavin, who reassured him all was well.

He checked on Miles, noting the door had been left open so clearly Gillian had checked too. He smiled, on his way to her.

When he found her, she was in bed, blankets tucked around her, reading a book on her digital book reader, those sexy glasses perched on the bridge of her nose.

"Everything all right?" she asked when he closed the door behind him.

"For now, yes. We'll open the door again when we decide to go to sleep. Gavin has moved to the living room at the end of the hall here and there's another guard coming that I've hired before. He'll be here in several hours."

She nodded. "All right." She patted the bed. "Come here. Let me give you a massage. You're stressed enough as it is. You have a big day tomorrow. Don't let one idiot with a camera ruin that."

For a little woman, she had great, powerful hands. Probably the years of piano playing. But she straddled his ass and began to work her fingers and the heels of her hands into the knotted muscles of his back. And he let it all go as she worked through all the stress and bunched-up muscles, leaving him relaxed, warm and mad to have her.

"Do you know what I noticed when I first saw this room?"

"I'm sure there's something sex related in this story," she murmured, kissing his shoulder before rolling off and landing next to him on the mattress.

"You know me so well." Slow but total need coursed through him as he reached out to draw his fingertips down the pale, smooth line of her neck, between her breasts and then down over her belly.

He doubted he'd said anything more true than that in a very long time.

"I need you in me. Lose yourself in my skin. I want your hands, your teeth and lips. Definitely your cock."

"There you go, English, with your filthy mouth, undoing me."

"You're not naked. You still have pants and underpants on. This isn't a reasonable stance to take."

She said it prim and proper, and his cock went from seven to twelve on the hardness scale as he managed to get his muscles working enough to get his clothes off.

"Your pupils just got so big. And you bared your teeth at me." She blew out a breath and then swallowed hard. The breath stuttered from him as he plunged into this moment with her. Let it take over.

And his mouth feasted at her throat as he slowly slid the buttons from their holes, spreading the front of her pajama top open to revel those magnificent tits. Leaning back, he took her in fully as he got to his knees.

She looked up at him through fuck-drunk eyes, her lips parted, tongue darting out.

"I can't figure out how to look at your face with those lips and big brown eyes and those breasts at the same time."

The corner of her mouth slid up enough to bring out her dimple and he fell in love with her all over again.

It was good here. This place the two of them had stumbled into, each of them fighting it here and there but always coming back for more until they gave up and let themselves have a relationship.

She was his family. The mother of his son. And it meant so much that he'd have loved her just for that. But there was more because she was his. That's all he could say to himself that felt most true. He'd looked at her and his entire being had gone taut and he'd thought, *Mine.*

So she was his mate. Something he'd craved after watching his friends and family find their love and make their own families.

"Out of those pants. I want you on me."

Her gaze roved over his body, pausing to look at his tattoos, at the piercings and the muscle, the softness of that hair and that gorgeous face of his.

"You are every single filthy bad-boy fantasy rolled up into one, and I'm quite aflutter with it."

He grinned up at her when she straddled his body.

"I am?"

"Oh yes. You are the motorcycle-riding, tattooed, pierced, bad-boy rock star. You're as alpha as they come and you manage to do it all smooth-like so half the time I'm so befuddled by how absurdly attractive you are, and your voice does that thing and it makes me wet. Because you are that bad boy but you're not when it comes to me."

She kissed him, slow and deep, her hands braced on his shoulders. His hands played over her thighs and back, over her ass and up into her hair.

And then lower, the edge of that scruffy beard when she shifted to the hollow below his ear and then up the row of hoops.

Down his throat and across his chest so she could lick and tug on his nipple with the ring. She breathed him in, tracing the lines of his arms and the point of his elbows as she continued to kiss her way downward, over the lines of the tattoo on his belly. His flat, hard belly.

Positively light-headed, that was what he left her. By the time she slid her tongue across the slit of his cock, there was only the way he made her feel.

She let her hair fall around her face, knowing how much he loved her hair and when he got that partial view of what her mouth was doing on his cock. Swirling licks and sucks, she drew him in deeper and deeper.

She wanted to bring him pleasure to distract him from his stress. Wanted to minister to him the way he had her so often.

And so she poured everything she felt about him into every touch. Every kiss and lick.

Over and over, she took him as deeply as she could, keeping him wet, massaging a slow, circular slide over his asshole as she continued to suck his cock. Her inner muscles skittered when he groaned.

That need to please was a powerful thing. In those moments with him like this, the dark things they both craved and found in the other, the raw sexuality of their energy—there was no fear or hesitation. She wanted to bring him pleasure. Wanted him to find it in her.

His dominant side rose slowly, building. But he'd already been halfway there, already in protective mode from the incident with the media earlier. He was sure. Aggressive. His fingers in her hair tightened as he guided her the way he wanted.

And she loved it.

He growled and thrust upward when her lubed fingers had found his prostate and began a slow stroke each time she pulled her mouth up.

She lost herself in the scent of him, the feel of his body, the way he tasted, and concentrated on pushing everything but pleasure from his brain.

This had to be the best blow job he'd ever had. And Gillian was a fucking genius with her mouth, so that was a big deal. She had him on the edge of orgasm and he was just about to go over but she felt so good and looked so fucking hot bending over his cock he didn't want it to end.

And, as he sailed into climax three minutes later, he was pretty sure he might have blacked out, he came so hard.

"When I can move my anything again, I'm all over that pussy. Just sayin'," he managed to slur.

She laughed and snuggled into his body. "You never told me what it was you saw when you looked into this room."

"The posts on the bed. I'll need to use them when we work up to round two."

17

If he never rode in a helicopter again, he'd have the memory of Miles's face when they walked from the back of the house to where the ride the label had sent to pick them up waited.

"This is major," Miles breathed out, eyes as wide as saucers.

"It is pretty awesome, I agree." Gillian grinned at their son and Adrian put an arm around each one of them and walked them over. This made the hassle of fame worth it. Being able to share such a thrill with Gillian and Miles.

"Come on then. Let's see Miami from the air." He held his guitar and the case, the same as he had over and over. But the nervousness over the meeting with Reg was something he hadn't felt in a very long time.

As if she sensed he needed it, Gillian reached out to squeeze his hand.

"I've never been in a helicopter before. Mum either. This is beyond." Miles was all eyes as he strapped in. Gavin grinned at him and strapped in next to him.

"I've done it before several times but it's always cool."

Miles took in Gavin's considerable size and nodded, as if reassuring himself. Adrian hid his smile.

Gillian grasped his hand so tight he made her let go so he could put an arm around her shoulders. He'd never seen her this spooked by anything, but the way she melted into his side and averted her gaze from what was going on outside the window as they rose and left the ground made him glad he was there to comfort her. Glad she turned to him for it.

"We should arrive shortly," the pilot said via the headsets they all wore. Jeremy had stopped by for breakfast and had met Miles and Gillian. Gillian had charmed him easily and Miles asked rapid-fire questions about the industry that kept Jeremy on his toes, but if the zeal on his face was any indicator, he'd enjoyed the discussion.

He also hated helicopters, so he and Merrill had headed to Reg's about twenty minutes before the copter had arrived. Gillian's mouth had flattened into a hard line when Merrill had been there after they'd woken up. One bodyguard and she'd been all right, but two and she'd understood the gravity, which he knew hit that mother-worry bull's-eye.

But she'd straightened her spine, held her hand out to shake Merrill's, and by the time breakfast had ended, Merrill looked at her with the same fucking cow eyes Gavin already did.

She was as larger than life as Erin was, but in her own way. It only made him more fascinated to watch how she interacted with people. Her quiet way seemed to calm Miles, and though he hated to admit it, he finally understood what she'd meant when she tried to talk to Adrian about structure and how Miles thrived with it.

He turned to kiss the top of her head. Love was alchemy too, he realized. It had changed him right down to his toes.

So when he walked into that room with nothing more than his guitar and a notepad to meet Reg Thorne, he knew for sure that whether or not Thorne agreed to produce, he'd make that CD anyway. And it would be the best thing he'd ever done.

When he'd gone through two songs, Thorne rapped the table with his knuckles. "You don't need anything more, mate." Thorne had an accent that made Adrian's fingers itch to touch Gillian.

He paged through an appointment book. "I haven't worked in Seattle for a very long time. Do you have a home studio?"

Adrian hoped he looked calm when he managed to find his words. "I do, yes. I also have access to a larger studio should we need it."

"I'll send my assistant out to yours in March to be sure it's up to snuff. We'll start work in April. I want you to get your sister on this one. You and she have a rhythm, it's good for you to keep that when you make a leap."

Thorne's gaze locked onto Adrian's. "And you *will* make a leap, old son. You ready for it? This stuff is going to take you to a whole new level. I gotta admit to you that I've not been this excited about a project for at least a few years."

Relief warred with excitement of his own. "I'm more than ready. And Erin is in already. Working in Seattle will make it even easier for her. And for me too since my family is there."

Reg nodded. "Good. Just so you know up front, I'm not a label lackey. I don't play with keepers, so if the label wants that, you make them understand that's not going to happen. I don't want anyone in that studio who will muck up my work. You're a big enough property that this probably won't be an issue, but it needed to be said anyway. You have drug problems?"

Adrian snorted. "I don't have the time for a drug problem."

Reg stood. "Glad to hear that. I'm not a song doctor. I can't fix your fuckups. But this is good material and you're not a newbie so you know how to do that yourself anyway. You're going to hit your audience with a face full of your inner life. Send me the songs as you begin to polish and I'll send back from time to time with notes. When we get into the studio we will work as long as we have to to make the record."

Adrian nodded. "I'm amenable to all that."

Reg held out is hand and they shook on it.

"Don't let this go to your head or anything," Reg began as they walked out to where Jeremy waited with Gillian and Miles, "but I've wanted to work with you for years. I asked around, never heard an unkind thing."

They paused as they entered the room and everyone's gaze swung to the two men.

"You must be Miles." Reg held a hand out and Miles, gobsmacked, took it and gave his arm a few pumps up and down.

"I'm a big fan of your work, sir."

"Nice job raising a kid with some manners." Reg looked to Adrian, who redirected his attention to Gillian.

"I can't take credit for it. Miles's mum did it all. Gillian Forrester, please meet Reg Thorne."

Gillian shook his hand. "It's a pleasure to meet you."

Reg's crusty reserve melted away when he heard Gillian's voice and Adrian managed to stifle his laugh.

"Darlin', whereabouts do you hail from? You're working the Queen's English, but that's not your roots."

Blushing, she managed a quirk of a smile. "Newham."

"Ah, a London girl."

"Born and bred. You're not though. You're a Geordie."

Reg's delighted laugh cut through any remaining tension. "I am. Six generations of us from Newcastle. What's a fine-looking woman like you doing here in the States instead of back home?"

"Came here when I was fifteen."

"Have you been back to visit? Do you still have people there?"

"None I'd want to spend time thinking on." She looked to Miles and then Adrian. "Everyone I want to see lives here."

"Ah, that's the way of it then. My wife is Welsh and she keeps me coming back to England again and again. I should bring her with me when I'm in Seattle later next year. You'd get on with her, I think."

"You're a right clever man to be working with Adrian."

Adrian stood with Miles and Jeremy as she flattered and joked with Reg. In Thorne's company her accent had deepened and it was damned sexy. Nearly as sexy as the way she talked Adrian up with such pride.

"Aye. He's a good one, your man. I certainly won't be questioning his choices now that I've met you and the lad."

She laughed, patting Reg's arm. "Aren't you the charmer."

"The wife says so and I never argue with her because she's always right. Though you can't tell her I said as much. It'll only go to her head."

"How long have you been married?"

"We'll all take lunch together." Reg made this pronouncement and a young man leapt up to make it happen.

Later, as they watched Miles frolic in the pool, Adrian put an arm around her and pulled her to his side. "I think Reg has a crush on you."

She laughed. "Our Reg loves his missus very much. He also loves your music. The two of you will work well together."

"From your mouth to God's ears."

"You have these wonderful songs. He wants to work with you. You want to work with him. It's fate that you two should come together and make something amazing."

"Your faith in me means a lot."

"You have great talent, Adrian. I'm not the only one who feels that way. You feel it too. Of all the things to worry about, you don't often seem to fret about your music. And there's a reason for that. You're confident of your music and that's how it should be."

The ability she had to see past all the smoke and layers of shit he had to erect to continue to be able to make his music always set him back, even as he appreciated that ability more than he could say.

"Never saw much need to pretend. I love making music. I'm lucky to be able to make it and that I continue to be able to make it. My success means a lot to me." He paused to watch Miles for a bit. "Up until September it was pretty much the most important thing in my life. I have other priorities now. But music is still one of them."

She didn't speak, but he knew she listened.

"I'm glad he suggested Seattle. He normally works out of three cities, Portland being the closest, and I wasn't sure how it would be to work in New Orleans while you and Miles were at home. Before September this just wouldn't have entered my reality. But I can't imagine not seeing you or Miles for months."

"Good. I can't imagine not seeing you for months either. In fact, I'm utterly sure I'd hate it." She shrugged. "But I'm a realist and I know you'll have to tour to support the record. So you will be away for months. We'll get through it. Miles and I will be waiting when you get home."

He couldn't put into words just how happy it made him that she referenced a future with him in it.

"I can schedule it for when Miles is out of school and you can come with me. Erin has mentioned a possible willingness to go out on tour as well. Bringing along Todd, Ben and Alexander. It could work."

She smiled, open and thrilled. He kissed her because there was nothing he wanted more than that.

"I take it you're in for such a project? They have tour buses that are pretty nice. We can set you up a wireless workstation. Obviously you'd be unable to do piano lessons while away from home. But there are pianos in most venues so you could play regularly. Miles can have his own room. A bodyguard would travel with us. That's part of all my tour contracts and it's nonnegotiable."

"Stop being so gruff with me. I already agreed." She stood and jumped into the water. "Come on in. Play for a while with me and your boy."

18

Adrian watched Miles as he struggled to stay up on his snowboard and then managed to do it after wiping out several times.

Gillian wisely kept quiet until he reached where they'd been waiting for him, and then she threw her arms around their son and gave him a kiss on the cheeks. "You did awesome!"

Miles's grin was infectious as he looked to Adrian. "Yeah?"

"Totally. I can't believe yesterday was the first time you've ever been snowboarding and you're already kicking ass."

Gillian elbowed him in the ribs.

"Er, butt."

Gillian had never been snowboarding either. She had picked it up a lot faster than Adrian had assumed she would.

Elise, Brody and Rennie had all decided to ski while Erin stayed back at the house with Alexander, Ella and Martine. Ben stayed back with her, and Todd was out on the slopes for a while before they all went back for lunch.

It wasn't just Christmas but also Brody and Elise's first wedding anniversary. Adrian loved that they were all together and that Miles

and Gillian could be there as well. It was his favorite present so far.
Well, actually, his second favorite, as Gillian gave him a scarf and hat
she'd knitted herself. He wore them both right then and planned to as
often as the weather permitted.

She'd made something for him with her own hands. Which was better
than anything else he could have wished for. Of course she'd also given him
a huge box of yellow lined writing pads. The ones he always used for song-
writing. Several boxes of the pens he preferred, blank CDs and new strings
too. Everything he needed all the time, but he usually had to get himself.

Of course she appeared befuddled with how much he liked it. But
she seemed to be easing a little on other things. She'd accepted, quite
happily, the new parka he'd given her, and currently wore the earrings
he'd put on her pillow that morning when she'd been in the shower.

Spoiling her was his new favorite activity outside hanging with Miles.

"Let's go on another run and then we'll head back to the house,"
Todd boarded up to where they all stood. "Erin just sent a picture.
Everyone is having a great time. Ella sends her love. Cope brought in
more wood, she says."

"I'll head back now, if you don't mind. My eyes hurt from the glare
and I'm too old for this." Gillian grinned and reached out to squeeze
Miles's hand.

"We can all go back." Adrian didn't want to watch her go.

"That would be silly. Erin is fine. Ella and Cope are there with her.
Miles is getting the hang of this now. Go on and have another run
with Todd. I'll see you boys later." She kissed Adrian quickly.

Todd tossed her a set of keys. "Take my car back. I'll ride with
Adrian and Miles."

She nodded her thanks and Adrian watched her go, holding her
board, looking more beautiful than any woman had a right to be.

"Don't worry, she had a good time," Miles said as they got back
into the gondola to head up for a last run.

"You think? Also, am I that obvious?"

Todd's guffaw told him he was indeed obvious.

"It's obvious you want her to be happy." Miles shrugged. "Shouldn't you? Isn't that what you're supposed to do?"

He put an arm around his son. "Indeed it is."

"So you love her, right?"

He paused. "Yes, I love your mother. I wasn't joking when we talked about living closer or with each other."

Todd looked him over. "Good. You two are good. You three are meant to be a family."

Adrian sighed. "I think so too. But Miles and his mom have a life on Bainbridge and it's not as easy as consolidating our households. We'll take it up again after the holidays. If I know Gillian, she's thinking on it now too."

"She's not much for making snap decisions. That's what they did. She doesn't want to be like them."

Adrian didn't have to ask who "they" were. He knew Miles meant Tina and his grandmother. Since Adrian knew Gillian never would have spoken ill of either of them in Miles's presence, he had to have picked it up on his own. Which made Adrian proud and a little sad.

"Making sound decisions is a good quality, kid. It's her job, you know, to make well-thought-out choices that are best for you." Todd said this idly, but Adrian knew it had come from his heart and he knew Todd's words would help Miles too.

"I know."

The gondola doors opened and they shuffled back out into the cold to grab that one last run before they went back to the house.

When she walked into the living room where Erin lay on the floor, Marti sitting at her left and Alexander on her right, building a block tower, Gillian found herself filled with love for Adrian and his family.

"Joo!"

Which is what Alexander called her.

"Hello there, little man." She walked in and moved to sit with them. "They went on one last run and they'll be back," Gillian told Erin as Alexander patted her knee with his pudgy little fist.

"Yo, Joo."

"Yo, Alexander. And how has your morning been?"

He pointed to the blocks.

"What a fine builder you are. Show me more?"

He nodded enthusiastically and moved back to the blocks.

Ella walked in with Cope. "Hey, Gillian. I just made some hot chocolate, would you like some?"

"That would be lovely, thank you."

Gillian picked up Martine and situated her in her lap. She'd put her down when it came time to drink the cocoa, but for the moment, she sucked up all the baby goodness.

"And what are you up to today? Still working on the crawling thing? It's important to keep up with Alexander, I know."

Martine clapped hands and bounced a bit, swinging out her chubby little sock-covered feet.

Ben came in and Alexander hooted to get his attention, as if it was ever very far from the baby. From everything Gillian had witnessed, Ben and Todd doted on their son as much as Erin did.

"Hey, Gillian."

Ben Copeland was unbelievably handsome. And utterly in love with Erin and their son. They made the kind of family few others could manage, and yet they made it look easy, which Gillian knew it couldn't be.

"Ben, I'm supposed to tell you that Todd beat your time record and you are expected to bow down and give your obeisance."

Ben snorted. "Yeah right. When we get our turn this afternoon we'll see who will be bowing down."

She hadn't breathed a word to anyone, but she'd seen Ben and Todd making out just the day before. Outside, both men in big coats as they moved wood for the fireplaces. She'd been in the bedroom and heard the sound, moving to the windows to see what was out there and she'd seen them.

And she'd never forget it.

Hot. Hot. Hot. Mouth to mouth. She'd stood there, stunned and breathless, as Todd had grabbed Ben by the hair and shoved him back against a tree, never breaking the kiss once.

Erin was a fortunate woman to be able to see that every day. Of that Gillian was sure.

"Did you hear that? Daddy and Pop are going to have a contest of manliness. Aren't they silly?" Erin got nose to nose with Alexander, who laughed.

"Pop? Pop?" He looked around, looking for Todd.

"He's snowboarding, monkey. He'll be back in a bit with Uncle Brody and Uncle Adrian too."

"Boo?"

Gillian laughed. "Yes, Miles too."

"Nee?"

"Yes, baby. Rennie, her mommy and daddy. Adrian and Miles and Pop too."

He looked at Erin, wearing a serious face she'd seen on Brody a few dozen times.

"Okay."

Shortly after that, the rest of them came through the door, laughing and bustling with all that Brown energy. Miles's cheeks were rosy with cold and excitement and Gillian shooed him off to go change out of his wet clothes. Rennie was full of news of the new run she'd conquered as Brody filled in the story with details of his own.

As Gillian stood there with Adrian, his arm around her waist as everyone chattered around them, she took refuge in his body. Snuggling into him.

He hummed, pulling her even closer. "Hey. You all right?"

"Mmm, yes, I am. You smell like winter." He just made her feel better. Made her feel at home. She should be ashamed of how much she needed him, but she couldn't be.

Once Erin, Ben, Ella and Cope had gone to the slopes, taking Miles with them and leaving her a little nervous, Adrian drew her upstairs to his bedroom.

"She's a mother too. She's going to be sure he's safe. Ben promised to be with him the whole time and he's a good teacher. Miles will have a great time."

Of course Gillian knew this in her head, but her heart was another thing entirely.

"Let me take your mind off things." He got that look and she allowed him to draw her closer.

"I should point out to you that this is your solution to every problem. But then you might think I had a problem with that and I do not."

Laughing, he spun her and managed to get her sweater off in one deft movement.

"You're so good at that."

"All practice for you, English."

With that, he dropped to his knees and yanked her pants and knickers down so she could get out of them. But instead of moving her anywhere else, he simply pressed his face to her pussy and breathed her in.

He banded an arm around her body, across her ass, and held her in place as she squirmed.

That's when he opened his eyes and looked straight up her body and into her face. While she watched, utterly still, he used the tip of his tongue to slide between her labia and tickle her clit until the breath shot from her lips.

But she couldn't tear her eyes from the sight.

He pulled his face back, his lips shiny with her. She swallowed, motionless and waiting for what he'd do.

"People downstairs. Babies sleeping all around. You're going to have to be so quiet. Can you manage that?" His whispered words played against her already wet and swollen clit, his lips just barely not touching her body.

She nodded, not knowing if she could, knowing she had to. Knowing it really worked for both of them.

He motioned to the bed with a tip of his chin and she moved to it. The windows were open and it was still full day outside. But the glass was also smoked and he'd assured her no one could see in, a fact she could verify herself when they arrived and couldn't see in any of the windows.

"On the edge. Spread those thighs for me," he murmured, turning to kiss the inside of her knee and further rendering her to quivering jelly.

He pushed her thighs open even wider, leaving her totally exposed to his attention. At first the touches of his lips, his tongue and even his teeth were gentle and whisper light. But then he moved closer and changed his pace.

She sifted her fingers through his hair, tugging and urging him closer. He chuckled against her pussy and echoes of pleasure rippled through her.

His thumbs slid back and forth at the hollow of each hip, mesmerizing her.

Little flicks and licks and his tongue stabbed into her cunt, fucking into her body. She had to swallow her gasp, holding it in with the back of her hand pressed against her mouth.

This time she squeezed her eyes shut. It was too much to watch him devastate her with that mouth of his as he worshipped her cunt there on his knees. It was too much to watch the way he touched her with so much reverence and care, even with a rough dig of fingers, he didn't harm.

Long licks, short licks, quick flicks of the tip of his tongue let her get complacent with his lovely pace. And that's when he sucked. Oh. She nearly shouted, it felt so good. He sucked her clit in between his lips over and over. Her muscles labored and trembled. She bit into her bottom lip to keep from crying out though it was all she wanted to do.

Other than come, that is.

Orgasm seemed to roll her over and suck her under, pulling her in and holding tight as he continued. She had to yank on his hair and scoot back after the second, smaller aftershock climax.

He kissed her belly, and though her eyes were closed, she knew what he was up to even before she heard the crinkle of the condom wrapper.

"Open your eyes. I want you to see whose cock is in your pussy. I want you to see who's giving you your pleasure."

She obeyed, overcoming her lethargic muscles only to find him standing next to the bed, his cock in his hands as he'd lined it up, nudging against her gate. And then he was in her and they both sucked in air as if they were drowning.

The muscles in his neck held a tension she could see as she watched him. The late afternoon sun behind him framed him like a corona.

He was so beautiful. It wasn't just the outside of him, it was the sum total of Adrian Brown that drove her to her knees. Humbled her. Inspired her.

Because he knew she watched, he held her thighs wide, the glorious muscles on his forearms corded, pulled taut. She watched his tattoos, the way they stretched.

"Touch yourself." His whisper was harsh and low.

She took her time, knowing from his pace that he'd be there a while, and she had no problems simply enjoying the moments they had.

Licking her fingertips, she played across her nipples, delighting in the way his lips parted and he began to breathe a little harder.

She rolled and pinched them and he watched, eyes on her like a physical thing. "Yes . . ."

The clasp of her cunt around him when she played with her nipples nearly pushed him over. But he didn't want to yet. He wanted to luxuriate in her. Enjoy her body this way. Take this time they'd stolen from the day and just be with one another.

Surreal. Beyond sexy to see her there so bold as she took her pleasure without any shame. No one else got to see this side of her. Damn, that undid him.

Her pussy tightened again as she slid her right hand down to where he thrust into her body over and over. She played around the base of his cock, getting him even wetter as she got herself lubed.

And then he heard the soft moan she made when her fingers found the clit he'd been licking only minutes before.

Tearing his gaze from her hand, up her belly, lingering on the jaunty bounce of her tits and up into her face, he caught sight of the way she bit her bottom lip to keep from crying out.

Hot damn, that was seriously sexy.

All the filthy things he wanted to say boiled up, but he had to swallow it back. Not that anyone would have cared if they heard. But Gillian would, and that was important.

She was lush and petite all at the same time. Gorgeous. Sexy. Smart. Funny and shy too. And he'd never met his match in bed until her. She'd ruined him for all others, and that was fine since he didn't plan to have any others but her.

Her *unh* when she began to finger her clit in earnest was just a puff of air, and yet he heard it like she'd said it in his ear.

That he had to fight to stay silent was foreplay in and of itself when he wanted to bend down and take a nipple in between his teeth and tug. He wanted to pull out and roll her over and fuck her from behind. He loved it that way. Loved being able to see the bounty of her body, loved the way her breasts looked as he thrust especially hard. Loved to control her by her hair.

"You're thinking something very naughty," she whispered with a smile.

"I sure am."

She laughed, low and sultry. "Can't wait."

"Getting closer, English. Make yourself come."

She licked her lips and his gaze let go of her face, looking down at where his cock disappeared into her body over and over, returning dark and slick from her cunt. Her hand was between her legs, fingers on her clit, squeezing lightly, and he nearly lost his mind, knowing how much she loved it when he did that to her.

She arched, tipping her head back, exposing the long line of her neck, stretching so that her tits looked insanely good as her cunt squeezed down on him so hard he grunted.

Two thrusts later and he joined her, fucking into her pussy, now even slicker. Her inner muscles still squeezing here and there as climax worked through her.

He came so hard and so long he wondered if it would end, and finally was able to pull out and leave her for just a moment to deal with the condom and come back, getting on the bed and bringing her close to his body.

"Better than the slopes any day." He nuzzled the back of her neck and she sighed happily.

"Indeed, Mister Brown. Indeed."

19

The jet-setting thing made Gillian tired. But she couldn't deny that all the close-knit family time she'd had with Adrian and Miles over the last ten days had rocketed them forward in their relationship.

She could believe they had a future. Could tell him she loved him without hesitation. Could receive his love in return without worry.

"You're finally back!" Jules looked up with a smile when she came through the front doors of Tart.

"I am." She unbuttoned the coat that had been one of what felt like a million presents from Adrian.

"Come and sit. I'll get you some tea and we'll catch up. When does Miles get back?"

She sat at her favorite place at the counter and watched Jules move in her own precise and graceful way.

"Tomorrow morning. Adrian took him to some sort of all-ages show and then they played video games with Brody and Cope until far after midnight apparently. He sent me an e-mail about it." She laughed. "Today?" She shrugged. "I think they're going over to Seattle Center and the EMP."

"Look at you! Letting him go a little. You okay with that?"

"Adrian is good with him. Brody is a great dad too. He likes being with them. You should see it." She smiled. "At first I was worried, you know? I worried Miles would get lost amid all those big giant male personalities."

"Not the case?"

"No. You and Mary were right. He's thriving with them in his life. They don't push him so hard he feels bad, but they encourage him to try new things. It's good for him, and I think maybe good for them too."

Finally, all customers had been served and the tea was ready and Jules slid into the seat next to Gillian.

"Okay, get to talking. You texted that he liked the scarf. I told you he would. How did he react?"

"I felt so stupid giving it to him. You should have seen that place on Christmas morning, Jules. Those Browns and Copelands sure do know how to throw a holiday party. But yes." She smiled, remembering Adrian's face as he opened the box with the scarf and watchman's cap she'd knitted for him.

"Fuck that." Jules waved it away. "He digs you. Like, major. Your knitting would have meant more to him than an expensive present and you know it."

Gillian blushed. "He wore it every day we were there. Of course he gave me this coat and more things than I can list. I've given up trying to tell him no. He's like a child!"

"Good. On the giving-up-telling-him-no stuff, I mean. Jeebus, Gillian, he's not any of those jerks your mom brought home. A new pair of boots does not mean he expects pussy in exchange."

"That's good since I already gave it to him for free."

Jules tipped her head back and laughed. "I miss you when you're gone. Texts aren't the same."

"I missed you too. *I like them*. I do. They're fun people I enjoy being with. Miles adores each and every one of them and they adore him right back."

"But?"

"They're all so close-knit." She sipped the tea Jules slid in front of her. "They have this ease with each other and when I'm there I know Adrian wants me to feel it too. But how can I? I feel guilty. And then I get angry that I feel guilty because they've had years and years and I've had four months. It takes time to build relationships like that. It's not as if I'm off by myself when I'm with them. That's not it at all. I laugh and have fun and all that. But—"

"But you're not that person. You're not instant intimacy. Oh sure, you have it with Adrian, but that's something unique in your life."

"I try. I do. They're so close and they share everything and I just can't sit and gossip and spill all my details with them. Not like they do with each other."

Jules squeezed her hand. "Baby, they understand. They can't possibly expect you to be as close to them as they are with each other. I don't know them as well as you do, obviously, but they seemed to like you. Has anyone said anything?"

"No. Of course not. They're all very nice people. And I *do* like them and want to get to know them better."

"You need time, and they're not dumb. They'll give you that time and you'll all get to know each other, and one of these days you'll be as comfortable as they all are. You're worth the wait to get to know. Did you have fun at least?"

She sighed happily and dug into the slice of pear tart that had appeared before her. "My favorite. I missed this too. As for fun? I did. I feel like a character from a novel. He sort of swept me off my feet. A helicopter ride. A house with a pool *and* a boat dock. Though we also had paparazzi. I didn't like that part.

"Still, Adrian took us for lavish dinners and filled our bedroom with dozens of roses. And he continued the scary movie campaign, as if he needed to. Every night at his place in Whistler we had a movie marathon. I'm already head over heels in love with the man."

"Aw, he totally loves you. He wants to spoil you."

"I know. It's adorable. But, I haven't told him about my father yet. I know I should, so get that look off your face. But I can't. I start to bring it up and then I freeze."

"I didn't get any look. Not like you think. I feel like this is something you should tell him just because it will eventually come out and you should control the how and when of it. But your father is not part of your life. He never was. Ronnie Pete was some dude your mother boned for a while and then he pushed off and did his own thing for another fifteen years until it all caught up to him. You don't know him. You are only his daughter in the most minimal sense. Stop trying to own what he did as if you had any say."

Gillian had known Jules would say what she needed to hear. This was the kind of connection the Browns and Copelands had. It was what kept Gillian going even on days when she was absolutely sure she wasn't going to make it. And she couldn't leave it behind even if she wanted to.

"I love you."

"Right back atcha, sister. Now, tell me true, are you going to move to Seattle to be with him?"

That was the big question, now wasn't it?

Gillian found herself on her hands and knees, hair covered by a bandana, scrubbing her kitchen floor because that's what she did whenever she needed to think. That or ironing, and she didn't want to face that today.

There were things she knew to be totally true. First, that Miles needed his father. If that hadn't been apparent already, the way Miles and Adrian had bonded on the holiday trips they'd all taken would have made it so. They clicked. Adrian made Miles happy and it definitely went the other way too.

Adrian had to make some dad-type decisions while they were in Florida and then in Whistler. Enough to make himself the bad guy on more than one occasion. Miles had been startled, but afterward, he'd been even more at ease with his dad. As if he knew Adrian really was his father and would take care of him.

It had been a bittersweet realization for Gillian. She wanted them to be close, but it was hard to share the governance of Miles's life with someone else.

And yet, sharing him, being a family the way they had, had lodged in her belly. Miles was still with his dad in Seattle, opting to spend one more night there. Adrian had wanted her there too, but she needed some time to think.

Things between them had gotten very serious.

Four months they'd had, and at least a month of that time she'd spent fighting with him and thinking he was a jerk. It was one thing to have this romance with him. But moving in meant a whole new level of commitment and intimacy. More than she'd ever had with anyone before.

The way she felt for Adrian wasn't just a crush. It wasn't just love. He was that puzzle piece she'd been missing. He was, to be blunt and all since she was scrubbing the floor and this was a discussion in her head, her mate.

That meant something. It meant something to that girl who never had much of anything or anyone until Gran had come into her life. Never understood that depth of love and devotion you could feel for another person until she'd held Miles. And even that wasn't the same. Not the same as the way Adrian made her feel. Tough and ready for anything. Safe. Loved. Confident.

A tattooed, bad-boy rock star with a big, tight family and a heart to match. There'd never been a more unlikely man for her! But they made sense, despite all their spats and the way they fought and then fucked. They worked. They clicked. She *knew* she got him in ways most others didn't. She also knew he did the same with her.

She didn't doubt they could live together well, though there were still problems.

The biggest problem was that she didn't want to move away from Bainbridge and the relationships and community she and Miles had built there.

She was sure that made her selfish. After all, Miles probably would flourish at a private school. But it had taken the boy a long time to make the friends he'd made and it wasn't as easy as *starting a new band* as Adrian seemed to think.

She was a lot like Miles, she supposed, in that it took her a long time to totally feel comfortable in a place or with people. She had that here. Had a community.

But . . . she wanted to be with him. She wanted to live in a house with her son and his father. Location was something they could work on. So what was the real problem, damn it?

Fear. She loved Adrian so much it scared her.

She sat back, arse on the floor, resting her head against the cabinets. It took her *years* to love someone, and with Adrian it had happened so fast. One part of her was okay with that. Love was a certain kind of magic and she accepted it as such.

Miles had been instant love. The moment she held him against her chest she'd loved him so fiercely it had filled up everything.

And that had been enough. More than enough. She'd loved being a mother more than she could have ever imagined. She made mistakes with it, of course. But even if everything else in her life had been out of sequence, she and Miles had been in sync.

Adrian had changed *everything* in much the same way Miles had. And, she supposed, she loved him in much the very quick way she'd loved Miles. He felt like family.

When she'd been growing up, her mother had thought she was doing a favor for Gillian by keeping her expectations low. A girl like her wasn't pretty like Tina, so she could play piano and be a good enough wife and mum for some bloke who'd sit and watch footie every night down the pub with his buddies while she handled the home life.

Low expectations had been her main dish as a child. While she'd had Miles and had found an avenue for her passion with the piano, the ugly, unvarnished truth was that she'd never expected to have a love like she had with Adrian.

Fucking was hard enough. But letting someone into her soul? Past all her defenses into her very heart? The unvarnished truth was that he was there already. It wasn't a matter of decisions on her part. It simply was true and at the end of the day, she accepted it. And it strengthened her. She also knew that.

She could see herself and Miles living in Adrian's house. It was big and bright and had a gorgeous view. She could most definitely do her work there. She might even be able to expand to some new avenues around the area.

But the yard, while lovely, wasn't the kind of yard a boy could really run around in. Not that Miles was much for sporting around in the back anyway.

It would only be half an hour from her friends. Not the same quick ride over to Mary's or down to Tart, but it was doable. She could still go to dinner and hang out and they could come to her as well.

She didn't like parts of his life. The constant exposure troubled her. Quite frequently, people camped out at the base of his drive. Just outside his gate on any given day there'd be fans. Most were very respectful, though she had her doubts about the level of obsession of people who came to find his house and then camped as if they were in the forest instead of a neighborhood.

Instead of going to get coffee nearby his home, he headed to the café Erin owned. He didn't do anything in his own neighborhood as a matter of fact. And it was a nice neighborhood!

But his face was too well known there, and while the people he lived around seemed just fine with his celebrity, that didn't stop the camping out and the occasional paparazzi.

Twice since Miami, photographs of Gillian and Miles had ended up on gossip websites. That was a whole new level of exposure and it pushed those buttons she'd had for a very long time. She had enough of that when she was young and everyone knew her mum was the town bike and her dad was a drug dealer who liked young girls.

This country had brought her relief from that. She'd reinvented herself away from that, and the idea of people looking at her and judging her for what others did or didn't do made her sick.

Was it all about her? Was she so self-centered that she'd make it all about how she felt when clearly Miles and his dad deserved to be together?

"Get it together, Gillian," she muttered, going back to scrubbing the floor. Dithering never got anyone anywhere. Period. She needed to make her mind up and go forward from there.

So she refilled the bucket with clean soapy water and got back to work.

"Lookie here, Miles."

She glanced up from where she'd just finished cleaning the baseboards to find Adrian and Miles standing there, grinning.

"I thought you two were off for the day with mischief in mind." She got to her feet, peeling off the rubber gloves after pouring out the dirty water.

"We missed you." Miles tromped over her freshly scrubbed floors, but it was to hug her and so it didn't matter.

"Hey, love. I missed you too."

Oh, beautiful love. Love flooded through her, that warm, bone-deep mother-love. Filled her up to bursting.

And when he stepped away there was Adrian, also tromping across her freshly scrubbed floor.

She knew she wore a fool's smile but it didn't matter.

"Mister Brown. I trust you have not broken our son?"

"I do my best, English." He leaned in to kiss her, a sweet sort of smooch that made the backs of her knees tingle.

"Miles and I were hanging out and all after we woke up and we both decided we needed to see you." He leaned past her to put a bag on the counter. "You have no idea how hot it makes me to see you this way," he murmured softly.

Oh, he thrilled her right to her toes.

"We brought shrimp, corn on the cob and potatoes. I think we can work with this combo."

"I think we can, yes. I'll make a pasta salad to go with. We'll do a boil, don't you think?" Gillian shooed them both from the room while she re-mopped and dried up quickly.

"And we can eat out back with a fire." Miles stooped to pick up Jones to give him a snuggle. Fat Lucy had been annoyed he'd been away so much, so she coolly ignored him.

"Call Isabel." She indicated a note on the counter. "She called for you. As did Jason. Feed the turtle."

"Jeez."

"Guess you don't miss me as much now."

He grinned. "Nah, I still missed you." He put the cat down and headed out to feed the turtle.

She turned to dig out the pot to boil the shrimp, corn and potatoes in, and another for the pasta as Adrian slid into motion around her, moving to the sink to clean everything up.

"Just so you know, I'm going to be all up in you ten minutes after he goes to bed."

"Just so you know, I'm on board with that." She pressed a kiss on his shoulder as she filled the pots with water.

When she'd turned the heat on beneath the pots, he spun her, backing her against the door to the pantry. "I'd planned to apologize and ask if you were all right with us coming back early. And then I saw your face when you caught sight of Miles when he told you we missed you. The look on your face . . . beautiful. I love you."

"Oh, you say the dearest things. It's impossible not to love you right back. I want to be honest with you—it scares me to need you so much. I haven't stopped thinking on how to make the moving-in thing work." She needed to say it fast so she wouldn't chicken out and not say it at all.

He nodded. "You're not alone. I wake up when you're not with me. I can't sleep as well alone now. There's a Gillian-shaped spot in my bed. And in my life. I want you in it. I want you with me. I want our family. I'm also thinking on the moving-in-together issue. I want it, but I want to do it right."

Miles let the back door slam and they moved apart, back to making dinner.

"Mum, can Jason come to dinner? His parents are away and his older sister is being mean to him."

Gillian restrained her need to roll her eyes. Mean to Jason was probably that she ordered pizza instead of making him burgers or something. The boy was prone to exaggeration, though Gillian often considered him one of the family.

"Of course. The boy knows he's welcome. Tell him he can sleep over too."

Miles's quick grin told her that was the next question anyway and he tore off to make that call.

Adrian hummed and sang as he worked. A few minutes later, Miles and Jason spilled into the kitchen, chattering and laughing, talking over one another. Jason already got over his starstruck phase with Adrian, so he was just another parent.

Something she knew Adrian enjoyed and was proud of.

Gillian paused to simply let it wash through her. It was beautiful, this thing they'd built together.

20

Brody looked up as his brother entered the front door. Rennie tore toward Adrian and he caught her up into a big hug. His brother was a damned good uncle. Without Adrian, Brody was totally sure the transition with Martine would have been a great deal harder.

He'd changed since Miles had come into his life. Since Gillian. That sort of restlessness that even the time off hadn't cured had actually calmed. He lived in that moment, appreciated it.

Adrian was in love in the best kind of ways. With his child and with the woman who was his other half. Brody knew full well what that meant because he'd had it himself.

He'd never expected Elise. Not to fall in love with her the way he had. And he'd most assuredly never expected Rennie. He'd fallen for her too. Fallen for being a father, and though she wasn't his biologically, he was her father in every way that counted. And that was enough.

"Yo, Ms. Irene, what's shakin'?" Adrian put her down and followed her into the living room and through to the kitchen where Brody and Martine were.

Rennie took a deep breath and Brody caught sight of his brother bracing himself for the torrent of words he'd be swimming through in less than a second.

"I got a part in the play. It's not a big one, they chose *Jamie* for that." It was clear what Rennie thought of that particular idea. "But I get to sing and dance. Momma's gonna make me a costume. She has a lot of pretty costumes still in the back of the closet. They let her keep them, you know? When she stopped dancing? And then we can use them for templates for when the school does a performance. *Oh!* Did Aunt Gillian tell you that she's going to play piano in *Carmina Burana*? Momma is going to dance in it. She doesn't usually but her students talked her into it and I'm super excited because she's such a great dancer and all. Where's Miles? Will you be there at the play and also at *Carmina Burana*?"

"Yes, I wouldn't miss your play. Yes, I will be at *Carmina Burana*. I'm also excited to see your mother dance and to hear Gillian play piano. She's actually practicing with the other piano player right now so no we won't be seeing her and Miles tonight. What play is it?"

"*Peter Pan.* I'm a Lost Girl. They said I was a Lost Boy but hello! I am not a boy. I do not have a penis."

Brody coughed and Adrian made a heroic effort not to laugh.

"Absolutely correct, my dear Irene. You do not. Lost Girls are just as good. I'm sure Miles and Gillian will come too."

Marti, who'd been happily sitting in her high chair eating cereal until she was not paid attention to by her uncle, issued a loud screech to get Adrian's attention.

Adrian kissed Rennie's head and moved toward Marti, kissing the top of her head too.

"I see you, ma'am. Do you think I'd ignore you?"

She calmed right away, placated for the time being.

"Doesn't matter their age, if it's a woman, you'll charm her." Brody shook his head. "Just made a fresh pot of coffee, if you'd like. You staying for dinner, since your woman and your boy aren't around tonight?"

"He's got a test tomorrow and she's practicing with her partner for the show. I'll stop by after school to see how it went."

"All right then. How was your day?"

"Managed to meet with Erin to work on some songs, so my day was productive too. Yes to dinner, thanks."

Elise wandered in with an armful of clean laundry. "Hey, it's my brother-in-law." She paused to turn her cheek up to receive a kiss.

"Pizza for dinner, I think."

Rennie jumped for joy at that one, and seeing it, Martine squealed and clapped her hands.

"There's your answer to that question, eh?" Adrian grinned. "I'll do it. The usual?"

"Yeah, and then you can tell me what's up." Brody looked back to Marti. "You have more food on your face than in your stomach, baby girl."

She grinned. "No, no, no!"

"You're growing up, all right." He wiped her face and she laughed.

"Out." She pointed to the ground.

"All right. You can free range awhile in the living room."

They'd gated the entire living room, putting most of what they didn't want her to touch outside it. She crawled like a flash to keep up with Rennie, so he and Elise knew it would only be a matter of time before she figured out a way to get over, under or through the gates.

But parenting was a day-by-day venture anyway.

He cleaned up her messy face until she started to get grumpy. She was off like a shot once he put her down and she caught sight of her big sister, who was busily pulling open the box of Marti's toys.

Rennie played with Martine, both girls laughing as they made a great big farm with chunky horses and cows.

Elise came out and took a look toward Adrian and then back to Brody. "I'll hang with the girls until dinner arrives. Go see what he needs."

He reached out to slide a fingertip over her lips. "You're one of a kind, you know that? I love you."

She smiled and he grinned down at her. His woman. In their house with his children. Life didn't get any better than that.

"I love you too."

He kissed her and turned to head back into the kitchen where Adrian was.

"Half an hour. I'm passing on the coffee. I need to sleep well tonight. Topped you up, though."

"Thanks." He sat and pushed a chair out with his foot. "Sit and tell me."

"Am I so predictable?"

"I know you, Adrian. Like I know Erin. Like I know the people I love. You're happy. Happier than I've seen you . . . well, ever, I suppose. But there's something else. Something's bugging you."

"I asked Gillian to move in with me. To bring Miles and make my house theirs. I want this, Brody. I want feeding babies in high chairs. I want to wake up with her every day. I want to be with my son the night before a test and to eat breakfast with him while I quiz him."

"Why aren't you there, then? Why are you here in my kitchen instead of there, in hers?"

"I have stuff to do. I need to work and my studio is here. Why isn't she here?"

"Because your son is in middle school in another city. That's where the life she built for him is. Christ, Adrian, you know this. What is it really?"

His brother sighed.

"You know you can tell me anything. Right? I'm not going to judge you for having feelings. But I will kick your ass if I think that's what you need. And I will tell you you have spinach in your teeth too. You'd do the same for me. Now, what is it really?"

"She holds back. Okay? Haven't you noticed that?"

Brody sat back and sipped his coffee.

"What I've noticed is that she likes us. She comes to our events. Listens to stories about stuff she wasn't there for and people she doesn't know. She does this with a great sense of humor. And she does it for you and for Miles."

"Do you think she just puts up with it then?"

"Just tell me straight, Adrian. Are you looking for a way to fuck this up or are you looking for a way to make it work?"

This was why Adrian had ended up on Brody's doorstep instead of Erin's. Erin was perfectly capable of kicking his butt when he was wrong, but it was Brody who would sort him out in a more unflinching way. Brody, who was his mentor, his father figure and the person he looked to more than anyone else for advice and an example.

"I love her. She loves me. This is not in doubt. I'm good with that. More than good with it, actually. It's the best thing in my life. I have a son and he's a great kid. He and I are building a relationship and I'm not fucking up too very much, I hope. Gillian would tell me if I was." He laughed.

"She's a warm, lovely woman. But she's shy and it's going to take time. What makes Gillian the perfect woman for you is the fact that she's unique. Right? There's no one like her and she gets you."

"So you think she's not holding back?"

"I'm not in a relationship with her. I can tell you what my observations are. She's reserved. She's not going to discuss favorite sexual positions with Erin and Elise. At the same time, she understands family. She sees it the way we do. She has that with her friends. I saw it firsthand when we went to the lunch at Mary's last month. I also saw Miles with them. They're his family just as assuredly as we are. So of course she wants the boy to keep that and you should too."

Adrian knew all this, but it helped to have Brody say it. Gave him some clarity.

"She tells me she's working through the moving-in-together stuff and I believe she is. I believe she wants to and I know I do."

"So what's the problem? Huh? You admit she's not the kind of woman who will be buddy-buddy with strangers right off. And yet she is working on it and she does fit in just fine. You admit she loves you and that you love her. You say she's working through the geographical issues, which you and I both know are a bigger deal than you're admitting. She's good for you. You're good for her. Miles is great for you both."

Brody looked at him carefully as the sound of Rennie's laughter and Elise's voice came from the other room.

"Why can't it be easy?"

Brody barked a laugh. "I don't have the answer to that one. I just know that nothing worth having or doing is easy. Nothing." He paused. "Do you trust her?"

Adrian took a moment to think, because it wasn't an easy question to answer. But there was only one and it was utterly clear. "Yes. I do."

"You've seen her several days a week for months. And you've gotten to know her as a mother as you've found your own way into being a father. It just occurred to me that you've gone backward with your lovely Gillian."

Adrian paused and then laughed along with Brody as he realized the truth of it.

"For an old guy you have some big brains. Yeah, that's it. I need to date her. Stuff that's just the two of us. Stuff you all did when you first started out with your husbands and wives, too. Like the tavern."

"Exactly. You know how much we love Miles. Elise and I would love to have him overnight. He and Rennie get along. We'd totally have a great time. You know Erin would love the same. God, they'd jam for hours. The point is, you have lots of options between us and I'd bet her friends too. Go on a date. Take her to dinner and a movie. Whatever. Just normal things. You both need it. To have that part of a relationship."

The worry eased. "I was telling her that I never fought with women before. Because mainly I didn't care for any of them enough to bother with it. But with her, with that, that—"

"That holy-hot-wow thing you and she have with the little battles of will you play? You two have *chemistry*, man. You cannot pretend it. It's not something you can fake."

Adrian nodded. "Yep, that's it. Little zings of electricity between us. When we fight it's never about things we totally disagree on. It's about things we agree on but the problem is the how to get there. But it never feels dire or disrespectful. And yes, yes, it makes me hot when she loses that smooth veneer and shows me the side I know only I see. That is intimate and it blows me away."

"That's trust, dude. For a woman like Gillian to open up the way she does with you? Do you know how she looks at Miles?"

Adrian smiled as he pictured it. "Yes. Awesome, isn't it? It's how Elise looks at Rennie and Marti."

"She opens up and all those reserves fall away and she just can't not show how much he loves him. She looks at you like that. With that same open joy."

She'd shown him over and over how special he was to her. But somehow hearing that just sort of set him back on his heels.

Brody snorted. "Exactly. We love Gillian for who she is. But even if she wasn't a really cool woman, we'd love her for the way she looks at you. Dumbass. We have no problems with Gillian and how she is. She fits in just fine. You're worried, but no one else is."

"Pizza's here," Rennie called from the other room.

Adrian stood and rubbed his hands together. "Just in time. I am suddenly totally starving."

Brody stood, shouldered his brother from the way and all was right again.

21

It had been a very long time since she'd been on a real date. She looked at herself in the mirror again. Daisy had shown up with an armful of packages full of clothes the day after Adrian had asked Gillian on that date for pool and beer with him.

A chic pair of tapered-leg pants and a black, boatneck blouse that was positively vintage. Still, the pants seemed to hug her butt just a bit more than she was sure worked.

It was Jules who was doing the pre-date Gillian-sitting that evening. "I think you look so lovely. That outfit Daisy gave you for your birthday is *humina-humina* hot."

She looked back at Jules. "Do you think? It's very . . . snug." She ran her palms down her waist and over her thighs.

"It's vintage. Boatneck so you can't even see a hint of your dirty pillows. The only skin you're seeing is arms and yours are gorgeous. You're going to wear a sweater over it anyway. As for snug, that's the way it's supposed to fit. You don't look like a sausage. If that's your worry. You look absolutely gorgeous. Feminine. Classic. I promise."

She looked back again. Yes, it was lovely. Sexy without being sleazy. Fitted without being tight.

"Wear that necklace he gave you for Christmas with it. And the tangerine cardigan I gave you a few years back."

"I need you with me every day to make these fashion choices for me."

"Whatever, girl. I'm just here to gawk at your hot-looking man when he arrives." She snapped a picture with her phone.

"Hey!"

"I promised. It was the cost for not having us all here."

She tried to look severe, but it wouldn't work anyway. Her doorbell rang and she blushed. "He doesn't have to do that. He has a key."

"I'll let you get it. That's always the fun part. I lied about the waiting-to-spy-on-you part. I just wanted to get a gander at you." Jules squeezed her hand and headed out the back door before Gillian could argue.

She was still smiling when she opened the door to Adrian holding a bouquet of flowers so large it obscured his face.

"Come in."

He peeked around the flowers and waggled his brows. "You look amazing. Is Miles here or did he already go to Jason's?" She took the flowers with a kiss.

He took them away from her, placed them on her table and eased her against the door. "Now then, I ruined it by asking about Miles first."

"Be quiet. He went straight there after school and says he'll see you tomorrow. Now you may kiss me."

"Now who's cheeky?" He bent his legs and dipped to kiss her.

He nipped at her bottom lip and a sound she didn't remember making came from deep in her throat.

She sucked his tongue into her mouth and he groaned, squeezing her a little tighter.

"Now," he said, putting her away from his body, "that was a better introduction. You look beautiful."

"Thank you. These are gorgeous and you also look really tasty. You sure you'd rather play pool?"

He swatted her butt on the way past. "Get those in water. You and I are going out. Pizza. Beer. Pool. It's going to be rockin'. There's going to be karaoke tonight too apparently. Erin is all buzzed about it."

"If you say so." She made it extra prim and set about putting the flowers into two vases since the bouquet was so large. He couldn't seem to resist crowding her, but she wasn't complaining about it. She loved the way he smelled, the heat of his body as he stood so close.

She loved being irresistible to a man like him.

He helped her into her sweater and coat and then into his car like a total gentleman.

On the way back over they chitchatted about their respective days. He told her about the song he and Erin had finished and sent off to Reg earlier that day. She leaned back against the heated seat and watched as he drove. Greedily took in his handsome features as he mimicked Brody or Miles. Loved his smile and quick laughter.

This was new for them. Despite the afternoons they had before Miles came home from school or the evenings after he'd gone to bed, this was the first outing they'd taken together just as a couple. It made her giddy with first-date anticipation even though they'd already made it to the thirteen-year-old-son part. And should be past it.

He reached out and took her hand, keeping it as he drove.

"I'm liking this dating thing a lot. I'm wondering what you're wearing under the clothes. Hoping you'll let me stay over."

She laughed, charmed. "Maybe. I don't want you to think I'm too easy. Perhaps I'll make you wait. What's the average wait time? A month? A few weeks?"

"Ha! Didn't you date when you were young?"

"No." She was so tempted to hold it there, but she wanted to try to be more open with him. "I didn't know any boys back home who were worthy of dating. The nice ones I liked wouldn't have given me a second glance. And then here? I chose piano instead."

"You were young when you moved to New York. I love New York City, but hell, even as an adult I find it daunting sometimes. How did you handle it?"

"I think it was that I didn't know any better." She laughed. "Really I was just so happy to be away from home."

"I'm sorry it was so bad."

"It's long past now. It made me into who I am today, which is good and bad, I guess. But it's not unique and it wasn't horrible. In truth, I think it makes me appreciate what I have a lot more than I might have under other circumstances. It makes me hyperaware of how I'm parenting."

He knew she was uncomfortable with the focus on her, but it made him happy she'd shared without any prompting from him.

"I was just thinking about this the other day. I use Brody as an example of what a good father is. Not the one I was born with."

"He's a good example to make. Then again, Adrian, you're doing a fine job yourself. It's hard to tell you've only been doing this since October."

Pride warmed him. "Really? I feel like an amateur next to you."

"Really. And I don't know why you'd feel like an amateur. I make mistakes all the time. Half the time it's Miles who teaches *me* how to do this."

He laughed again. "Do you know I think I laugh more with you than I ever have before, and I laughed a lot as it was."

"I bet you're agitated a lot more too."

"Yes. Can't deny it. Also can't deny it makes me hot. So be it, I'm a weirdo. I can accept it. Your prickly, buttoned-up-to-the-neck thing works my libido hard."

She sniffed delicately. "I may have noticed. It's a good thing for us both. Not many men have a bitchy woman fetish."

"I do believe you just made me guffaw with that one. They do say there's a lid for every pot. You're my lid, Gillian. Bitchy and all."

The ferry ride was quicker than usual going back to Seattle from

Bainbridge, and soon enough they'd arrived at the pub where everyone had gathered.

The pub was sort of dingy, but it was their place. A place where if he was recognized no one would bug him. This place had been a regular part of his life, part of the lives of their circle for years. Gillian belonged there with him on the cracked vinyl booth eating pizza and drinking beer.

Adrian moved through the usual Friday-night crowd, keeping Gillian against him to protect her from being jostled. It was during times like this one where he was reminded of how small she really was. And yet, she managed just fine. He shouldn't have been concerned; Gillian was a tough woman. But that didn't stop him from wanting to protect her.

The group was already there at their usual booth near the pool tables.

"Gillian, I really need to go shopping with you so I can find all the cute stuff you wear," Erin said as she patted the spot next to her in the booth.

"Thank you. I can't take credit for it though. My friend Daisy gave me this outfit as a gift. She claims it was for my birthday, which is three months away." She smiled. "Truth is, she just has a great eye and picks stuff up for me, Mary and Jules all the time and it shows up in our houses."

"I met her at the luncheon at Mary's house. I really liked her." Erin indicated the pitcher at her elbow. "Would you like some beer? We just ordered the pizza so that should be out soon. Wings should be out too."

"Awesome. I'm starving after spending the whole day working." Adrian took the beer his sister pushed toward him and Gillian sipped hers. He kept an eye on her, but so far she appeared to be having a great time and he was reminded of what his brother had told him about how the rest of them had zero problem with Gillian and how none saw her as holding back.

He was the one who needed to adjust his expectations.

"Now that everyone is here, it's time to draw straws for the first game." Brody held up his fist with the sticks.

"We all pick and those four with the longest sticks go first." Erin explained to Gillian, who nodded and proceeded to pull out a very long stick with a smile.

"When I was young, I'd play snooker down the local."

"That so?" Adrian examined her and she smirked, sending that jolt straight to his cock.

"It is. I haven't played in a long time. But there were pool tables at several bars near my old flat in New York, so we'd go play after school frequently."

Now it was Todd who leaned in. "Hmm, seems we have another shark in the water."

"They take their pool very seriously." Ella rolled her eyes. "I prefer to sit back here and watch them play. As they're all quite nice to look at, I think I've got the best seat in the house."

Gillian laughed. Just a quick, lyrical burst of sound. "Very true. Then I shan't be disappointed if I don't get in on the first game."

"No looking at anyone's ass but mine. That's the rules." Adrian picked his straw and it was a short one. Damn.

"That is so not a rule." Elise snorted. "That's an insane rule. Looking at you all is the best part of my night. Hush."

"I'm pregnant."

Their playful banter died down as everyone looked to where Ella sat with Cope's arms around her tight. Both of them smiling.

"It's early. We only just found out for sure this morning. We haven't told my family or the Copelands yet and we won't until I'm past the three-month mark."

The table erupted with laughter and congratulations and Adrian's heart, already full of love for these people, expanded a little more. They'd been trying for the last year or so, he knew.

"That's why you're drinking water!"

"Yeah." Ella's smile told the story of how happy she was with the news. "I just hope I don't have blood pressure problems like Erin did, because if I have to give up coffee, I don't know how I'll get through the day."

Adrian looked back to Gillian and knew he wanted that with her. Yes, they had Miles, and having a baby before they were settled would be stupid and unwarranted. But after they'd found a way to make living together work, it could happen. He wanted it to happen, damn it.

She caught his gaze and smiled, and he knew she'd been thinking the same thing.

The food arrived and after some beer and wings, the first crew moved to the table and began to play.

"Looks like I'm up." Gillian stood and Adrian didn't hide his need to watch her as she moved.

"You watch her like you're taking notes in your head," Todd said. "I know the feeling. Sometimes I watch Erin move and I'm sort of mesmerized by it. She has such purpose, your Gillian."

"She does, doesn't she? She moves like she's on her way somewhere. Always. Constantly running lists of things to do in her head, I'd wager. She's very capable. I love that."

"It's hard to love a woman like that though. When you want to do for them. Want to help and they can totally do it without you and you want to do it anyway." Todd shrugged. It couldn't be easy to be married to a woman like Erin. She was another capable woman. They all were, he noted, looking around at the women in his life.

Gillian did fit in, even when he was worried she didn't.

She also seemed to be a pretty decent pool player as she handily ended up in second place right behind Ben, who was nearly impossible to beat anyway.

"Here, take my turn," Adrian told Erin when Gillian returned to the table. "Pizza's here and so is my lady."

Gillian blushed. "You don't need to. I can eat pizza and chat with everyone here. I don't need a keeper."

That warm, slow flood of desire flowed through him.

"Yes, but we already established the fact that I do. Plus if I go play, I can't eat pizza. Really, it's the best of both worlds right here."

"All right."

They talked and laughed. Ella filled them in on the plans for the nursery in their house. Cope had already started on a bassinet that they'd keep in their room for the first months.

"Hand carving a bassinet? That's lovely. I can't imagine a more wonderful gift for him to give you. Other than the baby, of course." Gillian looked back to Ella, who was nodding.

"You should come to the house sometime for dinner. Bring Miles since he and Andrew seem to have the same insane love of *Burnout: Revenge*. He's done so much of the woodwork in the house himself. The moldings, banisters, chair rails, window casements. He's endlessly talented. Give him wood and his tools and look away and suddenly he's made something beautiful. I'm forever finding little boxes and things he's made for me."

Gillian's smile warmed. "That's a lovely thing for a man to do."

"I totally agree. So tell me about *Carmina Burana*. Elise shared earlier that you'd be playing the piano and how everyone is raving about you."

Gillian's eyes widened. "Really? Oh no, I doubt that."

Ella's laugh put Adrian at ease as she patted Gillian's hand. "She told me that she and the creative director of the choral group went to listen to you and the other pianist and you were amazing."

"Well, it's such a grand piece. Really, it's not me at all. I just play what someone else wrote. Rehearsals will start soon with the choral group. I haven't done anything like this in a while so I'm quite thrilled about it. Don't want to get rusty."

Adrian watched her. Listened to her conversations with the others. Joined in here and there. Maybe it was that when they were all together with Miles, her focus was on him so often she couldn't really engage as deeply. He didn't know for sure, but he liked seeing her this way.

Erin finally came back to their table, wearing a grin, and Adrian knew they were all in trouble.

"Karaoke night! Who's in?"

"Do we have a choice?" Todd's question was reasonable, but his wife rolled her eyes at him.

"Gillian, I think you and I should go." Erin held a hand out and Gillian tossed a desperate look back to Adrian.

"Say no if you don't want to, English. She won't make you. But I think you should."

"Only if you go too."

"Oh ho! The woman knows how to negotiate." Erin's pleased grin only made Gillian laugh.

"All right. I'll go next if you go first. *And*, I get to choose the song."

"No. You suck at song choice. You'll make us sing something stupid and I don't want to." Erin shook her head. "I'll choose and you'll like it and that is that." She took Gillian's hand and tugged her from the booth and both women moved to the small stage where they signed up and looked over the songs. Adrian watched as Gillian shook her head no to a few selections, and then they both nodded and laughed when he assumed they'd made their choice.

Erin slapped a pair of big old sunglasses onto Gillian's face and appeared to give her a pep talk as Gillian shook her head and appeared to finally relent.

"Fearless woman," Elise said.

"Fierce," Adrian corrected, noting how Erin stayed behind her when Gillian went up onto the stage.

And then she fell into the song and he fell into her performance of PJ Harvey's "Long Snake Moan."

"Holy shit." Ben leaned forward as they sang and it became totally obvious what a fucking kick-ass singer Gillian was.

And he had no idea.

Why had she not told him about this?

The piano was one thing, but she could clearly sing circles around a really difficult song. Enough that he could see she had received formal training. Probably at Juilliard.

He was impressed and proud, and at the same time, that he didn't know stuck in his craw, agitating him.

She didn't work the stage like Erin would have. Didn't dance around or act sexy. She simply owned her spot and that song as he sat there struck dumb by it all.

When the song was over she handed the mic off hastily and beat it offstage with Erin chattering at her excitedly.

The group cheered her and she blushed, but there was no hiding the big smile she wore. And he felt like an asshole, but the fact that he hadn't known she could sing only emphasized how much he didn't know about her. And how he couldn't unless she stopped holding back.

Still smiling, she turned to him, holding out the sunglasses. "You can wear them if you'd like. It's your turn. I think you should sing something like . . . Are you all right?"

"I just had no idea you could sing like that."

Her open, happy smile faded at his words. "Well, now you do." Still, she made an effort to keep it light even though she'd shuttered her gaze.

"Why didn't I? I mean, that's professional training." And even as he said it, he wanted to rip the words back. All he craved was to know her and he was fucking it up because he was caught off guard.

She looked from side to side, clearly embarrassed. Erin's brows flew up as she looked his way.

"Why didn't you what? Know I went to a performing arts school like we've discussed a time or two? The one whose diploma is on the wall of my office where you work a few days a week?"

"You're up, Adrian. Why don't you go on and choose a song?" Elise poked him in the middle of his back, extra hard.

"I just don't get why. English, all these months and you have a seriously rocking voice."

She licked her lips and got up. He'd hurt her, he saw that. His own lack of control had blown up in her face and she'd been embarrassed in front of others.

"I'm sorry you didn't know I could sing. Sorry to have upset you." She licked her lips, nervous, her voice very soft. "I believe I'm off home." She clutched her coat and her purse and looked to everyone else. "Thanks for letting me join you all tonight." And she headed for the door without fighting with him like she usually did.

Brody shoved him so hard he fell from the booth. "Go after her, you fucking idiot! What the hell is wrong with you?"

He didn't know. It had been a stupid, knee-jerk thing and he'd really fucked up. He scrambled to his feet, with the help of Ben, who pushed Adrian toward the exit.

She'd disappeared in the crowd so he headed toward the doors, hoping to cut her off. Her legs were short anyway. He'd catch up and throw himself on her mercy for acting like a dick.

He'd embarrassed her in public, something she hated and he knew it. Guessed some of the reasons why based on what she had told him. Revealed to him when he knew it hurt her to let anyone know what she'd endured and he made her feel like crap.

When she didn't stand her ground to fight with him, he'd known he'd overreacted and he'd tell her so.

He caught sight of her as she pushed her way out the door, through the crush of people. Suddenly, Brody was at his back, as were the others, everyone yelling her name.

And *shit*, he saw Larry Harold, a local journalist who'd clashed with Adrian in the past. The man hated Adrian and set about digging up dirt on him every time he could. Watched him catch sight of Gillian and smile, heading her way.

"Isn't that that reporter asshole?" Brody asked, pushing forward to get free of the doorway.

"Yes."

Shame flooded through her. She'd been so happy, she'd opened up with
his family like he'd wanted her to and she'd enjoyed it. But his reaction had been a slap and she struggled to process the why of it.

He'd been sulky about how slow she'd been to reveal her past, but
he'd never been deliberately hurtful except for in the very beginning
when he didn't know her. And tonight he'd looked at her with the
same suspicious eyes he had back when they'd met.

She wanted to throw up. Wanted to cry. Needed very badly to go
to Jules or Mary and they'd fix her. More than anything though, she
just wanted to be anywhere but there.

"Gillian!"

She heard Adrian calling her name but all she wanted was to get
away. There was a bigger intersection up ahead and she could call for
a cab and make the ferry.

"Gillian? Ms. Forrester?"

That was a different voice. She finally won free of all the people and
ended up passing by a man she'd never seen before but who clearly
knew her.

She continued walking but he grabbed her arm, halting her progress.

"My name is Larry Harold. I'm a journalist—"

She pulled free and sent him a look that he clearly understood the
violence in because he stepped back a little.

"That's really all I need to hear. I have no comment."

"But I think you might once you hear me out."

She shoved her arms into her coat and slung her bag crosswise over
her body. Ready to do some battle with this idjit.

"Is that so? And why would you think that?"

"How does Adrian feel knowing he's cozied up to the daughter of a
pedophile and a murderer to boot?"

Sickness hit like a physical blow. She should have told him. Should
have told him and now it would hurt him.

"That's none of your business. I've got nothing to say to you." She started to walk past as the thudding of footfalls she knew belonged not just to Adrian but most likely the entire group reached where she stood.

"Get the fuck away from her, Harold." Adrian shoved between them.

And it was like a movie instead of her life as the reporter turned to Adrian and began to speak through his smirk. Gillian knew it was coming, and if she'd had a clear shot, she was pretty sure she would have used her handbag to hit that reporter right in the face.

"I was asking your girlfriend how you felt about her father and if it was an impediment to your helping her with her music career."

She had to clench her teeth and breathe through her nose to keep from being sick as it all happened in what felt like slow motion.

"What about her father?" Adrian asked.

"It has *nothing* to do with him. Nothing at all." Gillian said it but knew it was fruitless. It was true, but it didn't matter.

"Oh yeah? So it's true then? You're producing this movie she scored? The director is trying to sell it using your name as a reference. Saying Gillian told him you were backing it."

"What? I never said anything like that. I haven't even spoken to Mel in well over a decade." Christ, she'd written that score when she was still in school. As a favor for a friend who was making an independent film. But it never went anywhere and she'd pretty much forgotten about it. Was he really trying to sell it and using Adrian's name?

This was a nightmare. His entire family had gathered in a semi-circle around the reporter as Adrian kept his body in between her and the reporter. Protecting her when her past was about to rip him apart. Which only made it worse. He was taking care of her, even though they'd fought, even though she knew it would be over in a matter of minutes.

"So it's true? You wrote a score you never told me about and are trying to sell it?" Adrian turned his head to speak to her.

"No! I mean yes, I wrote a score, but—" He put a hand up to silence her.

"We'll talk about it later." He turned back to the journalist. "As you can see, you're incorrect. Now shove off."

"Her father is in prison for drugs and for the murder of a sixteen-year-old girl he was shacked up with. A child killer."

Erin had been standing next to Gillian and she froze. Gillian closed her eyes against helpless tears.

"How do you deal with that, Erin? Your brother's new squeeze is the daughter of a guy like the one who killed your child. Does it come up at holiday dinners?"

Gillian turned to Erin. "Oh my God, I'm so sorry," she managed to say before she ran off. She ran and ran and then ran some more. Down through Queen Anne until her lungs burned and she managed to grab a taxi to head to the ferry.

22

Everyone filed wordlessly into Erin's place. Adrian felt caught between rage at himself and rage at Gillian.

"I can't believe she never told me!" He slammed his palm against the countertop. He'd fallen in love with a woman with some secrets. And those secrets had blown up in her face.

How long did she think she could get away with not telling him about her father? She had to have known he'd be extra sensitive to that sort of thing after what Erin had endured.

He began to pace as people settled in.

"Cope, take Ella home," Brody said quietly. "Ella needs to rest and not be upset."

"I'm not upset! Well, not by what you think I am. I'm not going anywhere." Ella crossed her arms and Cope sent Brody a look and took the glass of lemon water Ben handed to him for his wife.

"I need to know about this guy shopping this movie using my name."

"Todd's on it already. He started looking into it on the way back home," Ben said.

"She used me. All this time I thought I'd misjudged her but it was all an elaborate ruse. She deliberately didn't tell me about her father. She knew how I'd react."

"All those times I was in her house, all those times we were together and I told her about Adele and she never once mentioned it to me. I'm sick over it." Erin pressed a hand to her stomach and Ben rubbed a hand up and down her back.

"Let's all just take a fucking chill pill." Brody accepted the water he'd been handed. "This is getting out of hand. Baby girl"—he looked to Erin—"you need to get yourself calmed down." He touched her cheek. "It tears me up to see you this way and it's not going to help."

"He's right. I'm sorry Gillian ruined our night. I'm sorry I brought her into our lives like a poison. God, how stupid could I have been?"

That's when the water hit his face. Tossed from Brody's glass.

"You, boy, sit your ass down right now before I do it for you."

Shocked and a little humiliated, Adrian managed to get his butt into a chair as Elise handed him a towel, moving between the two brothers.

She sent her husband a look. "Brody, you take two steps back before this goes into a direction you didn't intend. I think we've seen enough of that tonight, don't you?"

Brody stepped back and took a deep breath.

Todd came in and looked around. "Do I need to break out the Tasers?"

That broke the tension a little.

"What did you find out?" Adrian asked, though he wasn't sure what he wanted to hear.

"I didn't do a lot of looking at her life in England because she was a minor. I knew enough that from what I could see she had no police record or outstanding issues. Her father is some character. Lifetime criminal, looks like. He's serving a life sentence for the murder of his sixteen-year-old girlfriend. She'd apparently been with him since the age of fourteen." He shuffled through the papers. "Gillian left England at fifteen, just as she told you. I also surprised this asshole filmmaker with a phone call at home. She wrote the score for him fifteen years ago, he says. He couldn't sell it so it's been in his basement. He saw her picture online and saw that she was your girlfriend and so, as he put it, he *used it like anyone else would have*."

"Except Gillian apparently. No." Brody pointed at Adrian, who'd been about to speak. "I'm talking now. You've said enough."

Adrian bit back his words.

"You too," he said to Erin. "You both rushed to judge her. No, she didn't tell you about her father in prison. But if you put together what Todd just said, it means she hasn't seen her father since she was fifteen. Probably longer than that, as he appears to have been shacked up with some girl instead of Gillian's mother. She came here with that hanging over her. And she made her own future."

Adrian heaved out a breath. He'd asked her if her father had ever been in her life and she'd said simply, no.

"She should have told us. My god, to be confronted with it that way in the street like that." Erin shook her head. "I trusted her."

"You know I love you and I'd do anything for you. But you're wrong." Brody leaned against the counter. "How do you go about revealing that story? You tell me, Erin. How does a woman like Gillian begin to share such intimate details when she knows they'll bring pain?" He turned that perceptive gaze to Adrian. "Hm? How does she tell you her father is a killer? At breakfast between pancakes and bacon? And do you for one second truly believe she held all this back to get your help selling an art house flick she wrote a score for fifteen years ago? Before she knew you? When she did actually entertain a music career as an option? You heard Todd. The guy hasn't even spoken to her. You overestimate yourself all while underestimating yourself."

"What the fuck am I supposed to think? She blindsides me with this amazing voice I never knew she had. There's a whole lot of *I never knew* in this relationship."

"Oh, boo-hoo. You acted like a total cock and started that entire mess with your reaction. Everything had already begun to spiral before she hit the door because you overreacted and she got embarrassed.

"And for what? Huh? You've known her four months! Here's a woman who grew up the way she did. She's got this shitty mother and a murderous father. She grew up in public housing, and I can imagine she got a lot of crap for who her parents were and what they were like. Then she comes here and she goes to school. Makes something of herself. But Miles comes along and what does she do? She's twenty-one years old and she dropped that career and came to Washington and made a life for her son. That's what you know, and it's more than a bunch of things she could have said. Who she *is* is all over her and your son. She is a good woman. Stronger than most people I know. And she loves you."

"She didn't tell you because she was ashamed. How can she not be?" Elise's voice was soft. "I know what she feels. I know what it means to live with secrets and to feel like other people's defects are your responsibility. I know the shame of having violence in my life, know the humiliation of that. And she knew about Erin and Adele, yes, which in my opinion made her scared because she didn't want to bring hurt into your life." Elise took Erin's hand.

"She was my friend."

"She *is* your friend. As am I, right? And I'm telling you, I'm sorry you had to be devastated that way in public. Hell, at all. But she didn't do it to you on purpose or to hurt you. She was victimized too. That reporter used her to hurt you, Adrian."

"I have to go." Adrian pushed from his seat and blindly grabbed his keys.

Brody caught up with him at the elevator. "When I was falling for Elise you told me you weren't going to let me lie to myself. And that saved me. So I'm going to do you the same favor right now. I'm sorry I threw my water in your face, first of all. I was frustrated and you were working yourself and Erin up too. But it was shitty and disrespectful and I shouldn't have done it. Second of all, don't lie to yourself just to save face. You love her and you misjudged her. Go make this right before you lose the chance."

"She should have told me about her father. She should have told me about everything. How can I trust her if she won't tell me everything?"

"I hope that's enough for you once you've lost her for good." Brody shook his head. "You're really going to let her go? You and I talked about how much you loved her not even a week ago and now you just walk away?"

"As long as I can see Miles, that's what I care about." He got on the elevator and didn't meet Brody's gaze as the doors slid shut.

Jules was waiting at the ferry dock, concern on her face, Mary at her side. Neither of them said a thing as they helped Gillian into the car.

"My house or yours?" Jules asked.

"Or the police station? What the hell is going on, Gillian?" Mary demanded.

And the words just came out, tumbling one after the other, even as they both helped Gillian up her front steps and into her house.

Once she'd finished, Jules rocketed from where she'd been holding Gillian on the opposite side from Mary and began to pace. "That sanctimonious prick! He accused you of—"

"Nothing. He didn't accuse me of anything there. But he left a message on my voice mail. He thinks I hid it from him deliberately and I did. I can't lie. I knew I should have told him about Ronnie but I never did. He never wants to see me again." Her tears started anew.

"You didn't hide it from him, for fuck's sake! You didn't open some past wound for his amusement. It had nothing to do with him. You didn't tell him about something that did not include him." Jules was fuming.

"But it did. His sister's child was murdered by a crazy person. His sister-in-law was nearly killed by her crazy ex. Violence is something that includes him and I should have told him. And now you're mad. I should have called a cab."

Mary knelt in front of her and shook her just a moment, enough to get her attention. "Of course you should have called us. You're in pieces. I've never seen you so torn apart except after your gran passed. You love this man. He loves you. Would you like me to call him? Explain things?"

Gillian shook her head and blubbered like an idiot.

"You can work this out. He was wrong to jump to conclusions but we know he's got that thing about reporters."

"What about her thing about being humiliated in public?" Jules countered Mary's statement.

"This isn't a bloody contest! I ripped his family apart and then he fell back to his original position about me. All this started because I sang well! We got into a tiff about it, or rather he was pissy and I wanted to just leave. But if I'd told him about my father, the stuff that happened with the reporter wouldn't have hurt him nearly as much.

"He doesn't trust me. He thinks I have to be with him every minute of the day and tell him every horrible thing in my past to be trustworthy, and I can't. I can't do that and I don't want to. Part of it is my fault. I own it. I should have told him."

She stood and they hovered around her. She was just totally and completely exhausted by everything. The truth about her father was out and she realized holding it in had been weighing on her heavily. She should have told him. She could own it and whatever damage she'd done. She'd sent an apology letter to Erin and arrange to be out of the house when Adrian was there with Miles.

"I'll have to find a way to tell Miles." She breathed out. She'd never told him either. Had simply said her father was a criminal and that she hadn't seen him since she was younger than he was now.

"Not tonight, though." Mary ran her hands up and down Gillian's arms. "Why don't you come back to my place and stay? I'll have Ryan run over and pick Miles up in the morning and I'll make everyone crepes."

"I must be in pretty bad shape for you to offer to make crepes."

"You're scaring me. I've never seen you like this before. You're the one who is always together and strong. It makes me want to punch him in the nose." Jules hugged her.

"Come back to my house. I'll even watch something that'll skeeve me out like *The Ring*. We'll have a slumber party, just us girls." Mary smiled hopefully.

She shook her head. "I need to be alone."

They both looked so worried she took their hands in hers. "I'll survive. It hurts like hell. I can't regret loving him and believing in my happily ever after, even if I'll miss it."

"Are you sure it's over? Gillian, he loves you. I know this. I believe it with all my heart. You two bicker all the time. How can this fight be any different?" Mary brushed the hair from Gillian's eyes.

"Because it is. I can feel it. Before we weren't disagreeing about the final outcome. Not really. This is not the same. He feels betrayed, and part of it is real because it has everything to do with his distrust of outsiders for doing exactly this."

"I don't want to leave you alone." Jules looked miserable.

"You're going to have to. I need a bath. I need some gin and I need some sleep. I have to get this dealt with and gone before Miles comes home tomorrow morning. Adrian and I started this relationship, so we can't just break up and not expect him to notice. It has to stay civil and not involve him at all."

"I'm coming by in the morning with the makings for crepes and you can't stop me." Mary sniffed.

Jules nodded. "I'll bring coffee."

"You have a shop to open in the morning." Gillian shooed them both to the door. "I'll call you both later. Thank you for the ride and for the shoulder to cry on. I'll be all right. I just need a long cry with the blankets over my head."

She locked up, including the dead bolts she never threw if she was expecting Adrian to visit—because she didn't have an extra key for those locks, which meant he had no way to get in if she used them.

She headed to the shower and gave in to tears again. The last few months had been the best of her entire life. She couldn't regret loving Adrian Brown. Even right at that moment she couldn't regret it. He'd filled her life with so much.

She cried and cried some more, standing there and feeling horrible until the water started to run cold and forced her out. The gin had hit enough to have taken the edge off the pain, but it was still there.

All she wanted was to get under the covers and go to sleep so she wouldn't have to experience this anymore. But she couldn't sleep. She needed something else, so she turned to go back downstairs to her piano.

Adrian slumped home. Empty. He'd meant that night to be a new step and it had started off so well. With a sigh he decided to work awhile. Why not? He turned his computer on, cracked a beer and sifted through e-mail.

Brody's words echoed through his head.

Erin's face as the reporter had yelled out his question to her also echoed through his head. The hurt of it, of wanting more of Gillian and getting it in the way he had, sliced through him.

Miles's e-mail address caught his attention. That was good. His boy was good, damn it. He opened it to find an attachment and a note.

Hey, Dad!

I forgot to send this to you earlier this week but we were just goofing around and I saw it on my phone. Just some video Mum took of us. I told you we would nail it after some more practice. Thanks for all the help.
    See you soon. Mum says we're all hanging out this weekend.

Miles

He clicked and watched his son and his band come to life. They played all the way through "Creep" pretty damned well, especially Miles. The boy was a natural, no doubt about it.

And then Gillian's voice. Laughing. Encouraging Miles. Teasing in her way all the while giving compliments.

He put his head between his hands and hit play again.

By the time he'd listened to Gillian for the fifth play, he was standing because he'd made a choice.

They'd worked out everything else. They'd work this out. She was his woman and they'd work it through.

Of course, he'd missed the last ferry, which meant he had to drive around. Which was fine; it gave him time to fight with himself and accept that he'd reacted badly and done some major damage. Especially the part where he called her and told her he never wanted to see her again.

He turned on the mini-recorder he carried with him everywhere and began to work on a new song as he drove the long way around.

It was late when he finally arrived. Long after two and heading into three. But he knew she was awake because he heard her piano as he walked up the steps. Sad. Soulful. His heart broke just standing there listening to it.

His key worked but the door wouldn't open. She had the dead bolt engaged. Damn.

He knocked and continued to do so. Miles wasn't home, he knew that much, and he wasn't going to wake anyone up because the houses next door were too far away to hear his knocking.

She continued playing, though louder. So he rang the doorbell and then started knocking again. He'd called and she didn't answer. He texted and she didn't answer.

"Gillian, open up," he said, his mouth close to the door.

He heard an abrupt jangle of piano keys and then the sound of what had to be stomping to the door she then yanked open, standing squarely in his path.

"Why are you here?"

Her face was red and swollen. She wore sweats and a ratty shirt and looked as miserable as he felt.

"We need to talk."

"Go home, Adrian. I've sent your sister an e-mail apologizing to her for what she had to face tonight. I'm sorry I didn't tell you about my father. I never wanted to hurt you and I have. That's really it. We've said all we need to say." She tried to close the door but he blocked it with his shoe.

"We said too much and yet not enough. The both of us. We need to work through this."

She straightened her posture and took on that starchy thing, but it wasn't erotic. She was deliberately putting him on blast. "Miles isn't home. I'll let him know you stopped by. If you wish to return tomorrow morning, I'll be gone so that can happen."

"Gillian . . . please."

He stood there on her doorstep looking so beautiful it was all she could do not to leap into his arms. She loved him more than she could express. And she wanted him to go before she did and they both embarrassed themselves.

"It's better this way, Adrian. Before we did something stupid like moving in together and something else comes up you can't handle." She closed her eyes. "That was uncalled for. But my past has ugly things in it. Ugly things I can't put down on a list for you so you can feel as if you know everything about me. This can't work. You need to go."

Her breath hitched and the sob was clear enough that even she couldn't deny it. He stepped toward her but she warded him off with a hand.

"No. It's for the best that this happened early on. You have trust issues and I'm not sure anyone outside the circle you already have will be good enough for you. I have trust issues and God knows I react poorly to being humiliated in public. They clash and I thought it could work, but clearly it can't. I won't stand in the way of you seeing your son, of course. I'd never do that. He loves you." Like she did. Tears were streaming down her face and she couldn't stop them so she simply ignored them.

"Don't do this."

"I hope you'll consider Miles's feelings in all this. He doesn't know about my father. Not the specifics. Just that he was a career criminal and not part of my life. Don't blame him for my faults or the faults of a man he never met."

She let herself touch him then. If only to push him back enough to shut the door and lock it again.

He put a hand over the place she'd just touched him. "Baby, please. English, I was wrong to be so harsh. I was shocked and I reacted wrong. I love you. I know you love me. I know you didn't tell me because you were ashamed."

He heard her crying, ached to help. Ached to make her feel better.

"This isn't over, Gillian. Just know that I'm coming for you. We will work this out because no one is perfect for me except you."

Her crying got worse and he put his forehead against the door, helpless against his own tears.

"Go. God, please. It's too much to have you there. I can't. *Please.*"

She turned off the porch light and he stood in the darkness as she turned off all the lights inside as well.

When she'd spoken to him she was not his Gillian. Her eyes didn't hold the light she had just for him. Her voice had lost the lilt she used to speak to him. Not even her prim British. She sounded empty and numb.

Being that he felt empty and numb, he supposed they made a great pair.

It was too damned cold to wait on the porch until morning. Worse, Miles would be coming home and he knew it was important to keep their son away from this mess.

He drove to a local hotel and though he lay in bed, sleep would not come. She hadn't seen her father at least since she left England. He'd not been any part of her life if Miles had no idea about the man. She had never returned to England since the day she left either.

Of course she must have gotten some voice training while at Juilliard. Now, with some distance from the actual event, he could see the truth of it. In his desire to know more he let himself get pissy over something totally stupid, which had cascaded into something worse because that reporter had been waiting for just such a moment.

His stupid overreaction had led to the spiral of insanity that had blown up in their faces. Christ, what a pair they were.

He'd seen her face when the reporter spoke to Erin. Had heard her tortured, whispered apology and watched her run away. She didn't run. She stood and fought when she thought she was right. She was like a little bulldog, she simply didn't let go until she won.

But tonight she'd run. She'd refused to speak to him and had shut down. And it was partly his fault. Okay, mainly his fault, though after listening to her on her doorstep, he could tell she held herself responsible. Which was his fault too.

No. Gillian Forrester was the one. She was his lid and he'd fucked it up but he'd not go down without a fight. He'd win her back and show her they could weather any storm.

Because there was love between them. He did have trust issues and she hit on an important point. His circle was his comfort zone. She didn't fit in it the way everyone else did and he'd looked for that to be a problem instead of just a process.

That he could see and hear the difference between how she'd been with him earlier, and the last months told him she *had* been sharing herself with him on her own terms. God, that she'd cried in front of him was major.

He had his own walls. They weren't as straightforward as hers were. He loved her, though. He knew it as much as he knew he loved Miles and his siblings. She was his.

So he'd be back in the morning and they'd hash this out and they'd be fine. In the meantime since there was no way he'd be sleeping, he may as well work on some music.

23

Gillian shuffled through the kitchen as Miles zoomed around. She'd called and begged Mary not to come over for crepes. She had to hold herself together for Miles, and if anyone showed her any pity or kindness just then, she'd lose what composure she'd managed to find at about five thirty that morning.

There was a knock on the door, but she was on the phone with a client so Miles rushed off, Claypool weaving through his legs like a fluffy road hazard.

Adrian.

She heard his voice and then Miles's surprised, happy response. It made her smile even as it broke her heart. She used to be part of that and now she wasn't.

She continued speaking, focused on her client and shutting out the beautifully sad sound of Adrian's walk through her house. She'd gotten used to it.

"Mum's on the phone," Miles explained when they came through.

She kept her back turned and headed to her office, shutting her door.

But that small peace was cut short when Miles barged in five minutes later, well after she'd hung up.

"Mum! Dad brought doughnuts and bear claws and stuff. Come on. I saved you one of those goopy lemon ones you like."

"No really, Miles, I can't. I have work to do today."

She looked up to find Adrian in her doorway looking a little rough. Served him right.

"Everyone needs a good breakfast. I know you tell Miles this all the time. Have some coffee. I brought you some."

She noted the box and the cup were not from Tart. He must have known the reception he would have received. Hmpf.

"I made a pot already." How dare he use the "it's good for you" against her.

"Come on, Mum." Miles grinned.

"Fine. For a few minutes, and then you and your dad should go to his house for a while. Or away for the afternoon. Whatever."

She followed Miles out, avoiding Adrian's gaze and his proffered cup of traitor coffee. She'd have to hide those cups deep in the recycling or Jules would have her head if she saw them.

The doughnut was probably quite tasty, but not just then, with everything she'd ever wanted just across from her.

Miles was seemingly unaffected by their tension as he chattered about all the fun he and his friends had had the night before and an upcoming band concert at school.

"Be sure to reserve enough tickets for everyone." Adrian spoke and that drawl of his caressed her skin, made her crazy to touch him so much she glared at him just for good measure.

But he was looking at her and caught her gaze. One corner of his mouth quirked up and she had to lick her lips. Which only made his smile bigger. The cad.

"Do you know what? We should jam while I'm here. I've been working on something new and it'll help if you two noodle around with me."

"Really?" Miles's eyes widened at the suggestion. "That would be awesome. Like how you and Aunt Erin do it?"

"Yeah. Only she and I have been making music together since I was eleven, so she and I have a distinct sort of rhythm. I thought it would be good to change it up with other people I trust and love."

She made to leave. How dare the man, really? Last night it was some vast conspiracy that she could sing and today he wanted to jam with her?

He preferred the fire in her gaze to the numbness he'd gotten earlier. Preferred anger to sadness. Fire he could deal with. Fire was something they did well together.

He'd been sort of annoyed at first to walk in and see her chatting on the phone as if nothing had happened. She'd turned her back and left the room even. But when he and Miles had interrupted her, he saw how wrong he'd been. Far from being unaffected, she had dark circles under her eyes to match his own, he'd bet.

"Please, Gillian? I really need you . . . to help me."

"Mum, please?" Miles already had his bass in his hand and he noted the way Gillian saw that too and her spine relaxed as she accepted the inevitable.

They all moved to the living room and she sat at her piano, waiting.

"This one I'm calling 'Indelible.' Starts off like this. You two just go with it." He started to play, falling into the song he'd written over the last several hours.

Looks can be deceiving
Fragile can hide strong
Her roots dig in
Dug deep like the rest
She's indelible
Scratched into my skin
Her scent on my fingers
Taste on my tongue

Yeah, try to forget, but you can't
She's indelible

He paused because he noted Miles staring at him and then back to his mother, who made a big deal out of not looking at Adrian.

"I need to call Jason about something. Be back in a while." Miles stood and took his guitar before bending over again to whisper in Adrian's ear. "Just say you're sorry and buy her something nice. But not like *your* nice. Normal nice."

Which made Adrian laugh because not only would Miles say something like that but Adrian understood it.

He ran from the room on thundering feet, leaving Adrian filled with so much love he thought he'd burst.

This is what she brought to him. This is what she was to him. Family. He could do this. They could do this.

He put his guitar aside and took her hand, pulling her to the couch. She settled at the far end and snatched her hand back and he simply scooted over and hemmed her in.

He took her hand back, holding it firm with both of his. "We need to talk, English, and you're going to listen to me."

She sniffed and, God help him, his cock got hard.

"So you know, as you've seen, I have sort of a crazy life. It's so chaotic outside, I've built a safe space for myself here in Seattle. My family, my few places, they're what I know and what I can trust. You saw the paparazzi when we were in Miami and even up in Canada. The people camped at my driveway. I just get exposed and it makes me feel helpless."

She looked up at him at long last.

"I'm sorry I didn't tell you about my father. Despite the fact that I did hurt you all, I never wanted it to come out like that. I wanted to tell you. I did. I waited for the right time, but there's not really a right time for it. I can't lie, I could have a few times but I didn't want to ruin things. I never wanted to hurt you and your family."

He sighed. "I know. I'm an asshole, English. I'm trying to tell this and then you go and apologize and make me feel even worse. You should have told me, if for no other reason than to share what had to be a heavy weight all these months. But my reaction was stupid. It was stupid because I love your voice and I was knocked back on my heels that I didn't know. And then it just blew up into a clusterfuck of epic proportions with Larry. I just flat overreacted when I should have stopped to work it out with you."

"I'm glad we can be friends."

He snorted, leaning in to kiss her hard. When he broke the kiss, she was short of breath and her eyes had gone dreamy. All very good signs this was on the right track.

"Friends? Fuck that. Gillian, I love you. You love me. Look, last night I realized some stuff. The big one was that all my anxiety about you holding back was really my own shit. I was holding you to a standard you couldn't possibly meet. I wanted you to be more at ease with people who've had, some of us, a lifetime to know each other. It was something you could never achieve and I set it up that way just to keep that bit of distance. But I blamed it on you because I'm a coward and I couldn't just admit I was scared to leave my comfort zone."

"My father is a murderer. He killed a girl just barely older than Miles. He sold drugs. He used them. He was a petty thief and a thug for money launderers and betting houses. He beat my mother and she let him come back over and over until I was about eight and he just never came round anymore. My mother was a drunk and a whore. My sister was a drunk and a whore. This is going to come out in the press, Adrian. I thought they'd leave me alone because I'm not exciting. But that's not the case. They'll hurt you and your family and they'll hurt Miles. I can't expose him to that. Or you."

"I don't care what he was or who he is. I don't. You aren't him or your mother. You're the mother to my son. The other half of my heart. You're my lid, English. I spoke with Jeremy this morning. I had to share some stuff with him, so I apologize for not getting your permission. But his suggestion was to do an interview so you can talk about it on your terms. We can control the spin and remove that from the media's hands. We can make this work, damn it. I'm not going to let you go."

"I did write a score for a movie, but I would never use your name to promote it or sell it. I tried to tell you last night but it just kept getting worse." She wiped her eyes with the back of her free hand and he knew she was still reeling to do such an uncouth thing.

"I know. Todd had a little word with the filmmaker last night. He won't be pulling that shit anymore. But I would like to see it. Just because I love your music and your creativity. The singing thing, I just handled it all wrong. Christ, last night was supposed to be wonderful and it all went so terribly wrong."

"It won't be the last time, Adrian. Things are bound to happen like that. You're a celebrity. They want to get a rise out of you. Want to hurt you for sport. If it's not this, it'll be something else."

"Yes, and I know this. I should have known it last night. This happened to me earlier this year. Only it was a piece on Erin and her two *love slaves* as the article termed them. The piece suggested Alexander should be taken away from her and her sex grotto."

Any doubts he might have had about her were gone when he saw the devastation on her face. On Erin's behalf.

"Yeah. It sucked. But we stuck together and it's fine."

"I can fight with you all the time. Really, it's rather like foreplay for us, I think. But I can't do what we did last night. I can't. If that's what it's going to be like, I really must say right now that we can't see each other anymore."

He went to his knees before her. "I love you. I want us to be together and married and as a family. Last night was a big wake-up call for me. The biggest ever. We turn to each other, first and always. That's my pledge to you." He held out a hand. "Pinky swear."

She eyed his hand and then his face again, narrowing her gaze. He wiggled his hand again and she sighed. "You're very bad for my

constitution. I find myself breaking all sorts of personal Gillian Forrester rules for you."

"From you, this is a great declaration of love."

"Hm."

"There she is."

She sighed. "Really, if you're a beast and you call me to tell me
mean things again, I will carve your bits off with a rusty spoon I've
sharpened against the pavement."

He was the best thing as he knelt there. Earnest and beautiful.
Loving. He wanted to make this work and she thought they might just
do it if she could let him in more and he could expand his life to include hers.

"Take a risk on me and I swear I'll spend the rest of my days making you smile."

She grasped his pinky with hers and crooked it.

"I love you, Mister Brown. So much I won't even tell Jules you
brought traitor coffee and pastry into my house."

He grinned. "That is love, English. Truth be told, I figured you
might have talked with her about what happened and I'd get chased
out. I saw how quick she can get over that counter. She'd be deadly
with a knife."

"Yes, well. It might be safe if you let me handle her and Mary for
a while. Though they both urged me to try to make things up with
you. Mary told me I loved you."

"And she was right."

"Yeah, she was."

"If Miles wasn't here—" He looked side to side and she couldn't
stop smiling.

"But he is! Stop it. None of that for hours. But when I get my
hands on you tonight, I'm taking all my feminine pique out on your
back and those arms of yours."

His grin was wicked. "Promise?"

"Yes."

It was nearly midnight before they found themselves alone. She'd gone off to shower and he'd hung out with Miles until the boy finally dropped off to sleep midsentence.

A lot like his mum in so many ways. Miles had seemed quiet and shy at first, but by that point he chattered and teased, and it made Adrian proud to be trusted.

Trust.

He moved to her, needing to reconnect after their fight. Needing the make-up sex portion of the program, not just for the physical release, but for the emotional connection as well.

There was a reason make-up sex existed.

He had to pause to catch his breath when he turned the corner from her room into her bathroom and found her, one leg on a stool, applying lotion. She wore the silky robe he'd given her for Christmas, the tie open at the waist, her bare skin just beneath gleaming from the heat of the shower she'd taken and the lotion she'd applied.

She looked up, catching his gaze. "Mister Brown, that look you're wearing might scare off a lesser woman." One corner of her mouth lifted and she put the lotion aside before moving to him at last. "Good thing I'm not a lesser woman."

"Much to my delight."

He danced her back to the bed and dropped on it to get out of his clothes and turn back to where she'd knelt on the bed, naked now and waiting for him.

"Hot damn."

"Well said." She held a hand out. "I need you." And she did. So very much.

Getting on the bed, he leaned in close to take a deep breath of her and then groaned. Each time he did that she understood what it meant to be cherished and loved. To be desired by a man who touched her with sometimes rough hands, but never intended to harm.

His hands on her kept them both anchored. To each other. To this moment. This would heal that last bit of the rift left between them. The heat they made together would make it all right again. They'd fight again, she knew it, and it was part of their energy as a couple. And so they'd fuck again and again, laugh as well.

"I'm going to use a blindfold on you next time. But for tonight I want to look into your eyes when my cock is buried deep in your pussy. So you know who's bringing you your pleasure."

A poke on her shoulder and she let herself tumble back to the bed as he followed her quickly. The teasing look had gone, replaced with stark, raw need.

She slid her hands down her belly and back up, taking the weight of her breasts, idly flicking her thumbs across her nipples just to watch him swallow hard a few times.

"Hold them for me." He bent his head to her, licking and then using the edge of his teeth over her nipples as she held them for him.

Her breath gusted from her lungs when he took her hands, banding her wrists in his grip and positioning her arms above her head.

"Yes, that sound." He licked the hollow of her throat and she made it for him again.

He held her bound in place as he spent long minutes kissing her. Lips and mouth. Jaw. Neck. It made her faint that he wanted her so much and yet took such exquisite time to taste her.

But his free hand shook a little. She knew he needed this as much as she did.

When the fingers of that hand brushed over her mound, she spread her thighs, rolling her hips. "Please."

He hissed as he spread her open and drew a fingertip from her gate up and around her clit. "You're so wet and hot. I love that your cunt is this way because of me. I love that here it's just you and me, Gillian and Adrian, and you are the finest thing I've ever seen."

He removed his hand and she gasped and then moaned when he licked his fingers and then kissed her. That taste, her pussy mixed with his taste, the way he changed her even at that most basic level, knocked her utterly off balance until she nearly spun with it.

"Please what?" he asked into her mouth.

"Put your cock in me and fuck me. Come inside me. I want you."

He rolled and was on her so she wrapped her thighs around his waist to keep him from going anywhere. And then he was pushing in. She should have been embarrassed at how wet she was, but there was none of that between them.

"Oh god, English, you're so good." He pressed all the way home and paused.

She writhed and he hissed.

"More!"

"I'm not going to last very long if you keep that up. I want to rut on you. Mark you. I'm trying to take this slow."

Oh. My. She shivered at his words.

She tightened her legs around his waist to draw him in deeper. "I don't want slow."

He let go of her wrists and grabbed the edge of the bed for purchase and, true to his words, let go of that control and began to fuck her in earnest. Not slow. Not gentle. And yet reverent. The tenderness even in such a raw moment brought emotion to her throat.

She scored her nails down his shoulders the way she knew he liked, the way she liked to mark him.

"Yes. Fuck yes."

He delivered a series of bites and sucks across her chest, leaving a love bite on the side of one breast. He moved on her, in her, like a man barely leashed.

She reached down between them and fingered her clit. He whispered something close to a curse and his speed picked up. This loss of control, this frenetic pace, the intensity of his thrusts as he fucked into her body made her swoon.

That he knew it, understood it and loved it as much as she did, was a gift she'd never cease to be thankful for. Even when he was a prat.

So close . . .

"I want to feel your juicy pussy grip me when you come. Do it," he whispered, his voice taut.

It was the hard nip to her left nipple that tipped her headlong into orgasm. She arched and rolled her hips over and over to meet his thrusts as he also drew close to climax.

Her body clamped down, inner muscles gripping him so hard that even without the way she writhed underneath him as she came around his cock, he'd have gone over. He came so fucking hard his head hurt.

Gaze locked with hers, with this woman he'd found in a completely unexpected way, he came home at last.

AUTHOR'S NOTE

I mostly have this tracklist on shuffle as I work:

"Daydreamer" — Adele
"Melt My Heart to Stone" — Adele
"Hometown Glory" — Adele (this one is Gillian's song)
The Goldberg Variations — Bach
"Is There a Ghost" — Band of Horses
Sonata no. 8 in C Minor for Piano, op. 13, "Pathétique": II. Adagio
    cantabilonata — Beethoven
"Ain't Nobody" — Chaka Khan
"I'm Every Woman" — Chaka Khan
"Dog Days are Over" — Florence + The Machine
"I'm Not Calling You a Liar" — Florence + The Machine
"King of the Rodeo" — Kings of Leon
"The Face" — Kings of Leon
"This Could Be the End" — Kings of Leon
"Pyro" — Kings of Leon
"Revelry" — Kings of Leon

"Blue in Green" — Miles Davis

"Starf*ckers, Inc." — Nine Inch Nails

"Long Snake Moan" — PJ Harvey

"Yuri G" — PJ Harvey

"Is This Desire" — PJ Harvey

"Corduroy" — Pearl Jam

"Go with the Flow" — Queens of the Stone Age

Piano Concerto no. 3 in D Minor, op. 30: I. Allegro ma non tanto — Rachmaninoff

"Creep" — Radiohead

"Soul Survivor" — The Rolling Stones

"The Weary Kind" —Ryan Bingham

"Depression" — Ryan Bingham

"Country Road" — Ryan Bingham

"Wishing Well" — Ryan Bingham

"Burn My Shadow" — UNKLE